After Before

After Before

Jemma Wayne

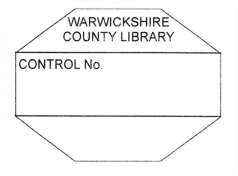

W F HOWES LTD

This large print edition published in 2015 by
W F Howes Ltd
Unit 4, Rearsby Business Park, Gaddesby Lane,
Rearsby, Leicester LE7 4YH

1 3 5 7 9 10 8 6 4 2

First published in the United Kingdom in 2014
by Legend Press

A CIP catalogue record for this book is available
from the British Library

ISBN 978 1 47128 671 1

Typeset by Palimpsest Book Production Limited,
Falkirk, Stirlingshire

Printed and bound in Great Britain
by TJ International Ltd, Padstow, Cornwall

MIX
Paper from
responsible sources
FSC
www.fsc.org   FSC® C013056

For James

PART I

CHAPTER 1

S he said her name was Emily. It had always seemed easier for English people to pronounce than Emilienne, and she refused to offer this part of herself, also, for sacrifice.

'Okay, do you have any cleaning experience Emily?' asked the thick-necked, white woman behind the desk. She shuffled the forms in front of her, impatience spilling into Emily's pause, but it wasn't a simple question to answer. The woman said it so easily, rolling off her tongue as smooth as the flesh beneath the skin of a sweet potato, the same as most of the words Emily had had thrown at her over the years: stupid, ungrateful, cockroach. Emily's mind ran over the dirty floors of her flat that she hadn't so much as threatened with a vacuum; then to the sparkling windows and door knobs in the house she'd cleaned and lived in once, belonging to Auntie; then tentatively to the dark puddles of blood she'd scrubbed from her father's floor.

'Yes,' Emily decided upon. 'I have experience.'

Her smile was gummier than she would have liked, and there was a gap between her front teeth, but it was important always to smile. It conveyed honesty, familiarity, trust.

'Do you have references?'

'No.'

The woman sighed. 'So you have no experience.' Tutting, she scribbled out the tick in what was now the wrong box on the registration form.

'You asked about experience, not references,' Emily clarified anxiously.

But the woman only smiled, as though such ignorance was what she expected. Emily smiled back at her. Ignorance didn't matter. Auntie had told her once. What mattered in this country was a willingness to work, to get down on one's knees and scrub stains out of floors too low for English girls. 'You'll be cleaning commercial properties,' the woman continued, lists of products and rules and company policies suddenly undulating out of her like a well-sung nursery rhyme. Obligingly, Emily nodded along to the beat until she noticed that the woman had paused and leaned forward. 'Can you remember all that?' the woman was prompting, smiling again, her over-padded wrists escaping the cuffs of her green blazer. The colour made Emily feel sick. The flesh made Emily feel sick. The woman's gritted grin made her feel sick.

'Yes,' Emily nodded.

The darkness of her skin seemed untidy against the neat, white piece of paper the woman pushed across the table for her to sign. Her hand shook as it hovered over the box where she was supposed to form the letters of her signature. It shook, and she shuddered, and her stomach grumbled queasily.

Outside, Emily wrapped her scarf around her neck. It wound three times and sat like a woollen brace that she rested her chin upon. Already the beginning of September, the first chill of winter was beginning to seep through the air into her bones and she knew she would be cold now until April at the earliest. It was impossible in this country to warm up once the cold was inside you and she would never grow used to it. But the scarf helped, and she liked the barrier it made between her long, skinny neck and the elements. Auntie used to try to get her out of the chunky knits she clung to and into more feminine shapes, but that was before she'd caused Auntie and Uncle so much distress, and they preferred her to disappear not just inside baggy clothes, but altogether.

A bus roared past Emily's right shoulder, her bus. She ran to catch it and smiled at the driver who paused long enough for her to clamber on and touch her Oyster card, but then accelerated with a jerk that threw her sideways. Emily was athletic once, strong, but now she was always a little unsteady on her feet and had to clasp the rail in order not to fall flat on her face.

She swung rail to rail down the length of the bus until she found a spare seat, avoiding eye contact with the other passengers who were just as furtively avoiding eye contact with her. It had been a shock when she'd first arrived in this country to find that people didn't greet each other in the street, or on the bus, or talk if they could possibly help it. Sometimes, sun-streaked instinct still got the better of her, but if there was anything she truly loved about England it was exactly this – the anonymity, the ability to live unnoticed, unidentified, undefined. There was a pleasure she found in the vast hoards of people whose names she didn't know, rushing obliviously past each other. There was comfort in the uniformity of floor upon floor of council housing like that of the building she lived in, her room on the fifth indistinguishable from the rest. There was tranquillity in the busyness of people's lives, in their individualistic pursuits and their self-obsession. There was isolation. Escape.

Emily alighted at Golders Green station. Her flat was still a 15 minute walk from there but she needed some groceries and preferred to buy them from the bigger shops with hundreds of customers rather than from the small convenience store on the corner of her road. She'd only been a few times but already the owner knew her face and asked her questions like, 'No avocados today? How about mangoes? I have perfect mangoes, you don't like them?' and, the week before, 'Where are you from?'

She picked up a basket outside the front of Tesco and dipped into the shop. She had exactly £4.73 left in her purse so had to make her selection carefully. The money needed to last until the end of the week and it was only Wednesday. Reluctantly she made her way towards the canned goods aisle and selected a tin of economy beans and some corn. Next, she found a loaf of bread that had been reduced in price because it was already at its sell-by date, and tore three bananas from a bigger bunch. Longingly she eyed the avocados but here such fruits were exotic and expensive. Emily picked up a small, hard one and quickly slipped it into her coat pocket. At the counter the cashier greeted her politely but without recognition, and Emily smiled. Rubbing the bunch of carriers between her fingers to separate them, she packed her few items into two bags so that the heavy tins could be divided and she could prevent the plastic handles from carving out valleys in her thin arms on the walk home. She always carried bags over her arms instead of in her hands. When she used to go shopping with Auntie, they would walk home with fifteen bags between them, and Emily would carry ten of them, each one balanced carefully an inch or two away from the next, all the way up her scrawny forearms, the skin pinching together as if she, like the avocados they'd bought, was being tested for ripeness. That was at the very beginning when she was grateful to Auntie for coming to her rescue, and naïve still to the reality that real rescue wasn't possible simply by escaping a place. Memories weren't rooted in the soil.

Emily realised now that Auntie had loved her then. She hadn't been able to feel it at the time but identified it later, like so many things, in its loss. They had done well to put up with her really. They managed it for three years and she knew even as it was happening that the screaming and the silences and the disappearances would one day amount to a final straw. Gradually, Auntie began to raise her voice at her, and Uncle hit her once. Which made everything worse. She wasn't surprised when they told her to leave. She told herself she felt safer that way anyway: alone, and running.

A white van was parked in front of the entrance to Emily's building. As she rounded the corner, she studied the men bounding in and out of it, unloading boxes. In Africa, they would be surrounded by people: newcomers were objects of curiosity to be scrutinised and assessed. *He who has travelled alone, can tell what he wants*, went the proverb, one of many that even after so many years, Emily was unable to rid from her mind. But the proverb held a truth, and it had felt natural for her, in another time, in a place that no longer existed, for strangers' stories to be tested and repeated, inquiries encouraged, questions asked. Emily shifted her shopping bags higher up her arms and walked past the van without a word.

The lift was broken again so she climbed the stairs, trying not to breathe in too deeply the stench of urine and beer. It amazed her still that a flat had been found for her so quickly, had been given so freely, by a nation who barely looked at each other in the street. Auntie had explained to her once about welfare, about asylum, about how she and Uncle had claimed both before the day came that with a job, and a passport, they needed neither. She'd told this story with pride, gratified by the distance they'd travelled, and though it wasn't due to a similar sense of aspiration, Emily always remembered this, and didn't mind sometimes having to hold her breath on the stairs. By the time she reached the fifth floor however she was gasping. Stopping at the end of the corridor, Emily rebalanced the shopping bags and dug into her handbag for her key. She always did this – stopped, prepared, felt the consoling piece of metal in her palm. An instrument of safety. Of power.

Emily looked up. A little way down the corridor, the door of the flat next to hers was ajar, a box propping it open, male voices inside. Emily had only ever seen the flat's occupant once, but she knew it to be a tiny, hunched-over old woman who seemed not to have any visitors and made noise only when her kettle occasionally whistled. Probably, Emily considered, the woman had died, because it was plain that the foreign voices she heard now were those of the men from the van, who it appeared were moving in. Emily wondered, briefly, how long the woman had laid dead next to her, whether her decomposing body had started to smell, who had found her; but then she heard footsteps on the stairs and quickly covered the last few feet of the corridor to her door, locking it carefully behind her.

The room was minute, the only windows facing directly onto a small courtyard with buildings so closely crammed around its edges and to such heights that it barely let in the light. Emily breathed deeply. She liked it this way. Rat-like. It was useful to be so far removed from the illumination of light, the transparency of sunlit days. Quietly, she unloaded her shopping, slipping the stolen avocado out of her pocket and onto the countertop to ripen, and placed a slice of bread into the toaster. She knew she shouldn't really eat the beans that night, but she was hungry so dug around under the sink for her solitary pan and, with a knife, pried open the tin before sense could change her mind. The dark red contents gushed with satisfying, hearty thickness into the pot. As it heated she opened the tap and let the water run until it was cold, then held a tall glass under it, allowing it to overflow, still finding pleasure, and promise, in this small excess.

When it was ready, Emily carried her meal over to the cushion in front of the TV. In a moment of charity – or pity, or guilt – Auntie had let her take it with her from the room she'd once slept in, along with the clothes Auntie had paid for over the years, and a wad of ten pound notes folded together and pressed into Emily's hand with a look of exhaustion at the door. Now the TV was Emily's biggest distraction from the dismal reality of everything else, and the floor in front of it had become a place from which she could watch laughter, glamour, optimism, frivolity, extravagance, romance, hope, dreams, success. She wished sometimes that she could be one of the happy people inside the screen, or even one of the girls who worked in the café around the corner that sat outside on their cigarette breaks, making jokes and throwing back their heads, light beaming from their eyes. There was a time when she would have given anything for that brightness, that spark, but the darkness that filled her seemed impossible to escape. Her anger was impossible to escape. Misery was impossible to escape. And for the most part, she no longer tried to.

Footsteps hurried past her door then returned a moment later, doubled and slower. Emily placed the remnants of her meal on the ground in front of her, turned off the TV, and slid from her cushion onto the floor. Lying flat she could make out the large, trainer-clad feet of one man walking backwards, and the sandals of another moving forwards opposite him. They were carrying something. The one wearing sandals was dark-skinned, though not as dark as Emily, and the wiry hair on his toes sprouted wildly, impervious to suggestions from the sandal straps of where they should lie. He called out to the other man in front of him and both pairs of feet stopped. Emily remained flat on the floor and listened to the muffled muttering between them in a language that wasn't English and that she didn't understand, then after a while the feet moved again, and disappeared from sight.

Emily began to weep.

It crept up on her slowly sometimes, and then there was time to make a cup of sugary tea, run a bath, or find some distraction on TV, but other times it hit her like this, abruptly. Angrily she hit back at the hot tears streaking down her face, but they only ran harder from her nose in polluted floods. She hugged her knees to her chest and forced herself to sit up, but then her mind wandered beneath the sink to the razor blade she had attempted to hide there, underneath toilet roll and toothpaste. The scar below her fringe throbbed, dizzying her. Her stomach tightened and contracted. Afraid that she might be sick she turned further onto her side, but couldn't muster the energy to reach the toilet, or even the bin in the corner of the room. All she could do was remain low on the ground, clinging to the hard, worn, reassuring carpet, until it was over.

When finally it was, Emily dragged herself back onto the cushion in front of the TV. The last beans on her plate were cold now and sickened her. She felt weak and listless. Her throat was dry and her head pumped after crying for so long, but she couldn't be bothered to refill her glass at the sink. She switched on the TV. A nature programme investigating the life of insects filled the screen and she changed the channel quickly. Now Jeremy Kyle appeared in front of her, arbitrating the trivial, meaningless, wonderful disputes that were enough to drive the families on the show apart. Emily curled her body inwards, hugged her knees to her chest again and rested her head on the cushion. When her eyes closed she was in a field of sweet potatoes, in a shallow dirt valley between the straight lines of crops, her face crouched next to the soil, her breath unsteady and unreliable, caterpillars taunting her from underneath the leaves.

She opened her eyes.

Another blink and there were voices screaming her name, shouts raised to a gruesome, fever pitch in exuberant anticipation of finding her. Darkness was in her mouth, dry, soil-smelling darkness. It scratched her eyes and covered them.

She blinked again. Her view cleared and suddenly, in the distance, she spotted her mother. Emily scrambled up. She ran towards her, fast, faster, her legs and arms flooding with acid, but somehow, the distance seemed only to grow. She shouted, but no sound came out. She waved, but her movements were slow and minuscule. She ran. But with every metre she covered, her mother fell further away, and the more she ran, the more pain filled the older woman's eyes, until finally Emily stopped and saw that her mother, on her unreachable plane, was undressed, and unhelped and unflinching.

Emily opened her eyes once more.

Her mother was gone.

Jeremy Kyle screamed on in comfort.

CHAPTER 2

She stares sometimes into the mirror. Minutes pass, she imagines. It might be seconds. Or hours. Sometimes she pulls faces at the glass, horrible faces, contorting her features into vile versions of themselves, making a beast of beauty. She has been told that she's beautiful. Luke tells her often. He brushes her wispy blonde hair behind her ear, tidying her, and touches a thumb to her lips, closing them, and tells her softly. Charlie used to whisper it hotly into her ear while fucking her from behind. He used other words – *beautiful* was not his domain – but somehow he seemed to mean them, and made her believe them, and excited her senses. She turns her lips inside out and scrunches up her nose and crosses her eyes and tries to see it still, beauty, shining from the inside out. She cannot. She says her name as though to summon it: *Vera, Vera, Vera*. She cannot answer. She calls again. *Vera.*

'Vera.'

Vera looks up. She wonders how long she has been staring past Luke into the reflective surface of the balloon. They are hovering over a field in

14

Hertfordshire a few miles from the house she grew up in. Luke is bent on one knee. There is a ring in his hand. 'Yes,' she tells him.

It has been 365 days since Vera first met Luke at a fundraising ball where she was doing PR and he was speaking on behalf of the government's Foreign and Commonwealth Office. PR, Luke had joked, was worse even than the jobs of journalist scavengers because it wasn't even hunting the truth but spewing out one-sided propaganda. Being a civil servant, she had replied, was a coward's route into politics: all of the power, none of the accountability. 'Ah, but we're all account-able to Jesus,' he had answered, and there was something about the mirth in the corner of his mouth and the earnestness behind his eyes that had her hooked in those first few seconds and made Luke her newest addiction. A year on and he has replaced the rest of them.

It is after all now 602 days since Vera last took cocaine, 433 since she's smoked anything heavier than a regular Camel Light – though Luke believes she's given these up too – and exactly 366 days since she's had sex. Charlie thinks the whole trans-formation is hilarious and won't last. She still speaks to him sometimes, although she doesn't tell Luke about it. It is something he asked of her early on, not to contact Charlie, and without much thought she'd agreed; but it is one habit she cannot give up. It is a kind of self-flagellation.

Vera leans forward and kisses Luke softly on the

mouth. He smells of coffee beans. The fairtrade Abel and Cole ones he powders with his manual grinder.

He smells of coffee beans.

If Vera's life were a film, there would be a lot of voiceovers. *He smells of coffee beans.* She wonders sometimes if she observes things that other people don't. She notices everything she thinks. *She thinks she notices everything.* Does everybody's mind have the time to rework a sentence five times in their head? She is paused, she ponders. Paused and in fast-forward. She watches herself from the outside. Her mind races. Do minutes pass? Has she scrunched up her nose again? Sometimes she feels as though she is still high. From his bent knee, Luke looks up and gazes at her as though she is some glittering trinket. As though she is brand new. *Of course I'll marry you.*

'Of course I'll marry you,' she whispers, then adds, 'but are you sure? There's no turning back once this baby's on my finger!'

'Put it on you silly thing,' Luke laughs, standing up and slipping it onto her wedding finger. Out of superstition, it has never been adorned with a thing, not even a Hula Hoop crisp. Luke has chosen a brilliant diamond set on a rose gold band that catches the glint of the setting sun and shines beauty directly into Vera's eyes, until she is blinded. Squinting slightly, she admires the costly sparkle. It is too big, but she makes a mental note to get the ring adjusted to fit. For the time being she

16

clenches it into her fist. The ring rubs slightly against her skin but she doesn't want to risk losing it. They are moving down now. There is a muddy field below them.

'I have something for you,' Luke announces once they are both seated, warming up inside the grand white limo he has arranged to transport them back to London.

'Oh good, 'cos I thought a diamond ring was a bit on the cheap side.'

'That's funny,' Luke laughs. Vera loves the way he pronounces his verdict on humour, as though physical reaction is somehow unreliable. Everything about him is definite, declared. She feels so safe wrapped up in his certainty. Vera is no longer certain herself if she is funny. People used to tell her that she was, and she used to work hard on telling a joke properly. It was an art form and she had wanted to master it, like her father. She tries now for Luke only and relies on his pronouncements to know.

Luke sits upright against the leather upholstery. He is out of place. Although he can afford better, he drives a second-hand Prius because it is saving the environment, and wears shirts that are years old or that his mother buys him, and carries a briefcase lettered with his father's initials with a tear across the front pocket. The extravagance of the day is a testament to the extravagance of his feelings for her. She smiles, and reaches for his hand.

Luke slips it away and reaches instead into the driver's section of the car. He seems nervous as he places a small, heavy object into her hands. 'I thought, well I hoped you might like this,' he begins. 'A new one of it I mean, a new . . . Well, read the card first.'

Vera does so carefully. Had she been alone, she would have dived first into the wrapping and torn it open like a child, but she feels Luke's gaze upon her as she slips the card out of its red envelope and takes in the oil-painted depiction of a hot air balloon on the front. 'Why a balloon? Bit random?' she grins, but the time for joking has passed and Luke says nothing. Inside, he has written just one line: *A three stranded cord is not easily broken.*

Vera thinks this must be from the bible. Somewhere. She has been going to church ever since they met. It was his thing, but it made sense to her immediately and she attends every week now. His church, with him. She even has a prayer that she says many times a day, like a mantra: *Dear God, help me to be better, to be worthy, make me clean. Dear God, help me to be better, to be worthy, make me clean. Dear God . . .*

Vera glances up at Luke before slowly inching off the paper. *To be worthy.* A book lays uncovered on her lap. A bible. The pages are beautifully bound in soft, black leather with gilt edges, the title embossed in gold leaf.

'For a new beginning, together,' Luke says. 'I know how much you've been . . . I mean, I've been so impressed by . . . And, well I thought you might like it.' Luke looks to her for reaction. His eyes are earnest, fervent, hopeful. All of the things that first drew her to him. And his gift says everything that Vera has been too scared to ask him: he forgives her, he trusts her, he has faith in her despite her past. *Despite the past.*

Despite the past he knew of her . . .

She lifts her head. He is waiting. And slowly, with a sincerity Charlie would never recognise, Vera finds herself looking into Luke's handsome, buoyant eyes and nodding.

'I love it Luke. And I love you.'

Outside, hazy fields drift by. More cars begin to appear on the road. A people-wagon, full of kids that peer out of misty windows to see who is inside the grand, white limousine. Luke puts his arm around Vera's shoulders, with his other hand hooks his fingers through hers, and Vera breathes him in. She rests her head on his shoulder. Safe. Secure. Affirmed. And as she imprints the moment into her memory, she ignores the squelching of her shoes and the slight stench of cow dung that has somehow found its way into the car. The camera in her mind pans away, *it was a day like no other,* and Vera pretends not to notice that there is a small red spot forming on her finger, just underneath her ring where the too-big band has begun to rub.

CHAPTER 3

Five weeks earlier had been Luke's father's birthday. He'd dropped in on his mother in the morning and they'd shared poached eggs with white bread and fried tomatoes, neither mentioning that this had been his father's favourite, nor that through this ritual they were marking anything in particular. And he'd walked with her to the high street where she'd pretended she wasn't going into the art shop to buy paints she never showed him, and he'd pretended he wasn't going to weave back past the graveyard. But of course they both had. And it was that afternoon, by his father's headstone, that Luke had imagined a good old chinwag with his long-deceased father who had never met Vera but would, he was almost sure, approve. Philip would have told him to buy the ring in secret. He would have urged him to be romantic. He would have asked him to make sure that Vera shared his passions and principles, which, it occurred to Luke, were the same thing.

He didn't tell his father about Vera's smile, or her tenderheartedness, or the heaviness in her eyes that sometimes made her seem so far away, so in need of rescue. Or the way that sometimes, when he was around her, he felt immeasurably flushed with hope.

Luke bought the bible before the ring. He bought the card in which to write his message before designing his proposal, using it for inspiration. He imagined the children they would have before the kind of wedding. If they had a son, he would name him Philip.

CHAPTER 4

Vera never used to be an early riser but has lately developed an uneasy relationship with sleep. The hotel room has thick, red curtains but there is a small gap between them and despite the early hour Vera is sitting up in bed, examining the colours refracted through her ring and onto the ceiling. All the hues of the rainbow dance over her in clustered dots she can manoeuvre with a slight turn of her finger and fill with promise. She feels the gold band as a promise. Not only to Luke but to herself. There is a folded piece of paper in her wallet that she will not open today. She hopes, *she promises*, to open it soon, one last time, and then to throw it away forever. She is happy, so almost happy. But first she must make amends. Vera crosses the chilly room for the new bible she's left on the dresser and returns with it to bed where she props up the plump hotel pillows, takes a deep, fortifying breath and snuggles for warmth beneath the satin duvet. Randomly, she opens the book to *Luke* and smiles at the accident.

Since just a few weeks into their relationship, it

has been a resolution of Vera's to read at least a small section of the bible every day. Luke, she knows, reads a passage or two every morning and it seems to set him up for the day, focus him somehow on goodness. It is more of a struggle for Vera. It is always Jesus this and Jesus that, and she cannot help but feel condemned by the passages, always the sinner Jesus is urging the rest to forgive. But she gets it. She gets the purpose. It is a set of rules, a set of principles, a way to live. Easier than painfully pondering each decision, or choosing, or making mistakes. And it is not difficult for Vera to cling to the teachings, as she sees Luke clinging. Or to wile hours away in buildings made of stone and dreariness. Or to: *Dear God, help me to be better, to be worthy, make me clean.* The words, like the bricks and mortar, are barriers against worse things. Against thinking about worse things. Against doing worse things. She gets it. She likes it. She is surprised she didn't think of it herself, before.

Luke was thrilled by her 'coming to faith'. She knows that had she not been a Christian he would not have proposed to her. For him, it is critical. But then he has been at it longer. There has been a lot of repetition. She is sure that by now the bible is ingrained into his soul. Vera has many more verses to read before this is the case for her, but she hopes that with enough practice, the light that shines from Luke's eyes will shine from her own.

In her movie, there is suddenly a cut away to her, in the meantime, seeking out the brightness of a chandelier to stand under. To fool him?

She blinks as though in the glare. She has not yet begun reading. *Luke* is still un-begun. Have minutes passed yet?

She dares not look away from the light.

The verses will speak of forgiveness, of welcoming home the lost son and of turning from sin. Merciful words, but the memory of what happened the night before brings no such clemency with the morning air.

Phase two of Luke's proposal had been a sumptuous dinner in the exclusive restaurant of the hotel at which he had also reserved two rooms. The place was a post-modernist creation far fancier than the places they usually go to, set within splendid Georgian architecture and decorated with every fabric and colour imaginable so that no two pieces of furniture matched. A uniformed member of staff had handed them each a glass of champagne as they'd entered the restaurant, though Luke subtly switched his for a non-alcoholic cocktail, and Vera had followed suit. Happily. She hadn't needed champagne anyway, she was intoxicated enough by the enormity of what they were doing together. By the new life they were so close to. Luke had ordered for them both, smirking mischievously as he dropped in the phrase: 'my *fiancée* will have,' and Vera had felt that the moment couldn't have been more romantic. They'd linked hands across the table, and found it was impossible to talk of anything other than their future wedding, which they did with a delicious feeling of conspiracy. They retold the afternoon to each other, and stared deep into each other's eyes. Finally, Luke had led her to her room, and then followed her inside.

She can remind him of that she supposes: *he* was the one who followed *her* in. It was *he* who had sat on *her* bed, *his* hand resting on *her* thigh, *his* tongue probing with unfeigned desire. She can remind him of these facts and lay them before him, like Humbert speaking of Lolita, dear Luke, dear reader. But Luke has always been a deceptively good kisser. The night they first kissed – on their second date, in a deserted street outside an independent cinema where they'd watched a film about a lost tribe in the Andes – Luke had kissed her, deeply, and then with just as much passion revealed to her that he was a Christian and a virgin, in that order, and that he wouldn't have sex until he was married. She had laughed. Putting her foot in it, she'd punched him on the arm and made him promise over and over that he wasn't joking. Until it reached the point that he was laughing too and unable to say it with a straight face, and she unable to believe that someone who kissed with such intensity was really a virgin.

But in hindsight, it had been barely a peck

compared to the powerful sensuality that Luke had pressed against her lips a year later, during phase two, last night. Because now they were engaged, she'd figured, and this had blurred the boundaries of what he'd always ruled out before. And he loved her. And it had been a perfect day. His hand had moved up her back and into her hair. His strong, cycling legs had pressed firmly against hers. His tongue had searched hard for an answer. And she'd wanted to give it to him. The answer was yes. Yes, of course it was yes. Yes, she wanted to fuck him, to be his first. She could barely believe they'd waited so long! Sex, he would quickly learn, was just as useful a distraction as prayer.

Excusing herself for the bathroom she'd slipped away and Luke had smiled knowingly. It had been a year and a day since Vera had last had sex and in breathy excitement she'd shed the faded cotton underwear that, unprepared, she'd selected that morning. The engagement ring felt heavy against her nakedness. Her blonde hair tumbled over slim, bare shoulders, still freckled from the distant summer sun. The tail of his encouraging eyes made her shiver. Time was speeding past. Moments were happening. Her body had finally caught up with her mind. And both, in sync, were focused only on him. She'd taken one last look at herself in the bathroom mirror before, resisting the pulling of faces, quivering with anticipation and nervousness and a love more urgent than she'd ever known, she'd reappeared before him, an effigy of smooth, pale flesh, uninterrupted but for a band of rose-tinted gold.

She can still feel the texture of the disdain with which Luke had greeted her.

It was a pockmarked moment.

Luke's eyes had narrowed at once into a hurt, harrowed, horrified expression, and then he'd come at her with one hand raised to shield his eyes and the duvet from the bed in the other, a weapon with which to conceal and tame her. 'To protect,' he'd insisted, disallowing her from running mortified back to the bathroom and forcing her to sit. 'From yourself. Sweetheart, I know we're engaged, but engagement is *preparation* for marriage, it's not marriage. Having sex now would be wrong, it would compromise our relationship, and our commitment to God.'

'What about your commitment to me?' she'd flailed in that first, hot moment. 'How do you think I feel to be rejected by my own fiancé?'

'I'm not rejecting you, I'm rejecting sin.'

The bible truly was ingrained.

Some way down the corridor the lift had beeped. It seemed to punctuate their dialogue and they'd sat in heavy silence while Vera raced through the emotions of mortification, rejection, anger, bewilderment and shame. In her head she called back all the moments that had preceded this one: his touch, his look, his tongue. Surely he'd been giving her encouragement. But then she thought back further. Luke had told her from the very start he didn't believe in sex before marriage, only that day he had given her a bible, thinking, or hoping, she was as dedicated as he . . . Did he realise now that she was only going through the motions? Wasn't he? Wasn't everyone? Weren't they all papering over something?

Thoughts snaked like poison through her mind. Snaking. Snaking.

She was the serpent. Still. It was her sin after all. It was because of her and not him that she felt so rejected and small.

'Look, it's no big deal,' she'd said finally, 'I just . . . I'm still learning the Jesus rules I guess!'

'I'm sorry sweetheart. Please don't feel bad,' Luke had reassured her. But he shook his head with minuscule movements she knew she wasn't supposed to notice, but did; tiny disapproving gestures that scared her. She took a deep breath.

'I'm sorry,' she offered. 'Forget about it Luke okay? Okay? Think of it as a preview. The main attraction's yet to come.'

'Exactly. Exactly,' he had agreed eagerly, and just as eagerly she had pulled the duvet closer around her and leant her head onto his shoulder, where she could feel his frame slowly relax as the danger receded.

'Tell me something true,' she had asked him softly, and Luke had smiled and kissed the top of her head.

'Jesus is truth sweetheart.'

★   ★   ★

28

Charlie would have thrown her onto the bed, offered her some coke afterwards and left hurriedly, possibly for another date. She would have felt better, and worse.

Vera closes her pristine new bible. The hotel phone rings. It is Luke. They arrange to meet for breakfast. Over toast and jam and fresh black coffee, they decide it is time to share their news.

Luke's mother lived by herself in a huge, rattling town house in St John's Wood just three roads away from Luke. She changed the window planters every season, had the façade painted every third year and dusted the whole house on Tuesdays. On Saturdays, she got up early, dressed in trousers, flat shoes and one of her husband's old shirts, unhooked her overall from its home in the pantry and made her way into the glass-topped extension at the back of the house where she remained until she lost the light, tenderly caressing canvases with a sable hairbrush. During the rest of the week, the door to this room was locked, and Lynn never showed anyone the vast landscapes and intricate portraits she created within, but she looked forward to Saturdays. So it was with some irritation that she told her son that of course he could pop in for tea, that she'd be delighted to see Vera.

Lynn replaced the overall, selected a dark blue dress from her wardrobe and snarled at her reflection in the mirror. She had been beautiful once. Men used to stare at her and whistle if she wore a short enough skirt. Women had envied her full breasts and tiny waist. Once, she was invited to be a model. Now her blonde hair was thin and white, the skin around her eyes too flimsy to take much make-up, and her breasts sat blithely on the waist that after two children, one caesarean section, and 58 years, was no longer so perfectly formed. Lynn pulled her excuse for hair back from her face and tied it perfunctorily into a low bun, before looking again.

It still startled her sometimes that she didn't see Philip alongside her own reflection. He had been handsome when they'd first met in the years after adolescence, between childish dreams and reality, before either of them had contemplated the existence of Luke and John. They'd met at Cambridge. Lynn had been amongst a new wave of women taking serious degrees and she and Philip had both read History, though she was more adept at it, despite the damning indictment of their final grades.

Together they had dreamed. Lying on the grass on the bank of the Cam half way to Grantchester, he'd whispered of Paris, Rome, the Sistine Chapel, of Notre Dame, of Mont Saint-Michel, the Coliseum, the great dome of the Pantheon, cafés and parks and churches and moonlight, all traced with gentle precision across the curves and valleys of her body by fingers that knew the future, or seemed to.

30

Sometimes she showed him her sketchpad. During those years she drew prolifically, each day stumbling across a new, life-altering emotion that had to be recorded in brave, sprawling strokes. In watercolours, she created shimmering, rolling landscapes. In charcoal, usually only him. But during that final summer they'd swapped their dreams for books that they devoured in chunks, feeding each other morsels, like wolves.

Philip proposed to Lynn three days before their first final. It was his birthday and they'd decided against a party since everyone they knew was studying around the clock. But the two of them managed to spare an hour to meet at their usual restaurant, a tiny bistro hidden at the bottom of an alley behind Lion's Yard that still used oil lamps and served hearty onion soup even at the height of summer. Lynn had been in the throes of the French Revolution all day and neglected to leave herself enough time to get ready. But she'd tied her long, thick hair into a playful ponytail and pulled on the yellow dress she knew was Philip's favourite, before remembering the matching silk scarf she'd chosen for him and wrapped weeks earlier, and cycling down the hill to meet him. He'd been wearing a pale blue shirt that she'd always remember, because in the midst of their celebrations she'd spilt red wine all over it and to make her feel better he'd joked that the stain wouldn't last anywhere near as long as their marriage. As it turned out, the shirt still sat in the attic in a cardboard memento box larger than the brass one in which Philip's ashes were entombed, the stain having proved permanent and their marriage less so. But that night the future hadn't mattered, or rather it had mattered, acutely, and was bathed in indomitable light.

At once, the French Revolution seemed irrelevant.

An engagement party was hurriedly planned for the day after their last exam before all of their friends went home, and Lynn spent much of the following week making lists of menus, sketching hairstyles and dresses, and not dwelling on History. It wasn't until many years later that she felt the depth and significance of this mistake.

Lynn held onto the banister as she made her way downstairs to the kitchen. The pain in her right side wasn't as bad as it had been the day before but nevertheless packed her with an exasperation that crept up on her every morning, swelling throughout the afternoon and poisoning her internal narrative. In the kitchen she filled the kettle, arranged some chocolate covered biscuits onto a plate, and set about making a round of triangular cucumber sandwiches. When she had finished, she pulled out a tray from under the sink and set it with teacups from her best set. She never used to use their best china. She and Philip had chosen it when they were first married and each year, on their anniversary, they'd added to it, in the beginning with an imperial feeling of expansion,

32

then later, with the sensation that she was trapped in a porcelain china cage. They had kept the set in a display cabinet in the dining room where Philip's urn now stood. Lynn had made space for it by clearing the top shelf and transferring its contents – cups and saucers – into the larger cupboards in the kitchen. Now she used the delicately flowered crockery every time she made herself a cup of tea, and every time contemplated the waste in not having utilised them earlier.

Lynn heard the door of Luke's new hybrid Prius slam before he rang the doorbell – out of politeness as he had a key. She switched on the kettle and moved to the hallway where through the small window, she watched her son's girl-friend dance towards the house. She was so young, so carefree, her son laughing delightedly at the girl's effervescence, she reaching her arms around his neck and he taking her hands in his, holding them between them then leaning down to kiss her forehead. It reminded Lynn of a day she'd spent once, in a park somewhere. She gathered herself to her full height before opening the door. Luke towered above her from the lowered doorstep. Behind him, Vera shifted her weight from foot to foot and smiled with irritating, youthful gusto.

'Darlings! How are you? What a lovely surprise! Come in, come in.'

She ushered them into the sitting room where Luke sank comfortably into the sofa and Vera perched as always on the edge of the cushion next to his. The girl seemed even more uncomfortable than usual, fiddling with her blonde hair, which wove itself around pale, young, angular arms. Luke nodded at her as though to lift her into assurance. On the other side of the room was a seat that used to be Philip's and still bore his dent.

'I'll be in in two ticks!' Lynn called from the doorway. 'The kettle's almost boiled.'

'Don't rush Mother, I'll light the fire,' Luke shouted back in typical can-do pitch, but he was still fiddling with the coals when she returned.

She tried not to smile. Placing the tray of tea, biscuits and sandwiches expertly down on the mahogany coffee table, with a flapping hand she shooed Luke away from the hearth, her deep blue buttocks waving at them as she manipulated the gas. 'Ah ha! There we are! A fire.' Triumphantly she sat down opposite her guests. In an attempt at politeness, Vera had begun to pour the tea but was struggling to manoeuvre the pot's spout without spilling. There was a knack, it had to be tilted slightly to the left, but Lynn decided not to offer this piece of information. She hadn't offered it last time either. Eventually, Vera managed to fill a cup.

'Milk and sugar Mrs Hunter?' she asked sweetly.

'Certainly not, just a little lemon.'

Vera handed the cup to her, spilling some tea into the saucer, and Lynn mopped it up with a serviette before placing it on the side table next

34

to her chair. 'Did you manage to get your washing machine fixed in the end?' Vera asked, starting to pour a second cup. But as she lifted the pot, Luke caught the girl's eye, the two of them exchanging surreptitious glances, and she spilled it again. Lynn knew that look. The two of them were conspiring over something. She stood up.

'Thank you Vera, I'll do the rest. I know how Luke likes his.' Vera conceded the pot with a smile, though Lynn was unable to tell if it was laced with gratitude or reluctant defeat. No official battle had been declared between the two of them, but she was the first girl Luke had ever dated who made Lynn feel the need to keep her guard. She raised her eyebrows, deftly poured out the remaining tea, and offered them the plate of sandwiches.

'Oh, no, I'm stuffed thanks, we've just had a huge breakfast,' Vera protested.

'I'll take one Mother,' hurried Luke, and Vera looked embarrassed.

'Don't if you're not hungry. I had them made already.'

Luke ignored her and took two. 'They look delicious.'

For a moment the three of them sat upright, sipping tea, listening to the sound of Luke chewing, and staring at each other. Usually Lynn would have asked after Vera's parents, or her job, or their weekend plans, but that morning she couldn't bear the thought of having to listen to the answers. Vera fidgeted in her seat, her eyes scanning the walls, lined with books that Lynn had read every one of, with the exception of the dictionaries, encyclopaedias, and a few of Philip's old law texts. 'So we have some news Mother,' Luke said finally.

'Oh?' Lynn put her tea down on the side table again, scowling with impatience at the pain that shot through her side.

'It's good news,' Luke clarified, noticing.

It wasn't his fault, she knew, but the confirmation of her distress reflected in his eyes angered her. She would have to tell them soon. 'Good,' she said curtly.

'And it's big news.'

'Well, what is it?' It was Philip's tendency and not hers to create decoration around plain facts.

Luke's hand wandered across the old sofa for Vera's. He uncrossed his legs, crossed them again, and coughed. 'Well, I've asked Vera if she'll do me the honour of being my wife. And she's said yes. Mother, we're getting married.'

The fire crackled. From the next room the kettle whistled, Lynn having boiled it a second time in anticipation of them needing another pot. Her side burned. She winced.

'Mother?' urged Luke.

'Are you sure?'

Vera flinched but Luke only laughed. 'Of course we're sure Mother!'

Lynn winced again, and tried not to frown. The

pain had never been this intense before. 'Yes, of course you are.'

There was a pause while they waited for her to continue. Lynn shifted uncomfortably in her seat.

'I think you've knocked your mother speechless,' Vera joked awkwardly.

'Aren't you happy for us Mother?'

'Of course I am.' Lynn shook her head angrily at the pain, picked up her flowered cup again and then replaced it. Usually she hid her symptoms so well. She stood up. 'Of course I am.'

'You don't seem quite happy,' Luke pressed.

'Don't I?' She punched her side gently, hitting back at the soreness, pretending to tidy.

'You're scowling Mother.'

'It's wonderful news, Luke,' Lynn affirmed edgily, trying her best to smile. She turned to pick up her tea and while she was facing away let out a small exhalation of stinging air, steeling herself before she turned back. But when she did, Vera and her son were swapping intimate, bemused expressions. Private entreaties. 'The thing is,' Lynn continued abruptly. 'I might not be here to see a wedding happen.'

Now Luke turned away from Vera and stood up. 'What do you mean Mother? We haven't even set a date. Are you going away?'

'No Luke,' said Lynn slowly. 'I'm going to die.'

Upstairs, Lynn lay on the king-sized bed she used to share with Philip and closed her eyes. She pushed a pillow underneath her feet and contemplated how much more comfortable she would be if she changed out of her dress and constricting tights, but decided against it. Instead she thought about Luke, for whom she had reluctantly agreed to lie down. On her oak beside table was a photograph of him aged four standing upright and serious in front of Philip, with John just a toddler in her arms; but she didn't need to open her eyes to picture either of her sons at this age. Already their personalities had been quite distinct. John forever clung to her, crying if she left the room, nervous, beautiful, expressive, sensitive; while Luke tried to follow his father to work, resisted being hugged, stood next to Philip in the mirror copying the way he wet his hair and slicked it back, and held fiercely to Lynn's hand when they were out shopping, protecting her. Now he was going to be married. To a girl still young and lovely, still in possession of possibility, whose unwrinkled fingers he'd lace with his own.

Downstairs, voices rose. Vera had left almost immediately. In those first, terrible moments, she'd reached for Luke's hand, muttered her sympathies and tried not to reveal her disappointment with the way the afternoon had turned out. But Luke had asked her to go. Then he had made Lynn give him the number of her doctor, and spoken to him for almost an hour. Finally, he had called John and forced him to leave his rehearsal, as though it was urgent, this thing she'd been keeping from them for weeks, as though there was something to be done. Now the two of them were sitting at the kitchen table, arguing.

It didn't surprise Lynn that her sons had already made this about them. *Their* pain, *their* responsibilities, *their* rivalry. This was what she'd been cheated out of all along – a story of her own – so it was apt that even her death was being appropriated by others. In the days after the doctor had told her she had cancer of the liver, and that it had spread there from her breasts by way of her lungs, and that she could have treatment but in his opinion she had only months to live, she had been thinking a lot about where she had lost her narrative, her life, where she had misplaced it. Because that's what it felt like: a To-Do list that had somehow been mislaid, a piece of lost property, out of sight but still belonging, staunchly, to the original owner, like those war veterans who've lost a limb but can still feel it flailing in the empty space, can still deceive themselves that it is there.

When had it happened?

There wasn't a moment, she supposed. It didn't come about like that. It was a progression: slow, undetectable, like the cancer. The contrast however between the days in which everything lay sparkling in front of her and then suddenly half-crumpled in her wake was sometimes too much to bear. Summers crept up on her. Days and days and years in which she was hardy and ambitious and the *new woman* everyone was either excited about or afraid of. She was one of the lucky ones, part of a generation in which things were possible, the whole world open to her if only she was bold enough to grab it. Nobody would have imagined then that she – clever, strong-willed, boyish – would choose an apron, a clean home, a set of china, the same life her mother had had. Not even she would have imagined it, or chosen it perhaps if she'd been aware of what she was choosing in those hours with Philip on the river bank; *that* she was choosing.

Was it his fault?

Lynn no longer knew the answer to this. A haze had descended without warning on her memories and it was impossible to decipher whose wishes she had been following, Philip's or her own, whose suggestion it had been that she stay at home, forgo her Masters degree, reject a career; whose doing it was that she sacrificed her story.

Mrs Hunter.

Those two simple words had filled her with such joy, pride and excitement. The day after they returned from their honeymoon in Cannes she had dressed in a new silk blouse they'd bought on the trip, and together they'd made a round of all the institutions that would require knowledge of her new status: the doctor's surgery, the council office, and the bank where they opened a joint household account, had both names printed on the cheque book, and where, when they left, the doorman said *Good day Mrs Hunter*, prompting her to run back inside under the pretence of having forgotten her pen just so she could hear it again. No, it wasn't his fault. She had been complicit.

She should never have taken such joy in baking. This was often what she felt the whole thing boiled down to: food, the substance of life. Right at the beginning when there was still space to mould their roles like the pastry she cut, she should have shaped herself as one of those women who got their husbands to help, or taken a job and hired someone to cook for them. But it was all a game then, being a wife, playing house, not real but a fantastical world like those she visited in the books she read and could dip in and out of at will. In the game, it pleased her to look after him. It pleased her to embrace the novelty of housewifery. It pleased her to see Philip tuck into meals she had prepared especially for him, develop favourites and request them, depend on her.

Luke knocked on the door.

It was quiet in the hallway. John must have left.

'You've been asleep,' Luke said as he entered. 'Mother, how are you?'

Rolling her eyes, Lynn sighed overtly back at him. Her son. One of only two accomplishments in her life. Not like women nowadays who could have it all. Like bright, career-driven, youthful Vera. Vera would live.

Lynn should have lived. She should have dared. The problem was she'd always liked to excel.

Having taken on the role of wife, mother, it followed that she should strive to be the ideal version of that. No affairs, no complaints, no help, no excess; just church and family and rules and principles and propriety, and everything done properly from scratch. Doing what was right, what was expected. Not that suddenly losing one's husband – and validation, and dreams, and future – was right, or proper, or expected.

'You'll have to look after John. When I'm gone,' she told her son.

'Mother, don't talk like that.'

'He's not as strong as you are.'

Luke took off his glasses and rubbed his eyes, half-filled with the green of hers. He looked a little like Philip as he rested his blond head in his hands, though John was the one that bore Philip's dark eyes and angular jaw-line and sometimes made her gasp when she was surprised by his silhouette. It was strange that Philip had never seen this likeness, that it was Luke who he filled with himself.

'John can look after himself, Mother. That's all he can look after.'

'John's sensitive Luke. And he looks up to you.'

Luke sighed again and replaced his glasses. He got that from her, his poor vision. Philip's sight had been perfect almost until the last and it had been comical to both of them when he'd finally succumbed to needing spectacles and they had clashed frames when they tried to kiss. They'd laughed a lot that last year. Philip had cut down his hours, finally, and twenty-odd years after they'd laid on the river bank of the Cam they'd been making plans again: Paris, Rome.

'Mother, we need to plan what we're going to do.'

A different kind of planning.

'Oh you'll figure it out. Remember that time John got his nose punched? You looked after him then didn't you? Saw to that awful boy, what was he called? Kevin Randall? Rundell. You stood up to him. Remember?'

'I'm not talking about John, Mother. I mean, we need to talk about what we're going to do about you, about your situation. I can't take time off work at the moment—'

'Well whoever asked you to?'

Of course she wouldn't cry. Many years had passed since there'd been any point in it, anyone there to mop up the tears. But her chest tightened as Luke spoke to her of practicalities. She hadn't thought ahead this far. For the last weeks she had been occupied with the past, with what she wouldn't ever now get to do, with the time she had wasted wallowing, mourning, regretting, but not with the disease itself, the silent, creeping sickness that was responsible for the final removal of choice and chance and possibility. The doctor had tried to tell her. He'd spoken about the 'decline' to come, about progressive symptoms, and now the worst of his warnings came back to her and struck her hard: she would need looking after. But by whom?

Who would buy the shopping when she could no longer make it to the supermarket, or even the little Indian-owned shop on the corner? Who would bring her her meals when she was too weak to fetch them? Who would change her sheets when she soiled them?

'I'm perfectly capable of looking after myself thank you,' Lynn frowned. Luke tried to reach for her hand but she slapped it away.

'Mother, you're going to need help. You already need help.'

'Don't be so ridiculous.'

'I wish I could look after you myself, but I just can't at the moment. Maybe, perhaps John could—'

'Don't you dare burden him with this.' Lynn pulled herself painfully into a more upright position in the bed. 'He has enough on his plate.'

'Why do you always make excuses for him?'

Luke stood up and paced around the room in front of Lynn's bed. His agitation was disturbing at first, but after a while it worked its way into a rhythm and his to-ing and fro-ing began to lull Lynn into another fog in which he was still there but smaller, and John was nearby, and Philip was crawling across the floor towards them in a swaying motion, pretending to be a ghost.

'Mother.'

She opened her eyes.

'You'll need someone to take you for your treatment Mother. And to look after you. You can't do everything for yourself. You – you won't be able to Mother. Already look how tired it's making you. I should have noticed. But – now – we've got to face it.' His jaw trembled in the same way it had when he was seven and being told off.

'Oh come here you silly boy.'

Luke sat down again, this time on the end of her bed and she took his hand. Removing his glasses, he rested his head on their clasped grasp. It seemed that if only they could remain this way, the moment would defy truth and time would pause, give them longer. But Lynn had to tell him.

'Luke, I'm not going to have treatment,' she said quietly. His head still bent, Luke didn't move. 'There's no hope of recovery. I'm sure the doctor's told you this. All it might do is delay things, a little, but it will make me much sicker, and I don't want to be. You know I'm no good with illness. So I'm not going to have treatment. And I'm not going into hospital. I'm going to stay here, in my own home, with my own things, where I've always been.'

It was just what her own mother had told her before her descent into nothingness. But such words had infuriated Lynn then, the stubbornness, the giving up, the admission of defeat. She'd wanted *her* mother to fight, to try, to prolong her life even if it was by mere moments. Now however she understood. This was the last and only stand that could be taken, the only way of exerting control, if not over a wasted life, then at least over death; not the whole story but the final chapter.

'I knew you'd say that Mother.' Luke left his head on their hands and wouldn't look at her.

'You mustn't tell John though, that there's an option.'

'Mother, are you sure?'

Are you certain? Her mother had asked her before the wedding.

'I'm positive.'

'Then we need to sort out some help here. Someone to look after you.'

She closed her eyes.

When she opened them again, Luke was gone.

She looked at the clock on the wall and saw that almost an hour had passed. Painfully, she shifted herself higher up the bed. The china cups and saucers were still in the sitting room, along with the plates full of crumbs and chocolate biscuits that would melt from the heat of the fire. It bothered her to think of the tea staining the pot and the inside of her cups, but she would have to deal with it all in the morning. There would be no returning downstairs that afternoon, or that night, and no return to her retreat at the back of the house; she was tired now. Lynn turned her head to study the photograph next to her bed once more. It had been taken almost ten years after that first, joyous wedding night with Philip, and by then there was a noticeable qualification in her smile, but the girl staring back at her was still naïve. She still possessed a faith that Lynn no longer indulged, and as she looked now at the hope in her youthful eyes, it filled her with scorn and pity, and a deep, grinding resentment for her former, innocent, culpable self.

CHAPTER 5

Emily didn't mind working in the evenings. There was a certain serenity to having whole buildings to herself, hallways and offices and corridors without another soul to contend with, and she preferred traversing the city at night. The problem was, it wasn't possible for her to sleep in the daylight; so she grew tired and had migraines more often and thought more frequently about the razor blade in the box under the sink.

Usually her shifts had started by five. At this time of day the council building she lived in was buzzing with sounds: of teens only slightly younger than herself crashing in and out of each other's flats; of mothers screaming at unruly children or unreliable husbands; of music blasting too loudly and rattling the walls; and she would move quickly then, without glancing up, glad in the knowledge that when she returned at two or three in the morning, a hush would have descended. Even in those dusky hours a few darkened figures might loiter in stairwells, and sometimes there was arguing, or the bass thump of music, or furniture moving in the room next to hers, but such activity always seemed muted somehow, made appropriate for the night. And this was when Emily sank into her bed, savoured the darkness and allowed herself to be lulled to sleep by city sounds that reminded her of where she was, and where she was not.

During the day, such calm was a futile hope. Even grey skies pushed colour through the tiny window into her room, and once lit, it was impossible for Emily to rid the corners and crevices of memories that hid there, waiting for her to look. The only solution was to move, and keep moving. And so she would brave the cold of her room to dress, make herself a flask of sugary tea, and hit the pavements of the streets that weaved around her. All day she would walk the cheerless roads, careful to avoid the areas where she used to know people, the building where she used to go to college, the road where Auntie and Uncle still lived.

The town hall was a place to go. Like museums, and galleries, places one could stand in for free and observe. It was something Emily was learning – the art of being a watcher without being watched. Evening shifts made it easy, scuttling about in darkened offices after people had left them, looking at their photos and their handwriting while never being seen. But in the daytime, no matter how firmly she set her fringe with wax, how drably she dressed, nor how flat her shoes, she could not shed the sensation of difference she had felt since coming here. Even at school, when half her class had been from other countries and many of the girls didn't bother to learn English properly so should have felt more different than she, there was an internal badge she could not take off that marked her out, made her angry and defensive, and kept her alone. It was memory, she supposed. Memory that jolted sharply through the London rain with hot, stabbing reminders of what had come before such comforting dreariness. Accusing her. Pointing at her. Making clear that she was not in fact so coolly disposed to talk calmly about the weather. To talk at all. *If you keep your problems in your stomach, the dogs cannot eat them*, her mother had told her once. Another proverb, etched in her head. And Emily clung hard to this wise instruction. She watched, and said as little as she could get away with, and kept her difference to herself.

Because nobody else noticed it, she was beginning to realise. It was her insecurity, her paranoia, her hard-learned lessons. Yet even in the town hall, where she sat amongst throngs of others darker and lighter and taller and shorter and thinner and fatter than she was, she needed a magazine to hide behind. She had taken this one from the doctor's office, and peeked out at the people from under it. It was a marvel to her the way they registered themselves. For all sorts of things: births, marriages, deaths, planning permission, social care, housing. She heard them talking in their twos and threes, or loudly over desks to council workers, explaining. So flippantly. Emily had applied for housing only because she had no other choice. She had loitered in the lobby for hours before joining the queue, and they'd had to ask her name three times before she had given it. Secrets should remain in one's stomach. She would not repeat the process to register for benefits. Still, she chose to come here sometimes when she had days free, to listen to other people's confessions.

CHAPTER 6

The red spot underneath Vera's ring has grown into a callous. She has not yet had the band tightened, though she has become obsessed with shining the rose-gold. She uses her jumper and occasionally strands of cotton catch on the diamond, only then making Vera aware that again, she has been shining. She is showing it off to her workmates. They think, she is sure, that it is the reason for her impending absence, though she has told them it is her own mother she needs time to care for.

Vera doesn't know why she is hiding the fact that it is Lynn. Lynn who is ill, Lynn who is dying, Lynn who she will sit with until that moment comes. Vera does not intend to be a silent martyr. It is purely for the credit that she is making the sacrifice. But perhaps she is mindful that it is Luke's loss and not hers. Or that death is not something to be bandied about. Or that the credit she wants is not from her colleagues. It is from the universe, or the power she prays to but does not believe in. It is from those great karmic scales, which currently lay toppled far too heavily to one side.

Vera smiles at the girls still cooing over her ring and begins sorting through the stack of files on her desk. It feels thrilling to be doing the right thing. Luke would never have asked it of her, but a trickle of excitement pumps through her stomach as she thinks about telling him. It is a truly generous Christian act. It is *better*. It is *worthy*.

'So, did you finally do the deed?' asks Felicity, leaning on the edge of Vera's desk. She lifts her eyebrows as she says this, and the other girls laugh.

When Vera returns to her desk after lunch, there is a message from her father. She hasn't spoken to him since the proposal. Nor has she spoken to her mother. It has been months since she last saw them, and only then because it was her birthday and they turned up outside her door. Vera texted her mother from the hotel room on the day Luke proposed but didn't answer when almost immediately she rang back. There have been no celebrations, no champagne, no meeting of in-laws, no reminiscing about how fast it all went and how grown up she has become. Vera's throat tightens as she thinks about this. She cannot bear the not seeing them. She cannot bear not hearing the sound of her father's soft, humour-filled voice. She cannot bear never sharing with her mother the bad haircuts and smelly armpit-men on the tube, and contents of her lunch, and other inane moments of her life that nobody else would care about. She cannot bear the thought that she will never again sit between them on the sofa and play Scrabble, all of them cheating. She cannot bear these things only marginally less than she can bear the alternative: seeing them, being reminded. *To be clean, to be clean.*

It was a stupid teenage rebellion that should have ended years ago. It was so stupid. So fast and unplanned. But all too quickly life changed from fields and mud, Journals and pink hair ribbons, her mother's tuna bake and A grades. And the piano. To a piano still but with Charlie, and her sat in her underwear on top of it. To dark rooms, hash that was too strong and made her sick, unbuttoned tops, unreturned phone calls, undone assignments, men, dawns, needles, ecstasy, abandon. And not her parents. And not herself, barely. But the start of everything that came next. And since it came next, she does not deserve to have what came before. The good is only a reminder of the bad. The past is a reminder of what has been. She can only survive by not thinking. And therefore the not seeing has to be borne.

Vera scrunches the message from her father into her palm and throws it under her desk into the bin. She remains still for a moment, her head bent. But she is too late. She did not act fast enough. She feels heavy.

'But this will pick you up,' Charlie told her. 'It's pure.'

Charlie reached into his wallet and handed the guy his share. Vera fished around in her bag for her mother's purse and produced a note from it. She would have left the purse and taken only the cash, but her parents had walked in just as she was rifling through it. They'd been at a dinner party across the road. Vera had been waiting at the sitting room window for Charlie's text. It was the summer holidays.

'Do you remember when you were 12, and we found you in here crying because we were home late?' Her father smiled, bounding into the room, enlivened by an evening of debate.

'You were so sensitive,' added her mother. 'You thought something terrible must have happened. We were only 10 minutes late.'

Vera dodged her father's kiss and stuffed the purse into her bag. 'I'm going out,' she told them.

Charlie had met her at Kings Cross. She didn't know he'd be with a girl. She was called Jane, blonde, pretty, innocent looking, like Vera had been. Behind them was a friend of Charlie's from boarding school. His father was a QC. His hair coiffed to the side hiding an early receding hairline. His skin was bad, his breath slightly putrid. Vera fucked him on Charlie's bed while Charlie and Jane giggled naked on the couch.

Vera shakes herself and glances purposefully up at her computer. Her screensaver is a photo of Luke. She locks her eyes onto his face and studies him, her soon-to-be forever: his jaw is well-defined, his nose hawked and masculine, his sandy hair slicked back with just enough gel to tame the waves, and his startling half-green, half-grey eyes

55

stare assuredly into the camera. It was she who'd been behind the lens, she who he'd been flashing his certainty at. His purity. His sincerity. Vera takes a deep breath, and sighs contentedly.

Dear God, make me better, make me worthy, make me clean.

She returns to the piles on her desk. There is one labelled *Home Care*. It was supposed to be her first solo account – a charity that provides carers for sick or elderly people in their own homes, runs activities for them, and is completely under-exposed and under-funded. Two weeks ago, she had been employed to change this, and although everyone agreed it was going to be a PR challenge, she had been excited by it. Vera checks around her desk for the advert she's spent three days mocking up. The woman in the photograph on it is not dissimilar from Luke's mother, and it occurs to Vera that Home Care would be perfect for Lynn, or for people like Lynn, people without a future daughter-in-law to depend upon. Vera feels another shiver of delight as she imagines the joy Luke will feel when he finds out that she has decided to look after his mother. He has been so sad since the news, sad and yet stoic, and more than anything she has wanted to find a way to console him. And he will be proud of her. She is for the first time in many years, a little proud of herself. Stapling the advert to the information pack on the top of the stack, she covers it in her trademark helpful yellow Post-its, and delivers the bundle matter-of-factly to Felicity.

Sorting through another folder, Vera tucks a few receipts and personal notes inside her top drawer before tidying the rest of the papers into a neat stack. It pleases her that there are no loose strands. She sees without opening it the edges of the piece of paper that is inside her wallet, in her bag, and for half a second considers taking it out. But in the end she kicks her bag further under her desk and glances around on top of it. The surface is already organised: a tumbler full of identical red pencils, which she frequently knocks over; an in-tray that she's alphabetised and organised with coloured dividers; and a stream of yellow Post-it notes that are like a map of her brain. At the beginning of the previous week, People PR had hired a new office cleaner and when Vera came into work she'd found her Post-its arranged in a vast floral pattern that covered her desktop. Every morning since there has emerged a new design, and every morning it has made Vera smile, but by 10 o'clock, or 11 at the latest, she is unable to resist the urge to restore them to their original contained lines. Whimsically, she removes one Post-it now and sticks it in the centre of her computer screen. She imagines a fat, jolly cleaner finding it there and laughing.

CHAPTER 7

The temperature had dipped again. There were two blankets on her bed, tucked in at the sides so as to keep out the icy air. She had not been feeling well. She had not been out walking. In the room next door, hushed voices rose and fell, feet scrambled. And Emily dreamed:

She smelled disinfectant and polish. Faceless computer screens winked at her. Rows of desks spilling their insides circled around and around, spinning her until she was dizzy and sick. Yellow stickers clung to her body like peeling skin. She sat down at a desk, back at her desk, Before.

'Hutus, stand up,' the teacher called. Thirty children stood, proudly, awaited the ticking of their names, the confirmation. They wore shorts or cotton dresses, their hair neat, their dark limbs gleaming with tiny droplets of sweat in the room that had no fans or air conditioning.

'Tutsis, stand.' This time there was a pause. Then hissing and laughter. Then slow, hesitant movements upwards and Emily, slinking down. Names called, ticked, noted. Then hers. 'Emilienne.' More firmly,

'Emilienne.' Reluctantly Emily raised her hand. 'Stand up Emilienne. Why do you not stand?'

'I don't want to stand with them.'

'You must stand with your tribe.'

'I don't want to be in that tribe. I want to be in Hutus.'

'You cannot be. You are Tutsi.'

'Why? What is Tutsi?'

Sniggers, laughter, jibes: big nose, lanky, parasite, cockroach.

'Ask your parents,' said the teacher, raising a hand to quiet the class. 'But now you must stand.'

She was eleven. She knew of course what a Tutsi was, but she didn't feel she deserved it. It was true, her family was not so poor as many Rwandans; they had a house with three rooms, her father had a job that paid better than tending the land like most of the village, but they weren't rich. She certainly wasn't rich. And she wasn't tall. She wasn't any of the things Tutsi was supposed to mean so why should she be called that name? Why should she be laughed at? Why should she be bullied and abused and told she wouldn't get a place at university, not even to bother, that she would never become a doctor, that she would never amount to anything.

Only Jean resisted joining in the jeering. She and Jean had been in the same class since she was five, he a year older, repeating the year. She had noticed him at once because his eyes danced with strange, brilliant colour – not brown like the rest of them, but half green and half grey. Ever since their first lesson together, in which the new female teacher had singled Emily out for asking too many questions and for the rest of the day made her stand at the front of the class, where to her mortification she had stuttered a sentence and once cried, Jean had stuck up for her against the other, less curious girls who thought her questions and tree-climbing and dirty knees made her not one of them. In return she had helped him with his homework, and mouthed him the answers to questions when the teacher put him on the spot in class. And they had become firm friends. Now, his green-grey eyes darted up at her apologetically from his desk, but he said nothing. She stood while he remained sitting.

'It is just what you are,' her mother told her that night.

'But is there something wrong with being a Tutsi?'

'No,' her mother softened. 'It is only what you were born. It does not mean you are any different from them. We are all Rwandans. You are just as good Emilienne. Better. Now say your rosary.'

'Can't I speak to God tomorrow?'

'Every day Emilienne. Every day. You betray God with such reluctance.' Her mother made a clicking sound at the back of her throat as she always did when she was considering an idea. 'You must not betray Him. Betrayal is the worst thing. It is a poison that seeps into everything, it grows and it spreads, it lives inside you, it controls you. Forgiveness is the only way to cleanse it and God will of course always forgive you if you are truly, truly sorry, but better not to betray Him in the first place. You will need Him on your side.'

'Why will I need Him?'

There was no reply to this. Only a hard rug filled with grass to pray upon, sore knees, stiff legs, boredom, fear of being hit if the boredom showed, questions, God never answering back.

Somehow later, she was younger again, seven. Her brothers chased her through a graveyard full of bushes and thick undergrowth at the back of their house. The grass was coarse and scratched at her bare legs. The air prickled with the smell of a hot, dry June. 'Emmy!' her brothers called. 'Emmy! Emmy! We're coming!' She ran wildly, the thrill of them finding her rising in a delicious bubble through her chest, making her pant ferociously, her breath too loud, a giveaway. Cassien pounced on her. 'I have her!' he yelled, and three more brothers ran jubilantly towards them, Cassien trapping her on the ground and tickling her until there was no breath left at all. Now she was theirs. And so she had to consent to their game: she was to be the judge, they the daring acrobats swinging from trees. She'd wanted to play it all along.

Mama scowled at the dirt when they arrived

61

home and sent the boys back outside again, curtly but with a half amused almost-smile. Emily was allowed into the house and helped her mother peel sweet potatoes and boil rice and be in charge. Her mother talked little, even when Emily tried her hardest to pry her open, but she loved these moments with her, these unlikely gestures of tenderness as they passed vegetables to one another. She loved the way that her mother listened to her incessant prattle: about climbing trees, and what game Cassien had promised her later, and long division, and how she and Jean were partners in Geography. And Emily loved how her mother smiled carefully, clicking her throat in encouragement as Emily lay out her childish hopes. Later, when her father arrived home, his face heavy with exhaustion, she would run into his arms and despite his fatigue he would hold her above him, his princess, and she would feel like one. Then, when her feet were safely returned to the ground he would go into the bedroom and remove the blue shirt he wore to work at the hotel, and put on his glasses, somehow replenishing himself behind them, and then it would be his turn to talk, sitting at the table while she and her mother sat nearby on the floor, passing vegetables, and now both woman and girl wore that same careful, inconsolable smile.

Suddenly a sunny day, maybe before or soon after. She was still young enough to have a gap in the front of her mouth where teeth had fallen out and not yet been replaced. A day out. A trip to Kigali. They were visiting Uncle Amani, their father's brother who though now widowed had married a Hutu, could speak French, was a brilliant scientist, and had secured a coveted job doing research for the government, despite the tiny amount of research being done in Rwanda and his obvious disadvantage in being a Tutsi. These were the facts often recalled to Emily and her brothers, and to their neighbours, and anyone else who would listen. Uncle Amani had no children but made up for it by remembering how to play kweti and introducing them to new gadgets he sometimes picked up from the Westerners he met.

The latest was a pack of cards with pictures of all sorts of cars on them, none of which Emily had ever seen in Kigali, and certainly not at home. She and her brothers were unable to understand the English type that accompanied each picture, but they recognised the numbers and Uncle Amani explained that it was a game in which these numbers were traded. They invented a set of rules and played ferociously while the adults talked about politics, and old times, and people they had once known. Emily couldn't help gazing intermittently up at them. Their faces flushed as they talked with a rare, untroubled animation, as though they were young again and didn't realise how raucous and ill-behaved they looked.

When Emily lost the last of her cards and had

to sit out of the game, she didn't mind her brothers' teasing. She sat silently on the floor and observed her parents. Her usually strict, no-nonsense mother sipped a coke through a straw, made unfamiliar coy flutters with her eyelashes, chatted enthusiastically, and told jokes that made Papa – ordinarily so tired, so headstrong and serious – wipe his eyes from laughter and squeeze Mama's hand, lying on top of the table for all to see. If Emily watched them closely enough, it was almost possible to snatch a glimpse of another time, and slip into their dreams.

In the afternoon, they walked through the busy town. Emily marvelled at the abundance of cars and people, and when they stopped, Uncle Amani bought them all a paper-wrapped cone of deeply fried frites, covered in a rich, buttery yellow mayonnaise that tasted like heaven. It was unusual for them to eat food in the street, but Emily gulped hers down even faster than Cassien, greedily scraping off even the slight mayonnaise crust that had built up around the edges and crunching it between her teeth. As soon as she had finished however, she regretted her haste and looked longingly at her brothers who had eaten more slowly. She should have saved some of her own. She should have taken home at least a couple of cold frites for Jean who had been ill recently, absent from school, and had lost weight. Every time she saw him he looked sad and listless, the usual playfulness somehow missing. He could do with tasting something as irresistible as the gooey mayonnaise whose flavour still lingered on her tongue. She had no money of her own and could not ask Uncle for more, not unless she wanted to be reprimanded by both of her parents in front of the bustling throng. But if only she could bring Jean something to cheer him up. A memento from Kigali. Then Emily spotted her opportunity. A colourful crowd began to file past them in the street and the men at the front were giving out flags: yellow, red and green. Jean liked green. His eyes were half green. He would like such a flag. Emily stepped forward to take one.

It was the only time that Gahiji ever shouted at her in earnest, or used the full force of his 15-year-old frame. Her hand hurt for whole minutes after.

Once more it was Before. Time kept jumping. They were outside their grandmother's house just a few hundred metres from their own. Emily circled Cassien as the rest of her brothers had instructed. The three of them were lying on the ground. She held a stick and chased Cassien with it, he grinning roguishly and scampering always a few feet ahead of her, deferring the end of the game; he was the last one.

'Come on,' Simeon groaned from the floor. 'Let her catch you now. Then we'll start again.'

'Can I be 'it' this time?' Cassien replied.

'Fine.'

Cassien slowed and let Emily reach him. In glee

she raised her stick and chopped at the back of his legs. Dramatically he fell to his knees.

'Now his head!' Gahiji cheered from his spot on the ground, slightly tilting his own head, like a bird, the way he always did when he was thinking or giving orders to his younger siblings, or creating a fantasy for them to believe.

Emily chopped lightly at his neck and Cassien rolled to the floor. She put her bare foot on top of him and stood jubilant, the conqueror. All five of them giggled. Then from the doorway of the house, a roar brought them to sudden attention.

'Stop it! Stop it this instant!' their grandmother bellowed. 'Come here. What are you doing?'

Humbly, eyes cast down, they trudged towards her, guilty they knew, but not of what.

'What were you doing?' she repeated.

'We were playing,' Emily offered slowly.

'What were you playing?'

'We were playing machete.'

Before Emily could blink her grandmother had raised her hand and slapped her, once, sharply. 'You should know better,' she glowered at the boys and lifted her hand again for them, furious but allowing them to run. 'Never again,' she told Emily who stood frozen and not understanding, holding her stinging cheek.

It was the embarrassment of the incident however that struck sharpest. When finally she felt that she could turn away from her grandmother, Emily looked up to find that Jean had appeared on the roadside. He averted his half-green eyes quickly and pretended to concentrate hard on the shapes he was making with his foot in the dust, but Emily knew he had witnessed her humiliation and the wrongdoing before it. It wasn't until many years later that she learned exactly what had made their behaviour such a sin, such an unwelcome reminder to her grandmother of unending Rwandan history. It was also not for years to come that she understood why she had been so ashamed to see Jean.

'Go away Jean. Stop spying. Don't you have better things to do?' she had shouted at him at the time in her mortification. She hadn't spoken to him afterwards for three whole days until he apologised for his accidental intrusion by showing her a small, imperfect circle at the bottom of his back that he had never dared reveal to anyone and which was inexplicably pure white.

Emily turned. Cassien and Gahiji were next to her. Gahiji had grown again, was tall now but thin, in many ways still a boy. It was his idea. He, the oldest, was always daring and they always doing his bidding. She and Cassien climbed the tree silently and threw mangoes down. 'Higher,' Cassien urged her, grinning impishly as usual, 'Don't worry, Gahiji will catch you.' Gahiji caught the stolen fruit in his T-shirt and peered through the lower branches, keeping guard. Their actions were laced with drama, but their breathing was steady.

'Take some bananas too, there is a very good tree three houses down,' Ernest declared abruptly from behind them. Ernest: their neighbour, the owner of the tree. 'I should tell your father about this.' They froze.

'Come on, come down. Emilienne, what are you doing up a tree? Shouldn't you be playing something more respectable with your girlfriends? I heard you were a smart one Emilienne, what is this? Cassien, I see you too. Get down. Come here. Gahiji, this is your doing, no?'

They shimmied down and stood heads bent before him, staring at the dry ground. Ernest watched them for a while, clicking his teeth. Then, 'Thank you,' he said, retrieving his mangoes from Gahiji's T-shirt. 'These needed picking.' Half-smiles began to creep across their faces and Ernest laughed sonorously, a deep-barrelled laugh that sounded as though it lived in the very bottom of his stomach and always tickled Emily. It made her think of long evenings sitting on the veranda with him and her parents and their other neighbours, or inside by the fireplace if it was raining, playing kweti with the children, listening to the adults talk. There was always a good feeling when Ernest was there, and often a piece of fruit or something else sweet; his laugh seemed to sweeten them all. 'Now, one each, and one for your mother,' he declared tossing them each a mango, the extra one going to Emily's charge. 'And next time, ask.'

They nodded their apologies and turned, running.

'And thank your mother for the salt!' Ernest yelled after them.

Emily giggled and received Cassien's grin, but she didn't follow him home. Instead she gave the extra mango to Jean who had grown that summer and was now the tallest boy in their class. His height had somehow given him a swagger and a wink that the other girls swooned at, but made Emily laugh when he tried them out on her. She still remembered the time he had fallen out of the tree in front of their house, and the time he had cried when Cassien, who was bigger than him then, had made him stay in goal for an entire game of football, and the day a few years earlier when he was still smaller than her and she had pinned him down in front of her brothers and made him laugh so hard that he started choking.

Emily wished they were still friends like that and had arm wrestles through which she could feel the heat of his lanky arms, and he join her brothers, almost as one of them, and was part of their games; but he'd started looking at her strangely lately, swaggering and winking, and now she felt uncomfortable under his lingering gaze. A green-grey gaze unlike any other. At school the week before he'd asked her, in front of a whole group of girls, if he could walk her home. Jean always walked her home. It was on those walks that the two of them and Cassien devised riddles they later tried out on Gahiji who tilted his head like a bird, and generously waited at least half a minute before solving them. But Jean had never *asked* to accompany her. And when he did this time everyone had started whooping and making kissing noises and embarrassing her so that for some reason she'd refused, and he hadn't spoken to her since.

The mango was a peace offering. He winked at her as she smuggled it into his hands and despite the strange, new, green-grey intensity, they laughed together and talked in familiar, animated tones until their fingers brushed and they fell unnervingly quiet again, and didn't move until Jean's mother called for him to come in, and sent Emily away.

She slept on her mother's chest. It rose and fell like water splashing the riverbank: gentle, reliable, lashing softly at the last pulls of the day. Her mother smelled of rice and coconuts. Her hands were coarse but tender. They played with Emily's hair. Occasionally they settled over her eyes, guarding her rest. Through the gaps in her fingers Emily could see the light fading, white and yellow flowers waving quietly from outside, her father smiling over the top of the thick book he'd promised to help her read when he was finished. Emily closed her eyes and sang to herself – a tune she and Cassien had made up, a tease-filled anthem to be sung obnoxiously when games between them were won. She practised it, looped it, smiled. Then something drummed against her temple, something loud and cold. Was it raining? Emily brushed her hand against the offending intrusion. It came back wet, and crimson.

She sat up. She was cold. She was alone. Her nose was bleeding. Her pillow was saturated in red.

CHAPTER 8

The reds were colliding. Not blending and complimenting each other as she'd planned, but crashing in and out of space like blood spattering, competing to make a mess of her creation. Lynn laid down her paintbrush and glanced at the clock. Vera would be arriving in 20 minutes. The thought of this in itself was irritating, demeaning. She had only agreed to it – why? Not because Luke had been so pleased at the solution. Lynn smiled as she realised the truth: it was malicious, unkind, powerful. It was the opportunity to visit her own poor choices on somebody else. Vera, the career woman, who could have had both, had forsaken her career already. For her.

Lynn cast one last stroke across the surreal canvas. It was better than the last and she would have liked to continue, but she did not wish to be caught so exposed. It would take at least 15 minutes for her to clean out the palette, and lock the door and make her way upstairs to change out of her painting clothes. It had been the only joy for Lynn of the past weeks – allowing herself to paint more often. At first, after Philip, it was a cathartic remedy she limited like medicine. She squeezed it carefully onto the palette.

The paint was a dark blue-black. Philip had been gone for three weeks. She said 'gone' and not 'died' around the boys and now even inside her own head. He had been gone frequently in the years they'd been together. When John was a baby, wrapped in her arms, refusing to be laid even for a moment in his cot, she would count sometimes the hours in which Philip was gone. Count them down, looking forward to the moment at which he would burst through the door filling her with support and company and friendship undimmed. Sharing with her the indescribable wonder of their sons that nobody else would ever quite understand. Creating with her four walls of sleepless, nappy-filled, unexpected . . . bliss.

He always came back to her then.

And told her when he was going. Gave her time to plan.

She picked up the brush she'd tentatively purchased from the shop in the high street. She had set up the canvas in her garden room at the back of the house and locked the door. John was still at school and Luke wasn't due home until the weekend, but she couldn't risk their finding a crack in her exterior. It was necessary for her to seem undefeated.

Luke had not cried, at least not in front of her.

John had wept for days.

She hadn't painted since Cambridge, since those endless days on sunny riverbanks. Why did she crave the brush now? To see him again. To remember him. To depict without decision the sweep of his hair, the gaze of his eyes, those early picnic dinners on student floors. When she was finished she stared at the images for hours. Longingly.

Lynn caught herself daydreaming and glanced around the room, inspecting the canvasses that she had begun that day. The paintings were like a diary of the last 15 years. Calmer times reflected in cityscapes, and beachfronts and forests from her youth. Other moments, regrets, frustrations, passions, in the sometimes-heady, sometimes-stricken faces of those she loved.

She shook her head. She should cover them. What was the point in remembering a happiness that no longer existed? It had been a foolish path in the first place. Family. Love. A career would not so easily have vanished.

Lynn closed her eyes.

She should have gone to bed earlier. It was unlike her to have stayed awake so late into the night, but the previous evening it had seemed necessary. Panic had begun to sweep over her often now: a sickly, hot sensation that made her kick off the covers or open a window or move around the room despite the pain in her side, for fear of stopping. Or noticing how fast her heart was racing. Or how pitifully nervous she'd become. *Poise,* people used to call it. She had poise. She'd had poise. Over the years she'd been told this often, and it was something people admired about her, aspired to, something that suggested intelligence and good breeding. She was glad that Luke and John, or worst of all Vera, had not seen her the night before: sweating, fidgeting, turning on the television. The *television*. She'd watched it until three in the morning, by which time she could hear birds already singing from the tree-lined street. There'd been a programme about reptiles that she'd watched for a while, the intrepid presenter somehow taming a ten-foot python, wild and beautiful, understanding it, showing it off before releasing it once more. After that there'd been only quiz shows, or rolling news of which she'd seen all the stories within the first 10 minutes and drew little satisfaction from the minuscule developments that were occasionally added. Still, she'd been compelled to watch something.

The result however, was this daytime haze that now enveloped her. She ought to shake herself out of it. She ought to clean out the palette and go upstairs. She ought to have done many things differently, and been different herself.

There is something about Lynn that makes Vera feel crumpled. Dishevelled, as though her clothes are in need of an iron. And condensed somehow, folded, like the piece of paper in her wallet. She sits on the tube, squashed between an old Chinese woman and a slightly pungent teenaged boy, and tries in vain to straighten herself.

She knows that Lynn dislikes her. Lynn barely managed to hide her horror when she and Luke told her about their engagement, and sometimes when they are together, sipping tea and making small talk, Vera catches Lynn glaring. She doesn't hold it against her. Vera suspects it is because Lynn has seen through her. Luke tells her all the time how good his mother is, how self-sacrificing, how astute, and Vera fears that for all her church-going and toeing of lines, Lynn has somehow spotted her wildness. Her evil.

It is for this reason that leaving work to look after Lynn is so perfect. It will not be easy. It will not be fun. It will be Vera's punishment, and redemption.

Despite knowing this, Vera has spent the past week concocting improbable fantasies of how things might pass – cosy confidences, raucous moments of laughter, a passing down of womanly secrets. A sharing of son and fiancé. Luke was so thrilled by her offer, touched and effusively grateful. Squeezing her arms beneath his coat he volunteered a 'something true', and told her that thanking God for her presence in his life is the first thing he does each morning. Then he kissed her square on the lips in the middle of the park and for once didn't seem to notice the people walking by. Vera can't quite quell the spark of hope that has been rising inside of her ever since. If only she can truly befriend Lynn. If only she can be there for her, and for Luke too, be useful, needed, do something good, help him, help them, help ease the transition between now and eternity. *Dear God, make me better, make me worthy, make me clean.*

Vera so wants to be clean. She wants to be good. When was she last good? She doesn't mean church and charity and abstinence and all that. She means something else she can't quite finger but knows she has lost. Purity? Innocence? Humanity? When was she last pure? Who last met *that* Vera? Not Luke. Though he has no idea.

The train shrieks to a halt. Lynn's house is the next stop.

Of course it was Charlie.

Charlie.

It's best to start with his name because so much about him seems to unfold from it. Charlie as in Prince Charles and aristocracy; Charlie as in Chaplin, the joker, the entertainer; Charlie as in cocaine. When they met during their first day at university, Charlie called her V and instantly, with one letter, dismembered her from her previous era, detaching her from the sensible, loving daughter she had once been, and setting her free. Or so she had thought for three blissful, electrifying, terrible years, the two of them filling the void of life, of growing up, of becoming, with chaos and noise and drug-fuelled decadence. Feeling youthful and brilliant, soaring high, until . . .

Luke fills his void with Jesus. His goodness shines out of him.

★ ★ ★

Lynn does not smile when she opens the door. Leaving it agape she moves to the lounge where she seats Vera in the comfy chair and insists on making their tea herself. She winces as she lifts the teapot but will not allow Vera to pour. She opens the window for Vera who is hot, then rubs her own arms from the cold. She is a wily old bat. Vera has a momentary vision of Lynn fanning her arms like bat wings. Luke would not find this funny but despite her nerves, or because of them, Vera laughs at the imagery. Lynn raises her eyebrows. Perhaps she thinks that Vera is laughing at her frailty with the teapot. Vera cannot explain. She avoids eye contact and scans the room, trying quickly to spot something to bond them, some nugget to offer up for friendship. It is important that they begin on the right note. Lynn sips her tea silently. Against the delicate china cup, Vera's own lips feel large and clumsy, and she cannot quite stifle the slurp. On the mantelpiece, a brass-tipped clock ticks loudly. In Vera's movie version of her life, tumbleweed is rolling by. She can see it moving across the rug and squeezing underneath the coffee table. Vera blinks. She can actually see it. Lynn is frozen, while dried, globular strands of plant creep over her, consuming her, progressing while she is paused. Or is it Vera who is paused? Slumping into the soft cushion, she feels herself folding. *She is folded. She is about to fold.* On the side table, there is a photo of Luke. Smiling. Smiling with certainty. The photo has pride of place. Lynn is looking at her looking at it. Vera's mantra circles her head. The silence has become unbearable.

'You must teach me how to make that soup Luke loves,' Vera ventures finally, plucking a thread of conversation from the air.

'You mean before I drop dead and can't cook it any more?'

'No – I . . .' Vera pauses, again, uncomfortably. *Like her life, there is an uncomfortable pause.*

'Only the way he raves about it anyone would think you've got a Michelin star.'

'I'll make you a pot,' Lynn replies, leaving Vera to nod gratefully into yet another silence and reach for more tea, which she spills over the antique coffee table. At least it is a reason to escape to the kitchen for a cloth, away, briefly, from Lynn and her disdainful looks, which have a way of dismantling Vera. It is already harder than she had imagined. It is one thing to play a part to willing audiences, to people predisposed to think well of her, but Vera finds Lynn too much of a sceptic to keep up the charade. Especially when, when it comes to her own character, Vera is a sceptic too.

'I'm sorry about that,' she mutters, returning with the cloth.

Lynn stares at her silently for a while, then concedes a nod. 'Well, I suppose you might as well get used to mess,' she says, pushing a strand of hair back into place with fingers that Vera now notices are stained red.

Vera pauses from wiping the table. She is taken aback. 'I won't mind,' she offers eventually, tentatively, putting down the cloth and thinking how brave it is of Lynn to admit her fear of the untidy end. To share it with Vera. 'And it might not be as bad as you think.' She steps closer, reaching slowly for the discoloured hand.

But at once this enrages Lynn.

'When you marry my son and have children, is what I mean. Children. There'll be more mess then than someone like you will ever be ready for.'

'I'm not ready,' she tells him.

'Nor am I.'

'I don't want it,' she whispers.

He says nothing.

'I won't keep it,' she sobs onto his shoulder. It smells rancid: wine and smoke and sex and sweat.

Vera breathes in deeply.

Someone like you, Lynn had said. Who is she like? Not herself. Not that girl she was for a while. *Help me to be better.*

When you have children, Lynn had said.

Help me to be better, to be worthy, make me clean. Help me to be better, to be worthy, make me clean. Help me to be better, to be worthy, make me clean. Help me to be better, to be worthy, make me clean.

Lynn taps her foot against the chair leg.

'Did you ever work, before children, before you

had Luke and John?' Vera asks, exhaling hard. She passes Lynn a crumpet.

Lynn butters it, adds jam, and then laughs, pityingly. 'I had no interest in such things. My choice was to be a wife and a mother.'

Vera flinches, too visibly. But perhaps because of it, to her surprise, Lynn softens: 'You'll understand dear, now that you've given up your job.'

'Oh, I haven't given up,' Vera replies quickly. Her mind is still whirring uneasily from their previous exchange but Lynn has offered an olive branch. Now is the time to capitalise, to clarify that she doesn't plan to live off her son, that her feelings for Luke are authentic, that leaving work to care for her is a sacrifice not a desire. 'I've just taken a sabbatical. I'll be going back.'

Lynn drops part of her crumpet into her lap. 'A sabbatical?'

'Yes.'

Angrily Lynn snatches up the fallen crumbs and empties them onto her plate. 'A sabbatical,' she repeats. 'So how long is this "sabbatical" to be? How many months have you allotted in which for me to die?'

'Oh, I didn't mean—' Vera begins, but Lynn has already taken her plate into the kitchen, and then too slowly to be really dramatic, but perhaps more potent because of the pain it is obviously inducing, storms upstairs, away from Vera.

★　　★　　★

Lynn lay alone in her bedroom, staring at the ceiling and noticing a chip in the paint that she wouldn't bother, now, to repair. Downstairs she could hear Vera moving about, tidying up, trying to be quiet, but every sound shot through Lynn's nerves and filled her with a seething anger. It was bad enough that Vera had arrived early and made her rush from her painting, leaving her dishevelled and imperfect for the rest of the day. But having her there, in the house, right in front of her was like being taunted by her worst demons. Slender limbs without age-spots. Hair still bright and voluminous. Naïvety and hope in abundance. A career. That had been the last straw, to learn that Vera had not been as stupid as she. That, after all, Vera would not cast herself into the periphery. Into dependence. She would marry *and* live. A whole life still unwritten.

Lynn's own money ran out a month after their eighth anniversary. She'd had a fund set up for her by her grandfather that she'd drawn from only slightly during university, but with their marital home to decorate and children to clothe, she'd pilfered from the top more and more regularly until there was no longer a top as such, but a fast-approaching bottom. She scraped the last of that to buy Philip a new briefcase made from the soft leather he'd been admiring with his initials embossed just above the buckle. There was a conversation soon after during which Lynn suggested half-heartedly that she apply for a

82

secretarial position somewhere, or something part-time as a supplement. But they both knew that she was trained in Plutarch, Tacitus and Thucydides, and the thought of undertaking a career so far below the options that had once been open to her, filled her with dread. Philip – who by then was earning quite enough salary for both of them and had acquired a number of rising expectations along with his rising status – wouldn't hear of it anyway. Not *his* wife. A legal aid perhaps, or something else professional and suitable to her intellect, but that would take further qualifications, and when she pointed out it would also mean the need for a housekeeper and a nanny and an end to his nightly three course suppers, he didn't push the matter. Instead, he presented a simple solution: a new fund, topped up monthly by him.

But it wasn't so simple. All of a sudden every penny she spent was accountable to Philip. Not that he asked, but when he ran through the accounts each month she felt a need to explain why they'd required a new toaster, why she'd purchased a new set of curtains, who she'd been at *Henry's* with three times for lunch, what was the occasion for which she'd bought her mother chocolates. It was as if all at once she needed his permission for everything she did, and the more often she requested it the faster she felt herself shrinking, submitting, forgetting almost the girl who'd once debated Engels and excelled at Cambridge, and been cleverer than her husband.

The first time she used her new fund to buy anything extravagant for herself, she unveiled the Givenchy dress she'd pounced upon in delight at Harvey Nics as they were getting ready for bed one evening. 'It's the new style,' she informed her husband, holding it up excitedly. 'Longer. What do you think?'

Philip was in bed reading a law journal, as if to emphasise the disparity that now stretched between them, a gap across which it was becoming increasingly difficult for her to fly, but he put the heavy book down to consider his wife.

'How much was it?'

Some words are heavy. They can drag a person down.

Although, in hindsight, it was possible that he'd never meant the question to be an indictment, Lynn could still feel the amalgamation of guilt and resentment, which in that singular moment clipped her wings. At once, she began to pack the dress back into its plastic. 'It was quite expensive darling, but I did need a new dress. We have the party next week don't forget.'

'Of course,' Philip agreed. 'I'm just curious, how much?'

It had cost twenty pounds. In those days that was a lot of money. It still, to Lynn's ears, sounded a lot and it shocked her when Luke didn't blink an eye at paying that much for dinner somewhere, for each person, for each course.

'Twenty pounds!' Philip said no more than that.

He'd always been mild-mannered, like John, but there was accusation in his eyes, or she imagined there was and concocted his thought process: *I work hard all day, I provide for us, and what do you do? Spend my money like it's nothing.* His unspoken words stung her through the silence.

'Put it on,' he said suddenly. Sitting up in bed now, Philip had taken off his glasses and tidied the journal onto his nightstand. Lynn was already in her nightdress, her hair set in curlers, her confidence dented.

'Not now darling,' she said. 'It's late. You don't really want to see it now.'

'Put it on.'

Lynn hung the garment onto the door of the wardrobe and turned to face him. She was unexpectedly exhausted and no longer felt like parading in front of him in the dress she now hated. But it had been bought with his money. This, she supposed was how she was to repay him. Philip nodded and so, slowly, she removed the protective material, sliding the dress off its hanger, stepping out of her nightdress and lifting the new outfit over her head while he gazed on. Silently she took out the curlers. Her hair tumbled free. She slipped her feet into a pair of heels. And then she stood, fully clothed now but feeling more naked and exposed by his eyes than ever before. With an abrupt, determined movement, Philip raised himself from the bed and walked rapidly over to her, his hands feeling for her waist and turning her in front of the mirror so

85

they were both looking at her reflection. Her skin was pale and she was still thin after a bout of flu. The dress skimmed her breasts and hung loose.

'It's stunning,' Philip whispered.

From behind her now, he hitched up the new long-length material, slid his hand underneath, then kissed her neck hard. Slowly she turned to face him again and just as slowly Philip lifted the twenty-pound dress over her head and threw it unceremoniously to the floor, so that she stood before him wearing nothing but a pair of heels. It was by no means the first time. The nights they had been naked together since their wedding were by then too numerous to recall and ordinarily, with both boys asleep, Lynn would have reached eagerly for Philip, for the buttons of his shirt, the string of his trousers, what lay beneath them. But this time the occasion felt contrived, an unequal exchange, her nakedness a gift and payment for him alone to enjoy. She let him trace her body with his hands and squeeze where they liked while she remained motionless. For the first and only time in their marriage, as he tenderly made love to her, Lynn felt tears stream down her face. Oblivious, Philip whispered his usual sweet nothings, *my darling little one*, but Lynn felt herself suffocating underneath his strong, capable frame, and as he moved on top of her she stared not at him but over his shoulder, fixing her eyes blankly on the then unblemished ceiling above their bed.

★   ★   ★

86

Vera knocked gently on the door before she left at five. When Lynn didn't answer, she knocked again, then retreated downstairs.

Lynn sat up. When she was sure she had heard the front door close, she slipped on the overall she'd hastily stuffed under the bed that morning and walked slowly to the window on the landing. Vera was already halfway down the street, occupied by her mobile phone. Light. Flippant. Unmoved by the fury her presence had sparked. Lynn felt red creeping back up on her. She made her way downstairs, stopping in the kitchen for a glass of water and noticing that Vera had left a small dish of pasta on the counter under cling film. Lynn left the dish where it was and returned to her painting. She pushed the canvas she had been working on to one side and started another. She used reds again, but this time it was a portrait.

It could have been a bigger disaster. Lynn could have asked her to leave, or told her outright that she hated her, or worse, told Luke. Of course if Vera had been thinking of Lynn and not herself, she may have pre-empted the insensitivity of the sabbatical issue. *Someone like* Luke would have realised.

At dinner, Luke reassures her. He tells her that his mother is scared, and used to being capable, and says she must simply keep on trying. He does not say that *he* is scared, and used to being able to fix things, and that he doesn't know what else to try; but Vera sees the fear behind his eyes, and carries his request for perseverance heavily. 'Perhaps, perhaps let her see that everyone is frail in some way,' he suggests. 'That we're all frail, and Jesus knows this. I don't know, maybe knock over the teapot?'

'Already done that,' Vera grimaces. But she knows of course all about frailty, vulnerability, weak spots. Worryingly, Lynn has begun to hit hers.

She walks home instead of getting a bus, forcing her legs to move steadily. Her mind feels hazy, her body too slow, her being trapped in a strange confusion of stopping, pausing, and running, running, running. *Children*, said Lynn. *Children, children, children*. Luke walks sluggishly in the other direction. They are both killing time. Killing the thoughts that surface when one has time. It is almost winter but the plants are not yet dead, the leaves not all fallen, as though petrified into a state of in-between-ness. Vera stays up late watching episodes of sitcoms she has already seen. She drinks coffee and Red Bull. Eventually, canned laughter lulls her to sleep.

The following morning, her head is groggy. Nevertheless she is up early. She has decided to read the bible. She decided this at 3.57am, but forced herself to lay with closed eyes until six. Twice she drifted off, but her dreams then were short, contained, not devastating. She picks a verse she has laboured through before, embraces the sensation of accomplishment that comes with understanding it, allows ancient thoughts to drown out her own, and arrives at Lynn's armed with determination. At the well-kept door however, Lynn tells her that really she isn't needed and would do better to go home. Lynn is pristine today, her hair in place, her cheeks perfectly rouged, her fingers un-coloured. On the doorstep, Vera's feet feel cumbersome. She moves her weight from one to another, aware suddenly of the messages going from brain to muscle to make them lift. She twitches her finger and is aware of thinking that she should twitch her finger. Pushing her shoulder forward, she is conscious of the test she is setting herself and no, she is not able to push forward her shoulder without following this thought process too. There is no mirror, but seconds are ticking by. Lynn taps her foot against the arch of the door like a metronome.

A breath, oh for a breath.

Vera exhales a conscious breath. Politely, she replies that she'd like to stay.

As though having anticipated this, Lynn nods and steps aside, but again Vera is disallowed from making the tea or fetching a blanket, or preparing lunch, and in the end she simply follows Lynn from room to room like a stray dog, offering strands of conversation that with a roll of the eyes are flapped away.

It is an absurd dance and they both know it. Lynn is without real occupation. She is busying herself, lifting books and opening them to random pages, feigning design. Vera's pursuit is even more ridiculous. The dance however continues. The rooms are cold. They are filled with a lifetime's clutter but a chilliness has settled upon the chaos like a film of dust. Vera wonders if Lynn sees it too, if with her movements she is trying to wipe it away, if under the trinkets and plant pots and photo frames, she is looking for some lingering warmth. For Life's heat. She returns frequently to the fireplace.

Eventually, Lynn sits. She holds her side as she does so, although she attempts to hide this. Then she closes her eyes pretending sleep. Again, Vera tries at conversation, but Lynn winces with every one of Vera's efforts, so in the end Vera decides to say nothing.

She leaves half an hour earlier than planned. Lynn raises her eyebrows towards the clock but Vera feels herself folding more quickly now. She has to get out. There has been silence for too long. Her mind is racing too fast, her mantra losing ground to the other noises inside her head.

Summoned noises. Summoned from the depths. Not from the depths. Vera shakes her head. Yes, from the depths, but so unexpectedly by Lynn, by her stillness today, and by her words of the day before. Words like 'children', cutting through Vera's thoughts. Vera watches her own arm as she raises it in slow motion to shift her bag higher up her shoulder. Her fingers curl around the strap like a reef fluttering in the undulation of shallow water.

Folding. Unfolding. Folding. They let go, they release, they move gauchely back through the air. Vera needs occupation. Or distraction. Or both. *Dear God make me better, make me worthy, make me clean. Dear God make me better, make me worthy, make me clean.*

Clipping quickly down the street, she scrolls through her phone. Charlie's number is conveniently always near the top of her list of contacts. Luke's is further down. Vera returns her phone to her bag and thumbs the worn seam of her wallet. She knows she must open it, take out the piece of paper, unfold it in order to unfold herself. But what if it undoes her altogether? What if it undoes them? Her and Luke? Her hope, her happiness, her sanity, her redemption. Her bag is heavy. She is carrying the new bible Luke gave her and it takes up most of the room. Vera sits outside the tube station and fishes beneath the bible for her pack of cigarettes. She lights one, thinks of Luke and stubs it out against the crumbling wall. The tube station is busy. People are jostling. Vera lights another. This time she inhales deeply, a dirty, smoky, cloudy breath. Her fingers feel better for being occupied, though her spare hand lingers over her wallet. She will smoke another cigarette before she boards the tube. She is not yet sure which way she will go.

Lynn had not planned for John to be their buffer. After three days of tension and silence the friction had seemed insurmountable and even Lynn, who had created it, wondered how long any being could last amidst such tautness of air. The days dragged, weighed down like gravestones. If she had been alone, Lynn could at least have been painting, or watching TV, or staring into space lost in her thoughts, but with Vera there she felt an impetus to feign occupation. And to make elaborate meals that really she was too tired to cook, not hungry enough to enjoy, and later felt the impact of, having stood for so long.

On the Wednesday, perhaps having noticed this, Vera turned up with pre-prepared food from a deli, and Lynn rather fancied a half of the egg and onion bagel, or some of the lemon-topped salad, and the ease of it all. For a moment she even found herself thinking that it was good Luke would have somebody so bent on providing sustenance. But she could not bring herself to accept Vera's offerings. Galling Vera was her only amusement.

Then John turned up unannounced that Thursday and regaled both of them with stories of blunders from his rehearsals, and did an impression of the power-mad director, and made them both laugh. At the same time. About the same thing. He insisted on a glass of champagne with their three o'clock tea, and by the time he left at four, something had dissipated. Lynn found that she could tolerate Vera without scowling. And to her credit, Vera had not given up on conversation. Her attempts were awkward and unskilled, but she was persistent. Really, Lynn should have put her at her ease, the way she used to with the new wives she met at Philip's law functions: include her, welcome her, let her in. The women always told her, later, how intimidated they'd felt by her – Philip Hunter's smart, beautiful wife – and how grateful they'd been for her friendship. They'd loved her for that. Lynn should let Vera love her similarly. But she could not bring herself to help the girl who already had everything. She let Vera scrabble.

'They're very different aren't they? Luke and John?' Vera tried, picking crumbs from the carpet near the chair John had sat in.

'I suppose they are.'

'You must be very proud of them both.'

'Of course, I am.'

'And that the family is so close, is a testament to you.'

Lynn nodded, thinking in fact how rare it was for the three of them to congregate together, how she had never once been to John's flat, how there was so much about him she had pretended not to notice. Were they close? Should she have noticed? When he was a teenager –

'I don't see my parents often,' Vera offered into the long pause, and Lynn snapped back into focus. She was noticing these lapses of hers more and more often. It was growing harder to stay engaged in conversation, in the present. Ridiculous for a woman not yet 60.

'Why not? You don't get on?' she said briskly.

'Well, we disagree these days.'

'All parents disagree with their children's choices.'

Vera flinched, and Lynn noticed the sting of her remark. 'My mother for example, despised my choice of churches,' she added.

Now Vera smiled and sat in the chair she had finished brushing for crumbs. 'My father doesn't believe in God at all. If I told him I was going to church now he'd think I'd lost my senses, or stopped questioning things, you know?'

'Not everything should be questioned,' mused Lynn, not convincing herself, but watching with not total irritation as Vera brushed wisps of blond hair from her naïve, freckled skin.

'No. But well, that's not the only thing that's come between us.'

'Most things are fixable with time. If you *have* time,' said Lynn pointedly.

'Yes,' mumbled Vera apologetically.

'Which *you* do.'

'Yes.' Vera looked down at the crumbs in her hand. 'It's just – well, there're things I've done, before, terrible things that if my parents knew about, if anyone knew about . . . But of course they've been done, so . . .'

Lynn rolled her eyes and tapped her nails impatiently against her teacup. Just as she had begun to imagine she could bear the girl, here it was, Vera's recital: an account of adventure and passion and cleverness and adversity, and things that

94

shouldn't have been done, in her youth, in her recklessness, but nevertheless had been and made her who she was, and made Luke love her, and were times she would tuck away and store and feed off.

'I'm sure it's very exciting my dear, but really everybody's done similar, haven't they?' interrupted Lynn, a little brusquely now.

'Well, no, I don't think so. I think of it every day . . .'

'Goodness such dramatics,' laughed Lynn, unable to stand it, the very sight of Vera sitting there prickling her again. 'You didn't murder anybody did you?'

Vera looked up at Lynn nervously.

'Well?'

She said nothing.

'Well?'

'I . . . I was pregnant once.'

Now Lynn said nothing.

And Vera said nothing. Nothing more.

Lynn was shocked by the revelation, and no doubt Vera saw this. Saw the surprise, the amazement, as though Lynn knew nothing of life, of living.

'Mrs Hunter . . .' Vera said finally, slowly, beginning again to pick at imaginary crumbs.

Silence.

'Mrs Hunter . . .'

At last Lynn looked up. 'Well, abortions are ten a penny these days aren't they,' she said.

*　　*　　*

95

What was she doing? What had she done? Panic sweeps up Vera's throat and loiters in the back of her mouth.

It is only the second time she has told anyone she was pregnant. The first time of course was to Charlie. She has not told Luke. She swallows hard. A nauseating liquid continues to trickle into her mouth.

She supposes she must tell him now, now that his mother knows. Vera cannot believe she revealed so much to Lynn of all people. Was it the champagne? No. Of course not, she doesn't get drunk on such small doses. But it is true that her mind is hazy, has been hazy all week, full of it all, full of loss and buried pasts, and perhaps she had felt in that moment between them a small opportunity for trust, for newness, for building a relationship upon. And for those redeeming cosy conversations she had imagined, as though the living room were a confessional and Lynn might prescribe a few Hail Mary's and clean Vera's soul. *To be clean. To be clean.* She knows that it can never be that easy. *Stupid. Stupid.* But Lynn's response was surprisingly kind, flippant almost, with her usual dismissiveness making an abortion seem the commonest of things.

If only it had been an abortion.

Not *only*, but better than the truth.

Of course abortion was still murder, in a way. Or not, but at least that's how she had felt then. Not back at school when they debated it in Health Education and liberally agreed that every girl should have choice, choice over her life . . . choice over Life? But when it was her choice to make, her body, her baby inside her. Still there were people who would accept it, understand it, condone and justify and even commend it. A task Vera just could not quite accomplish. Then. Now. And that was why it had all got worse. And crashed down around her, into pauses, and sleepless nights, and flashed in front of her – sanitised rooms and needles and nurses, refusing to be sanitised themselves.

Beginning with needles she herself had wielded.

Charlie had supplied the cocaine, bought from their favourite dealer. By her third year she as well as he a connoisseur. And the high had been amazing. All of the best feelings of energy and sexuality; none of the hallucinations she had suffered once in the corner of a nightclub and still scared her, though not enough to stop. They had been in Charlie's room getting ready for a party. They were talking at the speed of light about it, disparaging the poor, dense friend who was providing alcohol for everyone and whose birthday it was. She had thrown something at him. A wet tissue? And he had chucked something back. Ultimately they'd ended up on top of each other. Charlie's bed felt softer than marshmallow. His stubbled cheeks rubbed against her like an exhilarating exfoliation. His skin smelled so manly, so delicious that she wanted to taste it. She remembered biting him. He had slapped her, roughly across her cheek. And then torn at her skirt. They'd both wanted to feel each other so hadn't bothered with a condom.

By the time her period didn't arrive, the high had long gone. She and Charlie had been arguing on and off for weeks. Making up and waking up in passionate embraces, then unravelling again when things grew too serious and one of them did something stupid to prove their commitment to flippancy. It was their third year, and such signals were needed. They were like swans during that time. Not in the poetic sense of heart-shaped, life-long figures floating in unison on still waters, but in the sense that after their philandering and solo trips down the lake, they seemed unable but to return to each other.

But Vera was alone in the loo. She had waited for several days before buying a pregnancy test. They were expensive, she told herself, and she was broke. The cashier in Boots stared at her accusingly as she counted out coins. Then she sat on the loo in the sociology block waiting for a blue line, or a lack of it. Though she already knew which it would be.

It was an odd place to confirm that there was a baby. That there was an independent life inside her. That, like the different social classes and statistics and peoples being discussed in the lecture theatre, she was as human as everyone else. As powerful. As vulnerable. As absolutely scared.

★　　★　　★

'It'll be okay V,' promised Charlie.

He had taken her to the clinic and she lay on the bed staring blankly away from him. She'd left a voicemail on his phone the night before, late, two whole weeks after she'd found out herself, telling him that she was pregnant, and that it was his. And he had arrived at her room early the next morning unshaven and scruffy from a night spent in another girl's bed. He had not flinched when she told him she wanted to have an abortion. Charlie, usually so vociferous, suddenly wholly compliant. *Had she wanted him to flinch? To say something?* His silence threw her, but he didn't criticise, or oppose, or ask her why her hand barely left her belly. He simply booked the appointment. And drove her there. And shared her bewildered glances when the nurses were as brusque as if she was there to whiten her teeth.

'These help the lining detach before the surgery. You'll get some cramping. Take them two hours before we start,' said one nurse, handing Vera some pills and taking her blood pressure for the second time while smiling sympathetically at Charlie.

There was still four hours before the surgery was due to begin. They slipped into familiar, mindless conversation and, for the last time, it felt almost normal. But then the nurse returned to remind her about the pills, and she went into the bathroom to take them, and after that, conversation stopped. Vera turned her face towards the pillow. She could not help crying. It is the last time she has ever cried. Charlie hid his own face behind a magazine. She closed her eyes and immediately darkness flashed in front of them. She placed a hand on her not yet empty belly. She glanced towards the sun-soaked window and wished it would be raining. Then, Charlie began humming. Quietly, from behind his magazine, he hummed 'Singing in the Rain'. It had been their favourite movie, and now the melody came like droplets. Cooling. Helping to drown out hot, black, niggling questions, like whether she was making the right decision and, if she should tell him. The anaesthetist appeared to take her down to surgery.

'It'll be okay V,' Charlie whispered.

And that's what she had thought of as she told the anaesthetist that she hadn't in fact taken the pills, and was not going to have the surgery, and was going to keep the baby, and to please tell her friend not to wait.

Riding the tube home from Lynn's, Vera scrolls through her phone and pauses on Charlie's name.

They had not seen each other for months after that, the end of the university year hurrying them through final exams and packing up. And a 'trip to Paris' excusing her from farewell parties she would otherwise have been at. Then the summer arrived and took them away and apart and hid things that needed hiding. But he had called her 12 months later, precisely, to the day. He pretended a booty call but of course he had remembered, which made everything worse. *Make me better.*

She'd thought she was doing the right thing.

Vera pulls her wallet roughly from her bag, yanks out the carefully folded piece of paper, then pauses.

Her life is a perpetual pause. Though it began with rushing. With haste.

She was never going to keep it. She was young and she was meant to have a career, and be with somebody who loved her. But perhaps she could have tried, seen if she was any good as a mother. Attempted to be one. Or at least she could have gone through the proper channels. Made sure of things, faced the people in charge. But that would have meant facing herself, and she wasn't herself. And it would have become real, and it wasn't real – what she was doing, what she had done, what she was getting rid of.

He was a boy.

He weighed seven pounds.

He had a full head of dark, determined hair.

She left him wrapped in a blanket outside the children's home. The tag attached to his wrist said his name was Charlie V.

She had not even given him her full name.

Vera puts the piece of paper back into her wallet. She doesn't need to read it to remember what it says, though she looked at it only once all those years ago – snatched it out of the newspaper she'd been reading over somebody's shoulder on the tube.

He was found at the bottom of the stairwell. Three days after she'd left him. Much too late.

Vera gets off the tube a stop early and stands in stony silence on the platform. Minutes pass, she imagines. It might be seconds. She catches sight of herself in the CCTV and sees a glimpse of what she must look like from the outside: hunched, a little gaunt, strangely not moving. *Unmoving. Unmoved?* There should be tears. In a movie there would be. But Vera has none. She cannot cry. She is not a woman but a monster made of stone. A mother with a teenaged daughter stops to ask if she's alright but Vera cannot break her arrest to answer and eventually the woman leaves her alone.

She will tell Luke that she had an abortion. The rest is too much. For now. Forever? He knows that she has had sex before and it practically killed him. He has been 'praying on it'. It is something he has had to work through.

She must find the right time before Lynn does.

It had taken all of her strength not to hit her. Not that hitting anybody was something Lynn had ever done, but she wanted to. She wanted to knock down that brazen modernity, that boldness, that riskiness that she herself had not grabbed.

When she had found out she was pregnant with Luke, it was the last time she could have turned back, returned to academia, made a different life. After that, she knew it would be nappies and

buggies and cooking and housewifery and all the
other domesticities she had quite happily been
playing at, but this time forever. In the minutes
before she told Philip she was pregnant, there had
been a pause, the very briefest of moments. And
in it had been the fleeting thought that she might
not carry the baby.

That was all it was. A flicker in her mind.

Vera arrives at Lynn's the next day, half an hour
early and laden with cupcakes. She has not slept.
She has not spoken to Luke. He'd called during
her bath the previous evening and she'd stared at
the phone, dripping water just next to it the whole
time it rang, imagining him needing her, needing
somebody to distract him from his own chasing
demons; but she could not talk to him. Not yet.
Not until she knows what she will or won't have
to reveal. She is desperate to persuade Lynn to
keep her secret. Hovering on the doorstep for a
moment, she stares at the cold paving beneath her
feet, wishing she could un-tell the half-secret she
has told. Wishing in fact, if she is making wishes,
that she could undo it altogether. Not the telling
of the secret but the secret itself. Or at least if she
could modify it, have had the abortion, ended
the life before it was a whole one. Or had the
baby but had it adopted properly, safely, respon-
sibly. Not stupidly. *Stupid. Not stupid. Evil.*

Vera knocks on the door but Lynn doesn't
answer and in case she is napping, Vera avoids

the doorbell, takes Luke's key from her pocket and lets herself in.

'Hello?' she calls gently in the hallway, before sticking her head into the sitting room and the kitchen and the dining room, without finding Lynn.

Deciding that she must be upstairs sleeping, Vera sets about putting the kettle on and arranging the cupcakes on a plate. She has chosen vanilla over chocolate, thinking that this is more Lynn. She hopes she is right, that she has not misjudged her future mother-in-law. She can barely breathe with nervousness. In a matter of hours she will be meeting Luke for dinner and he will ask her how things are with his mother, looking at her in that way he has that demands earnestness. His eyes will be sad. They are sad lately, his smiles less frequent and less certain. But his strong frame will offer her an anchor from the spiral that has been engulfing her overnight: grief, regret, panic. And noise. So much noise. Her head is so noisy. It is full of sirens and church bells and nursery rhymes, so many nursery rhymes. Noises that should have been. Luke will mute them. Luke will anchor her. It is what he has always done – drawn her back from the brink with his flicker of unearthly goodness. The problem is, to grab it, him, will mean telling him at least the half-truth, and that will mean risking everything.

She cannot risk Luke.

But the only other option is to persuade Lynn

to stay silent. And then, to somehow stop thinking about him. Not Luke, but the boy, the baby, Charlie V, who she knew for three days and cannot forget. *I love you, I love you . . .*

'I love you,' she whispered closely into his ear.

He smelled of milk – formula, not hers. And warmth. And a slight sweatiness from the layers and layers of blankets she had wrapped him in. It was a mild January, but she could not risk him being cold. If she could cry, she would have wept relentlessly onto his slightly spotted cheeks – milk spots they had told her: *Just watch, they'll go in a few weeks.* But she would never see them disappear. And she had not been able to cry since she'd made her decision at the clinic.

'It's for you,' she muttered, holding him tightly to her. 'I'm not ready for you. I'd be a terrible mother. I'd muck you up, I know it.'

He opened his eyes then and yawned gently.

Vera smiled at him, in apology, convinced that he understood what she was saying, and did not believe her. She rocked him back and forth until his eyes closed, then she waited until she saw somebody go into the building.

She would have liked him to wake up again before she left him. One last chance to persuade him that it was for the best. One last chance to see his still-blue eyes. She willed them to open. But she had to leave him while she knew somebody was there in the building to find him, and he was sound asleep when she placed him and his layers of blankets on the doorstep. He was sound asleep.

'Hello?' Vera calls again from the bottom of the stairs.

There is still no response and Vera mulls for a while whether Lynn, too, is sound asleep, or if she is somewhere upstairs lying dead. She cannot be quite certain which scenario she is hoping for, but gambling on the former she wanders again around downstairs and begins opening the undrawn curtains. After the sitting room and the dining room, she comes to a room at the back of the house that she has never been into. She remembers trying the door once before when looking for the bathroom, but it had been locked and Lynn had quickly directed her away from it. It is a laundry room probably. It would be nice for Lynn if Vera was able to do a pile of ironing before she wakes up. Vera hates ironing, but she pushes down the handle and opens the door.

Inside, Lynn is sitting in an overall, her hair dishevelled, a look of wildness in her eyes as she holds a paintbrush to a canvas. Vera glances around the room. It is full of canvasses and colour.

'Oh my goodness,' she breathes in amazement. At which point, Lynn looks up. 'Mrs Hunter, these are wonderful, they're—' But before she can finish her sentence, Lynn is on her feet and storming towards her.

'Get out!' she orders, ripping off her overall, throwing it over the canvas she's been working on, and frantically smoothing her hair. 'What are you doing here? Get out at once!'

Vera steps back. She has never before heard Lynn shout. 'I'm sorry,' she mumbles. 'I didn't—'

'Stop looking! Get out. Have you no manners? Get out, get out, get out!' Lynn grabs Vera's arm and with surprising force, marches her through the doorway into the hall.

'What? What?' is all Vera can mutter. 'But Mrs Hunter—'

'Get out!'

'I am out. I haven't seen anything.'

'No,' Lynn seethes. 'Out of my house. Altogether. Go. I tried to weather you, I really did, but I can't do it. I don't need help, especially from someone like you.'

To be clean.

Vera stands, frozen.

'Go. Go back to work,' says Lynn. 'Your "sabbatical" is over. Leave me alone.'

She flaps her hand authoritatively towards the door and in the process a long fingernail slits sharply across Vera's neck. Vera touches it and immediately there is blood. Now both women look a little taken aback. Lynn opens her mouth awkwardly as if to speak, but doesn't. Her eyes are seething. She cannot tame the fury, but there is a need for something. It was an accident and they both know this, but still there is blood.

Lynn says nothing.

Vera says nothing.

She catches sight of herself in the hall mirror. It is a bright day but she can see only darkness. Seconds begin to tick, but she shakes herself. She takes a faltering step back towards Lynn. 'Mrs Hunter,' she tries one last time.

'Get out,' Lynn says quietly.

CHAPTER 9

The priest made the announcement and the congregation turned genially towards them. *A pillar of our community.* Lynn nodded modestly and Luke beamed. *One of our most active members . . . has found his life partner . . .* Vera smiled too but looked uncomfortable, as she had done all morning. Neither woman had mentioned the argument of the day before. It embarrassed Lynn to think of it now, to think of herself unravelling; worse, to think of Vera of all people having seen her artwork, having learned something so intimate that she had never shared with anyone, something that revealed her weakness and her regret. Lynn reinforced her smile and nodded to the priest appreciatively. He was young, this one. The third Lynn had seen come and go at St Anne's, but he'd grown up here, remembered Philip and always made a point of taking her hand at the end of a service and paying his respects. He conducted sermons now in modern language, trying to be *accessible*, but Lynn thought him a tad foolish. There was little left in the bible that she counted as true, no matter how you wrapped it up; better then to preserve its mystery so that other people wouldn't also notice the contradictions, the false hope, the passivity of the teachings that had led her to this.

Lynn was having a bad day. She was in pain and hadn't slept properly and could feel herself snapping. Luke had picked her up at ten as promised but hadn't warmed the car so the cold had seeped into her bones. And Vera was there. Silent for once, not wrinkling her youth and beauty with awkward chatter, but full of the power of it. The power too that she held over Lynn. A scarf was wrapped demurely around her slim neck, for now hiding the evidence, but she fiddled with the tassels on the edges as though cautioning Lynn as to how easily this cover may be removed. And John was absent. Vera slipped her hand through Luke's, as though sensing his disappointment in his brother. Just as she had *sensed* she should have an abortion, and *sensed* she should only take a sabbatical. Luke rubbed the palm of her hand with his thumb, and Lynn glared.

John was rarely available on a Sunday, even less often at church, but this week he had promised to come in order to hear the marriage announcement. It wasn't his fault – only that morning he'd discovered he had rehearsals he couldn't miss – but Lynn knew Luke would feel it as a snub. A snub he'd nurse with memories of all the times previous that John had let them down. A patted hand however was not something Lynn was good at. And conversation, proper conversation, was not possible with Vera there, or the watching church. She would have to wait. Wait. Such a waste of precious time.

Yet it was exactly what her mother had urged when she and Philip announced their decision to marry that first summer.

'What's the rush darling? You've only just graduated. Weren't you going to think about a Masters degree?' she'd said.

But Lynn couldn't contain her haste then. 'I still am,' she had protested, certain. 'I still will. Perhaps Philip will find a job in Cambridge, or perhaps I'll continue my study in London.'

'You won't have time darling, not once you're a wife.'

They had been flicking through bridal magazines. Lynn could envisage the scene as though it was yesterday. Wearing jeans and sitting cross-legged on the floor opposite her mother who was sorting through a pile of stockings that needed darning, she had been carefully cutting out pictures of dresses and flowers to stick into her wedding book, not really listening. She could still hear her voice so dismissive and sure.

'Oh don't be so old-fashioned Mummy. It's almost the 70s. Things have changed. Women can have careers *and* be married. Ooh, look at this one!'

But her mother had shaken her head. She had known already what it would take Lynn years to learn for herself.

The first autumn that she deferred her place on the History Masters back at Cambridge, she'd honestly believed it was just for a year, so that she could take charge of settling them into their new home while Philip studied for the bar. The second autumn, when she managed to find an alternative course in London that she also deferred, she held faith that the delay was temporary, and purely necessary until Philip was more established, and besides, her choice. But three years later, when she finally let the university know that she wouldn't be taking up her place after all, she began to realise how quickly her earliest ambitions had slipped away and been replaced by others she hardly recognised.

Then however, there was no regret. Wrapped up in Philip's arms, the busy evenings and weekends they spent together made up for the days in which Lynn was often without occupation and alone. Besides, while she may not have been adding new works to the great pool of historical analysis as she'd once imagined was her destiny, new priorities constructed themselves around her. Their foundations rested robustly upon that single new word, *wife*, shooting taller with each passing month so that it became harder and harder to peer over them as they arched into a protective dome above her, their oculus, that ever-present possibility of another word, *mother*.

It came just a few years later. Too fast. Before she'd had a chance to decide if she really wanted it. Philip had been thrilled. She had been overwhelmed and very much in need of her mother who sighed deeply and immediately began knitting. Eight months later, Luke arrived. He weighed just six pounds and was jaundiced, but she and Philip cooed over their tiny yellow baby who had ten fingers and ten toes and everything in the right place working the right way, as though he was the first perfect being ever to enter the world. And when they took him home they placed him in a white crib they'd built together, in a lemon-coloured room at the centre of the house, directly beneath their oculus.

When John burst forth into their lives via an emergency caesarean section 42 months later, he received Luke's old crib, hand-me-down clothes, and considerably less awe; but John had a gentler temperament from the very start, barely cried, and demanded nothing. Lynn theorised that it was because he had been snatched so quickly from the womb; his rapid arrival had denied him the kind of slow transition that allows one to prepare, to arm, and so he had not yet formulated his plans for the world but was tugged along by it. Philip tried to express as much enthusiasm over their sensitive second son, but Luke always embodied first hopes, always lived up to them, and could always do everything better than his brother, and so won all of their father's praise. And expectation. To make up for it, Lynn slipped extra biscuits or slices of freshly baked sponge cake into John's lunchbox.

Lynn could not help thinking of these days

constantly now. She saw the boys as two impish faces that sometimes blurred into one, dashing around the house, scraping knees, needing her. Philip was frequently there, his presence always at the helm of her memories: giving the boys rides on his strong back, teaching them to thread string through conkers or later, how to shave, reaching out for her hand underneath the table at dinner parties, watching her as she entered a room, smiling in her direction, his *darling little one*. But her sons made up the soundtrack to those busy, oblivious years and pervaded everything. Her husband's aura was a quieter strength, the ghost of it ever-present but silent, appearing more in shapes than in sound: in the angular faces she found herself painting over and over; in the brown, threadbare dressing gown of his she'd never thrown away and sometimes found crumpled on the floor; in the dent of the pillow next to hers where if she closed her eyes she could see him, blond and tanned, or greying at her whim.

Until she opened them.

And was without Philip.

She glanced again at Luke, whose hand was still interlaced with Vera's. Vera, who had made different choices. Lynn looked away. She was no longer needed by anyone. She was nothing, except for the mother of two sons, and the wife of a dead husband who'd earned all of their titles and left her nameless: Mrs Hunter, Mrs Late Barrister, Mrs Deceased Respected Pillar. Like the Wife of

Potiphar whose story was not her own but a reflection only of her husband's and Joseph's, and was another example of how the bible was written by men and therefore left out half of the truth that her mother had known all along.

The priest finishes his list of community announcements and the congregation creaks up from the wooden pews to raise their voices for the selected hymn. Luke turns to help his mother stand and Vera glances quickly away. She hasn't been able to look Lynn in the eye all morning. Despite the itchy mark on her neck, she is sure it was her own fault somehow. She intruded, she imposed. On a sick, vulnerable woman she was supposed to have been helping. *To be better.* Vera rubs her temple with her forefinger. Her head is still noisy. Rhymes and regrets are circling. Luke turns back towards her and raises an eyebrow in concern, but Vera shakes her head and smiles, *it is nothing.* She has told Luke nothing. Not about the way Lynn screamed at her, or grabbed her, or despises her. Or why. She plans to find a moment at church to talk to Lynn, to apologise and put things right; and if that fails, to trade the scarf around her neck for the secret Lynn could hang her with.

Ten green bottles, hanging on the wall. Ten green bottles, hanging on the wall. If one green bottle, should accidentally fall . . .

Vera squints her eyes together and opens the

115

well-thumbed hymnbook. She studied her beautiful new bible again the previous night, searching in earnest for answers. But today, all the fanciful, ethereal passages about forgiveness, grace and renewal seemed to crumble to nothing when set against the solid, forceful words of the minister during his sermon – *evil of fornication, sanctity of marriage, abomination of sodomy, sin of abortions, 'Be sure of this, that no fornicator or impure person, or one who is greedy has any inheritance in the kingdom of Christ and of God.'* Lynn had glanced accusingly at Vera as the priest had spoken, and she could feel her condemnation burning into her. *'They're ten a penny,'* she had said. *One a penny, two a penny –* But of course, Vera now understands that Lynn hadn't been negating the sin of abortion, merely pointing out the frequency of it. If only she knew the rest.

If only Vera could forget the rest. Now that she has begun she cannot stop playing it over in her mind again and again, like a home movie, or a lullaby. How could she have done it? How could she have told it? *How* could *she* have *done it?* Was it even her?

Her heart sobbed the whole way back from the children's home. Her eyes made no tears but her heart sobbed. It had been sobbing for months. For herself, she knew that. For bad choices and unfulfilled ambitions and unfair situations. And it was still about herself because of course she would be a terrible mother, a drug-taking, irresponsible, sex-obsessed, jobless, too-young, awful, awful mother. But only now, too late, had she even considered that she might miss the baby, that she might want the baby, that The Baby was her son.

Her hand hovered over the stop button. Perhaps a tear would have moved her, unstuck her with warm, salty liquid. But she did not get off the bus. Unmoving, she let herself be moved.

The congregation begins to sing heartily.

Do they know the things she's done? Do they sense how far from their pure path she's strayed? Can they see it in her face? Is that why their smiles, just like Lynn's, seem laced with disapproval and judgement? *Sing a song of sixpence, pocket full of rye . . .* Vera pulls her skirt lower over her knees and fidgets with her scarf, wishing she'd had breakfast. She feels in the wrong place. Church! How ridiculous for her to be at church! It is making her remember not forget. It is no longer papering over but pointing out every sin she has committed. Even the things she didn't think were sinful. And there is enough real sin to do without mere mindlessness.

At least Luke loves her. Glancing up at him she studies his face until eventually he feels the weight of her gaze and looks at her, and smiles, smiles through his own growing sadness. He reaches for her hand again and anchors her. Reminding her why she is here. Then she notices

Lynn watching their exchange, a frown spreading across her forehead, and at once Vera feels inadequacy and terror rise through her body again. *To be worthy*. Her hands shake as they try to hold the hymnbooks.

> *Look unto him, ye nations, own*
> *Your God, ye fallen race;*
> *Look, and be saved through faith alone,*
> *Be justified by grace.*

Vera feels hot. She can feel her face flushing. Little Charlie's face was flushed from crying. She reaches for the crook of Luke's steady arm. He squeezes her hand. They sing on. Voices pushing through the scripture, sure, sonorous tones bouncing off stone walls and stained glass and the wrought iron cross that hangs over the pulpit.

> *Awake from guilty nature's sleep,*
> *And Christ shall give you light,*
> *Cast all your sins into the deep,*
> *And wash the Æthiop white.*

Vera glances towards Lynn again and finds her still staring, the frown spreading as she directs the words carefully and deliberately at her. The heat spreads. There is a stabbing pain deep inside her. Vera puts down her hymnbook and, too loudly, clattering her bag against the pew, rushes out of the chancel.

And Jill came tumbling after. And Jill came tumbling after.

She has never met Sally-Ann before. A few of the faces at Luke's church have begun to look familiar, part of their circle, but Vera doesn't remember Sally-Ann's when she nudges open the door to the cubicle.

'Are you okay?'

Vera accepts the dampened tissue and leans her head against the tiled wall of the antiquated bathroom. Flattened bars of soap languish on the sides of sinks where liquid dispensers should be, and the hand towels are made from thick, blue, almost cardboard textured paper like the ones they had at school. The coolness of the tiles quietens her head a little.

'I'm fine. Thank you. I just got a bit hot. Must've been the holy spirit!'

Sally-Ann doesn't laugh at the joke and Luke isn't there to tell Vera whether or not it is funny. Instead Sally-Ann moves closer. 'Are you pregnant?' she whispers.

Vera isn't usually the kind of person to laugh nervously, but she does so now, a rough, stuttering chortle that lands in silence. 'What? No I'm not, I'm just . . . I mean, God no! Pregnant? No, I'm not.' Has she managed to answer like a good, Christian virgin? 'Who are you?'

'Sorry. I'm Sally-Ann,' the girl laughs, then pauses. 'It's okay if you are.' She shakes her tousled hair, balancing a hair band in her teeth as she casually pulls the unruly mop on top of her head and waits for Vera to answer. Now Vera notices the girl's short denim skirt, her electric blue tights, and suddenly, she lets out a loud, incongruous laugh.

'Don't tell me I've actually found an actual Christian who's actually had sex!'

'Um, actually, no.' Sally-Ann passes her another tissue awkwardly. 'I mean, obviously I don't agree with sex before marriage, but if it's happened, it's okay is what I mean, your community will still be there for you.'

'Oh.' Vera accepts the tissue with a grimace. She doesn't look at Sally-Ann but dabs at her flushed face. Finally she paints on a smile and with faux cheer spins back around towards her. 'Are you serious? This lot?'

'Okay, maybe *they* wouldn't,' the girl concedes. 'In fact, they'd probably be after you with torches and pitchforks, but there're lots of communities that would be fine. Like my church, St George's in Marylebone. I don't usually come here. But it's Mum's birthday. Anyway, what I'm saying is lots of people make mistakes. What's important is facing them, and not turning away from Jesus because of it. He'll forgive you and so should everyone else.'

Vera stands up. 'I'm not pregnant.' She throws the wet tissues into the bin. Her face is regaining its colour but the scarf still itches. She would like to take it off. *Off again. Sukey take it off again.*

120

'Oh. Okay. Good. Sorry,' Sally-Ann hurries. She eyes Vera curiously and Vera wonders if she is mouthing the nursery rhymes clattering about in her head. Is she saying them aloud? Did Luke hear them? 'I just thought . . . You know, you should come to St George's sometime.'

'I'm not pregnant.'

'I didn't mean that. Just, most people there are very, questioning, so there're loads of extra study groups and seminars about relevant issues, and lots of activity. You should come.' Her face has come alive now, almost as vivid as her tights, too intense for the dreary walls of the toilets at St Anne's, and Vera cannot help but be a little enchanted.

'It sounds lovely,' she says, turning towards the door. 'But Luke's been coming here all his life.'

'But you feel judged here.'

Mid-step, Vera freezes. 'That's ridiculous,' she manages to retort finally. 'How can you know how I feel?'

'I know about your abortion.'

Now Vera's hands move unconsciously but directly to her stomach as though pulled there by a latent, placental magnetism. Sally-Ann has caught her off guard, without armour in a place that already feels dangerous. She tries to laugh, but can say nothing. She can hear an infant crying.

'My mum whispered it to me as soon as the minister announced your engagement,' Sally-Ann confesses softly. 'Mrs Hunter told her before the service this morning.'

121

'Mrs Hunter?'

'It shouldn't be like that Vera. I'm just saying try St George's. Grace is a gift for everyone, you don't want to miss it. You have to be careful; church can crush as well as liberate.'

'Mrs Hunter told her?'

From outside there is a knock on the door.

'Think about it,' Sally-Ann says.

Moments later, Vera and Luke are sitting on a bench outside and without being asked, Luke takes off his jacket to wrap around her shoulders, leaving him shivering in shirtsleeves in the winter sun. It is still morning but already it feels as though the sun is sinking. *Row row row your boat.* And time is ticking. *Tick tock. Hickory Dock.* Lynn has already spilled Vera's secret, it is only a matter of time before she tells it to Luke. Luke rubs her cold hands between his. Vera hesitates. It is difficult to chip away at such a perfect thing.

'Luke, there's something I have to tell you,' she begins finally.

'It's okay,' he says instantly, brushing an escaped wisp of hair behind her ear. 'I know you find this tough. Don't be embarrassed. I love that you're trying, that you want it for yourself.'

Vera stops.

'Shall I tell you something true?' he continues, prying open her hand to hold it. 'I'm proud of you Vera.'

Weakly, Vera smiles. Across the courtyard she

can make out Lynn talking to a group of women, every now and then pointing at her and Luke. Vera feels herself filling with fury. And shame. After a moment, Lynn catches her gaze and this time Vera looks her straight in the eye and raises one hand to her scarf, but the older woman only holds her stare defiantly. Daring her.

'You remind me of her a bit, if that's not too weird,' Luke smiles, noticing the direction of her eyes.

Vera drops Lynn's stare and snaps back into focus. Luke seems so happy sitting there in the churchyard, between his two women, so much happier than he has been of late. *If you're happy and you know it* – Luke claps his hands together to warm up.

'Did you want to tell me something else?' he asks, studying her. 'Is something wrong?'

Vera looks up at him. His two-tone eyes are full of concern and responsibility; they seem so easy to hurt. In the distance Lynn laughs with her gaggle of women. *Goosey goosey gander* –

'Mother's had years to get to know everybody,' Luke offers, misinterpreting her gaze. 'Don't worry, it will come. She didn't know anybody when she first joined here either, but look how loved she is now.'

Luke smiles in the direction of his mother, *Old Mother Hubbard . . .* And nervously Vera watches the man she adores. She glances again at Lynn, the bastion of his childhood, the manipulative snake, whom he loves unconditionally. Who reminds him of her. *Mirror mirror on the wall* . . . Who will soon be gone. *Mirror mirror* –

'Luke,' she says finally, shaking her head to rid it of the noise and tapping him lightly on the leg. 'There *is* something I have to tell you.'

'Yes?'

'I'm sorry, I've tried, but I can't do it. I miss my work too much. I can't look after your mother.'

CHAPTER 10

Emily's headaches were getting worse. Dizzying. Nauseating. But she forced herself out of bed, up and inwards, towards the city. To Euston, or Kings Cross, or Victoria. She had three cleaning jobs now. But the destination she travelled to most often was Kentish Town. She had seen the advertisement for the charity on a desk at one of the offices she cleaned, and she had picked it up, plastered with yellow stickers, and stared for long minutes at the photographs of happy, elderly faces, frail but slipping slowly into incapacity. A gentle demise. The carers with them looked strong and confident, and capable, almost like doctors. *If you're building a house and a nail breaks, do you stop building, or do you change the nail?* she'd heard, in her mother's voice, in her head. So after five days of hesitation and procrastination, she had finally made a nervous phone call to a person to whom she'd never spoken, and had supplied her name, and the following morning begun a training course to become a carer.

During the first class – learning Health and Safety, and how to use a fire extinguisher, and how to wash her hands – Emily had found herself drifting off, dreaming of days in which her ambitions had amounted to far more. But after that they got on to the moving and handling of the sick and elderly, and medication, and catheter care, and there were talks about the ethics and principles of health care. And now they were doing emergency aid, which felt like a real skill, and soon she would be assigned a Buddy and begin her stint of shadowing. And so far nobody had asked her about her childhood.

The course distracted her from it. It filled the too-bright days. And when she allowed herself to consider it, fleetingly, she found it was good to be learning something again. Still, time persisted and there remained long stretches of daylight when things felt uncontained and uncontrollable. And so she took the bus and clung to the crowded, protective, urban sprawl.

No longer limited to places one could stand for free, with her new wages from her cleaning jobs, Emily bought herself soup or a sandwich and sometimes a sweet piece of cake, eating it alone at the windows of different cafés. There, with glass between them, she watched real people strolling by, oblivious to her, oblivious to the others like her who existed now only inside her head.

Like Cassien.

She tried not to think of her youngest brother. But in and out of the cafés came friends swathed in greetings and goodbyes, and Emily could still feel the warmth of his arm when he placed it casually around her shoulders.

So she stood. And she sat.

She imagined reinforced glass.

She walked. She walked.

Clicking her tongue, her mother said: *You can outdistance that which is running after you, but not that which is running inside you.*

And inside her, both she and Cassien were running fast.

Once, Before, about two years before the violence began in earnest, they had found themselves caught in a riot. It was difficult now to imagine that they had ever been so naïve, but they didn't believe anything would happen then, not to them, not really. It was true that things were changing – the adults said nothing though all the children could feel it – but at the beginning it was still like one of Cassien's stories, the kind that hovered tauntingly on the brim of their consciousnesses but they would never truly see: like monsters, or landing on the moon, or America.

They were on their way to school when they saw them. Cassien had been carrying a football – new, bought for his birthday, prized – intermittently dropping it on the floor and dribbling it through yellow-flowered bushes. She had a satchel slung over her shoulder on top of the neat, cream school uniform of which, having only just been admitted into senior school, she was excessively proud.

There was a pale blue trim around the edge of the sleeves, and as Emily swung her arms she liked to catch flashes of it, like a promise just to the side of her of calmness and cool.

The men in the street were uniformed too but in louder, hotter colours. Flashes of green and yellow were emblazoned across their chests, tied around their heads, and raised on flags that flapped atop spears and masus and machetes. *Hutu Power*, they chanted. *Hutu Power*, followed by more words that were angry and aggressive and aimed, suddenly, at them. Emily had seen these men before in smaller groups or from a distance, but never with such empty space between them. Putting his arm around her shoulder, Cassien moved them carefully into the void. He was a year older than she and a foot taller. The football was now tucked securely under his arm. His jokes had been replaced by an unnerving silence. Emily knotted her hand into his shirt and pulled back slightly, but without conferring they both knew they had no choice other than to move towards the road upon which the sweaty, raucous men were assembled. It was their only path to school and Mama and Papa reminded them daily how fortunate an education made them.

They drew closer. As they did so, the volume of the men's chants increased and Emily felt her limbs involuntarily tighten. Still, she didn't truly believe that the men would harm them. Not an unarmed child and his scrawny, barely-there sister.

Not them. Not so near to home. Not until Cassien fell.

Cassien.

Turning frantically, the first thing Emily noticed was that his football had rolled away and was already lost in the crowd of stamping feet. Instinctively, she began to go after it for her brother, but from the floor, Cassien yanked her back.

'Cassien!' she protested.

'Shush Emmy.'

The man who had smacked him towered suddenly over them both: tall, broad, wild, stinking of beer and lust and power. Cassien, at 12-years-old drew himself up before him. His nose was bleeding.

'*Inyenzi Inyenzi!* Cockroach!' the man bellowed, spit spraying from his mouth. Other men grew interested and moved closer.

'We are not.' Cassien wiped his face with the back of a hand that to her horror, Emily noticed was shaking. She looked up. The men held masus, clubs spiked with nails, and bottles of beer. One of them was fondling a spear grotesquely. Cassien took his sister's hand and kept her tucked behind him. 'Come on Emmy. Let's go back.'

'But school,' she protested. 'We'll miss school. And your football—' Some of the men were kicking it now between them.

Cassien's glance back was only fleeting, his last seconds of childhood rolling away as fast as his prized possession. As they ran, the dirt and dust kicked up from their feet settled over her new uniform.

At home, their father took one look at Cassien's nose and started shouting in language he never used and they were not allowed to. But he didn't go after the men who had harmed his child. Instead, he ran to the factory where Gahiji worked, and to Simeon and Rukundo's school and brought all of his boys home. Then he bolted the doors and told them they were not to leave the house. Mama fussed over Cassien and heated a pan on the stove to make them all tea with muffins. She suggested they sit at the table and play a game, and for a while it was almost as if their togetherness was due to a public holiday, or a birthday, or Christmas. They even laughed. Emily sat next to Gahiji and puffed up proudly when in his bird-like way he tilted his head and declared that she was to be on his team. Cassien's nose stopped bleeding and the drama of the afternoon seemed to melt beneath the hot liquid in the mugs so that soon it felt almost like an adventure survived, and a reason for festivity. But Emily hadn't realised that this would be her last memory of them all sitting together like that, smiling, though even then they knew deep down that the smiles were only for each other's sake, because it was better than crying, and because they hadn't yet seen the first body in the street.

That would come in the morning. And that was the day that Mama made the rules: *If they come, run. Be quiet and run. Into the graveyard behind the house. Into the bushes. But not together. Never together.*

No matter how scared you are. If one is found, at least the other survives. You run, you be quiet, you hide alone.

The adults spoke directly to their offspring now, they told them what was what, they gave them warnings. It was too dangerous to keep them hidden in cotton-padded childhood.

Sometimes, before her first cleaning shift began, Emily returned from her new course, or from her city wanderings, to her flat, lay a blanket on the floor, and prayed the rosary. *'I believe in God, the Father Almighty . . .'* she began, making the sign of the cross and sitting on her knees, just as her mother had taught her. *'. . . He shall come to judge the living and the dead. I believe in the Holy Spirit, the Holy Catholic Church, the communion of Saints, the forgiveness of sins, the resurrection of the body and life everlasting . . . forgive us our trespasses as we forgive those who trespass against us . . .'*

She meant none of it. Not anymore. When she used to kneel with her mother, solemnly bow her head, and utter the sacred words, she felt she was whispering to a trusted confidante. Infallible. Unerring. God was her friend then, her saviour. But how could she trust Him now? How could she trust in anything? How could He even exist and let what happened, happen? She didn't believe in Him. Or in resurrection. Or in some ethereal supreme judgment. It was as cheap a promise as democracy, or community, or help from the UN. Besides, she didn't want to forgive. She wanted to

131

cling instead to her fury and her hatred; it was all she had.

When she said the rosary now it was with defiance, as a gauntlet, and because it was her only means by which to talk to her mother.

CHAPTER 11

Underneath a patchwork quilt onto which her mother had sewn roses in a deep, passionate red because they are her daughter's favourite flower, Vera holds the phone to her ear and listens to her fiancé unravel his anger and unpick the last remaining threads of her armour.

'She's dying Vera, she needs us.' His voice is urgent, insistent. Vera imagines him sitting at his desk with neat piles of papers and bills and post laid out in front of him, a pen in his hand hovering over a lone piece of scrap paper on which he's written, *Mother*. If only she could contain all of her anxieties to one sheet, to one word. She thinks of the folded piece of paper in her wallet.

'She needs *you*. You're her son,' Vera responds tentatively, standing up from the sofa and turning towards the mirror. This is the third time in a week that they've had this conversation. On the first and second occasions she tried to justify her decision with arguments about work and falling behind and missing a promotion; but without telling him what his mother did, and why she did it, and what she knows, and what demons are running wild because of it, there is no real way to explain. *She cannot explain. She will not explain.*

Explanation is illusive.

He pleads. 'You know I can't leave my job.'

Vera stares into the glass. She has found that if she fixates on something small, something present, a mole, a freckle, it is easier to block out the nursery rhymes and other noise. She studies a fine hair that has strangely appeared on her earlobe. The face in the mirror answers: 'There're other people who can look after her Luke. This charity I'm working with for instance, Home Care. I've told you that's what they do. Why don't you call them? Or let me arrange it. Let me help that way.'

'She doesn't want a stranger. And I thought you wanted to do this? For me?'

'I did. But I can't.'

Luke sighs. 'But you offered. *You* offered. And now you want to unsettle her? While she's deteriorating? You made a commitment. Is this how you treat your commitments? I suppose it's good to know.'

Vera's chest tightens.

'You barely tried Vera. It was only a week.'

'Exactly, it was only a week. And now she's been alone for a week, and getting sicker, so you do need to find somebody. But she'll be fine with somebody new.'

She must have somebody new.

The agreement has not been spoken aloud, but

Vera is clinging to the idea that so long as she stays clear of Lynn, and hides the lingering mark on her neck, then Lynn will not tell.

Luke's voice grows thinner. He begins to quote biblical passages. He has never done this before, in argument. Vera feels inadequacy welling inside her. *To be better.* She surrenders the ear-hair for a moment and lights a cigarette. Why does he have to pull the Jesus card? There've been many months now of trying to get something profound from all the hocus-pocus, but she doesn't know Jesus, she hasn't 'met' Him. Religion is to paper over. To glue together. To cut out. Either that or to hound into compliance. She gets that. She had thought that would be enough. She is ready to comply. With Luke's verses raining down on her however, she could do with the comfort of really believing. She could do with that feeling of surety and redemption. She could do with Luke.

'You're going to be my wife,' he urges. 'And she's my mother.'

'I know. That's why . . .'

'I thought you loved me,' Luke says. 'I thought you wanted to be a Christian.'

Wanted to.

Vera glances down at her ring, which is in need of cleaning, and considers that probably he is right. Probably, despite what he doesn't know about his mother's behaviour, despite the hold that Lynn has over her, and despite the debilitating noise, she should agree. *Not despite, because of the noise, she should agree. Not because of the noise, because of the murder.* Since Lynn used the word, Vera cannot get it out of her head or off her tongue. It tastes strong and sickly and makes her choke until she can't breathe. *So she should not breathe.* She should hold her breath for the duration of the time that Lynn has left. After all, Jesus made the ultimate sacrifice and if she really wants to 'come to faith', to be clean again, good again, good enough for Luke, then surely she should embrace the crux of what being a Christian is about.

Vera stubs out her cigarette, lights another and leans against the sofa and her mother's quilt. Briefly, she wonders what her mother would advise. The thought of her mother tightens her chest further and if she was able to cry, tears would have welled in her eyes. She looks up. The woman in the mirror looks pale and drawn. *As though she has been drawn. As though she is a rough sketch, not quite right, still needing colour.* It is hard to pick one aspect to focus on.

'Why won't you do this for me? For us? I know how good you are Vera.'

She sighs and rubs her head, scratching herself accidentally with the diamond of the ring she still isn't used to wearing. The woman in the mirror flinches, then pulls a hideous face, in one motion plucking the fine hair from its lobe. Outside the open window, a flock of pigeons circle. Vera feels dizzy. The drone of Luke's voice both lifts her up and weighs her down.

'Well I don't want to shock her to death if I refuse another of her sandwiches.'

At Luke's end of the line there is silence, then slowly, inching through the plastic his voice comes, cold and quiet. 'That's not funny.'

Vera sighs nervously.

'Are you smoking?' Luke asks.

A cigarette between her lips, Vera inhales deeply and walks. There is no destination, only an intangible need to move. She walks south from West Hampstead, through St John's Wood, around Regent's Park, down Baker Street and into Marylebone. Crowds of late shoppers barge past her with energy and purpose and surety. Without any of this, Vera walks close to the street, out of their way.

She would like to keep out of everybody's way, Luke's particularly. She knows he is going to find out. Find her out. Cast her out. *Baa baa, baa baa*. A black sheep. Nursery rhymes again. She should concentrate, or rather, distract herself. *She should distract herself by concentrating*. On him. Or on Lynn. Or at least on how she can fix things with him after what happened with Lynn. But since it happened she cannot stop thinking about someone else. Or seeing someone else. Or listening to and hearing someone else: the baby, her baby, if she even has a right to call him that.

When she closes her eyes, even for a second, his emerge vivid from the darkness. Blue, *still blue*, *forever blue*. She never found out if they would have remained that way. She hears him too, a phantom howl – in the water of the shower, in the wind through the shoddy window glaze, in her head more and more and more. Why did she tell Lynn? Why did Lynn ever have to speak to her of children? Why did she let herself look back? She doesn't look back. That's the rule. That's the trick. But now, now, now she cannot stop thinking about him. And about Charlie, and the lie that she told him. The lie she has now repeated to Lynn, *or not quite repeated but let her believe*, the lie that is beginning to resurface in her world that was supposed to be fresh and new. And clean. *To be clean*. Luke's clean verses batter her brain. She cannot tell Luke. She cannot tell Luke. She cannot tell Luke. But she is sure that at any moment it will explode out of her, splutter from her mouth and smear itself into the cracks between them, cracks that began, again, with abandonment. Again. This time of Lynn.

Vera turns a corner and crosses the street. In front of her is a rank of taxis. Once, too pilled up to get home, Vera slept in a taxi office.

The memory hits her unexpectedly.

She looks up.

And that's when she sees it. At the end of the road, the tip of a grand dome has crept into view. She feels her eyes straining towards it and suddenly, with a peculiar deficit of surprise, she realises: it is St George's, the church that Sally-Ann urged her to try. Until this very moment, Vera wasn't even aware that she knew where St George's was.

For a reason she can't quite locate, Vera's hands begin to shake. Inside her bag, next to her wallet with the folded piece of paper, is her bible. She looks down and both seem to taunt her. She looks up and the church confirms it. She closes her eyes. 'Ridiculous mumbo jumbo,' she tells herself, and then hears herself repeating the words out loud. She opens her eyes again. The dome of the church glows warmly. 'Come on then,' she challenges it. 'Come on then. Let's see.' And defiantly, she strides towards the enchanting hemisphere of stone.

The structure is vast. An old, stained glass window paints the steps beneath the imposing arch of the façade. Inside, there is a gentle bustle of people despite – Vera gathers from the sandwich board at the front – the evening service still being almost an hour away. She hovers by the entrance and notices a sign for a café in the crypt.

Downstairs, the walls are flooded with declarations: *Let Alpha change your life! Learning to live! Embracing prophecy! Be a Healer! Words of prayer! Becoming a leader! Exploring the difficult verses! Marriage Preparation!* She feels deafened just reading them, exclamation marks hitting her with judgement. She starts to wonder why she even came in. But then, at the end of the room, bounding down the stairs appears Sally-Ann.

'You came!' she exclaims.

Taking her by the arm, Sally-Ann shows Vera around and one by one they dip into screening rooms and discussion nooks and lounge areas. The place feels more like a fancy conference centre than a church – Christianity for the 21st century – and without the traditional iron crosses, Vera begins to relax. Slowly, more people drizzle into the building and they collect in puddles around the room, young, vibrant, and enthused, just as Sally-Ann had promised. They are dressed in jeans and casual tops, and look like they've come straight from a bar or an indie music gig. Looking at them, Vera guesses that not all of their journeys towards Jesus have been without bumps. The thought consoles her, *Baa baa black sheep* begins to quieten, and for the first time she considers that perhaps such trials are the reason their conviction is now so strong.

Innocents. Vera cannot help but think this. And laugh at this, to herself. *Did she laugh out loud?* Vera shakes her head and purses her lips tightly shut. But they are innocents. *Or are they sinners?* Like her. Doesn't the bible say something about everybody having sinned?

Back upstairs, Sally-Ann leads her into the main body of the church. Georgian splendour shapes the space with pillars and balconies, tall, arched windows, a walnut floor, and the domed roof that attracted her from outside encasing everything below it in a warm light. At least 500 seats are laid out facing the altar, in front of which is what can only be described as a stage. On it, stands an electric keyboard, a couple of guitars propped up next to microphones, and a full drum kit.

'Are you expecting a band?' Vera jokes.

Sally-Ann merely smiles.

Together they settle into seats half way up the hall. A few of Sally-Ann's friends file in next to them and one by one the chairs are filled. Vera sits back and waits. On stage, the band take up their positions and gently begin to play, growing gradually into a soft rock ballad to which the words are projected onto the stone walls of the church and the congregation begin to sing or hum or sway to, some standing, some sitting, some with their eyes closed. Vera shuffles in her seat uncomfortably and can't help but look at those around her, her gaze not towards the altar, not towards the cross on which Jesus hangs, but to those who unlike her, feel His grace, who are so enlivened by it, so sure. Like Luke.

How can he be so sure? Since he got the news about his mother, Vera has so wanted to console him, to hold him, to take him in her arms and tell him that even though his world is falling apart, it will be alright. When she reaches for his hand however, he draws it away, placing it instead on the bible he clings to. And so Vera never knows quite what to say, and on the phone today she said all the wrong things. And cannot even complete the task of helping with his mother. Because of her own lies and secrets and secret lies. And his faith still seems like a secret to her. She has told him she is a Christian now, but all his hope is pinned to a book and a faith that if she is honest, still seems like a bad joke. Where was Jesus when she needed him three years ago? Where was He when she was choosing drugs and deceit, when she fell pregnant, when she made her stupid, stupid, stupid decision that she thought was the right thing? Where is He now?

From the front of the church, the band plays on and a peculiar lump begins to work its way up Vera's throat. It is an unfamiliar sensation, not sore but bulbous and she wonders if she has a lozenge in her bag. When she looks up to read the lyrics and tries to sing them – *We love you Jesus. For death and life and freedom* – the lump grows and chokes her. She coughs. All around her, more and more of the congregation are singing, rocking rhythmically, lifted by the music. Vera feels possessed and paralysed by the lump inside her. Sally-Ann glances in her direction and smiles. The music plays on. *We can't contain our love. We turn it up loud.* Louder and louder it comes from the stage: guitar, bass, drums. Voices. Noise. Clapping. Crescendo. Then suddenly: peace. Vera swallows hard. The room swirls around her, not quite real. Everything seems suddenly to be moving fast. Not paused. Not unmoved. Moving.

A solo guitar strums on and the minister steps forward, inviting the congregation to offer a song

142

to God, anything that is in their hearts. *Who has a song?* Silence. Then, quietly, from the back of the hall, a single female voice begins, strong and hopeful. *We praise you. We praise you Jesus. We praise you.* The band joins in. The congregation joins in. *We praise you.* Vera's mind flies to Luke, dawdles again over her incapacity to help him. Or to be worthy of him. *We praise you.* Her thoughts move to Lynn, complicated, ruthless, fearful Lynn. *We praise you.* To her own forth-coming marriage, devoid of input from her parents. The lump in her throat throbs and pushes higher. To her baby. Her child. The hymn buzzes in her ears. Her son. She grows hot and worries she might faint, but just in time the sound ceases.

The minister approaches the microphone once more and the congregation stills. He begins to speak of responsibility, of Christian responsibility, of Jesus' revolutionary nature, his political activism, his charity, his example of standing up. Vera stands up. Sally-Ann pulls her hand and she sits down again but her head is muddled now, her mind whirring, her soul in some kind of upheaval. Poor Lynn. Poor Luke. So hurt. So good. And she so sinful. Unheeded infant cries tumble through her head. And so sorry. *Forgive me Jesus. Help me to be better, to be worthy, to be clean.*

The band starts up again. This time Vera stands and sways with the others, the words in her head marking the tune where her voice cannot. *Forgive me. Help me.* They tumble over each other, churning, clearing, reshaping. *Help me.* The minister takes centre stage again and invites anyone who feels in need of a prayer to move towards the pulpit. And suddenly, Vera finds herself moving. Without meditation, or self-consciousness or doubt, she pushes against the paralysing lump and walks where she is called to, as though somebody's hands are resting on her shoulders, guiding her.

Sally-Ann stands up and follows her. A small group gathers, their brows furrowed, their eyes sore, a collection of aching souls. Around them clusters another group – experienced members of the congregation with a gift for prayer. Sally-Ann is amongst this contingent. She touches Vera lightly on the shoulder and without a word of explanation begins to pray. Her eyes close and her voice is soft but it possesses a quiet confidence, as though her words are for someone she trusts, an intimate. Vera looks up. Another woman joins them, then one more, each of them placing their hands on her shoulders and asking God to help her. She does not know them, they do not know her, but their appeals seem like gifts, all the more potent because they come from strangers who are not obliged to care.

Now Vera closes her own eyes. She thinks of the sterile abortion clinic and the hospital and the steps of the children's home, and Charlie, and her little Charlie, and charlie. And wanting to tell her parents she is sorry and that she loves them. And wanting to tell herself that she is sorry. And wanting to tell her baby she is so, so sorry and that she regrets it every day and loves him still and has thought of him every second since she left him in that blanket, on those steps, even when she is distracted, even when she is paused, even when her reflection in the mirror is twisting and writhing and making a mess of reality. She clenches her eyes tighter. She is without music now, but the words crawl again across her tongue. They are not beautiful or eloquent, they do not possess poetry or prophecy, but they are there, and she means them, and she is no longer saying them merely to stop herself from thinking of other things. They are not a mantra but an earnest prayer. *Help me.* Her head is awash with a hundred different memories that she watches as they run through her. Memories she has blocked for too long. Her baby's blue eyes blink at her helplessly. She continues to pray: *Help me, help me, help me.*

She whispers the words patiently, expecting nothing except perhaps a moment of calm, of quiet. Then all at once the lump in her throat pumps harder and spills upwards. And Vera can't breathe. Around her, the women praying seem calm and unconcerned as she tries to yank air upwards. Again and again she heaves her chest for breath, but still she tastes only density until at last, in a moment of panic and surrender, she opens her mouth to gasp for air a final time and instead, an unmistakable sound escapes it: a sob. Startled, she touches her hands to her eyes. They come back wet. Tears stream down her cheeks and streak her make-up. In disbelief she examines her mascara-stained fingertips, then puts her hands to her chest to feel it rising and falling in quick, successive bursts. Slowly and one by one the women praying over her put down their hands. Sally-Ann gives her shoulder one final squeeze. 'Don't rush away,' she whispers. And Vera, who has not cried since she lay on the hard bed at the abortion clinic, stands at the front of the church, alone amidst a group of evangelicals she would a year ago have ridiculed, and she weeps.

CHAPTER 12

As he summarised the recommendations of his DRC health initiative to the minister, who would probably read only the first few paragraphs of the 132-page policy document, Luke Hunter felt the weight of the world resting heavily on his shoulders. If he didn't explain things with sufficient clarity, with enough of a structured imperative as to what must and must not be done, it was likely that the minister would lose sight of the message altogether, or at least his fervour for it, and announce something half-hearted or distorted to the press. Then, thousands of innocent children in the DRC would suffer longer and needlessly, and Luke would have failed. He could not fail. He had to save them.

'I believe that if we follow this framework closely, we've got a genuine chance to save her life here,' Luke concluded.

'*Her* life?'

'Say again?'

'You said *her* life,' the minister repeated, lifting the first sheet of the heavy document and scanning the page underneath, in what Luke knew would probably be his closest inspection of it.

'Oh,' Luke floundered. 'Yes, sorry, by *her* I mean *Africa*. After all, she's a raped woman.'

The minister angled his head up at him, considered this for a moment, and then chuckled to himself. 'I like that,' he told Luke. 'I'll use that.'

The Freudian slip did not however escape Luke. At lunch, he shunned the department canteen and walked instead away from the vast government buildings to a small Italian café where he sat alone at a table in the back, ordered a sandwich, and bit the flaking skin around his nails until it arrived. When he discovered that the sundried tomatoes he'd ordered had been substituted for fresh ones, he called loudly across the restaurant to the harassed waitress and sent it back.

'Why is it so difficult to do what the menu specifies?' he asked her, aware of his unreasonableness, and knowing that he wasn't really talking about his sandwich. But it had never been difficult before – doing what was prescribed. In fact it had been the one thing that made things easier and certain again.

After his father died – of a sudden, massive stroke, aged 45 – Luke had struggled with uncertainty, unanswered questions, and a world spiralling out of his control. Philip had not only been his father but his mentor and inspiration. When there was a decision to be made, it was he who Luke consulted, his approval he sought before deciding

148

what his own opinion would be; and though it had never happened, he'd known that if he was ever in trouble, ever in need of help, it was his father who would rescue him. When he died, Luke was 19. He'd just embarked on his first serious relationship and was in the process of selecting which modules to read the following year. He'd been planning to sit down with his father to thrash it all out when he visited him at his old Cambridge college that weekend. Philip had, with some amusement, been planning his bus and train adventure to get there because the car was being serviced, and Luke had already pulled out his sleeping bag so that his father could have the bed. But the journey, of course, had never been made. Philip had never told Luke what he thought. Luke had spent the following month clenching his jaw to prevent tears he was terrified might choke him. And there had been nobody to come to his rescue.

That was when he'd turned more heavily to Jesus. Philip had always been involved with the church so it felt like an apt way to continue his legacy. But more than that, Luke realised that if he followed the scriptures diligently, if he lived by Christian teachings and did exactly what the bible told him was right, then he would not need to wonder what his father would have thought, or explore that gaping space inside. Slowly, over the years, the void was filled with rules and passages and teachings that at first gently guided his choices, then hardened into principles, and gave Luke strength, solidity and order.

But now, it was all crumbling again. For no matter how diligent he was in his bible study, how much money he gave to charity, how often he prayed, or refused alcohol, or abstained from sex, he could not control the pace at which his mother was deteriorating. Endlessly he searched the bible for answers, but something intangible had been shaken and he could feel his might wavering. At night, he lay awake and worried how he was going to hold everyone up: his mother. John. Vera. Africa!

Vera, he knew, needed him. He didn't blame her entirely for abandoning his mother. She had never been quite ready. From the moment they'd met he could see the pain that crept so often into her distant blue eyes, the self-doubt that undermined her obvious goodness. He could see her need for Jesus, and he'd wanted so much to help her. There were times of course when her shocking otherness had delighted him. When, weighed down by responsibility, he'd called her just to hear a hint of her recklessness, to listen to her endearing blunders, to remind him (since his father wasn't there to confirm it), of how far he himself had come. But more often, a spiritual awakening was what he'd wanted for her more than anything. Now that she was trying so hard, he should be nurturing her. But he wanted her to get there faster, to be that pillar of strength he was lacking. And needed. He had agreed finally to let her call Home Care, his mother would have help, that wasn't the issue. The issue was that Vera had fallen short. She had disappointed him. She had hurt his mother. And of course all of that was *his* fault. Her failures and mistakes and selfishness only mocked his own weakness.

Luke felt tired.

It was his weakness after all. He should be guiding Vera and instead he was picking on her, pushing her away. He was letting her down. He was letting everyone down. He had to find a way to stem the chaos. With the effort of a shorn Sampson he lifted his head as the waitress returned with his replacement sandwich.

'Mozzarella with *sundried* tomatoes,' she announced. 'Exactly as it says on the menu.'

Luke nodded and took a bite. It didn't taste as good as he'd imagined.

CHAPTER 13

The bus was late. Emily didn't like waiting. It made her feet twitch and forget that sometimes they were needed only to stand upon as well as to run. But it made a change to have a predetermined destination. It gave her purpose and a forward momentum. It helped her not to look back. She wrapped her jacket tighter around her thin frame and stared up at the morning October sky: blue but somehow paler than in her memories of clear, sunny days. A single cloud meandered boldly across the horizon and Emily watched it. There was a time many years ago, when she and Cassien would lie in the graveyard next to the house and spot lone clouds as they appeared above them, taking turns to decipher their shapes, to invent stories for them and make the other one laugh: a haunted house, an elephant, a two-headed dog, a smiling face. Once, later, in a dark, sky-less place, she'd thought back to these never-ending afternoons and would have given anything for the luxury of such a lazy moment. She'd have done all she could and everything for the freedom of even a few seconds to stop, un-harassed, safe, and notice a cloud in the sky.

Emily stared hard at the cloud now: a worthy entity for study. It streamed out in a thinning line as it floated eastwards, its edges changing as the seconds ticked by; but Emily could not think of a single shape that it resembled, or a story, and so it remained merely a blur in the blue.

Mrs Lynn Hunter's was the first home that Emily had entered since Auntie's. She didn't count her own; it wasn't a home so much as a hole in which she hibernated. Though she didn't hibernate really. She couldn't survive for long without food, without air; she knew this acutely.

It wasn't Lynn who answered the door. Despite having never met her, Emily knew from the people at Home Care that Lynn Hunter was not elderly but a cancer patient, a widow, and in need of light assistance around the house with the probability of increased nursing care as her condition deteriorated. The person at the door was a man, young, white, with dark eyes, a slim frame, and something about him that made him spectacular. And unthreatening. He stepped at once to the side of the corridor and with a debonair sweep of his hand ushered her in, closing the door delicately behind her.

'My mother's not in the best mood this morning,' he whispered confidingly, taking her coat and scarf and hanging them on a grand wooden coat stand, whose branches she noticed were polished to perfection despite the base being covered in dust. 'It wasn't her idea, to have help, you see. It was my brother's. But she's been fending for herself for a few weeks now, and well, struggling, so she's going along with it. Barely. Don't be offended if she's a little gruff.'

'Gruff?'

'Oh, sorry, are you not British?' The man was reassessing her now, playing back her accent inside his head.

'I'm, I . . .' Emily froze. Instinctually she stepped backwards. It was always the same questions that triggered such unsteadiness. What *was* she? The only thing she wanted to be was human, and sometimes she wasn't even sure about that. But everyone seemed so fixated on defining themselves and everyone else. Must she too? She held a British passport but what would happen if one day it was bad to be British? It was better to have no label. If blood was spilled, a label would not damn the flow. 'I just don't know the word,' she managed finally.

'Gruff? Oh, I suppose it is a little old-fashioned. It just means harsh, abrupt. You understand.'

Emily smiled. It was unusual for people to make such an assumption of her.

'Yes.'

The man smiled back at her, an easy, charming smile she suspected was used often. Oddly, the presence of this man made Emily feel reassured.

'Let me show you around and introduce the two of you,' he said, making that gallant sweep of his hand again. 'Oh, and I'm John.'

They shook hands. John's were soft, his fingers long and elegant, squeezing her rougher palm tightly to register his sincerity. Cassien, Simeon, Rukundo and her father had had altogether tougher palms, and Gahiji's had been like leather, calloused underneath from working at the soap factory, which she always thought was ironic. Sometimes Gahiji rubbed milk into his hands in an attempt to soften them, but even when the hard blisters had diminished she winced dramatically when he hugged her, joking, 'A snake! A leathery snake!'

She followed John into the kitchen. The house was at least four times the size of Auntie's and everything was old. Not in the sense of being dirty or threadbare or in need of replacing, but ancient, as though it contained history, a personal one. The floorboards creaked underfoot but were made of solid wood that had obviously been cared for. There was a slightly dank smell to the kitchen, as if it hadn't been used properly for a while, and when she opened the cupboards she saw that old packets of biscuits needed to be thrown out and everything inside dusted. But there was no washing-up in the sink and the surfaces were clear, except for a teapot with two teabags already waiting at the bottom for boiling water to be poured upon.

155

The lounge was oppressive. Books were every-where: lining shelves on the walls, stacked upon coffee tables where they acted as platforms for small antique lamps, and on the floor, leaning against steel sculptures whose strange angles made the balancing act look precarious and like a piece of art in itself. It would have been impos-sible, she thought, for one person to have read so many books, or at least, to have read them and lived a life as well. John pointed out the television and showed her where Lynn kept her CDs.

'She likes music sometimes,' he said. He didn't mention the array of awards in the glass cabinet, or the grand chesterfield armchair, or the pictures of glamorous looking white people above the fire-place. Instead, he led her back into the hallway and apologetically showed her where the cleaning products were kept. 'My mother was so house-proud,' he said. 'She was famed for it.' Then finally he took her upstairs.

Lynn was sitting up in bed holding a book in front of her, though there was something about the way in which her eyes gazed through the pages and not across them that made Emily suspect she was not really reading at all. This was a woman, she realised at once, who inhabited two separate worlds: the one her eyes could see and the one only her mind could navigate, somewhat like Emily herself. On the bedside table there stood an empty glass and a bottle of pills, but this was the only hint of the woman's illness. Clothes were put away, cupboards were shut, and beyond the bed a curtain had been tied neatly, the window behind it opened just enough to expose the small garden at the back of the house below. From the doorway Emily could make out a great, wide tree at the end that made her think about swinging on branches, and so of Cassien.

John pushed the door open wider and Lynn looked up. She put down her book and Emily suspected that this was a relief. Her wrists were as spindly as twigs. She wore a wool cardigan despite being wrapped up under a duvet in bed, and her hair was set on top of her head as though she was going to a party. When they entered, she jumped as though being caught looking at herself in the mirror, but she barely glanced at Emily. Instead, her eyes grew suddenly furious and bore directly into her son's.

'This is Emily, Mother. From Home Care,' John ventured quickly, imploringly through the awkward quiet, but Lynn quelled her rage only long enough to take a breath before speaking. When she did, Emily expected her voice to be weak and thinning like the rest of her, but instead it came out solid, steady and severe.

'She's far too young John,' Lynn stated.

It was decided that it would be best if Emily began with simple cleaning. It was John's idea. Lynn didn't want her 'touching things' and at first made a show of throwing back the covers of the bed to escort Emily out. 'It's not you,' John assured her, intervening, but waiting outside the bedroom door Emily heard Lynn telling him that she didn't want a barely grown girl she didn't know in her home, scurrying about like a cockroach.

Cockroach.

The word stunned her. She hadn't expected to hear it again, to be called it, and the incongruity of it imbalanced her and made her head throb. It had been a while since she'd had a headache this bad. The pain was blinding and sometimes she blacked out from the force of it. Now, she sat on a velvet stool on the landing that was almost as large on its own as her whole house in Rwanda had been, and tried to draw sense from the bleakness. She'd wanted to help. That was what had been so attractive about Home Care: it was a way to heal, someone else if not herself, a way to care for someone again without the need to trust them, without expectations of reciprocity. But she supposed that after all she had expected something back because she'd imagined that Lynn would be a kindly old woman who was gently appreciative. She hadn't anticipated anger and abuse and dangerous words.

John suggested some 'tidying up' downstairs. Did she have any experience cleaning, he asked her.

It was a relief to return to chores that didn't require thought. The methodical back and forth of mop against wood gently lulled Emily into a calmer frame

158

of mind. When John left, she managed to say goodbye quite pleasantly and busied herself afterwards, content in her solitude. At first, the place seemed tidy and proud in its order, but once she began cleaning deeper – making sure to move objects quietly so as not to disturb the beast upstairs – Emily slowly discovered chink after chink in the glossy veneer. The surfaces had been wiped but nothing upon them lifted in what must have been many weeks. Book and toaster and vase-shaped patches of grey dirt dotted the house like a rash. Emily removed the grime with satisfaction and poked about further. Inside, the cupboards were a disorganised jumble: shelves that began at the back with neatly-lined tins and packets deteriorated into a mess of unconnected objects that had been stuffed wherever they could fit. In the dining room she opened one drawer to find it filled entirely with elastic bands. As she cleaned, curiosity began to get the better of her and soon Emily was speeding around the ground floor unaware of the noise she was creating as she studied photos, picked up trinkets and wiped away the thin layer of dust that at first obscured everything. She didn't know why she was suddenly so driven, but had a vague idea that she was trying to construct something, or reconstruct it: a life, a personal history, a story that belonged to the woman who was lying alone in bed. Picking up a small, silver elephant, she was reminded for a moment of her own history, of a park she'd been taken to once, and proprietorially she slipped the ornament into her pocket.

Only one door was locked. John hadn't shown her the room behind it, or directed her towards the key so she presumed this was not a place she was meant to clean. She wanted to though. Peering behind someone else's door had lit something in her, something she hadn't felt in many years: Curiosity? Interest? Appetite? Zest? She couldn't quite place the taste of the emotion but she ran her tongue over her teeth and enjoyed it. Then, reluctantly leaving the locked room behind, she returned to the corridor where she'd first entered. When she ran her damp cloth over the coat stand, the base turned out to be silver.

'I can't reach down there,' Lynn announced suddenly.

Emily jumped up. Behind her Lynn was standing, leaning slightly to one side but dressed immaculately, the remnants of beauty fluttering against her pale, thin skin like an echo. 'It's been driving me quite mad for weeks, that spot on the bottom, but I wouldn't ask that girl to do it, and the boys don't see things like that do they?' Emily was speechless. 'I'll have a cup of tea in the lounge,' Lynn continued. 'Lemon. No milk. Make a pot. You'll have one too.'

Emily found two china cups and used the pot with teabags that had clearly been left on the kitchen counter for this purpose. Lynn was wilier than she looked. It was obvious now that this détente had always been the plan, but why had she put on such a show of anger for her son? Was she pretending then or now? Was she hateful or merely hurting? Pain, Emily knew, had a way of corrupting one's emotions, but she needed to spot the one that was authentic. She could not fail her first job for Home Care. There was the money to think of, and also that pale sliver of light.

Lynn received the tea with wiry hands, tutting that there were no biscuits. 'I can get some now,' Emily offered but Lynn shook her head and waved her into the chair opposite, insisting that she would make do. For a while, the two of them sat without speaking. A vagueness had overcome Lynn's face, an unsettling illusiveness that was both intense and distant, as if while scrutinising Emily she was also somewhere far away. It was like being viewed through a telescope. Emily tried not to fidget with her fringe and stared back at the woman whose poise made her feel as though she was sitting in front of a teacher, or an immigration officer. 'How do you feel today?' she managed to ask finally.

Lynn let out a little noise of impatience and flapped her hand dismissively by way of an answer. 'It's mild today,' she said instead, glancing out of the window as if the weather and not her health was the reason the two of them were there, sipping tea across the generations and racial divides and stories that neither of them yet knew.

'If you need me to do anything, if you need help, I can,' Emily persevered, hoping to remind the elder lady of her newly-acquired nursing credentials, her usefulness, but this was apparently the wrong thing to say.

'This whole situation is preposterous,' Lynn exploded, her serene posture suddenly unbalanced. 'I'm perfectly capable of looking after myself. I don't need a girl like you snooping around my home. Have you taken anything?'

'No!'

'I'll find out,' Lynn continued. 'I'm sick but I'm not senile. They only want you here so they can feel better you know.' Anger spewed out of her, contorting her face and stripping it of beauty, the heat of her wrath erupting like pent-up lava.

'I only meant—' Emily began but Lynn didn't trouble herself to listen to the rest. Her mind was made up already.

'They don't care what I want, but what I want is to be left alone. It's my life after all. It's my death. And I can manage it perfectly well without you.'

'You couldn't manage the coat stand,' Emily dared.

Lynn stopped abruptly. With a great effort of leaning forwards she put down her tea, stirring it with a teaspoon whose clunking sound filled the gaping space Emily's remark had cut between them.

'How very impertinent,' she declared finally, slowly, regarding Emily without the distance of before and then suddenly chuckling in a soft manner that turned into a cough, for which she needed to dig out the cotton handkerchief she kept balled up inside her sleeve. Emily wasn't sure now whether to smile or remain serious, to offer help or to look away, so she did nothing. 'You can come to clean,' Lynn conceded finally when she had composed herself. 'I could do with some help cleaning I suppose.'

'I am not *only* a cleaner,' Emily pressed nervously, but this was too much. Lynn threw the teaspoon onto the tray.

'You may clean only. Three times a week,' she declared firmly. 'From nine until one. It is twelve-thirty now. You may clear this away and make me a bowl of soup before you go. Not too much. Small portions are more appetising. There are tins in the cupboard.'

The last time Emily had prepared a meal for anyone besides herself had been at Auntie's. Auntie made a fuss of cooking proper Rwandan food every Saturday, usually making enough to last for the whole coming week. She had enlisted Emily's help, bossing her around the kitchen as though she was born for such power, her whole physique broadening and lengthening in a way it didn't when she came to and from work. At first Emily had resented this. During the days and weeks when she had first arrived and wanted only to sleep, and most of the time was allowed to, she viewed these sessions in the kitchen as punishment. Auntie's nagging was oppressive. She didn't want to be made to do things, or talk, or listen to Auntie's gossip; she wanted only to be allowed to retreat into her silent world that deafened her. Whenever she could, she crawled beneath the covers of her bed and lay there, alone, any attempts to marshal her into action being met with resistance and tears and, in the end, screaming and kicking and her throwing up. She didn't control these outbursts. She didn't intend them. It was as if her whole body had shut down, like a person in a coma whose total energies are focused on healing the damage to the brain and whose small actions are merely reflex. Except that Emily was not in a coma and, conscious of the thoughts in need of healing inside her head, found she was unhealable.

For many weeks her hibernation was tolerated but eventually Auntie began to insist. 'You need to get moving,' she told her, dragging her by her arms into the kitchen and putting her to work. 'Chop that up, you're not useless,' she would say. 'Don't tell me you can't peel a few potatoes? Don't tell me you can't boil the rice? Don't tell me can't.' Assailed, Emily began to force her fingers into movement. It felt impossible to begin but somehow she managed to peel vegetables, she dried fish, she boiled beans, she began to handle a knife, and after a few days with barely any direction she was mixing together aubergine and corn and spinach because they couldn't find cassava. Meanwhile, she listened to Auntie. Mostly her monologues were filled with the details of her day-to-day life and structured in the form of a sing-song lament – the cold weather, her underpaid job, her busy husband, the stupid bus that was always late.

Emily correctly understood this fault-finding to be a pastime, proof only of Auntie's love of talking, and paid little attention to her plethora of sorrows. But one day, in the midst of stirring the stew, Auntie sat down at the table where Emily had been enlisted in her usual task of peeling, and said,

'Your mother was a very wonderful woman Emily.'

Emily was unable to say anything. Instead she stared hard at the potatoes, though her hands had stopped working on them and the peeler dropped to the table where it splattered tiny fragments of skin across the veneered top.

Auntie continued. 'You know she was my cousin?' Again Emily didn't answer but Auntie seemed not to notice. She appeared not to need to be listened to so much as to talk. 'I knew her since she was born,' she said, making a clicking sound at the back of her throat just like Emily's mother had done. 'Your father too. He was a friend of my brother you know. He was a good man. He was very clever, like you, no? Your mother wrote that you were very clever.' Auntie picked the peeler up from the table and took over Emily's job, clicking still. 'She always said I was crazy for leaving. She said how could I leave Rwanda? She loved that country too much. She loved the people. Not me. I didn't hang around. Even at school, I didn't like to be contained anywhere, I didn't like all this rigid structure, all these rules. I told my mother no, I was leaving, even when she begged I said no, I had a ticket. Not your mother. She sent me letters. She told me how things were. She wrote when my mother died. She was the one who'd been with her.' Auntie wiped a tear from her eye that she pretended wasn't there. 'She was so strong,' she said, standing up and returning to the stew. 'I'm very sorry for you Emilienne. Girls are not meant to lose their mothers.'

After that, Emily had retreated deep into herself again and Auntie saw this. She didn't bring up her mother any more, although a few times she tried to encourage Emily to talk about herself. In a morbid, uncertain way she wanted to know what had happened, and she nudged her way into the landscape of Emily's recollections: had there been a fire at that old church, she asked one day. But eventually she stopped talking about Rwanda at all, and stuck to cooking food whose smell knotted up Emily's stomach with a smarting grief that devoured her appetite and left Auntie with bowlfuls of remains.

Uncle steered clear of her altogether. He knew stories. Not *her* story but the political narrative. He knew therefore that hideous things had befallen her, he saw the scar on her forehead, which back then still seeped puss occasionally. He knew what might have been done to her, put inside her to poison her, and he treated her as a pitiable animal: a poor soul to feel sorry for and care for out of a moral duty, but not to engage with, damaged as she was. Over dinner, he sometimes asked as if out of interest and encouragement which dishes Emily had made, and then she watched as he left them tidily on the side of his plate.

Emily concentrated hard on not overheating Lynn's soup. She'd found a tin not yet past its sell-by date, and added carrots and a little flour to thicken what seemed to her to be a very thin broth. From the lounge, she heard the TV blaring. Emily arranged the soup on a tray, poured Lynn a glass of water, and as a final thought added a saucer with three biscuits arranged on it. As soon as Lynn saw the contents of her lunch she rolled her eyes.

'I said a small portion,' she admonished. 'And people here do not eat biscuits with soup. Where are you from anyway?'

Emily helped Lynn – who was flapping her away – to balance the tray on her lap, then made a great show of collecting the tea things, as if this was occupying her attention too fully for her to answer the question. Lynn however did not pick up her soup spoon or return her eyes to the television, but stared insistently at Emily.

'Well? Where are you from?'

'I live in Hendon,' Emily conceded finally, thinking fast. 'It's not far from here. 20 minutes.'

'Don't be so silly, I mean originally.' Lynn reprimanded, shaking her head at Emily's stupidity. 'I know where Hendon is for goodness' sake.'

'Oh. I grew up in Africa,' Emily relented attempting now to sound flippant, breezy, but still she hadn't revealed enough.

'Whereabouts in Africa?' Lynn demanded. 'I had many friends who went to Africa after university, doing charity work mainly. They came back with all sorts of tales. And trinkets for me. Elephants and giraffes and the like. Whereabouts?'

Emily hovered with the tea things while interminable seconds ticked by, and felt the silver elephant heavy in her jeans pocket, visible she feared. Finally she spoke. 'I'm from Rwanda,' she smiled, grinning broadly.

At last this was enough and Lynn said nothing. For the third time that day she examined Emily, scrutinised her, made her feel like a piece of evidence or a rare archaeological find, a testament to a former civilisation, which in some ways she was. Across Lynn's face crawled titbits of recall and understanding. The word *Rwanda* was like that; it was unable to be impotent. *Rwanda: that is the place where all those people killed each other,* people thought, wondering inevitably if Emily was a killer, since she had obviously not been killed. Or else they were full of shock and intrigue and pity, the kinder but no less discomforting emotion. Turning with the tea things towards the door, Emily left Lynn to select one of these two responses and retreated to the kitchen where she fished the teabags out from the pot, carefully washed the inside, and put it back on the kitchen counter. She spent a long time meticulously cleaning the china cups, telling herself she was only moving so slowly because she didn't want to break them, then finally she returned to the lounge.

'Shall I clear that away before I go?' she asked Lynn, gesturing at the barely-touched soup. But Lynn only flapped her hands again in the exasperated fashion Emily was already growing used to, then looked her straight in the eye.

'How did you get your scar?' she queried, boldly.

Emily was not prepared for this. In defence, she took a deep breath and sidestepped.

'Do you need me to help you with that?'

Lynn let out an irritated exhalation of breath. The woman obviously did not like to be treated like an invalid, her frailness her own embarrassing scar that showed too much. And suddenly realising this, Emily pushed on. 'Do you need help back upstairs Mrs Hunter?' She offered her arms but again Lynn slapped them away.

'Was it a machete?'

'Or I could run you a bath?' Emily pressed, now in open defiance, her tone deliberately consoling.

'What happened to your family?'

'I'll prepare some dinner for you shall I?' They were trading blows. 'Here, let me take that before you spill it.' Emily dived for the tray but Lynn clung on, reaching for Emily's wrists to keep her there. Emily twisted them away. She reached over once more and tugged at the tray and again Lynn resisted, but finally could hang on no longer, loosened her feeble grip and, victorious, Emily escaped to the kitchen. When she had finished washing up, this time she armed herself with coat and bag, ready for a fast exit, ready to run. By the time she stepped back into the lounge however, Lynn had turned up the volume on the TV, pulled a blanket around her and barely acknowledged Emily at all. In those missing minutes the distant preoccupation of earlier had returned to her face. The fight had left her.

'I never used to watch television,' she mused almost to herself in response to Emily's nervous goodbyes.

Slowly, Emily backed away into the corridor. The change in Lynn was unsettling. Emily wondered if it was okay to leave her. She wondered too if the woman was pretending again, plotting something, perhaps she'd decided to ring Home Care to cancel Emily's visits, maybe Emily should appeal to her. But then abruptly, without her saying a thing, Lynn called her back into the room. 'You'll come again on Friday,' she told her plainly. 'Be here by nine.'

★　　★　　★

On the jostling, traffic-plagued bus journey home, while fingering the smooth, stolen elephant, Emily noticed that the winter sun seemed to be poking through the cold air more strongly than it had that morning. She raised her hand to shield her eyes and looked ahead.

CHAPTER 14

It had been months since Vera had heard from Charlie. Last time, when she'd told him over the phone that she'd started reading the bible, he'd laughed hysterically, predicted it would never last and been sarcastic about Luke, who he nick-named 'The Messiah'. But when Vera arrived at her desk the morning after St George's, amidst the straight lines of yellow Post-its (the whimsical spirals having abruptly stopped), Vera found a small, white, handwritten envelope. Inside was a black and white postcard of Grace Kelly wearing a white dress and gazing seductively into the camera. On the back, over the lines for an address, Charlie had scrawled: *I hear you're getting hitched. Congratulations V. 'Today's a very special day.'*

Vera had spent almost 20 minutes at her desk gazing at the card. At lunch, she'd taken the folded piece of paper from her wallet and held it with the card, staring at them both over a cappuccino that eventually turned cold. An hour later the paper was returned, still folded, to its usual pocket, and Charlie's card was tucked carefully inside the back cover of her bible. But it has taken Vera almost four weeks since then to call him. It is a first step, and she is taking it gingerly.

The Alpha Course takes place at St George's every Wednesday and so far she has been to three. There is a great vine that caresses the wall outside the church and each week she has stood next to it, hovering, her progress feeling infinitesimally slow next to nature's showy changes. First green, then yellow, now a deep, confident red. But her encounter with what – without wishing to sound melodramatic or plain ridiculous – she can describe only as Jesus, or truth, has left her unarmed, and although she knows she has to see Charlie, has to tell him, she must take this time, she must restock her arsenal. Differently. The old bible story of the prodigal son keeps running through her mind, especially the moment in the pigsty when the son lifts his head and remembers that he has a home. It feels like a homecoming. But Vera has been totally unprepared for the cataclysmic shift inside her. It has enveloped her without restraint, and left her not with the sensation of peace, certainty and quiet contentment that she had supposed, but with a fire burning within. An inferno. The papering over she was so diligently doing at Luke's church, now smoulders at her core.

She wishes she could talk to Luke about it. On the surface they have reconciled, but lately, whenever she tries to demand his time he reminds her of the dying African children counting on his dedication. He doesn't remind her of his dying mother, or the fact that a stranger and not Vera is with her, but she knows this is the real occupant of his mind. Just as the dweller of hers is not in fact Luke, but Charlie.

She knows she must see him. She knows she must tell him. If anything has become clear since St George's then it is this. Of course there are her parents to tell too, and there is Luke. But it must begin with him. Like it or not, the truth is bubbling to the surface like hot blood, and she cannot quell it. Still, it is a question of when, and how, and what she will say. The Alpha classes are like defence missiles. She is stockpiling as many as she can.

They meet at a tapas bar in Soho. It is a Thursday evening. She does not tell Luke.

Charlie wears a crisp white shirt open at the neck and dangles an unlit cigarette from his mouth. Vera is in the simple trouser suit she wore to work and is without make-up. The lack of adornment was a conscious decision. She is there for confession, not complication. When she walks in, Charlie stands up to plant a soft kiss on either side of her face. He smells of something strong and sharp.

'My god, the virginal look suits you. You look sexy as hell V,' he says.

Charlie remembers her favourite wine – a full-bodied Spanish Rioja Alavesa – and orders them a bottle, but before they sit down Vera excuses herself for the bathroom and winds her way through the close, share-friendly tables into the lone cubicle. For a long time she stares at her reflection in the mirror. She doesn't pull faces, she doesn't fixate on moles or hairs – she has not, it occurs to her, done either of these things since St George's – but she instructs herself. Warns herself. Forces herself to recall all the times that Charlie has dumped her, or dismissed her, how he makes her feel confused and uncertain, how he introduced her to coke and one night slipped something stronger into her drink without asking. But that was the night they'd had the best sex ever. And since the, clinic, three years ago, they have not been alone together without ending up in bed. Their meetings are sporadic but conversation is furious still, they are good at small talk, at jokes and flirtations, and there are sparks, or perhaps embers. It is not a stretch for either of them to convince themselves into bed. Besides, she has never been able to refuse him. Sometimes, in recent years, Vera feels that she satisfies him as a payment, an attempt to fulfil a debt. But in any case the real collusion is not their bodies, it is their silence. Silence about the one topic they never touch. Silence about the topic Vera is here to lay straight.

Help me.

'So a bunch of evangelicals chanted their drivel over you, and now you're a born-again Christian?' Charlie declares with glee when they are midway through their second glass of Rioja. 'My god V, you've been brainwashed!'

'Charlie, I'm serious,' she cautions him. 'You can't understand 'til you've experienced it yourself. You should go to church. You should try it.'

Wine shoots out of his mouth. 'Do you really see me at church?'

She studies him. He is as handsome as ever. More so. Confidence spills out of him like cologne he can apply at his whim. A banker now, he looks respected, successful, but there remains a glint in his eye that she recognises from nights of raucous partying, hedonistic weekends in bed, whole days spent high.

'No, but a few years ago I wouldn't have seen me at church either,' she answers finally, tucking her hair behind her ear and taking another sip of wine.

'Me neither V.' He reaches across the booth and pats her on the knee, his fingertips brushing just a few inches higher before he removes them and takes out another cigarette. 'So come on then, tell me about Luka. What's he done to warrant this transformation? Good in the sack is he?'

'First of all it's *Luke*, if you don't mind Charles, not *Luka*. And I'm sure he's wonderful in the sack but I wouldn't know. We haven't slept together yet. We're waiting.' As soon as the words slip out of her mouth she wishes she hasn't said them.

'He's a virgin?!'

'He's a Christian,' she back-pedals.

'Oh my God. This is too hilarious.'

'And I'm a Christian now too.'

Charlie covers his eyes and tries to calm himself.

'I've had an amazing experience Charlie,' she urges earnestly. 'I felt it. I felt Jesus. I met him. It's a totally transforming thing—' It bothers her that she is finding it so difficult to articulate her coming to faith. Charlie is the first person she has really told, but his cynicism seems to taint it. Before it is strong enough to take assault. She stops. Slowly, Charlie dares a glance at her over his hands.

'So I can't tempt you anymore then V?'

'Charlie, I'm engaged.'

'I know, I know, but what if you weren't?' He gazes straight into her eyes and before she can stop herself she imagines the two of them falling into a hotel room and ripping off each other's clothes. His chest will be slightly tanned as usual – the remnants of the South of France, or the Amalfi Coast, or somewhere further afield. She will start with his shirt. 'Come on V, don't you miss the old rumpy pumpy?' He blows another cloud and winks at her. 'You must. You were very good at it. How long has it been?'

'Actually, since *we* last . . .' she guiltily hears herself confessing. But this is not the confession she is here for.

'My God. You poor thing.' He pauses. 'Well, if you'd like me to oblige . . .'

She smiles. The smoothness in his voice seems

somehow to sanction everything. Charlie slithers in between her strengths and weaknesses and mixes them up. She gulps at her wine.

Help me.

This is what he does. This is what he always has done. Not force her into anything, but make her forget, *welcome forgetfulness*, or distort, *but she would like life to be distorted*, or not know what she will live to regret . . .

No. It wasn't his fault. He knew about the 'abortion', he didn't know what came next. That was her. That was her sin. The worst of them all. Just the thought of it chokes her. She splutters on her wine. Charlie pats her back exaggeratedly. But the truth is not something that can be exaggerated into comedy.

'Thanks for the offer Charlie, but I love Luke,' she manages to say finally. 'And Jesus.'

Now Charlie coughs on his wine again. 'Fucking hell, you're an absolute riot tonight, V.'

'And that's why I have to tell you something,' she continues quickly, while she can.

Charlie takes a while but eventually stops laughing. He takes a slow sip of his wine and replaces it on the coaster. Finally he looks at her, bracing himself, and now he notices her nerves. 'Shoot, V,' he says calmly.

She takes a breath. 'Do you remember "Singing in the Rain"?'

Charlie takes an uncomfortable drag of his cigarette and doesn't answer.

'Do you remember humming it to me? At the clinic?'

He takes another sip of his wine, draining the glass. Then looks at her hard. 'Of course I remember. Why are we talking about this?'

Vera reaches for her own glass but there is nothing in it. She takes another breath: long, deep. 'I didn't have it.'

'I know, V. Wasn't that the point of the thing?'

Vera shakes her head. She wants to look away from him but forces herself to hold his stare. 'No. Charlie, I didn't have the abortion.'

'What?'

There is nothing else for him to say.

Vera inhales once more. There is no going back. Vera can feel invisible hands again upon her shoulders. 'I didn't have the abortion,' she repeats slowly. 'I didn't take the pills. I didn't have the procedure. I had the baby.'

Charlie cannot speak. He tips his head to one side. Vera waits. There is no disguising the searching in his eyes. Searching for the inevitable question that Vera has been dreading. Eventually he gathers himself enough to ask it: 'I – I have a child?'

There are other questions of course: where and when and how and what, and these will come, but this, Vera knows, is what it comes down to. She begins.

'He was a boy.'

Charlie opens his mouth to speak, but Vera doesn't know if she will be able to keep going if she stops now, and she holds up her hand.

'He was born on the 19th of January at UCH. I stayed in with him for two days. I called him Charlie. I—' Her voice is shaking. Tears are close. They seem always to be close now. 'I left him on the steps of St Andrew's Children's Home in Euston. I—' She cannot breathe. She cannot say it. Gentle sobs are choking her. She reaches into her bag and takes out her wallet. 'Thank you for humming,' she gulps between breaths. 'I'm sorry. I'm so sorry.' Slipping the folded newspaper cutting from her wallet, she unfolds it and hands it to him. Then without looking back, she turns for the door.

'*Help me,*' she whispers into the fresh, night air.

PART II

CHAPTER 15

In spite of a determination not to, Lynn had begun to look forward to Emily's visits. Aside from the brief debacle with Vera, it had been many years since there'd been another person in the house. Visitors of course – though it had been months since she'd agreed to see any of her friends, with their highlighted hair and Blackberries and reasons to keep up. There were her sons, but even they sat with her formally, being entertained. Emily was different. She might disappear upstairs for hours to change the bed and dust and vacuum, while Lynn watched television or if she had the energy selected a favourite book to read a chapter or two from, and they sometimes didn't see each other at all; but she could hear the vacuum going, or the quick shuffling of Emily's feet, and it was company, a witness to her existence.

She and Philip had spent whole days this way: he in the study turning pages that created a tranquil rustle, or tending young plants in the garden shed, while she was in the kitchen baking, or pottering about the house tidying the details of their lives. No words but reassurance. No dialogue but a promise of eternity . . . It was nice to hear a second pair of footsteps cross the wooden floors again and hands other than hers open cupboards, and exert a presence in her life.

Emily had been coming now for a month, three times a week. She knew where all the cleaning products were kept and exactly how Lynn liked the house to be ordered. She had learned the times and doses of Lynn's medication. She pretended not to notice when Lynn was feeling sick, but silently placed an empty bin near her chair. And she no longer had to be asked to bring the tea in at a quarter to eleven, but carried it on a tray with a slice of lemon on the side and two digestive biscuits for each of them. And sat in the chair that used to be Philip's.

'Don't you get bored of the same biscuits?' Emily asked one Wednesday.

They had been sipping their respective teas with the radio on, a countdown of all-time great jazz tracks. Emily didn't know any of them, but nodded solemnly each time Lynn pronounced the title during the opening bars. This question was the first time she had spoken all morning, and Lynn had the sense that she'd been working up to it. Despite the fleeting boldness of her first day, she was quiet this one, not like Vera with her excessive chatter. But John called her 'the angel': *'The angel's cleaned that ghastly vase'; 'The angel's made a delicious soup'; 'Will you take some brandy in your tea, Angel?'* And Emily seemed slowly to be warming to his mischief, unable sometimes to hide a smile. And just beginning to ask questions of her own.

'If I had money like you, I would buy all different ones,' Emily ventured again.

'What biscuits did you have in Rwanda?' Lynn asked. She'd been trying to get Emily to talk about Rwanda for days. Perhaps because of a not-yet-dead academic curiosity. Perhaps because the girl's existence somehow latched Lynn to the present. Perhaps because she had noticed that her tiny silver elephant was missing. Each time however, Emily found something to tidy away, or a light to turn off, or else she switched on the vacuum. Now, cornered by tea and jazz tunes, she touched her hand to her fringe and smoothed it down, but said nothing. 'You shouldn't cover it,' Lynn told her.

Emily said nothing, but glanced up in surprise.

'It makes you unusual.' *Beautiful*, she had meant to say. To Lynn, Emily resembled an African princess, or how she imagined one, full of exotic mystery. Her youth didn't grate on her as she'd thought it would, as Vera's did. Her otherness was more salient than ghostly taunts of girlhood. And aside from the scar her dark skin was flawless, her neck long and slender, her lips curled backwards as if in a state of perpetual restraint. Admittedly there was a small gap between her front teeth, and the fact of her constant fidgeting, but on the rare occasions that Emily sat still and smiled, the deep scar over her left brow extended the almond shape of her eye into a pool that rippled outwards. 'Beautiful,' Lynn conceded.

Emily blushed and lowered her head. 'We had ones like these. And Afterwards, they gave us special protein biscuits.'

'Afterwards?'

Emily stood up. 'Do you need something else Mrs Hunter?'

'I used to bake biscuits,' Lynn told her.

'My mother made muffins,' said Emily.

There was a short pause. 'We would need ingredients.'

Emily hovered by the door. The radio presenter's smooth voice cued in another jazz tune. Lynn shifted in her seat to test her side. It hurt, but not as badly as some days.

'It's not raining,' she considered.

As they rounded the corner of St Ann's Terrace and into St John's Wood High Street, Emily offered her arm to Lynn, who again refused it. The rain had stayed away, but the pavement was smattered with fallen leaves, trodden down by wet shoes and conspiring to form a thin, slippery coat of brown. Emily walked slowly and purposefully, unaware of passers-by who might be watching, heavy with the responsibility of Lynn. If the woman fell, she would be blamed for it. Even if Lynn had refused her help. Even if Emily had no way of accounting for uncleared paths. Even though Emily too felt unsteady and short of breath. *In a court of fowls the cockroach never wins his case*. Emily offered Lynn her arm, and was again flapped away.

Before they left the house, Lynn had made a fuss of Emily fetching the particular pair of shoes that matched her outfit. Under her wool coat she was wearing a simple navy dress with black tights, but she would not accept the brown flats that Emily first selected, nor the black loafers, which she laughed at, but demanded the navy heels with the rounded toe. They were sensible heels, well made, only an inch and not stilettos, but Emily wished that Lynn had not increased the distance from which it was possible for her to fall. 'One never knows who one might bump into,' Lynn had said with a glittering smile while buttoning her coat and checking her make-up in the hall mirror as though off to a party, and it had amused Emily, these ageless quirks; but now, even without supporting the weight of her, Emily could feel the effort the walk had become. She did not tell Lynn, but inside her bag were the loafers.

'Here we are,' Lynn announced, relief rubbing not quite imperceptibly at the boldness of her declaration, and frustration mingling with it as she felt the heaviness of the convenience store door. Just then, a young mother pushed out of it, a pram and nanny in tow, forcing Lynn to sidestep to the left. Emily noticed her wince as she did so and unexpectedly she felt a pang of protectiveness. She took a step closer, but then Lynn gathered herself and tutted at the mother loudly. 'I never had help with my two,' she told Emily.

They bought flour, vanilla extract, eggs and crushed almonds. There was butter and sugar already in the cupboard and neither of them were eager to increase the weight of the shopping bag with unnecessary goods. Emily's hands had been hurting that week, burning, perhaps from the cold. At the last minute, Lynn slipped in a bar of chocolate, a dark Green & Black's in navy wrapping. 'It's organic,' said Lynn. 'John thinks organic food's going to cure me. Of course it's absurd but we might as well humour him.' Emily carried the basket to the cash register, smiling at the thought of John who arrived sometimes, unannounced, in a whirlwind of hair and aftershave and harmless chatter, and often brought fresh fruit and vegetables, and seeds, and other things he had read were good for beating cancer. Lynn took out her purse, passing a card to the cashier, who she said good morning to, and deftly entered her pin number into the card machine.

The girl behind the counter did not respond to Lynn's greeting and was treating the interaction as a mundane obligation of her life. But there was a fleck of animation in Lynn that Emily had not seen before, a whisper of vivacity she had uncharacteristically on this shopping trip decided to share. And it rallied her.

'Good morning,' Emily repeated to the cashier,

pointedly. And surprised, Lynn looked at her, and chortled with such devilishness that Emily couldn't help but abruptly join in. Loudly. And for a long time. Emily couldn't remember the last time she had made anybody laugh, or laughed herself. The cashier shook her head and pursed her lips into a sneer. Delighted, Lynn laughed harder. It made Emily think of chopping vegetables with her mother.

Back outside however, the clouds had cleared and the sun had muscled its way onto the blue canvas, making Emily squint and abandon her fleeting feeling of elevation. The light danced around her causing her head to swim. A migraine had been threatening all day, and Lynn's questions that morning had already unsteadied her. She reached for the wall.

'We'll whip these up in no time,' said Lynn, perhaps noticing and letting the door to the shop swing shut. 'You look like you need feeding up. Here. To tide us over.' She dug with an exaggerated flourish into the shopping bag on Emily's arm and, with the whisper of exuberance still dancing around her face, pulled out the chocolate, breaking off a piece for herself and then offering it to Emily. But Emily had lost her appetite recently. She nibbled at Lynn's biscuits, but often couldn't stomach anything else. Suddenly she felt sick.

'Can we just walk please?' she said to Lynn tentatively, refusing the extended chocolate bar.

Lynn did not reply but she threw the chocolate

back into the bag and quickly began walking in a different direction to the way they'd come, her playfulness immediately dissipating.

'Where are you going?' asked Emily.

'Home of course. This way is quicker. It's almost one isn't it? You'll want to be finishing.'

Her voice betrayed hurt, and perhaps embarrassment, and Emily felt sorry for it, but Lynn was not to be argued with. She was never to be argued with. Besides, Emily could not deny that she wanted to get home, to be alone and shut out the dizzying light.

'Of course you should have told me how late it was,' Lynn admonished.

And Emily nodded, her head and stomach pumping as she followed Lynn dutifully through a series of winding streets that eventually spewed them out in front of a church.

With a domed top.

And the sun reflecting off it.

And outside, a man holding a lead.

And shouting.

And dogs barking.

'Emily,' said Lynn.

But it was too late. The eggs had smashed on the floor, and Emily was running.

Lynn's navy shoes were splattered with egg yolk. The man with the dogs pulled them to attention and moved on. There were no taxis on this road. It had been many weeks since she'd been to the shops on her own. Pain was stabbing through her side. In her handbag was a mobile phone, but she did not want to disturb her sons. Emily was gone. A slight flutter of panic crept across Lynn's chest. '*Poise*,' she instructed herself.

The pounding in Emily's head hammered harder and harder until she could hear no other sound than the fierce, insistent thumping. The thud of her feet on paving stones jarred and rattled, adding to the clatter, but she couldn't stop for fear that the noise would catch her. Slicing through the air. Knocking her down. Even with Lynn and ordinary shopping bags. Even here amongst the greyness and the coldness and the friendly unfriendliness that was not, after all, enough.

She was out of breath. A gate swung on its hinges ahead of her and Emily pushed through. The place was wooded and dark, part park, part graveyard. Crouching low next to a swing set, she loosened the scarf around her neck and clutched her legs, burying her face into her knees and rubbing her throbbing scar against them. It was the dome that had done it, the dome of the church, just like the one she'd run to once. And the noise: shouting, barking. Her throat stiffened and contracted. She was suffocating, she was sure of it.

No, she was cold, she told herself. She was in London where it was cold and she was cold, and the air was cold, and she could breathe it.

But her throat was hot, burning. And suddenly

she was spiralling backwards, too far, past the memories she controlled and so carefully rationed, past the recollections it was possible to sort and restrain, past, Before. And she was there again. In Rwanda.

They'd seen the men coming. Their small, wooden house sat on top of a hill, just in front of the graveyard where they sometimes played hide-and-seek amongst the trees and bushes, so it was easy to spot visitors across the fields as they approached. These visitors came wielding machetes and masus. One near the front carried a spear. He held it in front of him as though he was an old tribal warrior and shouted a chant the others quickly took up: *Hutu Power, Hutu Power.* All of them wore the colours – yellow, green, blue – threatening colours suddenly, detached from the flowers and the grass and the sky. *Green is for grass* . . . they were taught at school. No longer. Different lessons were needed now.

Rukundo had seen them first. They hadn't been to school that morning and instead had been loitering around the front of the house pretending to be doing something other than looking and waiting. For days it had been too dangerous to risk the streets. Gangs of Hutu Power supporters were gathering and chanting and stopping you if they knew you were a Tutsi, or if you looked too tall, or if they felt like it. Sometimes you escaped with words only. But the feeling was of something worse to come, like a pot of water slowly simmering, the boiling point as uncertain as it was inevitable. The only thing to do was watch, and stand as far away as possible from the heating pan.

They kept to themselves. Not even Jean sought her out as he once had, and they restricted their movements close to the house and to each other. Gahiji had left a week earlier. He had friends crossing over to Uganda to join the rebel army and he wanted to be part of the resistance. There, in numbers, with weapons, they could do something he said. Cassien – always brave, or rash, or in awe of Gahiji – had wanted to go with him but Papa refused and Emily slapped him for even suggesting such a dangerous thing. At least in Rwanda they were together, and had friends, and a home, and could be careful and survive. Still, her parents had kissed Gahiji goodbye and not stopped him, and ignored her screaming and then her tears, which fell first for herself and then more urgently for Gahiji's benefit as he resolutely packed up his paltry possessions, trying to avoid her pleading eyes; Emily had learnt at a young age of her eldest brother's weakness for them. When she was very little, she'd utilised this tool keenly. If their mother scolded her, even if she deserved it, like the time she broke Gahiji's new belt by misusing it as a skipping rope, her biggest brother was always the first to come to her rescue. The last time had been only a few months earlier after Jean had ruined everything with a kiss.

She and Gahiji had been walking home from church a little ahead of the others when she let it slip out. She hadn't meant to tell anyone, or anyone else (Jean had already seen to it that enough people knew his version of events), but Gahiji had asked why he hadn't seen Jean around for a while and without meaning to, Emily had told him.

Despite her attempts to normalise their interaction over the past months, Jean's mix-matched, swagger-filled eyes had remained full of that unnerving intensity, green and grey darting out at her in equally unsettling measures, and lately he'd started winking at her again. 'You look like you've got a twitch when you do that,' Emily had said to him this time, reaching for the cigarette they were sharing behind the schoolhouse, she still 12, he recently 14. Jean made a sarcastic face at her and took the cigarette out of her mouth.

'Well you look like a boy when you smoke,' he retaliated, blowing an inexpert cloud towards her.

Emily grinned. Such teasing was familiar territory, safe ground. She waved her hands through the puff. 'Don't. My mum will smell it.'

'She'll smell it on your breath anyway,' Jean laughed defiantly, taking a final drag before stamping out the stub. 'Here, smell mine.' Pinching her nose between her finger and thumb as though she could already smell the stench, Emily leaned in only slightly and conveyed the verdict with an exaggerated grimace, but Jean rolled his eyes, clamped a hand either side of her face and pulled it to within an inch of his. 'You have to come closer,' he told her. 'Smell it properly.' Now he opened his mouth a little and exhaled. His breath was warm and the heat of it did something funny to her stomach, something strange, as though she was about to jump from a high branch, or sit a test. And suddenly, although she wanted to lean back, the toxic air seemed to root her to the spot, while at the same time filling her with a keen, supernatural alertness that made her notice things like the early stubble on the top of Jean's lip, the single bead of sweat on his temple, the slight quiver of his jaw. She wondered if he still had that pure patch of white on his back. And then, too late, she realised that he was going to kiss her.

Emily was unprepared for the force of his lips on hers, the immediate, demanding searching of his tongue, not exactly horrible but disconcerting, alarming. Emily's face contorted. She was almost 13, but she didn't think of boys this way yet, not even Jean, who should have known this about her. When finally he let go, she pushed him hard.

'You stupid boy! What do you think you're doing?' she screamed, kicking the dirt between them and disturbing the cigarette stub. 'Why do you keep ruining things? You stupid boy! You're pathetic!'

He took a step back, tripping over his heel but said nothing, and for a moment the two of them stood silent beneath the dark cloth of her indictment. She wanted him to apologise, or tease her, or somehow unmake the minutes, but he merely looked from her to the wall behind her as though, without her to whisper the answers, he was desperately searching for them in space.

'Well?' she demanded again after long seconds had passed, because one of them had to speak eventually. But after opening and closing his mouth three times, Jean still offered no words to reply or reproach or justify. Instead, a second bead of sweat adorning his temple, he forced out an absurdly loud laugh, then turned his back to her, and silently, with a feeble attempt at swagger, walked away. 'Good! Go!' she shouted at him determinedly through the echo of his bravado. But as she watched him depart, Emily felt her fury quite unexpectedly evaporate, and gradually, as his silhouette grew smaller and smaller against the dying sun and the hills and the grass, it was replaced by a bewildering feeling of regret, and sadness, and loss. It was the first of many times that she felt the aching, pain-wrapped frustration of what might have been. But all she knew then was that she had to speak to him, and soon, if only to figure out why there was suddenly such a wrenching in her gut.

The next morning, a mass of cream-clothed students was as usual gathered outside the school-house. She'd left early without Cassien to go via Jean's house, but he'd already left when she arrived, or at least his mother had said he wasn't there.

He wasn't waiting for her by the gate, or on the path, or by the edge of the grass where sometimes he and Cassien kicked a football. Standing on her tiptoes amongst the throng, Emily searched for him, an urgency filtering subconsciously through her, but she couldn't see him. Instead, one of the girls she'd never liked and she and Jean had privately ridiculed, sidled triumphantly up to her.

'You're so sweet,' she crowed, laughing loudly for the benefit of the others, who Emily now realised had been looking at her and were all listening. 'To think that you tried to kiss Jean. But of course he wouldn't kiss you. He said he could never fancy a Tutsi.'

When Gahiji heard this, he doubled back past the church, found Jean halfway to the lake, threatened him with a fist and made him apologise right in front of the girls he was walking with and winking at. Gahiji always put things right. He always protected her. He always stemmed her tears.

On the day of his leaving for Uganda however, Gahiji only hugged Emily tightly, tilted his head, and promised to see her soon. Both of them knew they were words spoken for comfort rather than truth, but she clung to them anyway. Desperately. Rukundo ran shouting into the kitchen. 'They're coming. Men are coming. The Interahamwe.' Cassien and Simeon fell through the door behind him and Mama dropped the vegetables she was preparing: carrots and sweet potatoes that had been piling up in neat circles now tumbling across the floor, one slice of carrot rolling underneath the stove where it would never be found. Emily scooped the new baby out of her cot. Mary, a sister at last, had arrived four months earlier. Their father appeared behind them with a useless stick in his hand.

'We leave now,' he told them.

Out of the back door they hurried across the graveyard, their mother without the time to tie Mary to her back, bundling her in her arms, Emily chasing as close to Cassien's heels as she could. Rukundo and Simeon were far ahead, dodging through the trees they'd climbed together, but their father hung back, making sure they were all still running ahead of him. Once, Emily fell, but only for a moment. Then she was on her feet again, her hand gripped within her father's, her feet somehow moving.

By the time they reached the church, it was clear they were not the only families fleeing. Hundreds of other Tutsis were already crowding through the doors, the priests ushering them in like shepherds, the angels and saviours they'd always purported to be. Emily clung to her father's hand and mentally apologised to God for ever having complained about saying her rosary. Here He was, answering her, finally, loudly, when it mattered. Just as Mama had promised. Guiltily, Emily turned towards her mother, anticipating her pride at having been proved so conclusively right; but she caught the tail of a look that she had never seen before on her mother's face, a gaze not of triumph, but something between sadness and disbelief, between dreaming and reality, her eyes fixed not on the priests but on the streams of frightened people.

Mary began to scream. Dragging her eyes away from her mother, Emily let go of her father's hand and stuck her little finger in Mary's mouth. The girl's tiny body was swaddled closely in a white blanket Emily had helped her mother to bleach in the sun, but her delicate lips escaped the folds and sucked furiously for a few seconds until, calmed by Emily's familiar touch, amidst the jostling, wailing crowds, she hunched her neck down into the blanket and slipped off to sleep.

'She loves you,' observed their mother, all at once waking from her trancelike state. 'And I love you my daughter,' she added suddenly, starkly, with an urgent tenderness that was far more terrifying than everything else.

Emily clung harder to the swing set and let out a sob. Her body shook. She shouldn't have loosened her scarf. The cold air had crept underneath it and was controlling her, her muscles contracting involuntarily while her teeth chattered a rhythmic beat that paralysed her to the spot where she was crouched. She had to move. She had to get back to her flat, to a state she could manage. She had to close the door to the memories that were flooding her, forget Rwanda, forget Mary, not think about what came next.

But what came next was smoke-swaddled, seeping through cracks. Hot. Suffocating. Blurred by intensity. She remembered a petrified mob snaking into the church like Noah's Ark, in orderly channels of two or three, fear moving them to tidy regulation, to cling to what they knew, which was hierarchy and authority and chains of command. Rwanda. Emily and her family had joined the last of the convoy. In the distance, voices were beginning to ring out, exuberant voices, raised, intoxicated, chanting, baying, advancing.

Doors. She remembered doors closing and the priests standing in front of them, the hush of nearly two hundred people filling the church with the loudest prayer she had ever heard, spoken to God through sweat and silent tears and the sound of hearts racing. Now and then somebody coughed or a baby cried out, but its short infant gasps lasted only a few moments before somebody put a hand over its mouth, risking suffocation, usually the mother. Emily had again slipped her own finger into Mary's mouth so that she stayed silent. She could still feel the wetness of her lips, the heat of her sleeping body.

Wood hit wood as clubs met the solid church door. Glass shattered. People began to scream. Some of the women fell upon the priests who were

200

Hutus but also representatives of God: *save us, help us.* They pleaded. They kissed the priests' hands. And the priests smiled consolingly. Emily remembered that clearly. Their smiles. They nodded reassuringly, and Emily had loved them for it. They patted their flock. They blessed them, sanctified them. They stood in front of the heavy, protective doors.

And then, they opened them.

In their robes that identified them as priests.

With words that called out: *not us, we are Hutus.*

God's servants.

Pastors.

Friends.

From the back of the room, behind the altar where their father had hidden them, Emily crouched and watched as armed men rushed the building and the priests stepped helpfully aside. Smoothly. As if by prearrangement.

Then it was blurry again, and not blurry enough. There were machetes and masus. Blood was quickly everywhere. By their feet or hair, women were dragged outside. The door opened and closed and with every beam of sunlight there was another scream.

Then darkness. The men had fallen back and from the outside they heard the doors being locked. They were trapped, but at least the men were gone. Resting her eyes on her mother, Emily gave thanks. Now however, the screaming began in earnest. In the absence of light it resounded deeper than before, as though the pain was collective and had ripped through skin to the soul. It came in gush after agonising gush, fuelled not only by the freshness of terror but the stale, lingering devastation of loss: loved ones dead or soon to be, outside in the hands of killers; limbs missing; holes gaping through flaccid flesh; shredded skin spattering a bloodied, holy floor; skulls cracked like watermelons; humanity lost, vanished into a dark, domed void.

Outside, the men camped. They drank beer. Sporadically they took turns with Tutsi girls who no longer screamed, by now half-dead anyway, either from fast wounds or from the slow, deliberate end that in rhythm with the men above them pumped three toxic letters through their veins. H. I. V. H. I. V. A weapon of war more durable than gunshots. Inside, those alive cowered, locked in by keys safe in the pockets of priests. Some searched frantically for family. Some who'd escaped death by hiding under the bodies of those already struck down, dared not move nor answer even familiar calls. Above them the bodies turned cold.

During the night, the surviving adults spoke in hushed tones. They talked politics – the plane crash of the President, the broadcasts of Radio Mille Collines, the organisation and arming of the local Hutu Power gangs – whispered words that at the time meant little to Emily, only that this was why she was there, resting her head on Cassien's shoulder, clutching the hand of her mother who sang gently into her ear and smoothed her hair with shaking fingers. Few people slept. By dawn, the room stank. Children moaned for water. Adults gave up answering. Everyone waited.

It was many hours before the drunk hunters raised themselves, but when they did, the morning air seemed to fill them with a new bloodlust. Through the windows those inside watched as the priests obligingly unlocked the doors once more and the Interahamwe were upon them again. To her horror, Emily recognised some of them. In the frenzy of the day before she had noticed only their weapons and not their faces, but now she saw that they were local people, and she couldn't look away. A number of the boys were young and had been at school with Gahiji, some even with Simeon and Rukundo. She knew their names. '*Inyenzi*,' the men and boys taunted, waving their weapons like trophies, or school badges. 'Dirty cockroaches. Now we will cut you down to size.'

Blurry but not enough.

A routine developed. Not even the children were spared. 'They want to wipe us out altogether,' Emily heard a friend of her father's whisper. 'All Tutsis. They cannot risk leaving the children.' Emily clutched Mary tighter. From behind the altar, she and her family stayed silent as hour by hour the men returned. It felt complicit to do nothing, to say nothing, not even to scream. But what could they do? By evening, as many had been killed as remained.

Words echoed around the hall and inside her head. As transient as lasting. Departed yet enduring.

'We have to do something,' Emily's father implored them through the darkness. 'We have to fight.'

'With what?' came the whispered responses. 'Bare hands against machete and rifle and spear? Our small number against all of them? We will all die.'

'We will die anyway,' Emily heard her father reply, to which she covered her ears and pinched Cassien so he would pinch her back and allow her to feel a pain with which she could cope.

Then suddenly, there was no argument left to be had. The Interahamwe had a new idea and all at once through the windows came hurtling balls of fire. There was no more time. They would die now.

'Fire!' shrieked everyone. 'They're burning us alive!' Terrified people jumped up, abandoning their hiding places, pushing off the weight of dead bodies. Emily's father caught her hand and motioned for them all to stay down, but crazed and already coughing from the smoke, whole groups began to storm the front of the church, shoulders dropped ready to pummel against the bolted doors. Emily peeked out from behind the altar and willed them on, but her prayers were unnecessary. As soon as their shoulders hit the doors, they flew easily open. Emily turned to her father, puzzled, but the eyes of the stampeding crowd were glazed with triumph, euphoria, and hope. Hope's clarity blinding them. Propelling them forwards. They ran gasping into the fresh air, straight onto the sharp edges of waiting machetes.

The laughter outside was nearly as loud as the crying within. But the flames were the loudest of all. They crackled and roared and shrieked around the church while Emily and her family crouched closer to the floor behind the altar and coughed.

'We must escape,' her father shouted to them, his voice muted by the screams and the smoke that made him splutter. 'Not through the front door. We're going out the back.'

'There is no door at the back,' Mama yelled, spluttering too, her face frantic and unlike herself. 'There's nowhere to go.'

'We'll make a door,' said Papa.

Quickly, he, Simeon and Rukundo crawled to the back wall and began hammering at it with the single club they had between them, with a candlestick found overturned on the floor, with their hands. Their gestures became weaker and more desperate as they gasped for air, but finally, slowly, bricks began to budge. Cassien added his bare foot to the effort. Again and again Mama threw the whole force of her body against the loosening wall. Finally, they broke through. The hole was small but large enough for them to squeeze into. Mama went first, then Emily who jumped easily into the grass like she was dismounting from a tree and to whom Mary was hurriedly passed. The boys followed one by one and finally Papa appeared. They crouched in the grass, dotted with yellow flowers. The sounds of desolation hit them through thuds and screams and the exhilarated whoops of those inflicting it. Behind them, the church continued to burn. The smell of charred human flesh pervaded the air and Emily had the sensation of being in biblical times, the church some kind of living, animal organ being offered as a sacrifice to a vengeful god. She stared up at the building. The huge dome was lit by the glittering light of the fire within. Smoke-swaddled.

Cassien grabbed her hand. They ran in a zigzag close to the ground. Her heart pounded harder and harder until it felt as though it had risen through her body and into her head, where it was determined to drown out the terrible noises with its own thumping, vital presence. When they paused before dashing through an open clearing, her father turned and whispered something to her, stretching out his arms, but through the beat of her heart Emily could not hear him. Instead, she followed him into the clearing, fixed her eyes on Cassien's heels, clutched Mary tighter and kept running. The world dashed by, muted, until eventually they stopped in a thick area of bush where the trees provided temporary sanctuary and now her father spoke again, his face livid with anxiety. Still she couldn't hear him and so didn't answer. The world thumped. He spoke again, more urgently. Her heart pounded. Her ears buzzed. Slowly he came towards her. He reached for her face, stroking her cheek gently, brushing her hair out of her eye, saying something else, but everything seemed jumbled. His words reached her only as an incomprehensible hum and now she noticed that the others were turned towards her too. She sensed that she knew why but couldn't place it. They were looking and she was crying. She felt the tears streaming down her face. She saw her mother cover her eyes and Simeon's face fall. But it was only when Cassien lifted Mary from her arms, that she knew or could acknowledge that the baby, who had been quiet throughout the screams of the fire, and silent as she ran through the undergrowth, was no longer sucking on the finger she'd placed out of habit into her soft, still-warm mouth, and was not breathing, and didn't have a racing heart of her own.

Emily clutched her hands to her chest. The warmth of her woollen jumper alerted her to the burning iciness of her hands, but inside she felt hot, as though her insides had been shaken. She rubbed her face against the cold post of the swing set, the ropes clattering against it in the wind. Somewhere nearby, a small group of teenagers kicked their way past tombstones through the fallen leaves, brown and red layers over the soil, a protective mantle, a barrier to soften the way between life and death. Suddenly their flippancy maddened her, their disregard for nature's helpful tempers that she had never had. No cushions. No graves. No stones to carry some of the burden of memory. She scowled and they stared at her as they passed, but didn't understand. Not that she could either. The whole thing lay beyond the scope of her imagination, beyond humanity. Still pounding, she rested her head against the earth and dug her hands into the hard ground until the soil had worked its way deep beneath her fingernails and her knuckles had begun to bleed. The pain made her feel better; it rooted her to a time more manageable than the one in her mind and she scraped her hands harder against the dirt, contemplating how deeply she would have to cut herself before the bleeding would be unstoppable and complete. She pressed down harder, harder, deeper.

A hand that felt like Cassien's crept onto her shoulder. 'She's dead,' Emily mumbled, disoriented, still pushing into the hard earth. Until all at once she noticed that Lynn's navy shoes were in front of her. And it was Lynn's hand on her shoulder. Steady. Steadying.

'Emily,' the woman soothed. Behind her was a young man she had recruited to carry the shopping, staring inquisitively. 'Stand up slowly Emily. Careful.'

Emily stood up, snapping back into focus and attempting to hide her reddened hands. 'I'm fine,' she whispered. 'I'm fine.'

The man looked sceptical, and too curious.

'Well I know that,' said Lynn loudly, for his

benefit. 'Of course you're fine. Good gracious girl. But I'm quite tired of waiting for you. You'll arrive at nine tomorrow,' she told her. 'I think five mornings a week will do better. I'll call your supervisor. Now, see me to the road.'

Lynn held out her arm, and Emily took it, both of them ever so slightly leaning inwards as they inched out of the park. Lynn nodded sharply to the man behind them, who with a look of confusion, but obediently, followed the strange pairing with the eggless shopping.

Hours later, Emily climbed the foul smelling stairs to her fifth floor flat. Her hands were sore and stiff from the cold. Blood had dried in raised clots over her knuckles and cracked painfully as she dug into her bag for her keys. On an ordinary day she would have been holding them at the ready, but she seemed to be running in slow motion. As she fumbled, the door next to hers opened and a man stepped out. Without meaning to, Emily glanced up at him, and as she did so she couldn't help but notice that the dark-skinned man was excessively handsome, his face angular and puerile, angelic, his frame slight but coated in black, masculine, wiry hair. He wore white trainers that poked out from beneath a pair of navy jeans, and a grey hooded sweatshirt that framed a head of dark hair far sleeker than her own. Embarrassed, Emily looked quickly away but the man had already caught her eye and smiled warmly.

'Sister,' he said, extending his hand. 'So you're my quiet neighbour. Hello.'

Hesitantly, Emily took the man's hand, his fingers thin and delicate, easily broken, and briefly she allowed herself to look again at his striking face before turning back towards the door. She hated her meekness. It was not who she was, or who she used to be, Before. But it was better to be quiet and unnoticed. She turned the key.

'Sister, you're bleeding,' the man said, pointing to her hands.

'It's just a scratch,' muttered Emily, pushing unsuccessfully against her stiff door.

'I'm Omar,' the man persisted. 'It's good to meet you.'

Emily nodded. The door jerked open and she started to step inside but Omar stuck his hand in front of her.

'What's your name?' he grinned, leaning in to her flat and glancing quickly around.

'Um, Emily.'

'I like to know my neighbours, you know?'

Neighbour. The word made her shudder.

Omar shifted his body so that all of his weight rested on his forearm, which had now taken the place of his hand on her door frame. 'Hey, you should stop having fights with brick walls you know.' He grinned again, his teeth shining like those in the pages of magazines or on billboards, his smile lingering and then raising into an amused question mark as she silently looked on. 'You take care Emily,' he laughed and was about to leave when suddenly, Emily felt an urge to correct him.

'It's Emilienne.'

'Sister. Nice to know you.'

Omar removed his arm and stepped backwards. For as long as she could Emily returned his smile, but then abruptly she bent her head, closed her door and sank onto the floor in front of it. Reaching up, she locked the latch from the inside and slipped the key into her pocket where it would remain, safe, in her possession, until she was ready to face the world again. On the other side she heard Omar moving, his footsteps retreating, slowly at first, then faster, skipping down the stairs two at a time.

That night, Emily's dreams were vivid. They were filled with faces she knew: kindly, smiling, doting, laughing, friends, neighbours, teachers, priests. Then she saw the same faces again, distorted and strange, frightening in their mystifying mix of familiarity and evil. They floated above her dark and heavy, like shape-shifting rain clouds, then descended slowly until they surrounded her in a dense, disorientating fog that began to choke her. In her dream, she swiped at the smoky air, she gasped and fought and clung to life; but this was the easiest part of survival. These instinctual acts, this brawl over basic necessities, like air, these impulses that enabled her to subsist, this was not really living. It was existing. What came next was far harder, and a battle that began afresh every time she woke up.

She woke up.

The phone rang. The phone was ringing.

Few people had her number so Emily wasn't used to the sound and it jolted her from sleep with a start. Was she supposed to be somewhere? She didn't know how long she'd been asleep. One night? Two? Her body ached and her head throbbed. She lay back onto her pillow and closed her eyes. Without conjuring him, Omar's face drifted inquisitively in front of her. Then Lynn's, perplexed as she ran away.

The phone rang again.

She opened her eyes and strained to keep them that way. The animated buzzing seemed incongruous in the drab flat, lit by a lacklustre daylight that barely pushed through the paltry window.

The phone rang again.

With great effort, Emily pulled herself up to sitting and perched on the side of the bed staring at the ringing instrument, just out of her reach on the other side of the room.

CHAPTER 16

Charlie has been calling constantly. In the years they were together, and not together, and together again, he was never an advocate of phone calls. He said he preferred the romanticism of bygone eras, like in the movies they watched, where people just turned up at the designated time and place, and might not find each other, and could be missed, and plotlines could twist and turn powered by such serendipity, or lack of it. The mobile phone made for a boring life, he used to tell her. Nevertheless he always had his with him, simply screening the calls, and probably gave the same explanation to all his girlfriends.

Vera is screening her calls now. It will not be her parents, it is rarely work, and if it is Luke he will leave a message. Luke has been leaving Vera a lot of messages. As October freshness gave way to November chill, there have been more and more of them. About flower arrangements and which hymn will play first in the wedding service, and what canapés they will serve at the reception. The wedding has been moved up to January, for Lynn, to give her the best chance of being there. The day hangs like a beacon in front of Vera, still, promising her Luke, and happiness, which for so long have been the same thing. She cannot however seem to concentrate on the details. Or on him. Or on them.

It is a strange sensation, as though all that she thought was, wasn't, and the impossible is flickering into existence right before her eyes. Just weeks ago she would have given anything for mindless details to occupy her. Particulars of the now to distract her from what came before now, and to hide the fact that she was unable to imagine anything coming next. But suddenly, she is racing ahead. The nursery rhymes have stopped, the noise in her head has quietened. And she feels stronger, clearer. Guiltier and sadder too, more culpable; but more responsible, less evil, less alone. Not alone at all actually. That is the crux of it. There is still a cynical part of her that wants to laugh when she thinks it, but she knows now, *knows*, that she is not alone – she has Jesus. And from Him, present, future, past, she doesn't want distraction. With Him, she has confronted what she did. With Him, she has told Charlie. And with Him, as much as with Luke, she wants to move on.

But of course she is fooling herself. Because memories tend to drag and tie and weigh down and push backwards. And now that she has allowed them, they slip between her daydreams and hit her even more often, vivid and insistent. She may not be *alone* while remembering them, but they still require strength. Details she didn't know she'd even noticed swim before her eyes: the colour of little Charlie's hospital tag, the tiny fingers shaped like her own, the pudgy middle toe on his left foot ever so slightly raised above the rest.

And so it is clear. Whatever it is she needs to do to accept what happened, to accept *what she did* – tell Luke, tell her parents, tell the police? – she hasn't done. She is going every week to Alpha but cannot find the answers fast enough. She needs help. She needs Luke. She does not need distracting details. And she does not need Charlie's persistent phone calls, reminding her, reminding her, reminding her, ring, ring, ring . . .

The wedding invitations go out. Luke has selected them. He has chosen the wording and is the one to have called Vera's parents to ask them if they would like to be mentioned. Luke is paying for the small reception himself so there is no requirement to name them as hosts, but he feels that consulting them is 'the right thing to do'. He tells Vera this with an arched eyebrow.

Luke hasn't said anything, but over the creeping winter weeks Vera has noticed him beginning to look at her like this. And not only from beneath an arched brow. There are other tiny, barely perceptible differences that hit Vera at her core. Like when she makes a joke and his face stiffens. Or when she reaches for his hand, and he moves it away. It has been a long time since he kissed her.

One November night, he turns up late on her doorstep, and she can almost see the turmoil inside him bursting at his sensible seams. She has forgotten to call him during the day and hasn't checked her messages. It is possible that he has rung. But she has been trying to avoid thinking about the phone and who else might be at the end of it, or what that person might shout at her down the line. Luke tells her he has been at his mother's. Vera doesn't know what to say. She offers him her arms but he shrinks away from them. She offers him wine, but – with arched eyebrows – he shakes his head. He wants to talk, but not about his mother, or St George's, or them, or work, and nothing she says seems appropriate. He doesn't stay.

The following day he reminds her, over the phone, that she shouldn't be drinking wine. 'Do you not know that your body is a temple of the Holy Spirit?' he asks. 'And that you have a duty not to allow it to be mastered by anything?' It isn't a lot to ask, he says over and over. Not from his future wife. Silence follows this. She senses that she is meant to fill it, but cannot. She is not really thinking of giving up wine. It does not seem to her to be a prerequisite for loving Jesus. And besides, she is thinking of the red she drank at the tapas bar all those weeks ago, and listening to the beep on her phone line that is almost certainly Charlie calling again.

'Tell me something true,' she asks Luke softly.

Luke sighs. 'It's late Vera. I'd better call Mother before bed.'

During the night, Luke's words stack up around her. On top of her. Heavy. They terrify her with their judgement. She dare not even imagine what he would say if he knew the whole truth of what she has done. What would her parents say? What would a judge say? What is Jesus saying? Fragments of passages she has been learning at the Alpha Course run through her head. *It is for freedom that Christ has set us free.* She doesn't feel free.

Over and over Vera searches the bible. Over and over she ignores her phone. Over and over she prays, and smokes, and collects the ash into a small container that she waters with tears and intends to bury. Her lungs the only witness to the slow, gradual goodbye she has begun to say to the baby she longs for more and more, and longs to lay to rest.

CHAPTER 17

They had been playing Rummy before the boys arrived. Lynn would have preferred Kaluki but they would have needed a third, and even with the simpler game, Emily was proving a faster master of numbers and probability. Lynn had never been a great one for games of chance, or maths. Her strength had always lain in sideways thinking, in analysis, creativity and blind faith. But suddenly, numbers that gave definitive answers were more appealing than they had been. They left no room for doubt, no space for what ifs. Plus, in Rummy, there was the opportunity to gamble, to risk everything. While Emily collected straights and pairs and flushes, Lynn, with equal skill, gathered spaces between them into which she wove questions about Emily's childhood, about Rwanda.

The shock of seeing her curled up in the park the previous week had not quite left Lynn. Nor her words: *She's dead*. At night, the image flashed before her, unsettling, but replacing at least visions of her own demise. Emily's knuckles were healing and she'd regained her composure, that insurmountable, lip-curled restraint, but a knowledge had passed between the two women of darker things beneath bleeding skin. Lynn had not told her sons when Emily had failed to show up for work the morning after their trip to the shops. Nor had she complained to the agency. Instead, she had called Emily herself, three times before the phone was finally answered, and marshalled the girl back into the world of the waking. Without condemnation she had instructed Emily to return. And quietly, she had noticed the contriteness in the girl, the gratitude, the fresh nervousness and timidity. A bond of conspiracy flapped tantalisingly between them. But Lynn knew better than to start with the genocide. She asked Emily about what food they ate, about the dances they did, about the games played by children.

'But I am not a usual example,' said Emily, having been enticed ever so slowly into such a conversation. 'I climbed trees with my brothers, and played football, and liked to be dirty, not like the other girls.'

'You were a tomboy,' nodded Lynn, understanding. 'So was I.'

'You climbed trees?' asked Emily, smiling in amusement, looking up from her cards as if to draw the image.

'And once fell out of one. You see this arm?' Lynn raised her left arm, before conceding to a stab of pain in it. 'I broke it in three places.'

Emily grinned wider. 'I suppose it was strange for you then to have a boy so feminine.'

'Feminine?'

'John. Was he always so gentle? Was it a shock when you found out he was gay?'

'John is not gay,' said Lynn abruptly.

Emily looked up again from her cards. She shifted uncomfortably in her chair. 'Oh. Okay.'

'He's sensitive, that's all.'

'Okay.'

They both paused. Lynn threw a card away and Emily picked it up. 'Rummy,' she said hesitantly, laying down the proof.

Of course on some level, Lynn had always known it. In the deepest crevices of her memory was a day, a year before Philip had died, when John was just 15, and he had tried to talk to her, to tell her, to have her listen. But before he could wade into the pain of the conversation that was back then written so frequently all over his face, she had hushed him up. With silly questions about what he wanted for his supper, and if he had done his homework, and yes she did know his friend Tony, and wasn't he the boy whose mother had gone into a psychiatric hospital, and it was good of John to remain such a close friend to him in what must be a very confusing time. Philip had been in the next room and would have lectured John with Christian teachings about the sin of homosexuality. Which to some extent, Lynn had believed too.

So she had diverted the conversation, and thought she was sparing him. She pretended, later, that he had not been trying to tell her what she suspected. That with her omission she had helped him, guided him away from sin without having to judge it, or him, and unravel everything. She prayed that Luke and Philip wouldn't notice and knew that they wouldn't. She helped them not to and told herself again that there was nothing to see in the first place. Believed it. Ignored it. Ignored it. Ignored it.

'He's sensitive,' Lynn said again.

'Okay,' confirmed Emily.

Of course that was the moment that the front door slammed and John's voice sang up the stairs. It was past twelve but Emily had convinced Lynn that morning that it was acceptable for her to have lunch in bed, that in fact, it made it easier for her because Lynn's medicine was upstairs anyway.

'Mother?' came John's deep, soft tones. 'Are you up there with the angel?'

Emily glanced at her awkwardly. Lynn's voice was no longer strong enough to shout back, so she cued Emily to do so. Unable still to shout in front of her, Emily scurried to the door and stuck her head around it so that John could see her from the stairs. 'We're in here,' she told him softly. 'We're having a day in bed. With Rummy.'

'With rum? Oh, but I brought brandy,' John

221

winked appearing empty-handed. 'How are you Angel?'

'Fine, thank you.'

'How is she?'

'I'll leave you to spend some time,' said Emily. She followed John back into Lynn's bedroom and glanced meaningfully at Lynn before picking up the tray of lunch and making for the door.

'Hello Mother,' breathed John, settling into the vacated chair next to her bed. 'You look stunning.'

John was still sitting with Lynn, regaling her with the story of a botched performance the night before, when Luke arrived. Lynn supposed the lightness of John's tone, or of his life – in comparison to the weight of helping Africa's poor, and getting married, and looking after his mother – was grating to Luke. And perhaps this is what set them off. But it had been the same between them for a long time. When Philip had died and Luke had stepped so bravely and seamlessly into his shoes, John had still been tucked up in the bosom of childhood. Or so it must have appeared to Luke. John had had meals cooked for him, and school teachers to direct him, and did not seem to feel the need to take on any of their father's responsibilities at church. Like Luke did. Of course Lynn saw with searing clarity now that John didn't, because John couldn't. But she had pretended too well for too long. And what Luke must have seen all those years ago was his younger brother spending more and more time away from home, with friends who they never met, at clubs they did not go to, leaving Lynn alone so that Luke felt he had to come back from university to keep her company at weekends.

Two years later, at the first chance John got, he moved out of home altogether into a student flat, even though he could have stayed at home with their widowed mother during his time at the drama school which was only 10 minutes away. After that, he had never returned really, or made the effort to include Lynn in his life, and Luke was infuriated by this. By the contrast between his flighty brother and the expectations he demanded of himself. Lynn made excuses for him. She had always made excuses for him, and though she knew this angered Luke further, she understood now why she did it. Her eldest son however, couldn't comprehend the compelling force of culpability, and she could not explain it to him.

As they sat on either side of her bed, Luke and John bickered as usual, and looked to her to call the winner. Luke, who had raced over to see her on a lunch break from work and noted that John who had been free all morning, had only just arrived, preached Responsibility; John countered with Humility. There was a time when she would have knocked their heads together and been done with it, but the sound of their arguing made her so tired now, so wretchedly tired, and instead she closed her eyes. Their voices circled in a dizzying hum. In the end, it was Emily who silenced them.

'I heard shouts,' she said, sticking her head around the bedroom door. 'All the way from the kitchen. Is everything okay Mrs Hunter?'

At once the boys quietened. It had never been acceptable for family grievances to be aired in public and this was one value on which they all continued to agree.

'It's okay Angel,' John said brightly, smiling immediately. 'Thank you, everything's fine.'

'Mrs Hunter?'

Lynn appreciated that it was her opinion being sought and not that of her sons. 'Thank you Emily. I'm fine,' she said, looking to her quiet, seated offspring. 'They're behaving themselves now.'

But then, Luke stood up. 'Emily. Sorry, I wouldn't usually leave these things to my brother but – I've been wanting to meet you for some time,' he said as he volunteered an outstretched hand. And as Emily shook it, it was impossible not to notice how stricken her face was, how suddenly hunched her posture, how her hand trembled then flew to flatten the fringe over her eye. Even Luke, so easily confident, flushed red against her awkwardness.

'Well you made quite an impression,' John teased as soon as the door was closed. 'Got a way with the women have you Luke?'

'Be quiet,' Luke had retorted, pulling on his coat. But then paused, looking towards the door, then to his feet. Then to his mother. 'You are okay with her mother, aren't you?' he asked, fatigue or perhaps anxiousness dragging his voice into a whisper.

Lynn only flapped her hand.

CHAPTER 18

It was as though she was there all over again, standing, facing him.

It was his eyes: the half-grey, half-green duplicity of them. Not one thing or another, but two things at once. Lightness and dark. Trust and deceit. After and Before.

They penetrated her armour. They dug beneath Lynn and London. And she was there again, in front of him.

Of course, Luke's skin was white, he had blond hair, and a far more angular nose. A black face, a brown face, even Omar's movie star, smiling face should have been a closer comparison. But the eyes, the eyes alone sent Emily running downstairs and into the closed room at the back of the house, the door for which she'd days ago finally found the key though not yet opened, locking it fast behind her.

She had no idea how long it took for her to calm herself. She breathed deeply, forcing the air into her closing lungs, and stared straight ahead of her at the panel of the door she rested her head upon. Over and over she told herself that she was safe, she was in England, she repeated it out loud. She conjured visions of snow, and skyscrapers, and trains, and puddles. She rubbed her wool-bound arms and reminded herself of winter winds, of grumpy bus drivers, of white faces. But her body wouldn't listen. It shook violently. Her stomach contracted and she vomited onto the floor. Emily's skin was cold but covered in sweat. Outside the room, she heard doors open and close, footsteps on the stairs, then slower ones, the creaking of the couch in the living room, the buzz of the TV; yet they could just as easily have been gunshots and the sickening slice of machete, the hum of laughter, the thud of her face on the ground.

At some point she must have passed out. It happened sometimes. More often lately. A shrill ringing would begin inside her head, growing louder until the pain of it was unbearable, and then finally turn everything to blackness. When she opened her eyes, they were caked in sticky reminders of her desolation, her left arm was numb from lying too long upon it, and the room stank of her own vomit. She looked to see if there was a window.

The room was covered in painted canvasses. Great, five-foot tall ones leaning against a table; smaller, square ones dripping from the walls and piled on top of each other in a careless fashion as if they were excess crates of beer; and a single, carefully positioned canvas set upon an easel, unfinished. Emily approached it and to reveal it better drew apart the heavy curtains that covered the great French doors to the garden, opening a window to let out the smell. There was something about this particular painting that drew her to it. The others were beautiful and intricate, whole stories conveyed in the wrinkles of angular faces, the sideways glance of an eye, or in the meandering paths in the distant corners of vast landscapes. But the unfinished painting was of a different style. It was a face only. Stark and stripped. A crown of wispy blond hair flew about the background as though the figure was in rapid motion, but the blue eyes were still, the skin pale and serene but for a spattering of freckles, and the expression on the mouth unremarkable. Yet the effect was luminous. Somehow full of hope and possibility and strength and courage. Emily looked down. Despite the impression of colour on the canvas, she saw that Lynn had used reds mainly; countless shades of them that must have been painstakingly mixed within the small pallet lying crusty and neglected beside the easel.

Emily's mother had loved art, though they never owned any, just as her father had loved books though in his job at the hotel he was barely required to read a whole sentence. To Emily's memory, art was not a means of expression that had touched her much in Rwanda, there was not a tradition of it. There was dance, there was song, but nobody in their village painted; perhaps for lack of tools or time. Still, her mother had taken her as a young child to an exhibition at a small gallery in Kigali and pointed out a painting that she herself had seen three times before. She told Emily that the painting gave her hope, though she didn't say why or for what reason hope was needed, only stood, staring at it for hours, long after Emily had been ready to go home. Emily's mother would have liked to learn to paint properly, she told her once, but instead she made do with making beautiful the lives of the children she'd borne, which was no small task in their village but exactly how Emily remembered it.

Luke's eyes flashed in front of her again, merged with another's. She raised her fingers to her scar, then she addressed the mess she'd made on the wooden floor, which she now noticed was covered with dust. Slowly, she turned the key in the door and edged her way out into the hallway, tiptoeing towards the kitchen from where she was hoping to retrieve a bucket of water and some disinfectant.

'Emily?' came Lynn's voice from the living room.

Emily froze.

'Emily? Can you come in here for a moment please?'

Despite a growing feeling of familiarity around the woman, there was always something about the way Lynn spoke that made her requests not questions at all, but imperatives to be followed. Emily moved slowly towards the living room.

Lynn was sitting in her usual chair, her head tipped awkwardly to one side so that she could view the television around a vase of flowers that Emily could only presume had been too heavy for Lynn to move. The woman had deteriorated rapidly in the past weeks, but she refused to bring her sudden frailty to anyone's attention, most of all her sons'. Instead, Lynn had Emily prepare in advance plates of (newly) assorted biscuits and asked her to keep the teapot ever-ready with a few teabags in the bottom, which she said was for the sake of efficiency, but Emily knew was for illusion. Any extra care that Lynn needed, any new ailment that crept up on her had to be spotted, and not mentioned but dealt with like a trivial inconvenience. Emily stepped forward now and shifted the vase of lilies to the left.

'I suppose there is a reason why you decided to lock yourself in my garden room?' Lynn proposed, keeping one eye on the TV and making no mention of the art that flooded the soft-lit space or why it was kept locked. 'And why you chose this as the place in which to empty your stomach?'

Emily said nothing.

'Are you ill?'

Emily shook her head.

'Pregnant?'

'No.'

'Have you met my son before?'

Again, Emily shook her head, but this time the

action seemed to swing her whole body with it, and the more she tried to restrain it the more out of control it became, rocking from side to side as if she was on a boat, or being tugged one way and another by a force much stronger than herself. She reached for the couch and tried to steady her legs, told herself to get a hold of herself, tried in vain to fight the fuzz, but by then the whole room had taken up the nauseating swaying, spinning relentlessly round and around. Lynn's voice echoed somewhere in the background, firm, steadying, but too far away. Then again, nothing but black.

The first thing she saw on waking up was the flowers. In her fall she must have knocked the vase because it lay shattered on the floor around her, the white lilies spread across the carpet, absurd with their heads dismembered on the ground and not reaching up towards the sky.

'John bought them,' Lynn said, and Emily turned her head to see Lynn kneeling awkwardly next to her. The frail woman had managed somehow to lower herself onto the floor and place a cushion beneath her head, and fetch a glass of water that she now held out to Emily. Emily sat up and took the glass. 'Funny though, I never really liked lilies,' Lynn continued. 'They were Philip's favourite. I kept them in the house for him. John always buys them for me now, but my favourites are daffodils.'

'Yellow.' Emily's throat hurt.

'They remind me of spring.'

'There were yellow flowers all over the hills in Rwanda,' she croaked. 'Yellow and white.'

'That sounds very lovely.' Lynn stood up, moving not towards her hard-backed chair but to the sofa where Emily had never seen her sit, and patted the cushion next to her. 'Come and sit with me Emily. It's time to tell me.'

'Tell you what?'

'Your story. What happened to you in Rwanda. What happened to your family.'

'*If your mouth turns into a knife, it will cut off your lips,*' Emily mumbled instinctively. Her throat clicked.

'Nonsense. It's time to let it out Emily. You can start with Luke if you want to.'

Slowly, Emily moved towards the couch and sat tentatively on the far edge. 'He reminded me of somebody. That's all. It's nothing.'

'Of who?'

Emily's stomach began to contract again. 'Don't ask me.'

'Of who, Emily? Who did he remind you of?'

'I can't—' Emily battled. 'I don't want to – I've never spoken about it.'

'Well, it seems to me that you have to.'

Lynn's voice had not raised but remained at that insistent, commanding level that ushered life in front of it, moved people to act. And suddenly, Emily began to cry.

'That's good,' said Lynn. 'Let it out. I'll make us a pot of tea.'

She was absent for many minutes and during that time Emily dabbed frantically at her face with the end of her sleeve, mortified, but the tears kept coming. It was shameful to think of burdening another person with her grief, yet oddly, it seemed to have infused Lynn with extra strength, with purpose, and she heard the old lady humming as she boiled the kettle and made slow journeys to and from the garden room, where Emily could only presume she was clearing up the lingering puddle of sick. When she returned, Emily helped her place the tray onto the coffee table but let Lynn pour their cups.

'Sugar?' Lynn asked.

'Three.'

They sipped in silence for a while, then eventually Lynn spoke. 'Begin,' she told her plainly. 'Begin at the beginning.'

'I don't know where the beginning is. I've never been able to put it all together, in order.'

'Then start somewhere in the middle,' Lynn pressed. 'We'll sort out the chronology later on.'

'No,' Emily shook her head. 'I don't want to remember it.' She knew though that this was impossible because she remembered it every day, even when she felt at her strongest. A mere flash of grey-green was enough. 'I just want to forget.'

'But you should not forget,' Lynn answered, with authority. 'You should set it free. It's your narrative

Emily, your story. You must tell it, you must make it history, just an account of something that has been, like a book. It's when it's caged inside you that it can hurt you; it eats at you then, it festers. It leaves you hunched over with bleeding knuckles.'

Emily clung more firmly to her cup and said nothing.

'It's my dying wish,' Lynn blackmailed.

Emily closed her eyes. She ventured another sip of her tea, allowing the sugary liquid to drip through her, then she filled her lungs with the warm air of Lynn's fire-heated lounge and looked back up to meet the woman's stare. Just a hint of a smile rested on Lynn's lips in testament to her knowing manipulation.

'Okay,' Emily said finally. 'I'll try. I'll try to give it to you.' Somehow, Lynn inspired courage. Still, she opened and closed her mouth three times before any words came out of it, because once they did there was no turning back, she would lose herself, she would let in the memories she'd fought for eight years to push away, she would go further back than she'd ever before allowed. 'You'll help me?' she urged, but even as Lynn nodded, Emily felt herself drifting dangerously fast, past the cave she inhabited next door to Omar, past the soft bed at Auntie's, past the chaotic plane journey, and the refugee camp, and the UN officials with their useless guns, past the graveyard, and then suddenly she was not drifting anymore but running, sprinting frantically through the undergrowth, away from a burning church, a dead baby in her arms.

There was no time to bury Mary. No time for the proper rituals. With his hands Papa dug a shallow grave in the earth beneath a Nim tree and Emily and her brothers helped to scatter dry soil and leaves on top of it. Their mother didn't move. In the days that followed, each of them would experience their own moments of paralysis, seconds in which their minds refused to accept what their eyes saw. This was her mother's moment: the first death of one of her children, the beginning of what for her was unimaginable. Papa and Rukundo had to steady her as they pushed on silently through the undergrowth. Simeon and Emily trailed close behind. Cassien was at the rear but only, Emily knew, because he wanted to prod her forwards if she slowed, catch her if she started to fall.

Then the men were upon her, pinning her down.

'What men?' Lynn interrupted from somewhere far away.

'Where are you?'

Emily stopped. She had forgotten the order again. Everything was jumbled. Her mind was blocking the story. It knew the danger.

'Go back to the undergrowth,' Lynn directed, a clink of flowered china in the background. 'Go all the way. You were running.'

Emily half-closed her eyes. Perhaps it would be easier to see only one world at a time, though she was terrified of losing her anchor to this one.

'You will tell me if I wander?' she asked Lynn, and again Lynn nodded.

'You were running.'

Perhaps they should have remained in the bush, but how long could they have lasted there? Already they were hungry and thirsty and so riddled with fatigue that they began falling over at regular intervals, and sitting for too long, and taking too much time to hear the voices calling for cockroaches. Twice Emily saw her mother fall and not even notice the scratches on her legs or the trail of red they made around her calves.

Night fell. Emily heard her parents talking frantically, pleading with each other for ideas, hoping against all probability that there was an answer they had missed, something simple, a way out. Sometimes Rukundo was consulted, but they never shared their conversations with the rest of them. It was not their way to talk to children about such worrying things. 'All will be fine,' Emily's mother promised, guiding her head onto her lap and stroking her hair, hiding her eyes as usual beneath the protective tips of her fingers; but when they thought she was asleep she heard the truth whispered over the other worrying sounds of the undergrowth. The truth was full of things they could not do: *They could not* try to cross into another village because they would be recognised immediately as outsiders, and identified as Tutsis. *They could not* try to head for a city closer to the Ugandan border where the rebel army and maybe Gahiji was entering from, because there were road-blocks everywhere. *They could not* stay in the bush where they would surely be found or die of starvation. At least in their home village, Emily heard her mother suggest, there were Hutus who were their friends. They had neighbours like Ernest who would look after them, who would help them, who would hide them, who had not turned to stone. In the morning, Papa announced that they were going home.

They walked with a peculiar feeling of jubilation. Like when coming back from a long trip and the joy of a clean bed, a familiar chair, and a return to normality is anticipated with a pleasure that grows with every advance. Emily caught herself smiling at Cassien who prodded her in the ribs and smiled back. Even in this moment of danger, she and Cassien shared a fleeting happiness. His grin was the same as the one she'd looked upon her whole life – running through the village on their way to school, climbing trees, spotting clouds, telling jokes from the bed next to her when they were meant to be sleeping – and it promised her that despite what had happened at the church, with the dead bodies and the fire and the crazed men who were not like men but monsters, despite the loss of their baby sister, somehow that incongruous levity would sustain them, and they would be alright. She held her brother's grin to her, with both hands.

When they reached the edge of the bush that backed onto the graveyard behind their house, Papa motioned for them all to be still and silent. Picking up a fallen branch he crept stealthily towards the house and pushed the back door open. Then he disappeared. In the minutes that followed, Emily's mother took three, deep, painful gulps of air. She held firmly to a low branch and didn't blink, even when a bold beetle scurried over her foot. Emily crouched in her mother's shadow and silently promised God that if only He would let her father reappear safely at the door, she would never do anything bad again. It was the first of many negotiations she had with Jesus, before she realised that such conversations were useless. This time however, she gratefully gave thanks.

It was better inside. The house wasn't large but it had walls, and windows you could close and doors you could lock. Without being told, they spoke quietly and said nothing at all when they caught sight of neighbours passing by in the distance. Three houses down there lived another Tutsi family but Emily saw nobody emerge from there and Papa told her to get down from the window. Mama went straight to the kitchen where she discovered that the larder had been raided and all their canned food and alcohol stolen. Still there were enough scraps for her to give some morsel at least to each child, which she presented to them in the same formulation in which they always sat, as if it was any other mealtime on any other day and Mary's absence was only because she was asleep in her cot.

As the day progressed, they allowed themselves the pleasure of slipping into old routines. Papa read one of his books, caressing the pages with his long spindly fingers. At one point he even called to Emily and made her read from the book out loud and discuss what she was reading, as if one day she might need to understand Machiavelli's musings on appearance and power. But she was too busy thinking about what had happened to her village, what could possibly have made Hutus she both knew and didn't know hate her so much. There was nothing to distinguish them, that was what she was stuck on. They weren't different colours, they spoke the same language, they lived together, they married, they shared their lives. Jean was a Hutu, and they'd been best friends, at least before he'd tried to kiss her. After that, she supposed, it was true that he hadn't spoken to her even when passing in the street, but that was different to believing that she and every other Tutsi must die. Jean couldn't believe it, surely. Not Jean to whom she'd, almost, been everything. Her father would have the answers and be able to explain it to her; but for the whole of that strange, surreal day, he preferred to talk about Machiavelli. She didn't press him. It was reassuring to listen to his voice, and cling to the promise within it that there was a future ahead of her for which she must be prepared.

When night fell, Mama and Papa called them together and told them their plan. Mama was going to slip out under cover of darkness and cross over the back of the house to their neighbour's. They had no more food, no water, they needed help, she said. Ernest would help them. Emily nodded. It was a good plan. Some Hutus had gone mad but Ernest was their friend, their neighbour, he'd been good to them 'til the last, he'd exchanged concerns with Papa about the riots on the streets and the boys joining the Interahamwe, she trusted the deep bellow of his voice and the laughter that followed the jokes he cracked at his own expense. He would shelter them, he would help.

Mama returned with her arms full of supplies: mangoes from Ernest's tree, a cup of rice, water. 'We're to watch for his signal – a candle at his window – and then we're to unlock the door for him. He'll bring us food,' Mama smiled, the relief on her face impossible to miss. 'The rest of the time we stay inside. Until this madness passes. It will pass,' she repeated, looking hard at her daughter, though even at 13 Emily sensed these words were as much for her mother as for herself. Because of them, the rice went down slowly, filtering with difficulty past the growing knot in the pit of her stomach.

During the night, Emily slept in sporadic bouts.

Asleep, her dreams were filled with screams and flames crackling; awake, with the eerie silence of her brothers, their wide eyes blinking white in the darkness. Once when she awoke, her mother was sitting at the end of her bed, stroking her ankle. 'Sleep my daughter,' she told her when she saw her stirring, but Emily couldn't. The sadness in her mother's eyes was too unnerving, her gaze too lingering, as if she was etching Emily into her mind. Emily closed her eyes and for her mother's sake pretended to doze, until at some point the soft strokes on her ankle did lull her into unconsciousness, and a final untroubled rest.

Emily opened her eyes.

Lynn had moved closer to her and was stroking her arm. Instinctively, Emily pulled it away.

'That's not the end, is it?' asked Lynn gently.

Emily shook her head. Weak London light slipped through Lynn's lounge window.

'Who does Luke remind you of?'

Emily shook her head harder.

'Go on Emily. Please, go on.'

But Emily could not speak. It was the furthest she could allow herself to travel. Lynn studied her carefully. Her face was full of sadness, and sympathy, and curiosity.

'It's past two,' she said finally. Slowly. 'I've kept you far too long. I'll have to pay you.'

'I'm sorry,' Emily stood up, shakily. 'I should never have begun.'

'Of course you should.' Lynn paused. 'Emily, I think perhaps I need you a little longer each day. I'll arrange it.'

'I'm sorry,' said Emily again. She backed towards the door, her two worlds dizzying her.

'Slowly,' said Lynn. 'Slowly Emily. I'll see you tomorrow.'

CHAPTER 19

With every frosty word from Luke, Vera is terrified that his mother has told him. They have been arguing again, or not arguing but always falling just short of understanding the other. She still intends to tell him, herself, about the abortion, or rather the lack of abortion, and everything that came after it. And yet November ticks by. Each night she plans it, practises it, steels herself to accept the fallout from it, but during the day the words just won't come to her. Jolted out of her head perhaps by the insistent buzzing of her phone. Early in the mornings, before the buzzing begins, she goes to St George's. She hopes that somewhere in the quiet, under the great dome, along the pews, in the pages of the books, the words she needs will be lurking, along with her redemption. Even after several unsuccessful visits, her hope is not diminished. She feels supported there, as though that light pair of hands is permanently upon her shoulders. Yet the loss of her baby remains fresh and unredeemable, and she has still not told him, and he is too much to risk.

Luke, untold, wants to know why she will not visit. He has brought coffee and her favourite date slice, and a careful gentleness to his tone. But she senses reservation and she has pressed him. 'I'm disappointed,' he tries to explain, tries to say calmly.

'Disappointed that I won't look after your mother?'

They have been walking through Regent's Park, a rare weekend morning spent together, and now they are sitting in Luke's car. Outside, remnants of a deep frost cling to blades of grass made razor sharp. Inside, the engine is on and they are warming up. A Bach sonata Vera once knew how to play clatters through the silence from the radio. Luke turns it down. 'Disappointed you won't see her. You don't visit her, even with me. It's been months,' he accuses finally, gently. 'I know how good you can be Vera, I don't understand it.'

Can be.

'I'm not sure she'd want to see me,' Vera offers weakly.

'Of course she would. My mother is very forgiving.'

Vera looks away from him and pats her pockets for a cigarette before remembering that she is with Luke and cannot smoke one. To steady the itch in her hands, she reaches for the dial of the radio and turns the music back up.

'Well say something then!' Luke demands suddenly, curtly, raising his voice over the melody.

It is the first time since she's known him that his face has flashed red, his sandy hair askew, his calm, reasonable composure altogether lost. Luke clenches his left hand and beats the steering wheel making the sound of the horn crash shockingly into the silence. Vera leans away. For a moment, neither of them breathe, and even the music on the radio seems to linger over a single note in uncertain anticipation of what may come next. But the shouting and swearing and aggression she has experienced from other men doesn't come. She forgets sometimes how different Luke is. How much better. If it had been *his* baby then maybe . . . Luke exhales. Everything about him deflates and gently, he rests his head on the steering wheel. The red rushes from his cheeks as quickly as it came and his face fades gradually to an ashen white. Pallid hands continue to grip the wheel.

'Please,' he says, without looking at her, his voice wobbling as it comes. 'I'm trying to help her. To do the right thing. At least for the time she has left. You're my fiancée, you should see her.'

From her bag, Vera's phone buzzes. Again. 'Work,' she lies quickly, turning it off. But Luke doesn't even lift his head. Has he grown used to it? Used to her being only half there? Only half true? Her stomach tightens. The thought of losing him hits her hard in her gut like a punch. Crouched over the steering wheel, he seems both weak and still so strong. Vera has an urge to touch him and tentatively she reaches for his arm. Through his thick winter coat she can feel his beating pulse. It is the most intimate they've been in weeks. And the thump of it is like an electric shock to Vera, a sudden propulsion.

'I should have visited,' she says abruptly. 'You're right.'

He breathes in heavily. Vera keeps her hand on his arm and feels for the rhythm beneath.

'I'll come Luke,' she says while the beat is strong. 'I will. But before I do, I have to tell you something.'

And she tells him.

That she was pregnant by Charlie.

That she almost had an abortion, and told his mother that she had it.

That she had a baby.

That she gave it away.

She stops. Waiting. Hovering. Deciding.

Luke looks up at her. His normally two-tone eyes seem almost black.

The pastries are almost a week later. Short, dark days have crept by and Vera has marked them with a succession of doodles that have now completely obscured the message on Charlie's card. At the time, after a long and uncomfortable silence, Luke thanked her for telling him, for allowing him the knowledge of the truth. Vera looked down when he said this but he didn't seem to notice her unease, or presumed probably that what she did confess was enough reason for it. He said he was grateful to her for enabling him to speak into her life with what he hopes will be help and illumination. And for a fleeting, uncertain moment, he squeezed her hand. But seven days have passed and he is yet to 'speak'. They have not been speaking. He has texted her a few times with wedding necessities – a sign she has taken as positive; but he has not answered her calls, they have not dissected what she told him, he has not unloaded her of her remaining secrets. She presents the sweets to Luke on Lynn's doorstep feeling a little silly in her grand gesture, but she has nothing else. 'I brought pastries,' she declares, stupidly.

He looks good. Tired, anxious, slightly more dishevelled than usual; but with grey-green eyes full of soul, and arms that if wrapped around her would solve everything. 'Perhaps I shouldn't have expected it,' Luke says quietly after a long pause.

'Expected what?'

'Expected more than, well, pastries. It was too much for you.'

Vera feels the sting.

'It was too soon for me to ask it,' he carries on, attempting to clarify, to temper. Then slowly he bends forwards and reaches for the box.

Accepting it. Accepting her? Accepting what she has done? *What he knows of what she has done.* Vera shakes her head. She wants to tell him the rest. The truth. She has come so far. But his breath draws close to hers flexing warmth through the cold air and Vera smells his familiar aftershave.

The desire to collapse into his forgiveness is too much. Breathing in deeply she wonders how she could ever have placed him in her periphery.

Then, of course, her phone buzzes. Always buzzing. Buzzing. Startling her like a police car or an ambulance siren. A flashing light reminding her of danger ahead.

'Come in,' Luke whispers. And she does, but without telling him anything more, without answering her phone that is blinking at her from the top of her bag, and without quite noticing his hand on her back, or the pain behind his eyes, or the way that he is watching her not watching him.

At first, Vera and Lynn greet each other with great fanfare. A fuss is made over the pastries, which Lynn insists be served on a particular plate that Luke has to root around for in the display cabinet in the dining room, and has to be eaten from matching dishes which Luke says he can't even recall, but finds eventually. The elaborate display of china seems to please Lynn and she insists on making a pot of tea with another delicate piece, despite their entreaties for her to sit and let them take care of it. Finally they all settle and endeavour to keep up the high spirits.

The older woman sits opposite Vera, loudly saying nothing. Her white hair is pulled back into its usual bun, her blouse freshly ironed, her cheeks lightly rouged, but the creases around her eyes and at the corners of her mouth seem to have hardened into the skin. Her lips are chapped and the first signs of undernourishment are appearing around the jaw. She seems far older than her 58 years. Occasionally, when she thinks nobody is watching, she winces. It is a peculiar feeling for Vera, to mix pity with trepidation. She tries to behave normally but hears herself talking several tones higher than usual and making jokes that nobody laughs at. Luke's face seems unprepared for laughter. He is absorbed in studying his mother and every now and then his jaw clenches or his eyelids blink in quickened succession. The sight of his bitten nails makes Vera swallow hard. She tries to catch his hand across the couch, but he folds it into his lap, then leaves the room. There is an urgent phone call, he apologises.

From the next room, Luke's voice rises and falls. Rises and falls. Rises and falls. Vera tries to steady her own breath with his and, alone again with Lynn, tries desperately to think of a topic for conversation, but she cannot come up with anything. Ever since her phone rang on the doorstep she has been thinking about Charlie, and even with Luke and Lynn and the agony of it all directly in front of her, her mind is almost wholly occupied by this, by him: the father, the ex, the victim, the aggressor. And by apprehension and anticipation of what sooner or later she will have to hear him spew – blame, and deserved reproach. She knows that the phone in her bag will ring again, will keep ringing, and she should have turned it off, but now in front of Lynn it would seem rude to fish around for the mobile. Vera endeavours not to stare at her bag too noticeably. The silence persists and she makes a mental note to prepare conversation in advance of her next visit. *What does one discuss with future mother-in-laws with no future of their own?* For her part, Lynn says nothing, and doesn't appear to be trying to. Perhaps, Vera supposes, there is simply little for them to say. They are too different. Lynn too pure and Vera too imperfect, still.

Yet they cannot say nothing forever.

'I've told him,' Vera announces to Lynn suddenly, out of nowhere.

There is no time for the older woman to reply before Luke re-enters the room.

He looks purposeful. The remains of a smile cling to his face and he seems refreshed almost. Vera watches him gladly, relieved that he is coping after all, that he has *been* coping without her attention. As he replaces his phone in his pocket however and sinks into his place on the sofa, his steady breath seems to leave him. He coughs slightly and asks his mother if she would like a blanket. She does not. He asks if she would like the window closed. She does not. He asks if she would like another pot of tea, but the one on the table is still half full and Lynn tells him so. Luke nods, and picks up his bible. He offers to read them passages from it, and finally at this Lynn assents. Luke grips the spine tightly. He recites verses that speak of tests of faith, and hard times, and healing. His voice is strong as ever, affirming, sure, but he rarely glances up at Lynn who sits still in her cream-coloured chair with perfect posture and respectfully listens, despite the faint frown that occasionally creeps across her brow, just fleetingly, before she remembers Luke and hurries it away. With the bible in his hand, Luke is no longer looking at her so does not see this. But Vera sees. And watches. Mother and son locked in tragic theatre. Mother sacrifice. Mother devotion. She cannot take her eyes off them.

After what seems like a very long time, John arrives. He flounces onto the sofa in his flamboyant way, and wraps his scarf around his mouth to indicate he'll be quiet, and although he rolls his eyes and slumps into himself as Luke reads on, he dutifully says nothing. And Lynn says nothing. And as they sit there, separately, bound only by teachings that she knows John does not believe, and promises from God that perhaps they don't all feel, and messages that she is beginning to learn come not from the book alone but reside in one's heart, none of them ask: *why us?* Or confess to each other what is all over Luke's face: fear and panic and vulnerability. They simply carry on, clinging on, letting Luke cling on for them, his voice growing ever more insistent and desperate and distressed until finally Vera's phone rings, again, as she knew it would, and at last she has a way to step in to save him.

'That's probably the minister telling us it's time to wrap up this service!' she declares jokingly. Then more softly: 'Luke, you don't want to bore your mother to *death*.' She smiles at him gently as she says this, a smile he'd once told her was sunrise-speckled.

'That's not funny,' he pronounces solemnly.

Vera's phone buzzes again.

John smiles in sympathy at her accidental choice of words but the others stare at her expectantly.

The phone continues to buzz.

'I mean – I meant . . .' She trails off. What did she mean? Only for him to stop, to look up. Luke is looking up now but does not attempt to rescue her. Vera can think of nothing else to say. She had not meant to be brazen or flippant.

The phone buzzes.

'Well then, it's interrupted us,' Lynn declares suddenly with a cantankerous flap of her hand. 'Don't you think you should answer it?'

Now everybody is waiting. Watching. The buzzing persists.

'Come on,' hurries Lynn.

Luke nods.

John nods.

Lynn nods vociferously.

Slowly, Vera retrieves the phone from her bag and puts it to her ear.

'Don't hang up,' says Charlie.

CHAPTER 20

Lynn sat straight in a hard-backed chair at the dining table and rested her hand on the stack of paper in front of her. The mono-grammed pen that Philip had once given her and she'd employed mainly for writing thank you cards, hovered, the tip ready and spouting a tiny bubble of blue ink. One of the lawyers at Philip's firm had already prepared the legal jargon of her will, updated to account for Philip not being there, John and Luke being grown-ups now, and Luke preparing to be married. Really, she should have restructured it years ago. Her lawyer had prompted her regularly, but she'd been barely 40 when Philip had died. Now she was not yet 60 . . . And she supposed she hadn't wanted to move on anyway, officially. Or couldn't. Just like Emily. Now she was forced to, and contemplated the great list of items she would soon no longer have a need for, the inventory of possessions by which it was possible to catalogue one's life.

The house would have to go to John. Lynn placed her hand on her chest. Since her Rummy-fuelled conversation with Emily weeks earlier, she had found it difficult to think of her youngest son without feeling a deep pang inside her. But there were practicalities to consider before sensibilities. John lived still in a one-bedroom flat that he rented, and was without a steady income. He was the one who needed a house. She lifted the pen. But Luke would undoubtedly feel snubbed, think she was favouring his brother, and remember this about her. She should tell him about it in advance perhaps. Or make him the executor of the will, the responsible one, the one she could always rely upon, and make sure he knew that, knew how well he'd held them up. She would be gone but these things mattered. They would frame the boys' memories, and be her last testament.

Luke would want Philip's watch. Lynn liked to take it out of its box each morning, shine it and lay it on her wrist. Listen to it ticking like a heartbeat. But Luke had always admired it. She moved her pen and made a note of this, carefully, in her best script. When she'd raced through her History exams at Cambridge her penmanship had drastically deteriorated, the style in which she wrote much less important than the content. But here, now, she was precise and spent time on the flourishes.

John must have the gramophone. They hadn't used it properly for years having long ago abandoned it for cassettes and CDs and in recent months an iPod Luke had bought her. But she kept the ancient instrument in the sitting room next to a stack of old vinyl records and every now and then, amidst one of his spells of exuberance, John dusted it off and set it working. Then they would put on Frankie Laine or Dickie Valentine and – before her side had grown too painful – dance together around the sofa as if they were at an old-fashioned dance. John had always been able to sense that Lynn missed this, this taste of what it was like to have a man on whose arm one could swing. Did John have a man to swing on? Was there somebody he loved? Somebody who . . .

What else? There had to be other things of value in her life, things her sons would want. The china. Lynn lifted her pen again and began to detail the collection. This should go to Luke of course. He was the one who would have a wife. She would appreciate it, and add to it perhaps, over time. *Should she specify Vera's name?* She had begun to come round again lately. It still irked Lynn to see her; she was young and rude and awkward, and in love, and young, and young. But she was persistent in her effort, Lynn had to give her that. She was amusingly forthright. And they seemed to have made a tacit agreement not to mention the mortifying exchanges that had passed before the arrival of Emily. But what if they divorced? It happened these days and considering Vera's background . . . Would Vera then pack her bags and in them place Lynn's wedding china? Maybe she wouldn't want it. Maybe she'd replace the floral pattern with something modern and classless. Maybe it would languish at the back of a cupboard or in a box in the attic and never be used year after year, nor be displayed, or even remembered.

Lynn wrote only Luke's name down as a beneficiary. Then suddenly she remembered the shares. And the offshore bank account Philip had created from which she still earned a salary. And the art. And her jewellery. She capped the pen and placed it on the table. Her side was playing up again and she felt nauseous and tired. There was too much to think about. She wanted to rest. But the documents would have to be cleared off the table somehow before Luke arrived, and the bed still hadn't been made, and there was a dirty, floral cup in the kitchen sink. And she hadn't finished her painting. And the agency hadn't called back about Emily coming on weekends.

Painfully, Lynn pulled herself up to standing and dusted the sheets of paper into a loose pile which she placed in the drawer of the side table she had always meant to fill with after dinner mints, or fresh sprigs of lavender, or spare greetings cards. It remained empty, save for a collection of elastic bands that Philip used to bind his post and she sometimes still found, inexplicably, on the dining room floor. And couldn't bear to get rid of. Steadying herself for a moment at the doorframe she made her way into the sitting room where she sank into her chair and closed her eyes, the sore rims thanking her with ready teardrops.

The night before she had been unable to sleep

again. There were twin terrors. First her body: nausea and headaches, and pain shooting through her arm. Then her mind: the future, the future, the future; that she wouldn't see and couldn't affect and was unable to control. It was filled with things like Luke and his need to fix the world. John and his life that she knew too little of, and had blackened with pretence, and the dwindling moments left in which to put that right. And, Emily. Most insistently, Emily. The girl shouldn't have mattered to Lynn as much as she did – she was barely more than a stranger – but Lynn found herself thinking of her constantly.

It was impossible to sleep when one of these thoughts struck her. Or, as was more frequent, when they all struck at once. Lynn opened her eyes and a tear slipped out of them. There was so much to do. So much she still wanted to do.

When she woke, Luke was there. He'd let himself in and was sitting in his usual place, opposite hers, watching her silently.

'How long have you been there?' she murmured.

'Just a few minutes.'

Luke's brow was furrowed, again. He was beginning to age.

'I only closed my eyes for a second. I've been busy all morning,' she told him, quickly checking her hair and sitting up.

'Are you feeling tired Mother? Would you rather not go to lunch?'

'Don't be so silly. I got sleepy sitting here waiting for you, that's all. It's hot in here.'

'I told John to check the thermostat.'

'I like it hot.'

'I'll check it now.'

Luke fetched Lynn's purse from her bedroom and didn't mention the unmade bed. 'You look beautiful Mother,' he said as she buttoned her sensible, knee-length black coat and made for the door.

John and Vera were both already at the table. John was dressed in a white shirt underneath a cream linen jacket with a silk scarf around his neck. For years, Lynn had bought him lumberjack shirts and woollen blazers, but that week, she had got Emily to pick up a fitted velvet waistcoat which she had wrapped for Christmas already, in case later there wasn't time. In case this gesture would have to say everything. When they entered, he was waving his arms around dramatically and Vera was slowly folding into her chair, holding her stomach in hysterics. She looked illuminated.

'Are we interrupting?' Luke queried, pulling a chair out for Lynn then kissing Vera – perfunctorily, Lynn noticed – and sitting himself next to her.

'John was just telling me about the cast in his new play,' Vera offered. 'They're very funny.'

'You didn't check the thermostat,' Luke told him.

★   ★   ★

They talked about themselves. All three of them seemed united in this end, though the lunch had been, Lynn knew, a symptom of their guilt at the fact she was dying, a desire to do something nice for her while she was still alive. All the while John and Luke made jovial digs at the other that weren't quite jovial, and didn't notice how cross this made her, cross with herself. She should humour them, act the grateful parent, but she couldn't help the surge of bitterness inside her. Particularly sour when the boys made it so plainly clear that she had done everything wrong. Every now and then one of them, usually Vera, made an inquiry into her health: was she experiencing any of those dizzy spells she'd been warned about yet, any sickness, any lethargy? This was the topic on which she was consulted, her illness, though even this was not something they considered her to be an expert in. They knew better it seemed. They were young, they'd been on the Internet, *Googled* it, had a better grip on these things. She was not yet 60. Philip had been 45 . . . They chattered on about work, friends, the wedding, John's play, Luke's promotion, the new church Vera had stumbled upon. They included her in these conversations but not as an equal; she listened but only with half an ear.

She didn't care. It allowed her more time to think about Emily. She had not pushed the subject of Rwanda again since the day Luke's appearance had prompted it. Such darkness could not be dragged out of a person, she knew. It had to be offered. Relinquished. Still, over the past weeks Lynn had been alert to opportunities to encourage it. She'd set them tasks over which conversation was inevitable, and sent Emily shopping for items that might provoke interest, like the waistcoat. And she'd purposely left open the door to her art room, uncovering a canvas she had painted some months earlier, full of blacks and purples and swirling angry markers of her own resentments and regrets. Signs that she might be a person to understand darkness. And wanted to.

The conversation between her children bubbled lightly on. Occasionally Lynn resisted the pull of her own reveries and said something controversial to shock them, but they only looked at her with raised eyebrows as though it was the illness talking and not her, a sound in their periphery. They didn't ask her about her hopes, her dreams, her ambitions. They probably assumed she didn't have any. They probably thought she never had, or that they were it.

Vera was full of enthusiasm all through the meal. Radiating even more youthful gusto than usual, a sugar-dipped energy dripping an elation that was driving Lynn mad. *The starters! The fish! Had they seen the fish?! The cheesecake!* She smiled constantly, particularly at Luke, trying in vain to infect him with her sickening excitement. Lynn noticed that Luke's demeanour remained solemn. Perhaps out of respect for her own humourless deportment? It made her wonder from where Vera's fervour had sprung.

'Cheesecake is not meant to be eaten after fish,' she informed her.

Vera ordered fruit.

Lynn's chocolate mousse was too sweet and reminded her of the sickly taste that was striking more regularly. She picked at it slowly. *Had she ever sent a dish back?* Philip used to do it sometimes, if something was overcooked or under, too salty or not hot enough, but this had always been an embarrassment to Lynn. She'd never wanted to offend, or point out the mistakes of others. *Let he who is without sin, cast the first stone.* But why? In the spirit of fairness? Since when had life been fair? It wasn't for her. It wasn't for Emily. Vera was the only one who seemed to have everything.

'When does your play open?' Vera asked John as the coffees arrived. 'And what's it about?'

Lynn handed her half-eaten mousse to the waiter and ordered a sorbet instead. She watched her coffee filter, the dark residue cleverly lifted from what was pure.

'It's a comedy,' John grinned over his own cappuccino. 'Luke, you'd like it.'

'Would I?'

John brushed the long, front strands of his hair gracefully off his face and smiled again, indulgently, as though he was about to confide a secret.

'It's about a man who's obsessed with himself,' he said. 'He can't see beyond his own person, you know.' He smiled mischievously at Vera. 'And he's

261

constantly exasperated because nobody's as good as he is. In the end, he dies in a car crash because he's looking at himself in the mirror instead of at the road.' John took another sip of his coffee without taking his eyes off his brother.

Vera laughed.

'That's a comedy?' Luke asked, with unusual quiet.

'It's very satirical. A lot of fun to play.'

'Well I suppose you can draw from—'

'It's Echo and Narcissus,' pronounced Lynn, reaching for her coffee cup. Refereeing. Again they'd all assumed she hadn't been listening, or forgotten she was there, and turned towards her now with evident surprise. She waited for the last drops of their attention to filter through, then slowly took a sip. 'Isn't it Vera?'

'Narcissus? Do you mean the flower?' Vera squirmed, touching her loose blonde hair, and Lynn laughed cruelly. But they were listening now.

'Didn't you do Ancient History my dear?' she said. 'Greek myths? At university?'

'I did Social Policy at university.'

'Oh. That's a degree is it? I thought that must have been an extra little course you did, or something.' Lynn's sorbet arrived and she dug into it, delivering a delicate spoonful of sour lemon into her mouth. For the first time all afternoon she didn't notice the pain in her side. 'Is *social policy* useful then?'

'Actually, it is quite useful at the moment,' Vera

replied, smiling tiresomely at Lynn. 'It's been helpful for the new charity I'm working on. There was a piece about it last week in the *Sunday Times*. That I wrote. I did the interviews.'

'You mean you wrote down the stories people told you?' Lynn queried.

'Well, I did a little more than—'

'Like a secretary? You must have impeccable shorthand.'

'Actually I recorded them on a disc.'

'Oh. I see. Well it sounds very high-powered my dear. Very clever of you.' Vera fell silent. Luke said nothing. 'So then, John,' she continued brightly. 'You were telling us about Echo and Narcissus, your play . . .'

To Lynn's disappointment, the hush she had created was not satisfying; she felt slightly embarrassed, as though she was a teenager again and had said something a little too bold, a little too crass. She was grateful when John delicately resurrected the lightness of chatter, and this time she didn't mean to interrupt it. But the pain came sharply. The cool taste of sorbet was replaced immediately by a return of hot, sticky sweetness and in the end Luke had to leave John his card to pay the bill so they could make a quick exit to the car. Back home, Luke wanted to call the doctor. He didn't seem to trust himself with her disease the way he did with finance or faith or politics, and he didn't trust her intuition either. Every time she made a sound, he made a fuss, but she knew the doctor would be as useless as they were. When Emily had gone with her to see Doctor Hammond the previous Tuesday he'd prescribed a few painkillers and recommended that she read about her particular kind of cancer, so that she'd be prepared for the symptoms when they began to manifest, but she hadn't wanted to waste the last days of her life reading about her death. And so she'd asked him to be succinct – *what could she expect?* 'Spell it out to me,' she'd demanded. But still he'd answered illusively: fatigue, nausea, perhaps pain, a deterioration of the cough she'd had for years, possibly jaundice in the latter stages, everyone was different. In essence, he didn't know. So Lynn also didn't know. Only that a doctor couldn't help, and that the pain would continue to get worse as she neared the end.

'Stop fussing Luke,' Lynn scolded him as he tucked a blanket around her on the sofa. 'I'm perfectly fine now. I'm not an invalid.'

He stood at the end of the sofa holding an extra cushion. 'Are you sure Mother?' She noticed his jaw quivering and that he clutched the cushion tightly. Lynn nodded awkwardly at him now and motioned for him to sit down. He did so slowly. 'Mother, shall we pray?'

Lynn closed her eyes. 'The kettle's boiled,' she answered.

While Luke was tending to it, Lynn drifted. It was warm under the blanket, like the summer that

John had turned two and Luke was sick with the chickenpox and the whole house had seemed in need of his cooling calamine lotion. Luke had been afraid of the doctor who made house calls and prodded at him with his stethoscope. He hadn't liked the red beard or the bushiness of his eyebrows, and when the doctor asked him questions he'd answered in a voice far smaller than he was. Somewhere in the distance the doorbell rang. The doctor?

'That'll be John forgetting his keys again,' Luke mumbled from the kitchen, and in her sleepiness Lynn noticed that his voice was deeper now. 'It is John,' he called from the hallway and she could almost hear his eyes rolling as he found her other son, as expected. Would he roll his eyes if he understood John's absences? Not that being gay explained forgetting his keys, but it explained why he had withdrawn from them, why he would not come to church, or rather her forcing him to hide his sexuality explained these things.

They all came into the sitting room and Vera poured the tea, remembering how Lynn took it and this time not spilling. They had filled the green teapot with the white crocuses, which Lynn never used, and she recalled without meaning to the weekend in Cornwall when she and Philip had found it. 'We'll use it for tea parties,' they'd promised each other as the shopkeeper wrapped it up for them carefully in newspaper. But it didn't match the rest of their set and they'd always selected the cream and red one instead.

'Philip, pass the biscuits,' she said to John, noticing the slip of her tongue even as she said it.

'Mother, I'm John,' he said. 'Not Philip.'

'I know, I know,' she snapped, taking a ginger crunch biscuit that Emily had bought. But she saw the boys glancing at each other.

They seemed to be waiting for something. All three of them were watching her carefully and speaking quietly as if she were as delicate as the china they were holding.

'Stop it,' she told them, and again they exchanged furtive glances. 'Stop it at once,' she repeated.

'Mother, are you in pain?' Luke fretted, hovering half-seated before her.

'No. I'm fine.'

'Is it your stomach?' John asked.

'I said I'm fine.' Suddenly she was the centre of attention, no longer peripheral, her every move watched and analysed; but this was not the narrative she'd wanted a lead role in. This was not what she'd been waiting for, sacrificed for, been promised.

'Perhaps she needs another painkiller,' Vera suggested to Luke.

Lynn dropped her teacup onto the floor. The china shattered at once on the wooden surface and the tea quickly soaked through the floorboards, into the nearby Persian rug, and up the sides of the cream sofa. Vera gasped.

'Don't worry Mother, we can fix it,' Luke declared, leaping into action and gathering the broken pieces.

'Leave it.'

'We can do it Mother,' John confirmed, the two of them finally, anxiously, united. Vera ran into the kitchen to fetch a damp cloth.

'Leave it alone,' Lynn demanded, but they ignored her, or didn't hear her, and carried on.

'We can save it,' Luke soothed.

'It's okay,' John hushed.

But all at once Lynn found herself bellowing.

'I said leave it alone!' she yelled, coughing as the strength of her command scratched its way through her chest and into her throat. 'It's broken. It's shattered. It cannot be fixed. That's the end of it. Clear up the mess and let's move on.'

'But I can save it Mother,' Luke ventured once more. 'If we just follow the pattern I can glue it back together, I can save it.'

'No you can't,' she decreed. 'It's too late. And I don't want you to try.'

The broken pieces were swept into a dustpan and transferred into the kitchen bin. Vera dabbed at the accusatory marks on the sofa, but only lightly. Nobody made an attempt at the stained Persian rug. Silence pervaded.

'If I were you, I'd get on with your lives,' she announced suddenly, opening her eyes wide, sitting up more and startling them all. 'This could go on for quite a while you know. I'm not dead yet.'

For once Luke was speechless, so it was John who protested for them. 'Mother, don't talk like that,' he said. 'Please . . .'

The phone rang. Letting out an overly irritated sigh, Lynn flapped a hand, feeling the need to be consistent in front of Vera who she'd chided for such an interruption a few weeks before. But she used to love the sound of that ring. And there was a time when *her* phone used to buzz as often as the young ones, with dinner invitations, with gossip, Philip just saying hello, her mother checking in – *Have you been resting enough? How are the boys? Are you eating properly?* – irritating queries she missed now with a burning sadness.

'It's a woman called Pippa, from Home Care,' John announced hesitantly, the receiver in his hand. 'Says she needs to talk to you about sending Emily on weekends.'

'I've already told them!' Lynn exploded again, this time not intending the excess of her reaction. She was aware that her poise was completely extinguished now; but she would not be an invalid publicly. She would not let on that she had already conceded to ask Home Care for more help. Taking a deep, painful breath, she glanced away from her sons towards the books that lined the room. The stories. *This* wasn't her story. In *The Secret Garden* she'd seen herself in Mary Lennox, not Colin; in *Great Expectations* she hadn't been Miss Havisham, but Pip; and in *Pride and Prejudice* she'd loved Elizabeth Bennett: bright, bold, unconventional. She was Elizabeth.

'But Mother, you're going to need more help,' Luke appeased. 'If not Home Care then even the church can—'

She would not slip without a stand into oblivion.

'If she doesn't want the carer more often, she doesn't want the carer more often,' John declared, quickly asking Pippa if they could call her back and putting the phone down on the side table. 'Mother, I have to go now.' He bent down to kiss her.

It was not over yet. She still felt a sense of purpose. Since listening to Emily, she should say, she felt again she had a task.

Luke stood up. 'John, you can't just say that and walk out. Take some responsibility.'

Her task was to help Emily. That was why she couldn't stop thinking of her. That was why, maybe, Emily had arrived at her door. That was why, perhaps, she'd gotten this sick, sick sickness. Too early. Too abruptly, like Philip . . . Lynn shook her head. It was too indulgent to believe in such a grand plan. Too romantic, too stupid. But nevertheless, perhaps this was her chance to leave a mark on the world, on Life – not in the printed word, but in the careful language passed between herself and just one other.

'I am taking responsibility, I'm listening to Mother.'

A language she'd learnt as a wife, as a mother. It had to be.

'You're not.' Luke's eyes were flashing at John, his hands in fists. 'You're ignoring how sick she is, and how sick she's going to get, and you're doing what's easy. Grow up John. She needs help. Are *you* going to look after her?'

'Nobody has to look after me.' Lynn interrupted, pulling the blanket indignantly around her and trying not to cough. Luke was looking to her now to referee, but she merely flapped her hand. She didn't have time for their squabbles. She had to find a way, quickly, to get Emily to open up. To deconstruct her barriers. Before time ran out.

'This is what you always do!' Luke continued at John. 'You leave all of the hard decisions to me and go off to live your carefree life. The prodigal son.'

She had to convince Emily to let out the truth. To speak it.

'My life is not carefree,' John admonished abruptly, his face suddenly dark. 'You know nothing about my life. You never *wanted* to know anything about my life, none of you did, so—'

Lynn looked up. Her youngest son was standing paralysed by the door, full of anger, full of injury. She sighed. Of course. Emily was not the only one who needed to speak the truth.

After John had left, Luke sat back down in his chair. Vera touched his shoulder but he shrugged it off.

'He won't think of anyone besides himself,' Luke said finally.

'He has enough to deal with.'

'Why do you always defend him?' Luke sighed heavily. A long time ago Philip used to do the same.

Vera glanced at the clock.

'Emily can come at weekends,' Lynn said finally.

CHAPTER 21

C harlie is waiting outside her flat. It is the third time that Vera has seen him in as many days and the hours between these encounters seem unbearably long. Today, he has promised that he will bring photos and Vera can barely contain her urge to skip and jump and leap down the corridor towards him. All afternoon during lunch with Lynn, and afterwards in her heavy, lifeless living room, watching heavy, dying seconds tick by, Vera has been looking forward to this moment. And replaying another in her mind, as she has been doing for many days.

She likes to tell it to herself again and again. She likes to say it aloud. She likes to hear it and feel it and cling to it with both arms. And laugh hysterically into the mirror where there is a not entirely disfigured woman laughing back at her. Even as she strides towards Charlie, she whispers it under her breath, his words: *He's alive Vera. That newspaper cutting you gave me, you didn't read it properly, you fool. It was another baby, a poor sod in Clapham. You said Euston, right? St Andrew's? I've been checking. I've been inquiring. I hired a lawyer. Vera, I've found him.*

Charlie waves and pulls an envelope from his pocket. She reaches for it, but Charlie lifts it above her until she has delivered a kiss to his pursed lips. She tears it open.

And he is there.

Alive.

Beautiful.

With eyes still blue.

CHAPTER 22

Luke sat in an empty pew at the back of the church and clung to his bible. There were no other congregants, only an assortment of children at the front waiting for choir practice, and the organist playing heavy chords. He had known there was no service but had nonetheless left work early. Deeply uncharacteristic, particularly on a day in which everything was going wrong and he was being looked to for solutions. Luke Hunter, who always had the answers. His Blackberry vibrated in his pocket. It might be Vera. It might be John, or his mother. It might be work. It might be all kinds of people for whom he didn't have answers. Who he couldn't help. Who he had failed.

Or pushed away. He knew that if he pushed too hard, Vera might never come back to him. They were slipping, slipping, further and further and in opposite directions. He longed to grab her arms, to wrap them around him inside his coat like she used to, to bury himself within them, to never let go. But he didn't know how to do it. He didn't know how to deal with her secret, with her son.

It wasn't the sex so much, or the pregnancy. The thought of both was like a thump, hard against his chest. But it wasn't those things; it was the running away, the abandonment, the abandonment of her flesh and blood. And the continuation of that abandonment. He could understand, almost, barely, a hormone-fuelled, fearful, momentary collapse. But now she was a Christian, and an adult, and supported – why didn't she want to find the child now? Why didn't she have that strength? Why didn't she even talk about him? If only she'd ask, he would support her, he'd be the father, he'd adopt. But it was without the excuse of youth that she continued to shut him out, and cut off her parents, and think nothing of her somewhere son.

Now, when her hand crept onto his arm or his shoulder, her nervous, tentative touch only reminded him of frailty. And so of his mother. And filled him with anger and umbrage. And perhaps Vera sensed this, because lately she seemed to have stopped reaching for him altogether, and didn't notice the needy twitch of his own useless limbs.

Luke clung harder to the closed book in his hand. The children at the front had started to sing along with the organ and the noise was unexpectedly stifling. Luke heard a door opening and the priest entering the hall. He stood up, clutching still to the bible. By the time he reached the car, his fingers were bone white.

CHAPTER 23

'Hey, sister!' Omar shouted as Emily hurried down the final stairs of her building and stumbled out into the impotent December sun. He was leaning against the wall opposite, locked in close conversation with a friend who wore flowing white trousers, a cream kaftan, and sandals despite the cold. Emily didn't know this man's name although he was always with Omar, but she and her new neighbour had taken to greeting each other like proper acquaintances. Most mornings he was there, propping up the building, and despite her apprehension, Emily had begun to look forward to bumping into him like this, though they never exchanged more than a few words and rarely ventured beyond the briefest of niceties.

'You're early for a Saturday?' Omar stated as a question, his intense eyes brightening slightly as he dug into his back pocket for a cigarette and waited for her reply. He stood as always making a triangle with the wall, his slender shoulders grazing the red brick, his head leant slightly backwards against it so that whenever Emily spoke to him she had to lean in. Smiling, she smoothed down her fringe, aware as she always was of her untidiness against his beauty.

'I work at weekends now,' she informed him.

'Oh?' Omar's face lit up with interest but his friend tapped him on the arm in an effort to direct him back towards their conversation. The man's indifference to her was nothing new. Emily was used to him crossing his arms when she appeared, or speaking on the phone, or simply walking away. He had never offered her so much as a handshake, but this time he seemed actively irritated by her presence, or at least fed up with Omar's continuing dialogue with her. Emily felt uncomfortable. Being inconsequential was one thing, unnoticed was good, but in the face of his seething acknowledgement, danger crawled beneath her skin.

'Congratulations, sister,' beamed Omar, flashing her his movie star smile to make up for his friend's rudeness. 'Does that mean no more night shifts?'

Emily nodded. 'I've stopped cleaning altogether. I am a full-time carer now.'

'You're practically a doctor.'

Emily smiled hesitantly, allowing herself to consider this assertion, how proud she was of it. And how, despite the difficulty in revealing some of her past to Lynn, despite how unsettled and dazed she'd felt for days afterwards, now she had begun to feel just the tiniest bit emboldened. Needed. Useful. Omar noticed her smile and his own grin broadened. She liked this grin, but then his friend hit his hand sharply against the wall, landing just short of Omar. 'I should go,' Emily mumbled, and turned towards the road.

'See you later!' Omar called after her. Called, but did not move. It seemed that nothing weighed heavily enough on his shoulders to pull him away from idling by a brick wall. Emily shuffled away without looking back, but at the very edge of her periphery she noticed Omar standing up from his eternal recline, bending his head towards his friend, scowling, and the two of them exchanging urgent words. Was it possible that Omar was castigating him on her behalf? Emily smiled again and quickened her pace towards the bus stop.

They were going to tackle the china today, Lynn had told her. Emily would take each piece out of the display cabinet and clean it, and Lynn would tell her where and when and who it was from. In Emily's bag, was a packet of Jammie Dodgers. And a silver elephant she had decided to return.

CHAPTER 24

Charlie has filed for custody. He tells Vera this in confession, in her flat, a week before Christmas, a few moments after she refuses him sex. She has decorated her living area with white tinsel and Charlie strokes it as he talks, every now and then a sparkly strand coming loose in his fingers. He has had the paternity test, he says, wrapping one such strand around his thumb and not quite looking at her. He has been visiting Charles (as he says he is known) for more than a month now. 'Presumption of Contact', he explains, as if this is an explanation. And during the weeks and weeks of, well, unreturned phone calls, he has decided that with or without Vera, he wants his son. Charlie's face glows as he says the word 'son'. He twiddles the tinsel strand into a ball, and flicks it into the air like a miniature basketball. Vera nods, her heart tightening a little, but says nothing. She watches the tinsel land and unravel on the floor. Now Charlie moves closer to her on the sofa. He puts his hand under her chin and leaves it there for a moment, studying her, tilting her face upwards. She lets him. It is great fortune, he continues animatedly, that he made contact with St Andrew's when he did. Charles has not yet been adopted but was about to be placed with his first foster family, which would have made the process much harder, many more legal hoops to jump through. His lawyer's pleased. He lets go of Vera's chin and waits for her to say something. 'That *is* fortunate,' she agrees quietly. Charlie smiles. The staff are stunned that he has only just learnt of his paternity, he tells her. At first they were sceptical but now they've covered him in plaudits for stepping into his fatherly role so willingly, and he likes this, he admits. But points out that he need not have also stopped drinking and smoking and taking coke – all of which he has done. All of which he has done, he repeats. She congratulates him. He could easily have continued in secret but he wants to be a good father, he reiterates. She nods. He never wanted the abortion. She nods again, slowly. He has thought about it ever since.

'So have I,' Vera mutters carefully.

Charlie frowns, and there is a long silence before he addresses her again. He has a girlfriend, he tells her now, but if Vera wants to get back together, be a family, then for the sake of Charles he will end the relationship. His hand has somehow made its way onto Vera's thigh. Gently, she pushes it away. And this is when Charlie mentions that the staff have also been asking about Charles' mother: *Has he seen her recently? How did he find out about the child? Does he want to prosecute?* There are legal consequences, it seems, for abandonment.

Vera does not respond and Charlie allows another lengthy pause before getting up and pulling her to her feet. 'Of course I'm not telling them V,' he winks, drawing her in for a too-long hug. 'Who you are, I mean. Cheer up.'

She smiles, obediently.

'But think about it, okay?'

'Think about what?'

'About us. About whether you want there to be an 'us'. A family. Because, well, it's all of us V, or none of us. It's the whole hog, or else, when I get custody, I'm taking Charles with me. I've got a job in New York. And there's no point mixing him up by introducing him to an absent mother. Don't you agree? It would be selfish really. Not a very *Christian* thing to do.

'I'll be a good dad,' he softens on his way to the door, when she says nothing.

The following day, a Friday, Luke announces that he is taking Vera to Venice. 'We need some time for the two of us,' he explains quietly when he appears at her work at midday, a surprise, both of their bags already packed in the back of his Prius. Vera has been sitting at her corner desk in the office surreptitiously Googling the law surrounding child abandonment and she clicks off the screen quickly when Luke appears. She would however like to go through the computer memory more thoroughly. She would like to make sure that the articles citing jail terms, and sites for legal help lines have been properly deleted. Not that it's the threat of jail that has been consuming her. Or rather, not most. Most, is the question she has been asking herself over and over since Charlie's ultimatum and cannot answer; the question of whether knowing her son is alive, is enough.

For so long Vera has believed him dead, and at her hands, that merely the knowledge of his living in the city, somewhere, is far more than she had ever dreamed. Far more than she ever deserved. And should, she supposes, be enough. But is it? She isn't sure now if she can stop with just knowing. If she owes it to her baby not to stop. If she owes it to Charlie *to* stop. And what the hell she owes herself.

Luke hovers. Vera glances again at her computer and takes her time tidying her desk. Under her stack of files is her bible. This too she has been searching surreptitiously. As she slips the book into her bag, Luke winks and Vera smiles at him. She would love to ask Luke what to do, what he thinks she should do. He would weigh her questions carefully, mull them, pass them through the filter of his goodness, and then he would solve them, with a few words tidying them away, tucked like a strand of escaped hair behind her ear. But he hasn't mentioned the baby since she told him about it, it is a bump she feels they are smoothing over, and besides she cannot declare to Luke that her son is alive (alive!), because he never knew otherwise. Vera touches her hand to her face, neatening her hair herself. Office chatter rises and falls around them. Luke waits patiently. Waits for her. To be clean. She picks pencils up one by one and carefully tears Post-it notes off pieces of scrap paper. And glances at her screen. Felicity and the other girls saunter over to her desk and grin at Luke with the same admiring look they once gave her engagement ring. Luke smiles and leans one hand against the wall, ever so slightly amused by the attention, or flattered by it? It is the same way he used to look at Vera. But she cannot remember the last time they had such light, fun moments, the last time they felt so close and easy, the last time she noticed him glancing at her in such a benevolent way. Abruptly, she feels saddened by this realisation, and guilty, and a little afraid. Vera shuts her computer down. A co-conspirator, her boss smiles as she is bundled away.

Once they are seated in the car, Luke turns to her. 'I know I've been distant lately, and impatient, and bad-tempered,' he says softly. 'Of course there's been a lot to think about, but I've been praying over it and asking God for a revelation, and I've realised that I've been unfair, and unkind, and I'm sorry. I'd really like to make it up to you. Will you let me?'

Vera's heart thumps. Here is the tenderness, the benevolence. Vera ventures across the dark interior to find Luke's hand. His nails are bitten painfully short. She runs her fingers over the uneven stubs.

She cannot tell Luke that she is meant to be meeting Charlie for lunch. She cannot tell him that today she is meant to be giving Charlie an answer – Luke or Charles. She cannot tell him how sick she feels for having barely even noticed the distance he is trying so hard to cross.

'Of course,' is what she tells him. 'Wow, Venice!'

Luke accepts her enthusiasm gratefully and changes gear. 'I love you, you know,' he says gently, a whisper of the old him dashing for a moment across his face. 'It's my something true,' he says.

CHAPTER 25

It was Lynn who had suggested Emily stay when Luke took Vera away for the weekend. To Venice, where she had always wanted to go but never had. Luke had wanted John to make himself available, to pop in to make sure she'd eaten. At first she'd tried to hide this new facet of her disease, but there were too many times now when she couldn't find the energy to make it down the stairs, or the inclination to eat if she had done. It was strange how food had become merely a requirement. Once, whole afternoons would be planned around cooking, tasting, savouring, sharing. But the ingredients of a meal had returned somehow to their most raw function, a necessity that filled, or stole, a few minutes of her day. Anyway, John couldn't pop in. His play had matinees at the weekends.

He was there however, when Luke came to say goodbye. She'd made it downstairs that day and was wrapped up in a blanket near the fire. Emily had let John in and she'd heard them joking easily in the hallway. Emily was less rabbit-like with John, less jittery and likely to dart. He had a way of doing that, of encouraging confidence; or perhaps, Lynn mused, it was because Emily felt unthreatened by his sexuality. Lynn, on the other hand, was petrified of it; terrified by the thought of the conversation she planned to have with him. *Had to* have, if there was to be a chance of making things right between them, and between him and his brother. *Had to* have, if she was to practise what she intended to preach to Emily: a conviction that talking, unloading, unravelling, truth-finding, was the only way to peace. *Was it?* Was there such thing as peace? There was no way of knowing but it had at least to be tried. If Lynn was sure of anything now, then it was this: try, do. Do something, that was the thing. Something . . . more. While there was time; if there was time. Lynn felt itchy to talk again to Emily. But first there was her son, her youngest, whom she had wronged so deeply with perfection, and spoiled with extra slices of cake.

They didn't know she was listening. Lynn, carrying a plate of homemade banana cake, stood at the door to their shared bedroom and smothered a chuckle with her free hand. Luke was teaching John about girls. They were seven and five. 'You have to say they're pretty,' said Luke. 'Even if they're not. Then they kiss you like this.' He smooched his hand dramatically. 'Except on the lips, and if you do it for a really long time then you have to move to France.'

'Mummy says you shouldn't lie,' John stated, seriously, wrinkling up his nose.

'That's true,' replied Luke, weighing this up against the other things he'd learned. 'But Daddy tells Mummy she looks pretty even when Mummy says she's so messy she's going to pull a hedge back into the woods.'

'No he doesn't. He says she looks *stunning*,' John corrected, again with complete earnestness.

'*Stunning*,' laughed Luke, practising the sweep of it.

'Stunning, stunning, stunning!' shouted John, dancing around the room, singing it louder and louder, in delight at his older brother's giggle.

They began a circuit of the room, sock-clad feet jumping from bed to bed to rug to toy chest. Lynn had banned this game in case of falling, but she waited a moment.

'Angel's cooking lunch,' John grinned as he came into the sitting room and sat down next to her on the big sofa. 'Smells good. I might stay.' He raised his eyebrows mischievously and Lynn wanted to relax into his jollity, to wait one moment more. But she nodded at him solemnly. He sat. 'Why ever are you on the sofa?' he asked. 'You never sit on the sofa. You'd be closer to the fire in your chair.'

'I wanted to sit by you,' she answered gently. 'I wanted to sit near you while I, tell you something.'

'Tell me what?' He leant forward roguishly, as though about to revel in gossip.

'I don't think a waistcoat is enough you see, of an explanation.'

John inspected her face carefully, looking she presumed for signs of delusion.

'I *know*, John,' she told him simply. 'I know. And I need you to know that I know, and that I've always known, and that I should have let you tell me.'

'Known what, Mother?' John asked, shifting uncomfortably.

'About you.'

He said nothing.

'I'm sorry I made you keep it secret. I'm so sorry. Please forgive me for it. I want you to know that, well, whatever your choices, whatever your, sexuality, I only want you to be happy.'

'Mother, good grief!' John exclaimed, clearly unsettled by the directness of a conversation they'd buried for so long. 'What *are* you talking about?'

'Are you happy, John? Do you, do you have somebody?'

'Mother, really. Angel, come on in with lunch won't you? We're going quite barmy with hunger!' There was a responsive clattering from the kitchen.

'John,' Lynn tried again. 'I made you hide yourself, I know that, but you needn't now. It's my fault. Church and chastity and . . . claptrap! I drove you away. From all of us. I understand that's why you keep things so private, so separate. I don't blame you for it, and if only Luke knew too he might realise—'

'There's nothing for Luke to know. Nothing at all to tell Luke,' John interrupted quickly, firmly.

Lynn stopped. John's eyes had turned to steel, barbed with darkness, and terror? She looked at him for a long time. There was so much she wanted to ask him, so many things she wanted to know. But she knew without pressing further that he would not allow her to fix it. She would die holding onto this mistake.

Slowly, she nodded her assent. She had kept her silence, misguidedly, for almost two decades, if he wanted it a few months longer, it was the least she owed him, the least she could do. Do. Something.

Emily continued to clatter softly in the kitchen. In the background, a Sinatra she and John both loved started up on the radio. Usually John would have hummed along, but today he was silent. Lynn thought about reaching for his hand . . . Then the doorbell sounded.

'I'll get it,' John announced. He stood up quickly and strode into the hall.

Alone on the sofa, Lynn lifted herself slightly and peered out of the window. Luke was on the doorstep. His car was still on, churning up cold air on the street. Vera was sitting in it.

'No rehearsals today?' Lynn heard Luke ask as his brother opened the door and together they made their way back into the sitting room. It was a genuine question, but the two of them had long ago stopped being able to decipher digs from authenticity.

'No,' John snapped back.

Lynn flinched. It was all her fault. She thought she had at least done this thing well, this thing that was motherhood, but –

Luke appeared at the door. She tidied the blanket over herself and attempted to look as solid as she could, but she noticed Luke's face clouding with anxiety at the sight of her.

'Good,' said Luke to John earnestly, staying by the door. 'It's good you came.'

'You're the one leaving for the weekend.'

Luke scowled and turned away from his brother. 'I can't stay long Mother, I just wanted to stop by before we left to check you have everything you need. Is Emily here? Is she looking after you?'

'She's making lunch,' Lynn affirmed. 'Your fiancée didn't bother to come in then?'

'I said not to. We have to hurry for our flight.'

'Of course.' Lynn flapped her hand towards the door. 'To Venice.' She was unable to resist the instinctive irritation. 'Off you go then.'

Luke hovered. 'But you're okay Mother?'

'Of course I am.'

'Emily knows about your night-time medication?'

'She's here every day Luke,' Lynn answered impatiently, unfairly taking her frustration out on him, he who could handle it.

He nodded, apologetically, heavily. It wasn't right

of her. But as he was turning to go an idea caught hold.

'Emily!' Lynn called into the kitchen. 'Emily!' She turned towards her son. 'No need for a messenger. You can give any instructions you want yourself.'

It was a necessarily cruel trick. The discomfort on Emily's face at seeing Luke again was obvious to all of them. Luke tried to negate it with extra enthusiasm but Emily's distress ruffled his own composure, and his false, raised tones seemed only to make Emily more nervous. At the first chance she got she scuttled for the door. Still, it had been at her most abject that Emily had last found the strength to talk. Perhaps, Lynn considered, looking to John, it was at their most abject when everyone found their greatest vigour. And so she was hopeful. And purposeful.

'You have the number for the hotel,' Luke said once Emily had left and John, who had decided now against lunch, had also made a rapid exit. 'I've left it on your nightstand. Call me if you need anything. Promise to. I'll be back on Sunday night.'

Indulgingly now, already half-thinking about Emily's reaction to her son, Lynn promised. But she knew that the only reason he'd receive a call was if she keeled over and died, and Luke hovered for a second more, clutching his coat tightly, clearly knowing this too. They stared at each other then, and Lynn could sense his need for affirmation, for comfort, for the touch of her hand, and almost, almost she spoke. But in the end neither of them said anything, and Luke turned for the door, away to Venice where Lynn knew he would forget all about Emily, and John, and his dying mother, as he lost himself in his youthful fiancée.

CHAPTER 26

They arrive by boat. It is sunset and the water laps against the sides of the *Paradiso* like liquid gold, carefully passing it forward. The men at the port have hauled their bags aboard and stowed them safely inside the sheltered cabin, but Vera and Luke sit in the seats at the rear, gazing at the perfection of the postcard they are entering. When the sea narrows into the Grand Canal of Venice, without realising it, Vera holds her breath and remembers to exhale only when Luke's bitten nails gently scratch against her palm.

The light begins to melt into the water as they wind their way around gondolas floating majestically in the molten darkness. She and Luke bounce malleably between the two worlds of density and translucence. Tourists are everywhere. They hold hands and board boat rides, wilfully letting the romance of the place whisk them into unreality while locals scurry through the shadows, propelled at a faster speed, charged with the business of their visitors' imaginations. It seems a necessarily protracted journey, the gentle rocking of the boat lulling them into the otherworldly atmosphere of Venice.

Lulling them like a lullaby.

Luke smiles. They alight opposite the vast dome of the Salute and leave the last remnants of their London existence on the boat to drift away.

Inside the hotel, they unpack in their separate rooms. Vera glances every now and then out of the window to the canal. Sometimes the flow of the water fills her with a welcome feeling of forward momentum; sometimes childish noises splash against her sides, dragging her back. Not that it is a case of forwards or backwards, past or future, truth or lies. But it feels like that. It is indeed one or the other. Vera tries not to think about Charlie who will be at the children's home by now. She tries not to imagine that he may have allowed her to go with him. He will have waited at the restaurant, she imagines, for half an hour or so before giving up on her. And by the time he received her text message, sent hurriedly from the parked car outside Lynn's house, he would undoubtedly have left, angrily. Vera remembers what Charlie is like when he is angry. Not violent, not loud, but a little cruel. He has not replied to her message.

Half an hour later, she and Luke meet in the lobby. It is their plan to stroll through the nearby streets that lead to St Mark's Square and Luke has bought a map for them to follow. He walks half a step in front of her and zealously calls out the road names as he finds them, whisking them around corners and through other couples who dawdle and mosey and create a lethargic bustle. It is useful for the landscape to occupy conversation for a while. Many weeks have passed since they spoke of the territory that is their relationship. Since learning about her son, it somehow fell into the periphery and now it has been a long time since Vera has even thought of it properly, or noticed it, or noticed it slipping away. Dragged away, she should say, dragged under, by the heaviness of lies, by an absence of truth. Luke calls out another street name that he has correctly located, his confidence in his navigation growing, and Vera longs for him to feel such certainty again about her. She quickens her pace slightly and tries to catch him. When she feels familiar hands touching her shoulders, it seems that they are helping to nudge her along.

Because of the cold weather, the streets are not packed and they find a restaurant with a table for two with relative ease. It is outside but under a canopy and surrounded by cylindrical heaters with the advantage of being exactly in the middle of one side of St Mark's Square. They sit facing each other. Behind Luke hangs the backdrop of the famous Basilica, like an oil painting on display. Vera takes out her camera and frames a photo. But in it, Luke's head is turned slightly to the side, looking over her shoulder, as though another painting is hanging there.

'What are you thinking about?' she asks him as the menus arrive.

'Nothing.' He buries his head behind the 'specials' insert. 'What a beautiful place, isn't it?'

'It's magical.'

The waiter appears and they order, Luke in Italian. Vera opens her mouth to speak but then closes it again. Around them, other couples clink their glasses of wine and gaze into each other's eyes and play footsie. She and Luke apologise to each other and make room when their legs accidentally brush.

'It's a rather small table isn't it?' he says. 'Everything here feels close, and interconnected.'

'Unified,' Vera offers hopefully.

'Perhaps,' he shrugs. 'But a little disorientating. Anarchic. This square's like the open expanse at the heart of a maze, but beyond it those roads we came through were so narrow and winding and all looked the same, and they all fed into this one spot, did you notice? It seems like this is the only place you can breathe and get a bearing.' He pauses. 'Would you remember the way back?'

'We came from over there,' Vera points but, as though slightly saddened, Luke laughs.

'Sweetheart, we came from the corner opposite that one.'

Their starters arrive: Luke's a sweet melon clothed in Parma ham; Vera's a simple salad. Tucking in, they exchange easy culinary raptures, Luke smiles at her and tentatively, Vera reaches for his hand.

'You never really know a place,' he says suddenly, as though there has been no gap in the conversation.

'What do you mean?'

'Perhaps the rest of the maze is misleading. How do we even know if we're at the heart of it?'

'Your map shows us,' Vera volunteers light-heartedly, but Luke doesn't seem to realise that she is joking. There is no pronouncement of funny or not.

'No, I mean, how do you ever know if the space you're occupying is really what you perceive it to be? Do you need to go outside it to look back in?' Luke holds her eyes now, imploring her to solve this confusing riddle as though the answer is urgent and necessary before he can return to the activity of eating his ham. Vera lays down her fork and tries to decipher exactly what it is he is asking. Does he want to go *outside* of their relationship to *look back in?* Does he know that she's been seeing Charlie? Does he know something more? Vera's leg rattles against the table. Abruptly however, Luke laughs. 'What a romantic city,' he says, overly brightly as he digs again into the soft, juicy flesh of the melon, and now Vera wonders if perhaps his reflections are nothing to do with her at all.

'Are you alright Luke?' she asks him.

'Romance makes me philosophical,' he replies, as if this is an answer. 'C. S. Lewis once said that good philosophy must exist, if for no other reason, than because bad philosophy needs to be answered. You should read some C. S. Lewis.'

'I have.'

'I don't just mean Narnia.'

Vera flinches.

Luke looks up at her, then shakes his head at himself. He looks devastatingly sad. 'Sorry.'

The main courses arrive. While they are eating Vera asks him about work and buoyed by the language of policy and politics, gradually Luke unfurls. He tells her about the latest progress of his health initiative in the DRC: they are going to launch a massive anti-cholera drive, help the country to develop a clean water system. The minister has finally been convinced, the Prime Minister is on board . . . His eyes light up green as he speaks, luminous in a way Vera only now realises has been absent, and slowly, in response, Vera too finds herself enthusing. She talks about St George's, about the journey she feels she is on, about finally being able to taste the first flavours of her own faith. And about the trouble she still has in knowing which path she should be following.

'It's just determination. You can do it,' Luke says, listening to her with what seems like fresh interest, and tucking into his pasta.

Vera smiles, hesitantly, savouring the affirmation she hasn't felt, nor perhaps sought from him in so long, remembering how empowering it is. But she wishes she could describe the paths honestly, tell him that while one fork leads directly to him, the other leads to her son, and there is nothing but brambles in between. She feels duplicitous. She yearns to talk to Luke about Charles. Even if he hates her for it, he would know what she should do. She opens her mouth. But then Luke looks up, his fork hovering mid-twirl while he weighs his next sentence. And apprehension churns her stomach.

'What?' she prompts.

'It's just, well, you do have to decide to have determination. It's a decision. And you mustn't abandon it, you mustn't abandon . . .'

'What are you getting at Luke?' Vera watches him selecting his words carefully.

'When it's challenging I mean . . .' She doesn't speak, and now he hurries. 'It's like going to church, my church I mean . . . You could have stuck with it a bit longer.'

Suddenly Vera feels indignant. 'You mean I could have stuck with your mother?'

'No.' Luke puts down his fork.

'Be truthful, Luke.'

'You be truthful.' He takes a breath. 'I don't want to do this now.'

'But you're angry,' Vera says, only just realising. She cannot believe that she hadn't noticed and wonders how long he has been angry for.

'Yes, okay, I have been angry about it,' he says, lowering his voice and staring at her meaningfully. 'But I've been angry about lots of things.'

Vera's stomach churns again. 'You haven't said a thing.'

'What do you want me to say?'

Vera doesn't answer and Luke allows a long pause. He seems tired.

'What do you want me to say?' he repeats slowly, as much to the universe now as to her.

But Vera doesn't have an answer. She has not counted on Luke's own lingering feelings about the existence of her son.

'What shall I ask you?' Luke continues. 'How could you have abandoned a child? How could you have kept it from me? How could you have lied outright to my mother? And then abandoned her too, while she's dying?!'

'I didn't abandon her Luke, she kicked me out!' Vera retorts abruptly. She knows that this is the least of the indictments, but it is the only one from which she has a corner to fight. 'She scratched me with her fucking, sorry Luke but *fucking*, long nails, and she told me not to come back. And then she told everyone at your bloody church about my "abortion".'

'What?'

Vera takes a breath.

'What?'

'She told her friends at your church.'

Luke pauses. He picks up his fork, then puts it down again. 'She shouldn't have done that.'

Vera says nothing. They sit like this for a long time.

'Everyone's fallible,' she murmurs finally. He nods and she is encouraged to continue. 'I mean,

there's no such thing as a good Christian, is there?'
He nods again. 'We're all sinners aren't we? I am.
And even you.'

Luke's eyes darken. She did not mean her words
as an attack but he seems to have taken them as
such. 'I've tried to be a good Christian,' he protests.
'I've tried. I've never had sex, or done drugs, or
stolen, or lied. I've followed God's teachings as
best as I can. I don't drink. I've always been to
church. I chose a job that would allow me to help
people. I've helped you, haven't I? Haven't I? I've
done my part in being a good Christian.'

Without meaning to, Vera laughs at this. His
defensiveness is stunning to her, he who is so
negligibly flawed.

'Are you calling me a hypocrite?' he demands.

'No Luke, no,' she laughs. 'I'm just saying that
everyone is fallible.'

'Well of course they are.' He speaks slowly,
restraining his voice from rising amidst the other
diners. 'Of course we are. *All have sinned and fallen
short of the glory of God.*' Romans 3:23. We know
that. We're human. Every human sins. But I try
not to, is what I'm saying. I *try* to be as good a
Christian as I can be. I try to follow Jesus. I try.
I've tried. Why are we even talking about this?' he
asks suddenly.

'Because you – I—' she falters.

'You think I should be home with my gossiping
mother?'

'What? No. And she—'

'You think I haven't been a good son?'

'That's not it at all.'

'You think I've neglected my duty to her?'

'Luke, you're a wonderful son.'

He stops. Suddenly deep lines spring across his brow. 'If I was so wonderful I wouldn't have left my mother with a carer,' he says abruptly, resting his head in his hands. His voice is riddled with pain and his eyes tip up at her nervously from their couch in his palms. 'I wouldn't have would I? I shouldn't have left her. I just – I can't stand to watch her deteriorate.'

'I'm sure the carer's amazing, Luke.'

'I know.' He pauses. 'I know she is.' He pauses again. And all at once his eyes harden and he is somewhere far away again. Vera finds herself struggling to stifle tears. They are still a little novel and she doesn't quite know what to do with them. With her thumb and forefinger she pinches her thigh so as to keep them at bay. Luke lowers his head as if in prayer, and despite the busy tourists around them Vera feels acutely alone with him, peculiarly intimate. Raw. She has a sudden, consuming urge to tell him the truth: '*I left my baby on a doorstep!!!! I thought he was dead!!!!*' She wants to shout it. Scream it. Confess it. *Truth, truth, truth, truth*. She feels herself leaning towards him, her lips poised to speak. But now? Now, while Luke is so fragile? She opens her mouth, then closes it again. Is now not the time for her to be silent and strong? Then again, perhaps it would

302

help him. Perhaps it would remind Luke that his sins, whatever he thinks they are, are as nothing. They are both flawed, they are all flawed, she and Charlie and John and Lynn and yes, even Luke, but Jesus loves them anyway.

'Luke, you're so much better than I could ever be,' Vera begins. But before she can continue he looks up, green-grey shining straight into her.

'I should have asked you about it,' he says. 'About the baby, about how you reached such a point of, I suppose, well, how you came to know it was the best thing for him?'

Vera shrugs, slowly, guiltily.

'I mean, I suppose, well, you were doing what was right for him? Making his life certain? Settling him? Not thinking of yourself???'

Vera does not hear the question marks. And so she says nothing.

'Tell me something true,' he pleads of her.

And it is time. She takes a breath. Then another. Luke smiles encouragingly. 'I – I've been seeing Charlie,' she begins. 'I've been seeing him because—'

Luke raises his hand. 'Too much,' he murmurs. 'Too much, too much.' He hangs his head low and shakes it gently. As they leave the restaurant and stroll out into the Piazza, Vera notices how the cathedral casts pools of golden light onto the square. People walk through them, unaware of the radiance that remains for a while on their shoulders. But Vera notices. And passes through it with Luke before leaving it behind. They walk together, separately, all the way from the Piazza back to the hotel and down the corridor. Vera's hands twitch for want of holding onto Luke's, but his are pinned firmly to his side. He is silent, and when they arrive at their rooms he gives her only a brief goodnight.

Their rooms share a bathroom, plush, beautifully tiled, and Vera closes both doors before sitting on the edge of the marble-clad bath to run it. She turns the taps onto full and tries not to wonder what Luke is thinking on his side of the heavy door. Or, while she is at it, what Charlie is thinking on the other side of the sea. Or what Charles has been thinking for three years about the mother who abandoned him. Does he understand that he has been without a mother? Does he miss a presence he cannot remember? Would he want her back, if she could come back, if she could bring herself to be at the mercy of a man she does not love and who would lord his power over her for the rest of her life? If she could bring herself to give up Luke? Luke. Who is sitting, silent, just feet and a door away from her. Who unlike Charlie she does love, and admire and respect and feel sorry for, and who she has ignored and neglected, and perhaps blown everything with.

Vera fingers her engagement ring, sheds her clothes and steps into the hot, cleansing water. The bubbles cover her with a welcome whiteness and the warmth of the liquid soaks into her bones. Immediately she feels calmer. Reaching for the purple hotel soap she begins to clean herself all over, then she closes her eyes and sinks further beneath the water. Without meaning to, she finds herself talking to God. *Help me*, she says, then in words with which she's been learning to articulate herself better: *Heavenly Father, in the Name of Jesus, I ask you to send your Holy Spirit to come upon me. I ask that I now receive your power by the Holy Spirit. I ask that the Holy Spirit come to live in me and be my heavenly Companion forever in life. Amen.* She feels a weight upon her shoulders, heavier than usual but warm – hands supporting her. She breathes in deeply. Then the weight moves forwards and down her chest. She opens her eyes. Luke is standing in front of her. She hadn't heard the door to his bedroom creak open, or his bare feet pad across the tiles.

'I—' he begins.

Vera sits up. Luke removes his hands from her chest but as she moves Luke smiles and she realises that her change of position had sent the bubbles flooding away from her, dispersing her frothy shroud. Rearranging them quickly she remains under the water and begins to reach for the nearby towel. 'What on earth are you doing in here? Didn't you hear the water?' she asks, whispering, as though this might prevent either of them from hearing or noticing what is taking place, but Luke doesn't whisper back. His voice is firm.

'Don't,' he says, intercepting her hand. 'I want to see you. I want to touch you. I don't want to wait anymore.'

'What?' she stammers in disbelief, then, 'We mustn't. We said we wouldn't. Luke, *you* said we should wait.' She continues to reach for the towel but Luke lifts it away from her.

'We'll be married soon anyway. And it feels right, doesn't it?'

'No.'

He keeps hold of the towel, but now lowers it slightly, offended. 'Charlie's seen you.'

At once, Vera feels tears threatening again. 'Don't do this Luke,' she implores him, opening her hand for him to relinquish the towel, and the moment. 'It's not the way you think—'

'You've given yourself again and again to Charlie.'

She reaches once more for the towel. 'You're just upset Luke.'

'You've been a whore for him.'

'Luke,' Vera hushes. She takes a breath. 'What's wrong?'

'You offered yourself to me before Vera,' he says in answer.

There is desperation in his tone. Something is happening within him, though Vera doesn't know what. Is his mother's disease making him feel impotent? Does it make him need to exert some kind of control? Is it his guilt at leaving her? (She knows all about that kind of guilt.) Or perhaps it is Charlie? Perhaps Luke has concocted some imagining of what he thinks has passed between them. Better or worse than the truth?

'I'm different now Luke. Now I want to wait.'

306

Only as she says this does she know fully that it is true. It isn't like before. She no longer wants raw physicality. Now, she wants intimacy, commitment, and to undress their souls slowly, so that they can be truly naked before each other. As husband and wife. She wants Luke. Forever. Quite how much she wants this is reaffirmed for her suddenly.

'Vera, come on. It's what you wanted.'

'How can you even ask me to?'

'How can you deny me?' He hangs the towel over the radiator on the far side of the room then sits on the edge of the bath, dipping his hand into the water and reaching for her thigh. She stands up. Luke smiles as she drips in front of him, an edgy, dangerous smile that months ago Vera would have done anything for. But now she storms over to the other side of the room and retrieves the towel. A choking sadness tightens around her lungs.

'How can you do this?' she demands wrapping the towel taut around her. 'After everything you've said to me? After all your rules and principles and values? Do they not apply because I've had sex before? Because I gave up my baby? Because I've sinned? Will I always be a sinner to you? Is there no coming back?'

Suddenly, Luke's smile changes. 'We're all sinners, aren't we?' he says, his voice wavering ambiguously. 'I knew that you had to see that. That was all. It was a test sweetheart. Just a test. And you passed it.'

With that he kisses the top of her head, leaves the bathroom, and closes the door. And Vera stands, wet, her whole body shaking.

It is almost an hour later that, while quietly collecting her toiletries from the bathroom, Vera hears the muffled sound of heavy, male sobs. Her heart constricts painfully and she rests her palm on the adjoining door. Hands push her forwards. But she shrugs her shoulders until they feel free of interference. She does not open the door. She does not say goodnight, or goodbye. She is careful not to make a sound long after she has walked the glorious corridor that takes her to the lobby, and into a taxi, then to the airport, and London again.

CHAPTER 27

Emily was hunched up, her knees to her chest in the corner of the art room when Lynn came in. The front door had sounded almost 20 minutes before, then Luke's footsteps on the path, and the only noises since had been the bubbling and then bubbling over of lunch, but still Emily had stayed where she was, staring at the paintings in front of her. Trying to swap these images for the ones in her head.

'I turned off the lunch,' Lynn said flatly from the doorway, without blame but rubbing her side and stooped over in a way that even a week earlier she wasn't.

Emily felt a wave of guilt, but she said: 'Why did you do that?'

'Because otherwise it would have been ruined,' replied the older woman.

'Why did you make me see him again?'

'I'm afraid I don't know what you're talking about.'

'You do know,' insisted Emily. 'Your son. You know he reminds me of . . .' she trailed off.

'Who?'

Emily was silent.

'Of course I *don't* know who he reminds you of,' Lynn said pointedly. 'But don't you think it's time you told me Emily?'

Still Emily said nothing. Luke's eyes flashed before her. Quickly she looked around the room. A new painting, swirling with unhinged colour was propped against the easel. On the walls and leant against them were the landscapes and portraits she'd studied now so often during her visits to this room. But the painting she had stared at the last time she had fled there, the unfinished one of the luminous girl, was now covered. It had been set by itself on a chair, and a heavy sheet was wrapped around it.

'It's not easy to uncover things that have been hidden,' Emily said to Lynn finally.

'I know Emily. But you must let your secrets out to be free of them. Trust me, you've inspired me to do that too.'

'Then why is that painting covered?' Emily asked bluntly.

Without answering, Lynn strode as quickly as she could to the canvas. With gargantuan effort she unwrapped and lifted the heavy sheet, then she turned the painting towards Emily. It was finished now. The blond, youthful figure stared out of the paper with boldness and fearless questioning. And such radiance. Emily looked up at Lynn.

'It is you,' she remarked carefully.

'No it's not me,' dismissed Lynn. 'It's nothing like me. I've never been anything like her.'

Emily looked again. 'It's you,' she repeated.

Now Lynn inspected the painting more closely. Her eyes traced the contours of the strokes as though seeing them for the first time, as though it was not she who had held the brush that painted them. Sadness and confusion crept across her brow. Slowly, she lifted her thin hand to her wrinkled face, touched her white hair, and looked at the image harder. Then she shook her head woefully, holding onto the chair for support. Crumpling.

Emily stood up. Her legs shook and a lump wobbled in her chest. Her head was reeling. She needed her own chair to hold on to. But she stepped towards Lynn.

'I will try to tell you,' she said resolutely. And taking Lynn's fragile arm, both women leaning in as they had grown used to, they made their way to the lounge.

They sat with tea just like the last time, fetching it slowly together and sipping for a long time before either said anything. Lynn waited patiently and seemed to regain her composure with the infusion of the hot brew. Emily shook. She felt she had barely survived the last encounter. But the important thing was that she had. She supposed. And grown even, a little, just as Lynn had promised. Lynn who had revealed herself. Who had trusted.

'Let it out,' Lynn encouraged.

Even in her weakness, there was such authority to Lynn's voice, such confidence and inspiration.

'Where was I?' Emily asked, the dizziness growing even before she had begun. Luke flashed again before her, then another two-toned memory. She shut her eyes. 'Was I with them?'

'You were with your mother,' coaxed Lynn. 'You were back home. Ernest was helping you. You had escaped from the fire at the church. You were alright. You were sleeping.'

'I was sleeping,' Emily repeated, un-calmed by this.

'You were sleeping,' soothed Lynn.

When she next woke up it was morning. Her brothers had already left their beds and were gathered with her parents at the table, except for Cassien who was standing by the window with his face flat against the wall so that it couldn't be seen.

'Ernest's candle is up,' he reported suddenly and moved quickly towards the door to unlock it for their neighbour before returning to his guard.

'Emilienne, there's some breakfast,' Mama said, pointing to a small bowl in which some of Ernest's mangoes had been sliced. Emily helped herself and let the sweet fruit slide against her tongue and down her throat. The slurping of its juice seemed loud and a little obnoxious. Rukundo and Simeon were silent. Papa and Mama said only what was necessary, but Emily felt talkative. The fresh light of the morning had calmed her fears and removed some of the rawness of the previous day. It filled her with hope.

'Can we play kweti today?' she asked.

'Cassien, leave the window. Sit with us,' Papa instructed, not answering her.

'I'm keeping watch,' Cassien responded.

'Come and sit Cassien.'

Reluctantly, Cassien began to move away, then all at once he froze.

'What?' Emily pestered, taming another slice of mango. 'What?'

But when he turned towards them, the terror on his face made her stop mid-bite, and he need not have answered.

'They're coming.'

Emily opened her eyes. Lynn nodded.

'I don't know if I can,' whispered Emily.

'You can.'

'I don't want to,' said Emily.

'You do. You know you do.'

Emily closed her eyes again. Want was not an option. She had begun. It had her.

'They're coming,' repeated Cassien.

They all flew to the window.

'They're coming from the side too. What shall we do?' Rukundo panicked.

Mama placed her hand on his shoulder.

'Run,' she said calmly, then she turned more urgently towards all of them. 'Now.' Emily reached for her hand but her mother shrugged it off. 'Get up!' she screamed at her, the way she used to when Emily didn't want to pray the rosary or when she tumbled into the house covered in scrapes. 'Get up! Run! Go now! But hide alone. All of you. Remember to hide alone.'

Emily's legs began to shake uncontrollably. She'd hardly begun to stand and already she was falling.

'Move Emilienne,' Cassien shouted now in tandem with her mother, then she felt him grab her shirt and pull her towards the back door.

Behind them, their parents didn't move. 'Mama! Papa!' she cried as Cassien dragged her away, but they remained where they were standing, her father picking up a small cooking knife, which was the only weapon they had, both of them calm, waiting. To their side, Rukundo and Simeon also loitered. 'What are they doing?' Emily pleaded in panic as she and Cassien broke through the back door, over the fence and into the graveyard. 'Why aren't they running with us?'

'You were sleeping,' he answered, pushing her on.

'What? What do you mean?'

'Nothing. Run Emmy.'

'Wait. Cassien. What about the others?' She slowed to look back.

'Run Emmy.'

'We have to wait for them.'

'No. Run.'

'Why aren't they coming?'

'They are.' He pushed her forwards hard. 'Emmy, they're coming behind us. I promise. Just keep running. Don't look back. Go faster. There, up that tree.'

Behind them, men's voices were beginning to clamour, then the clatter of glass shattering, and screams that were at once too familiar and too alien, disconnected from the bodies they belonged to, as though they'd been torn out from the inside.

'Cassien!' Emily cried from the branch he'd helped lift her onto. 'Cassien. Come up here with me.'

'No, we have to hide alone Emmy. Don't worry. Be quiet. I'll find you after they've gone. I promise. Just stay there Emmy. Don't move. Don't come down no matter what. Promise me.'

'Cassien!' Emily whispered again. 'Cassien! Okay, I promise.' But he was already gone. From her perch she could see him running again, away from her, away from the two Hutu men who had suddenly appeared beneath her tree. Gasping, she muffled herself with her free hand, clinging to the branch so tightly with the other that she felt a shard of wood sink beneath her skin.

'There he goes!' she heard one of the men scream in frenzied elation just feet below her. 'Come back you shitty little cockroach! You can't scurry forever! It's time you were cut down to size.'

The other man called her brother by name.

315

'Cassien, come out. Make it easier,' he bellowed, the voice deep with a hint of laughter that Emily recognised.

Ernest.

Gasping again, Emily clasped her hand more tightly over her mouth. She tried to stay quiet like Cassien had said to, but the mango she'd eaten, Ernest's mango, began to rise up inside her stomach, its sweetness suddenly reacting with her body like a poison.

I heard you were a smart one Emilienne, Ernest had told her once. *Take one each.* How could he have brought these men to them? He knew what they were capable of. He'd fretted over it with Papa. *One for your mother. And thank her for the salt.* Then the truth hit her. He hadn't brought the men, he had come amongst them. Emily threw up into her hand. The mango was still in chunks, undigested. She held the mess tight to her face to stop it from dripping. When she inhaled, it went back up her nostril and burned. Still she remained silent. Clenching shut her eyes, she began another conversation with God and finally the frenzied voices began to recede, to grow more faint, to seem less real. Nervously she loosened her grip on her face and allowed herself to exhale, but before she could so much as breathe in again the voices returned, and now they were louder than ever. Just twenty metres away she heard Ernest.

'Be still Cassien,' he was shouting. They had

him. The other man laughed and jeered and told him that if he didn't stop struggling they would make him. 'Where is your sister?' Ernest demanded, and Cassien, whose thin voice told Emily that he had already been badly wounded, promised that he didn't know, that she hadn't been with him. Through sharp breaths she heard him pleading with their neighbour, their friend who had once been so jovial and indulgent, *she wasn't here, please Ernest, Uncle, please, she wasn't with us.*

Suddenly Emily heard a grotesque slicing sound and Cassien screamed, a blood-curdling yelp, like an animal being slaughtered.

'So don't tell us,' the second man laughed. 'If we don't find her today, we'll come back for her tomorrow. Where can she go?'

'Let's return to the others then,' Ernest agreed. 'Bring him.'

'Get up,' Emily heard the other man demand of her brother.

From the tree, Emily peered between the branches and saw Cassien lying on top of a grave. He was covered in blood, both his ankles sporting deep gashes where his achilles tendons had been cut, but he looked straight into the eyes of his attackers and not once towards her. Instinctively, Emily's arms pushed away from the branch – she had to help her brother, she had to go to him – but his words echoed loudly in her head: *don't come down, no matter what, promise me, promise me.* She had promised. She froze.

'Get up,' the man repeated, knowing that he couldn't.

Cassien scrambled. He brought himself up onto his knees.

'Murderers,' Emily heard him snarl.

'Cockroaches,' the man spat. 'You are so high and mighty, you think you are better, but you are nothing but cockroaches, a plague on Rwanda, an enemy of our country. It was you who murdered our president. You are the murderers and you think you can get away with it, you think you are better than us. It is time you were cut down to size.'

With this final remark he swung his machete at Cassien and hacked at his bleeding ankles. Again and again he swung while Cassien screamed and writhed in pain and Ernest stood watching. Emily clung to the branch. When the man moved up to Cassien's wrists Emily closed her eyes and prayed fast, rushing through all the prayers she knew, then again bargaining with God, begging Him. When there was no answer, she began to sing to herself silently: their song, the winner's song with the irritating tune. She repeated it now with fervent sincerity, round and around, to drown out his shrieks.

For some time the slashing continued, the sound of bone being cut rivalled only by the thrashing sounds from her 14-year-old brother: screams that sounded sometimes like the child she remembered, and sometimes like the man he would never grow up to be. Emily removed her hand from her mouth and, her fingers webbed with vomit, tried to cover her ears, but she could only ever cover one ear at a time – with the other hand she had to keep hold of the branch – so no matter how tightly she squeezed her eyes closed and buried her head in the leaves of the tree, she could not prevent herself from hearing, nor imagining the sight below her.

By the time the killer had reached Cassien's neck, his shouts had been dismembered from him along with his parts. There was quiet, a deadly, deathly quiet, and cautiously Emily opened her eyes just in time to witness the final blow: a stroke just beneath her brother's young, handsome jaw; a mere formality of a slow, intimate slaughter.

'So there is one more?' the man asked Ernest, out of breath when he had at long last finished, but nonchalant, as though he was tired from a game of football.

'A girl,' Ernest confirmed, his voice faltering slightly. 'And another boy, with the rebels.'

'Well the girl can't be far. We'll return for her tomorrow. We'll need some more energy for her hey?' he laughed, and as they walked away Ernest laughed with him, a deep-barrelled laugh that made Emily think of the veranda, and her parents who by now were most likely lying dead upon it.

All day Emily clung to her branch. Everywhere there seemed to be Hutus. She could hear them calling to each other. Some voices drifted over the fields, trudged the route from school, and rustled through the leaves in everyday gestures of greeting and mundane activity – *bring in the washing, lunch is ready, call your brother* – surreal now in their normality, obscene. But others pierced the air in high-pitched shrieks: an absurd mixture of fear and euphoria. Emily couldn't move. Her fingers wouldn't work, though she had blown on them and wiggled them and tried to make them obey her if only to clutch more steadily to the branch. She had promised. To stay there until he came.

Guilt crept up the tree. She should have broken her promise. She should have done something. But what? The events of the last few hours had taught her quickly and acutely that she could trust nobody, and she understood that in a village swarming with Hutus and frighteningly absent of Tutsis, she could not descend from her tree. Perhaps later, in the dark, she could shimmy down, let the night cloak Cassien's remains, and make it inside and on to her Uncle's house in the neighbouring village. Perhaps later.

For the time being however, that tree, selected for her by her dead brother, was her only hope of salvation. She didn't yet have the courage to inspect what lay beyond its roots. The screams and wails that still echoed inside her head had been enough. She didn't want to see the reality behind them, to have it confirmed. Ernest returned to the graveyard three times that afternoon, calling her name, promising to look after her. She was sick twice more. The second time, only bile.

In the evening, the dogs arrived. Not domestic animals, but wild African dogs looking for food. Emily heard them barking in front of the house and shuddered. The year before, Simeon had had an encounter with a pack of dogs like this and lost a chunk of flesh from his calf to them. They appeared sometimes from the edge of the bush, their eyes black beads of ferocity laced on too-tight thread. Papa said they were scavengers, the worst sort of predator, and Emily lifted herself on the branch, craning her neck to see what they were scavenging now. Their tails were in the air as they sniffed at something on the veranda, licking, chewing and eating.

It was too much. Without pausing to think, Emily let go of the branch and slid down the trunk of the tree. Though there was no longer anything inside her to throw up, as soon as she hit the ground and saw Cassien's body, she gagged again. Flies buzzed around the stumps of his limbs. She shooed them away and wished his eyes would close, wished his mouth would not be upturned in that uncanny expression that looked almost like a grin, but his lips didn't move, and the insects returned immediately. She swiped at them again. They manoeuvred themselves a few inches away, then returned once more, mocking her. Strong in their numbers. Her body shook through fear and exhaustion, her legs grew unsteady, her arms flailed. Finally she could do nothing but leave her brother to his tiny persecutors.

The house was quiet. She stooped at the threshold and gathered a handful of stones and rocks, as many as she could carry, before pushing open the door. Across the floor were thick streaks of red where someone bleeding had been dragged, but no bodies, no evidence of the sounds she had heard. Without thinking she grabbed the bucket that stood by the door and a cloth from the sink and began scrubbing furiously, driven by an idea that if only she could get rid of the blood, then the truth too could be cleaned away. But the barks came again. Emily dropped the cloth, now dripping red, and pressed on. The door at the front of the house was hanging from its hinges and Emily nudged it open. Outside this door, she had once waited for glimpses of her father to return from work, she had sorted vegetables with her mother and bleached sheets, she had watched clouds and made up songs with Cassien, she had loved the world that unfolded hot and sticky and full of colour before it. Now, instead, three black dogs stood like shadows on the threshold tearing pieces of flesh from her memories.

Emily felt her stomach contract but she forced herself to look more closely and immediately she recognised the blue of Rukundo's T-shirt. It was new that month. He had liked the way his toned, muscular arms had tugged gently at the cotton, and although Emily had teased him she had secretly agreed that he looked handsome and strong, and a little like Gahiji. Now his arms were not poking through the sleeves where they should have been. On the floor nearby were Papa's glasses, shattered, and Mama's red dress, the one with the black trim, fanned out like the tail of a peacock. On top of it lay Simeon's body, his face collapsed in on itself like a broken doll, his back shredded, dark blood staining the soil around him. It was not possible to identify the rest of the remains. They were too badly disfigured, or strewn at angles so inhuman that it was impossible to say how they might once have been held, or moved, or used to run or cook or swing from trees or turn pages of a book or stroke her ankle.

Emily felt a roar welling up inside her, an explosion of feeling and horror, but somehow she stifled it back down and stepped closer still. The dogs snarled as she approached, but intent on their feast didn't bother themselves with prey still capable of fighting. Emily observed this, and as she did she was possessed by a sudden, reckless rage. Lifting one of her stones she launched it hard at the nearest dog. It yelped, then growled fiercely, but did not look up as it threatened her with a set of sharp teeth and continued with its meal. Emily lifted another stone and hurled it harder. This time the dog jumped and turned to face her, but she hit it again, then a second dog, then the third. Suddenly, it seemed to Emily that no matter what else happened, she could not let these beasts loose on her family. She could not let it happen. The men that had come, she was powerless against, but the dogs she must stop, and in that moment, she felt no fear.

One after another she threw her stones and when she ran out of them she scrabbled on the ground for more. The dogs leapt towards her but she pounded them again and again and again. When they tried to ignore her and return to their meal, she hit them on their noses. When they approached, dripping blood-tinted saliva, she hurled larger rocks harder. Eventually, they grew confused, and irritated, and finally began to back away. And Emily ran after them. She hadn't planned it, but all at once chasing them, beating these mindless, bloodthirsty beasts was essential, and the only thing she could do. The distance between them stretched. She ran faster. Her legs were weak and shuddering and filling with acid, but she struggled on blindly, shouting, cursing, running on and on even after the animals had long disappeared from view. Finally she stumbled into a field of sweet potatoes where abruptly she wondered where it was she thought she was going, and collapsed gasping onto the ground.

It was then that she heard the voices behind her. Raised, exhilarated voices, some of them calling her name. She recognised at least one of them but this time it wasn't Ernest's. Emily's head pounded and she couldn't think straight. She tried to raise herself to run again, to climb another tree, but there were nothing but sweet potatoes all around her and when she lifted herself onto her feet, they shook and she collapsed once more. Almost lifeless, her face lay flat on the cool soil. The voices grew closer. In her paralysis she wondered if there were caterpillars nearby, or snakes. She hated both. Again she tried to move, but the shaking of her body was convulsive and she could not tame it. She could not escape. She could not hide herself from the voices and when they reached her they laughed.

They ordered her to stand up. When she stood and fell they laughed again. Six of them, each bearing a machete or a masu or a spear, six intoxicated men leering and jeering, six faces that even through her mental fog she knew. Some were her father's age, some her brothers', one hers, almost, only a year older, a face she knew so well. The boy who'd once been her friend, her best friend, her almost more than friend, the white-patched kid who'd stuck up for her and played in her yard, and just months ago tried to kiss her.

His jaw was chiselled now. Taller than when she'd seen him last, he'd grown somehow into the body of a man. His green-grey eyes bore the same intensity of the past months, the same disturbing passion that had begun all the troubles between them, but now there was something else: fear, bewilderment, uncertainty – as though he was caught in the throes of a game that had got out of hand. As though they were up a tree together and realised they had climbed too high. At the flicker of such an old emotion, her heart lifted. 'Jean?'

He shook his head but she pleaded.

'Please, don't. Don't let them.'

Almost immediately she realised her mistake. The other men looked to her old friend with indicting question marks in their eyes, and all at once the uncertainty in his own clouded over with embarrassment and humiliation. She'd seen these emotions before too. And they were dangerous.

'Get undressed,' he told her.

The other men roared with laughter and danced about gleefully, but Emily didn't move. She couldn't. She stood, staring at Jean's familiar face, and Jean stared back. When he spoke, it was slow and with a new, unnerving menace.

'I said, get undressed,' he repeated, not taking his two-tone eyes off her. 'Take off your clothes, or we will take them off for you.' Jean, who in class didn't know what to say, who looked to her for answers. He took out a cigarette, lit it, and mockingly offered it to her. 'Come now, you think because you are a Tutsi you're too good for us?'

'No.' Emily wrapped her arms protectively around herself and the men jeered. 'I don't think that,' she said loudly for their benefit, and then lowered her voice to a whisper for him. 'I never thought that. Jean, you were my best friend. I only wasn't ready. Please, don't do this. Jean.' She should have stayed silent. The more she implored him, the more her familiarity seemed to anger him, and egg on the others. But she couldn't stop saying his name, beseeching him, as though she could somehow make him see the madness, and stop it: *Jean, please, Jean.*

'Shut up! Undress!' he shouted abruptly, waving his hands to silence her.

'No.'

He punched the air.

'Now Emilienne.' His demands were almost desperate, but she would not help him this time. 'Undress. Undress you cockroach!'

The words struck her like a slap.

'Fuck you,' she whispered, 'I will never undress for you.' His spitefulness seemed so childish. They could have been arguing again behind the school-house. But this time, months after the first, her rejection didn't embarrass him into retreat.

'Then we will do it for you,' he retorted instead.

At this, the men grinned, stepped closer and postured with their weapons, but while Jean stood there in front of her, she could not bring herself to beg again.

'Do what you like,' she declared calmly, over-come with a sudden, strange serenity. 'I'm not afraid of you Jean. Or any of you. I don't care what you do.' As she spoke, she felt herself growing in confidence and in that moment she believed her foolish words. She wasn't afraid, she didn't want their mercy, she wanted only to make them as angry as she was. It was obvious now that she was going to die, so it was better to make them mad, to fuse their tempers, to rile them enough to kill her quickly, to silence her in one blow, one shot of a gun, one strike from a spear, something fast and awesome and less painful than the slow torture she'd watched her beloved Cassien endure. 'You're all weak,' she taunted them. 'You're killing us because you're weak and envious. And pathetic!' she directed at Jean.

'Shut up!'

'Stupid! And pathetic!'

Jean raised his machete, took a running leap towards her, and brought it down hard upon her head.

'Emily?' Lynn was leaning over her, dabbing her neck with a handkerchief. 'Shush Emily, you're fine, you're here. I've got you.'

Emily realised that she was sobbing, and her clothes were wet.

'You fainted dear. You dropped your tea,' Lynn explained. 'Perhaps you should stop. Perhaps that's enough for today.'

'I'm sorry for the mess.'

'Don't be sorry.'

Lynn gave her the handkerchief. Deliberately she poured Emily another cup of tea, adding three sugars, and handed it to her.

'Luke reminds you of Jean,' she stated.

Emily nodded. 'They look nothing alike. Except

the eyes. Half green. Half grey. Two things at the same time.'

'Do you want to tell me what happened? Do you want to carry on?'

'I don't know. I've never told it before. You might think . . . I, I feel so—'

'You mustn't be ashamed. You're not responsible for what others do to you. Only what you do to yourself.'

Emily nodded. Tears continued to roll silently down her face. 'I'll try to tell you,' she muttered. 'I'm sorry if I cry. When I tell it, it is like I'm there again. And I can't stop it, I can't stop them, it comes so fast, but—'

'What dear?'

'I think you were right. I think I have to keep going now. Work it out, the order, get it straight.' She touched her scar. 'But I don't want to remember it.' She began to sob again. 'They all did – it pulls me back – it poisons me – they poisoned me – and his eyes were so, so . . .'

'Go slowly Emily,' Lynn said. 'Take it slowly. When you woke up, what did you see?'

Faces. Mostly Jean's, though it wasn't only him. They all took their turn and often didn't even wait for it, two or three of them tearing at her flesh at once, pawing her, stripping from her not only her clothes, and her virginity, but every last shred of her childhood and vestige of hope. For hours. Some of the time she fell again into unconsciousness, but the men kept slapping her awake, demanding of her.

'Beg, you Tutsi.' Or making her crawl before them. When she could distinguish it, there was fear still in Jean's voice, hesitation, but pleasure too, a wild, mad gratification.

'Who is pathetic now?'

She prayed that God would end it, she prayed she would die, she tried to embrace the haziness that seeped from the gash on her head. But what was happening was altogether too vivid. Their hot, rough hands all over her, inside her; pain ripping through her body, starting in the area between her legs that her mother had taught her to be protective of, then burning violently until she was numb; their laughter; the soil in her mouth when they pushed her face into the ground, its evening coolness; the smell of something sweet yet putrid; the taste of them; a tooth coming loose, spitting it out and noticing how dark her blood was; their hardness; the rosary that span round and around her head; their laughter; beer sprayed over her; blows to her stomach, her head, her bottom; not being able to breathe or speak or answer when they continued to make their demands; their laughter; her nose being held while they took it in turns to stuff parts of themselves inside her mouth; gagging; her nose breaking; her arm dislocating; blood; their laughter.

When they'd finally had enough, they ordered her to stand and get dressed, told her she was indecent and that they didn't want to look at such a vile animal as herself. She tried to stand but collapsed immediately.

'You don't want your clothes? You prefer to be an animal?' they laughed and again demanded that she get up and dressed, lashing the backs of her legs with the side of a spear as soon as she put weight upon them.

'Get dressed,' they demanded, and she tried again, fell again, endured their taunts again.

She looked through the muddled mass for Jean, but their faces had merged. Jean, even with his uncommon eyes, was indefinable from the rest.

'Why don't you kill me?' she eventually managed to whisper.

'We will kill you, be sure of that,' one of them replied. 'We'll get rid of all the Tutsis. But we've already killed your whole family today. We're tired. We need a rest. Besides, your friend Jean wants to wait until tomorrow.'

The one who had spoken moved and slowly Jean, standing head-bent a little behind the rest of them, came into focus. Green and grey. He nodded at her encouragingly, and then, then he did the most extraordinary thing – he winked.

Emily laughed.

Even in her pain, she couldn't help but laugh at him. Because his winking had always been such a ridiculous gesture to her, and now it seemed more bizarre than ever. He used it to convey what? Conspiracy? Sympathy? Apology perhaps? To

331

remind her of all the times they had spent together? To ask her forgiveness? Did he imagine himself as merciful? An extra day he had given her, his friend, his almost more than friend, one more day of life, and for this he expected her to be thankful? Emily pulled her eyes away from him and slowly trained them down her torn, naked body. This was not mercy. It was merely an illustration of how total and discretionary his power had become.

One of the men threw her clothes at her and painfully she forced her body into the trousers and shirt she'd been wearing. The material felt like lead against her bruised bones, but she clasped it to her, using a sleeve to plug her bleeding nose and dab at the gash on her forehead that was oozing some kind of substance thicker than blood. She felt Jean watching her grimace.

'Stand up,' he told her.

She stood.

'Move,' he said, pointing in the direction she was to go.

She began to move, pain shooting through her legs and hips and into her spine with every step.

'Faster,' someone else demanded.

She pushed herself forward faster, stumbling, continuing, obeying. The will to protest, to defy them, him, had disappeared into the sweet potato field. She no longer possessed any control of her life, no control even of her own body, there was no point in resistance. If he said go, she went now. If he said stop, she stopped. There was nothing left in her head, no plan, no hope, no ambition, no-one to trust, and no family to live for except for Gahiji who had probably perished too. No matter. They would kill her soon enough.

She didn't know how long she walked for. Her face stung against the air as she moved forwards and somewhere in her left leg a bone crunched. Perhaps they only travelled a few hundred metres, but it felt like many miles before they arrived at a makeshift camp that used to be the government offices. Outside, in a cage-like structure, were a mass of bodies, some lifeless upon sodden red soil, others alive but sitting heads bent upon wooden benches, almost as dead as those fallen untended at their feet.

'One more!' one of Emily's captors shouted to the two Hutus swinging great masus about the cage, and opened the cage door.

One of the men used a single strong hand to yank Emily inside.

'You're lucky,' he told her. 'We're almost finished for today. But you can be the last one.' He turned to his friend. 'I'm thirsty. We'll do the rest tomorrow.'

Emily didn't respond but glanced around to see who 'the rest' were. Opposite her was a young mother with two small daughters clasping frantically to her legs. Next to them was an old man, hunched and grey, the kind of man her father would have encouraged her to offer help to. There were no other men. The remaining ten or so people were frightened women and children, some younger than herself, some bleeding, some crying, some looking up at her with a mixture of apology and gratitude. And one woman, on her own, sitting stony still in the corner. At first, Emily's eyes passed over her as wearily as the rest, but something drew her sharply back. Liquid from the cut on her forehead was leaking into her eyes, but she squinted hard and looked again. She recognised this bruised, naked woman.

Her chest hurt with the incisive intake of air.

Time rolled back.

And in that sudden, surprising moment, Emily was a child again, not mangled, not abused, not in need of anything but to run into her mother's arms.

Her mother stood up. 'I will be the last one,' she declared defiantly.

Emily opened her mouth but the look in her mother's eyes warned her to stay silent. The top half of her mother's body was naked, except for a torn headscarf that hung limply around her neck. Emily knew she liked to wear this with the red dress upon which Simeon's bloodied head now lay. She was shivering and she was stained with blood, but she stood firm and strong and did not show her pain. She looked at her daughter. Her bleeding nose and torn clothes and gashed head, and Emily felt herself flush with shame. Clutching her dirty clothes to her body she wished she could hide what had been done to her, what she'd lost, what she hadn't been able to protect. She was more naked under her mother's gaze than she'd ever been with Jean and the other men who had undressed her.

The guard who had spoken to Emily laughed, and grabbed her mother by the chin. 'You stupid Tutsi. Don't you want to come back tomorrow?'

'I will be the last one,' her mother repeated.

Emily's heart pounded. She opened her mouth again but her mother glared at her sharply. From behind, the other guard jabbed her in the ribs.

'Move,' he told Emily, rallying her and the rest of the captives towards the door. But Emily could not look away from her mother.

'Move,' the guard prodded again, this time with the butt of his masu, and Emily's mother nodded, firmly. Obediently, Emily moved.

'You stupid Tutsi,' she heard the first guard laugh again, enjoying himself now and roughly dragging her mother forwards. 'Okay, let's have you today then! You can be the last.'

Emily glanced back. The guard was raising his masu, the huge club almost luminous against the dying sun, its nails catching the very last of the light.

She blinked.

Her mother's beautiful arms pushed heroically against the soil.

She blinked again.

There are times when it becomes impossible to believe in one's own existence, in the reality of what the eyes have seen. In the instant of her mother's death, Emily felt the last drops of life drain from her body. Her limbs felt hollow. This was her moment of paralysis.

'Keep moving!' The guard nearby lifted his club but the elderly Tutsi man shuffled forwards to take her arm and pulled her on. Emily let her feet follow his tug. It was irrelevant which direction she moved in now anyway. It was all fleeting and cursory and a way to kill time before it killed her. *Tomorrow*, they had said. They would kill the rest tomorrow. They had promised. She looked forward to it with all the emotion inside her, which was nothing.

'How did you escape?' Lynn interrupted.

'Do what you want,' Emily murmured.

'Emily? Come back,' Lynn urged.

'I can't. Everything's dark. There's a body on top of me.'

'No, you're here in my sitting room. In London. That's enough for today.'

'My mum died.'

'I know.'

'She wouldn't come back tomorrow.'

'She couldn't watch you die. She was your mother.'

'But I watched her. I saw. They smashed her. Then it was so dark. The compound was inside. I couldn't see the sky. Everybody was crying. I was cold.'

'Emily, stop.'

Lynn's voice was faint and far away. It had lost its authority. There were stronger voices calling her name. *Emilienne! Emilienne! That one! Emilienne!*

Jean was standing over her, his eyes not green nor grey but dark and wild as two other men pulled her to her feet. It was night still. The old man removed her head from his shoulder, looking down in apology. All the prisoners were silent as she was dragged away.

In a small room, bright with fluorescent lighting too dazzling for her bruised eyes, a man with a rifle slung over his shoulder ordered that she be flung into the chair opposite his desk, then slowly lit a cigarette before leaning forward to flick the ash onto her hand. She flinched but did not cry out. The pain was mere dust on the ground. Leaning back in his chair the man surveyed her. He was short and broadly set, with a small forehead that made his eyes seem menacing even when he smiled, his grin revealing gaping holes where front teeth should have been. Now and then he laughed obscenely, and Jean and the two others at the back of the room laughed with him.

'How old are you?' the man queried eventually, after he'd stared at her battered body for a long time.

'Thirteen,' she whispered.

'Thirteen. Hmm,' he rolled the number around his mouth. 'So shall we see what's underneath these dirty clothes?'

Panic gripped her. The only words she could find however were the truth.

'It is your choice,' she answered.

He smiled, titillated, and leant forward again so that his face was next to hers and she could smell his foul breath.

'Sir, the guns,' Jean chimed in.

Now the man spun towards him, and as if outraged by the interruption he glared at Jean hard, then walked around the desk to Emily where he placed a heavy hand suggestively on her shoulder.

'You wait outside,' he told Jean deliberately, slipping his hand beneath the neck of her shirt. 'I will get to the guns when I'm ready.' Jean cast his eyes down and obediently left the room. As soon as the door was shut, the man released her, grabbing her roughly by her arm and yanking her to her feet. Droplets of spit flew from between the gaps in his teeth into her face as he spoke to her. 'Where are the guns?' he demanded.

Emily felt her legs shaking. Speaking felt dangerous but remaining silent was worse.

'What guns?' she murmured finally, and at once the man's face was up against hers, his hand clasping her jaw so that she couldn't look away.

'The guns from your brother,' he snarled menacingly. 'The one who is with the rebels. Jean told us. Your brother sent guns to your family. We cannot lose these. You will tell us where they are hidden. Where are they?'

'There are no guns,' Emily replied, in a voice that was barely audible.

'What?'

'There are no guns.'

Before she could even see it coming he had punched her in the stomach and she fell gasping to the ground, the force of his blow knocking the air out of her small frame and at the same time somehow reigniting all the pain from her previous injuries, so that her whole body throbbed and pulsated. The man returned casually to his chair and smoked his cigarette while she writhed before him on the ground. Finally she caught her breath and mockingly he cupped his ear for her confession. But she had none.

'There are no guns,' she spluttered from her knees.

'Where are they?'

'I don't know.'

Calmly, the man signalled to the two others at the back of the room and one of them stepped forward to kick her hard in the stomach. Again she doubled up, winded and wheezing, but now her mind began to race. It didn't make sense. She couldn't think. Only hours before she'd had a family and went to school and was a child with dreams. Now this insanity replaced everything and removed all sense.

'Tell me the truth,' the man was demanding, but there no longer seemed to exist a truth. Only murder. Murdering and murdering and getting away with it. And not just by a few. By so many.

Even Hutus like Ernest and Jean. Even neighbours and priests and friends. And almost more than friends. Yet they were the same, weren't they, wasn't that the truth? They were all Rwandan, they were all people, weren't they? *Mama, why must I be a Tutsi?* It was only a name. It couldn't be real. This couldn't be real. It couldn't be humanity. A confused haze enveloped her.

'Where are they?'

'There are no guns,' she tried again.

Another kick to her stomach. Frantically Emily tried to inhale but no air made it beneath the surface. She started coughing and blood shot from her mouth.

'Please, there are no guns,' she pleaded. It was true. If she'd had a gun, by now she would have used it, but they hadn't heard a word from Gahiji since he'd left to join the rebels. Even Jean knew that, but Jean had told the men they were hiding his rifles, that she knew where they were. Why? To make sure they killed her quickly? To rid himself of her presence, of his guilt? But why go to such trouble? She would be killed the following day in any case. It didn't make sense. Then suddenly, as the man moved to kick her again, it hit her: Jean had done this to save her.

'There are guns, there are guns,' she reversed desperately, protecting her stomach with her hands. 'But they were moved. I can't remember where. I can't think straight. Maybe I can remember after I rest.'

The man who had been kicking her lifted his foot again but the one in charge halted him. 'Take her to the end cell,' he commanded from behind the desk. 'These guns are expensive. They will be helpful. We'll let her think about it for a while.'

Perception, it seemed to Emily, was an unwilling victim of suffering. As she continued to gasp for breath and they dragged her away, she tried to process her surroundings, to hook her survival to at least one hallway or building or blade of grass she could recognise and so use as an anchor. But time and space had become as illusory as everything else she'd thought was certain. When she was thrown into the cell, the thud could just as easily have been a movement of the floor as of her body, or she could have been lying on a wall somehow, or not lying at all, or not awake but dreaming, or not alive but dead, like all of the other people she knew and loved.

When she woke, she didn't know how many hours or days she'd been asleep for. Wracked with an urgent thirst her throat felt like sandpaper. When she tried to stand up a stabbing pain shot down her left hip and on lifting her jumper she discovered that her entire side had turned green. The cell stank. When she looked around she realised that she had soiled herself. A final indignity. It struck her with mere indifference. The emptiness inside her had now taken firm root. Nothing mattered.

At some intangible moment after that a guard entered the cell and placed a cup of water and a hard muffin on the floor. He held his nose at the stench in the room and looked at Emily in disgust, as if her example confirmed his worst expectations of what it was to be Tutsi. She wasn't embarrassed. There no longer existed such a thing. Impervious to his disdainful gaze she reached for the water and raised it to her lips, only then discovering that at some point during her unconsciousness, her jaw had locked. Jammed shut like a prison door. Gasping now for the water tauntingly before her she battled on, her struggle seeming to amuse the guard who snickered behind his hand. Finally however, after tilting her head all the way back, she managed to pour the liquid through the small, crusted opening of her mouth, and keeping her chin to the sky, it trickled down her sandpaper throat. Water turned into fire, but she swallowed, and glared defiantly at the guard. If only her stomach had been as stoic, but bubbling at the sudden influx of water, her insides exploded, and moments later filth ran in brown, gushing liquid down her legs, soaking through her trousers. The guard laughed. Emily lay her head on the floor and slept again.

For weeks she survived this way. Every time a glass of water was provided she drank it, and every time her stomach ran. The men took to throwing the food they gave her into the cell from a distance, anxious not to be close to her mess. Emily stopped smelling it. Her head throbbed all the time, the gash above her eye no longer seeping but crusting over and adding to the noxious air. When she lay on the floor she could feel her ribs and hips protruding into the hard ground. Gradually however, somehow, she began to grow stronger. Every now and then the man who had ordered her to be locked in the cell appeared and asked her in a cursory way where the guns were. But he seemed not to be able to bear the stench that surrounded her and didn't enter her cell to press for an answer.

Mostly she slept. Her dreams were filled with visions of her mother, naked, defiant, and of herself saying nothing, and of her father's smashed glasses, and the empty sleeve of Rukundo's blue shirt, and Cassien's arms and legs turned to stumps, and her not helping him, and Simeon's broken skull, and Ernest and Jean with machetes in their hands. Sometimes, when she opened her eyes she still saw these images, like ghosts leering in front of her, or clouds taking unearthly shapes, too distorted a vision to interpret or construct a story for.

She must have been in the cell for almost a month before Jean appeared in the flesh and not only in these nightmares. His hair was messy and longer, his face flushed as though he'd been working in the sun, and he seemed to have grown even taller since she saw him last, or else she had shrunk. He looked healthy. When his eyes met hers they betrayed all his disgust at the sight of what

343

she had become; but there was a reservation within his down-turned gaze that made her wonder if a small part of this aversion was reserved for himself.

'The killing's almost over,' he told her from the doorway in a tone somewhere between triumph and apology. Still she felt only emptiness.

'Who is left?'

'In our village, so far as we know, only you,' he replied, then, smiling ridiculously, as if he was still allowed this privilege, he added, 'nobody will want to kill you now. You are famous. People are saying it would be a curse to kill the last one.'

The last one.

One.

Infinite absence of another. Infinite loneliness.

Emily didn't smile back and Jean's face dropped. He ran a weary hand through his hair and disordered it. She said nothing.

'I've arranged for you to be hidden,' he hurried on more seriously, quietly, glancing back over his shoulder. 'A man you know has agreed to take you. I've bribed the guards. Someone will come for you tonight. Be ready. Can you stand?'

She nodded.

'Good.'

Emily said nothing.

She felt nothing.

She knew of course that it was a reason for hope, but she had none. She knew too that Jean was expecting thanks, but she could not give it. She had nothing left and nothing to impart. She stayed silent, and waited for him to disappear back into the world in which he still existed and she never could. Jean however, seemed equally unable to speak. He hovered by the door waiting, young and uncertain as she was, despite his manly frame. Running his hand up and down the door he seemed to be considering something, wrestling with it, and then finally, slowly, he raised his gaze from the brown-stained floor to her bloodstained eyes. 'I am sorry for you Emilienne,' he confided in a whisper.

Emily didn't respond. What did he want from her?

'I didn't have a choice,' Jean continued, but then abruptly he stopped. Because suddenly, Emily realised what he was after, and she found her voice.

It began with a laugh. An unsmiling cackle that hurt her throat and made her jaw click. For the first time in weeks there was something where there had been nothing. She could even name the feeling. As Jean stood there before her, a spear tied to his back, the keys to her prison in his hands, it grew stronger and stronger, and Emily realised that she hated him, and all those like him, with every ounce of strength that she had. And somehow it invigorated her spirit.

Standing up sharply, she stopped laughing. It was not possible for her to stand straight but she raised herself up as much as she could and held her head high. 'You had a choice,' she said firmly, channelling the boldness of her mother. 'It was I who had no choice. I still have no choice.'

'But I tried to save you.' His angular jaw pulsated. 'You are still alive.'

'I would rather be dead,' she spat at him. 'Living is not eating and breathing. You have stolen from me what life really is. You still have your mother and your father and your family. What do I have? What can I ever have now?'

Shaking his head as if to block out her words Jean moved closer, his eyes were dark, desperate, un-winking, his jaw quivering, a bead of sweat on his temple, but when he reached out a hand to soothe her she raised her own and he stopped in his tracks.

'Don't you see Emilienne, they made us do it?' he pleaded. 'I am a victim too.'

'No!' she yelled at him. 'You are not a victim! You are a murderer! Get away from me!'

And now, stunned, hurt, as though it was he who had been hit by a machete, Jean backed away.

Emily couldn't stop. Rage possessed her and held her up. 'You will be punished one day for this!' she screamed as he hurried to close the door to her cell. 'You will not be forgiven for what you've done! I will never forgive you!'

'Never. I will never forgive, never, never,' Emily muttered, oblivious to Lynn who was stroking her trembling hands. The clock on the mantelpiece chimed and slowly, fuzzily, Emily became aware of her surroundings. Somehow, her tea had found its way in safety onto the table and the curtains

346

had been drawn. It was late. Lynn leaned over to the coffee table and handed Emily her water, wincing as she did so.

'Oh no. You're in pain.' Emily noticed, the responsibilities of her present rushing back to her. 'I haven't been caring for you. You haven't had lunch. I'm sorry.'

'Don't be ridiculous,' Lynn responded. 'It's nothing. I'm not in pain. Not really. And it's quite plain to see that I don't *want* looking after. I would much rather look after somebody else than myself, exactly as you desire too.'

'Yes,' Emily admitted, amazed at how insightful Lynn seemed over and again to be. 'It's easier.'

'But it can't be avoided forever. There are consequences.' Lynn paused. She put her hand over her side and breathed deeply. 'I should have gone to the hospital months earlier. I knew there was something wrong.' She paused again and looked hard at Emily. 'You'll run a bath for me.'

Grateful, Emily nodded, took a deep breath of her own and stood up. She was still a little dizzy. When she tried to lift the tea tray her arms were heavy and as she moved towards the door her legs trembled beneath her, as though she'd been running all day. It was good however to have a task.

'You will have to forgive of course,' Lynn called after her as she reached the edge of the room.

Emily span around, the last of the biscuits flying off their plate.

'Haven't you been listening?' she heard herself yelling in a sudden wild fury she hadn't contemplated or intended for Lynn, and would surely get her fired. 'They killed my family. They killed thousands and thousands of people. They hacked my brothers to death. They destroyed me, my whole life. He betrayed me. They betrayed us. I will never forgive them.'

'Well you can't move on until you do,' Lynn observed calmly. 'It's what's trapping you in the past Emily. Your hate. Your mind is still locked in that cell.'

CHAPTER 28

Lynn lay flat in her freshly changed bed and let the tears roll freely from the corners of her eyes and down her cheeks, where they gathered in a pool of hot liquid in the crevice of her left ear. Occasionally a particularly distressing particle of a thought swam into the foreground of her musings and her face contracted in silent spasm, but the rest of the time she lay quite calmly as the sadness flowed from within her. A few feet away, in the spare room that Lynn's mother a lifetime ago used sometimes to stay in, Emily wept in more violent bursts, but just as silently. An hour earlier she had helped Lynn into bed though they hadn't spoken since the incident in the sitting room the previous day. The two of them had passed the time since then in quiet acknowledgement of the other's presence: Lynn nodding her head when Emily brought her her breakfast, Emily closing the door quietly in understanding of Lynn's morning headaches and a while later bringing her up the *Sunday Times*. Later Lynn had managed to make her way downstairs and switched on the TV to alert Emily to her presence, leaving the door open to convey to Emily that she was welcome to come in. And eventually, Emily had come in and sat silently, both of them taking breaths to start sentences and then never voicing them. But this friction wasn't the cause of Lynn's night-time tears, neither was the force of Emily's story. The tears were in memory of another night like this long ago when Philip still shared a bed with her, in recollection of how she'd sobbed then with the same frustration and bitterness, and because, because of Emily, she was finally letting it go.

The boys had both been teenagers. Luke, she remembered, had just taken the last of his GCSEs and John had been given a lead role in the school play, a production of Romeo and Juliet in which he was to play Mercutio. Philip had taken them all out to dinner to celebrate both feats. Only during dessert did he announce his own news: after more than fifteen years at his law firm he'd finally been made a senior partner. As a bonus, he'd been given an extra week's holiday, and, he informed them, they were going to spend it abroad. With the exception of a short trip to the South of France three years earlier, and the week they took skiing in Switzerland every January, in the years that they'd been married Lynn and Philip's dreams of exploring the continent had somehow been replaced by trips down to Cornwall, that could be fitted in last minute around unpredictable cases.

The prospect of a real, summertime holiday abroad was thrilling. She suggested Italy.

That night, she and Philip made gentle love, as they still did with reassuring frequency and afterwards, when he fit his familiar shape around hers as they lay down to sleep, her head was filled with the countless things she had to be thankful for: two successful sons, a loving husband, an upcoming holiday, health, financial comfort, God's love. It was the rare kind of day in which everything had gone better than expected and she felt she'd caught a glimpse of heaven on earth, her heart brimming with total peace. And then, without warning, she started to cry.

It had been an unpleasant shock to discover that she was unhappy in the midst of such apparent happiness. But there was suddenly a deep wrenching in the darkest regions of her soul that could not be mistaken for mere melancholy, or too many glasses of red wine, or a hormonal punch. It was instead a profound sadness, and though perhaps most stark in its juxtaposition to the euphoria of the day, Lynn recognised immediately that it was neither cursory nor something that had appeared from nowhere as it seemed. The happiness of that day, of her whole life she realised, stemmed from forces uncontrolled and uncontrollable by her. Because she had achieved nothing for herself. She had no career, she had written no treatise, her entire contribution to society had been the production of two sons – something she could have done a century earlier and seemed barely an accomplishment at all. Yet at every turn she was trapped by her own confusions, the dichotomy that ever since meeting Philip had resided within her soul: a longing to escape the confines of the domestic life she hadn't meant to choose, and the urge to fiercely protect it. Realistically, she hated being away from Philip and the boys, so she could never be the type of woman who flounced around the world, but, thus, she was trapped. She loved her life and also despised it. Yet she couldn't change it without destroying the very elements she most cherished.

Throughout that night, the constant evasion of a solution haunted her. The more her mind tossed around these circular arguments, the more powerless she felt, and the more desperate. And this angered her too. Looking down on herself – a slim, pampered white woman weeping silently in bed while her wonderful husband lay next to her in their beautiful home, while others starved and suffered real problems – she felt a repulsion for the egocentric obsessions of her mind, but she couldn't stop them. And this made her feel more incapable still, more pitiful and more disgusting. As it grew harder to subdue her whimpers she slipped from bed and sat staring into the mirror of the cool, marble bathroom. The tears staining her red face revolted her. She dabbed at them angrily and muttered to herself to pull things together, hoping desperately that Philip would not hear her. That would be the final shame. She couldn't bear the thought of having to explain it to him, of having him think that he and the life he'd provided for her weren't enough to make her happy. They should have been, she knew they should have been, yet she couldn't help longing for something more, something for herself.

For three nights, this silent weeping was repeated, leaving her haggard and tired in the mornings and finally making her so ill that she had to stay in bed and let Philip call for the doctor, to whom she pretended she had a cold.

At some point, perhaps days or weeks later, and typically without a defining moment or decision, she managed to calm herself. Gradually, she was able to lock away the pain she'd been harbouring, to dull her selfish desires, and tie her happiness once more to Philip and her sons and the ups and downs of their lives, to paint her face with happiness. To layer it over the dark creases of bitterness and regret.

Lying alone now, feeling the creases of her face, Lynn realised that this was what she had been carrying openly again of late, with all the scabs and ugly symptoms of the poison exploding out of her. It was an angry, venomous emotion and she'd been levelling it at everyone. Vera the most because, as Emily had so quickly seen, she was so much like herself.

Then however, there came Emily.

Lynn had not realised at first how powerful an encounter this would be, but getting to know Emily over the past months had fuelled Lynn's sense of purpose. Her sense of doing. Acting. Like Emily's mother had done. Real action. Real sacrifice. So she wouldn't have another 20-odd years; she had had 58 good ones. It had been 15 years since Philip. There had been time. It was time. If only she could last long enough to see it through . . .

As the pain in her side forced Lynn to roll from her back into a foetal position, she rallied herself. She had things to do, things to last for. As if in disagreement, her body gave way to another thrust of silent spasms, and a new pool of water collected on her pillow. Lynn allowed the tears to streak down her cheeks without wiping them, she allowed the self-pity, she allowed one final glance back. She knew however that in the morning she would get Emily to change the sheets, and then she would discard them, along with the last remains of all her bitterness and doubt.

CHAPTER 29

By the time Emily entered with her breakfast, Lynn was already awake and sitting up in bed with the telephone and a notepad on her lap. Immediately Emily was suspicious. She carried the tray of tea and toast and the vanilla yoghurt Lynn favoured carefully to the bed, laying it gently on top of the covers before shaking Lynn's medication from the six different bottles arranged in height order on her nightstand, and handing it to her with a glass of water that was already standing waiting.

'I have something for you,' Lynn announced, taking the pills into her cupped hand and breaking the silence that had engulfed them over the past day.

Emily raised her eyes and the older woman triumphantly tore a page from her notepad and held it towards Emily. In beautiful, artistic script a name had been scrawled across the top of the page and underneath it was an address and a phone number. 'Gensur?' Emily read tentatively. 'Who is he?'

'It,' Lynn corrected, with difficulty dropping the pills into her mouth one at a time, concentrating hard on swallowing. 'Not a person, a

355

charity. GENSUR, Genocide Survivors.' She paused, but the explanation meant nothing to Emily. 'For people like you Emily, for survivors of the genocide in Rwanda. I have a friend who used to work for the government, we were at university together, I've been on the phone all morning tracking her down and . . . anyway, she gave me the number. She said they're wonderful. That they'll help.'

'Help with what?' Emily ventured, holding the piece of paper at arm's length from her body.

'Help you to work through what happened. Help you move on.'

'I don't need help,' Emily retorted, her hands shaking. 'I'm fine. You are the one who is sick. Is there something *you* need?'

Lynn however no longer seemed willing to trade provocations. 'You are too proud,' she said earnestly.

'I'm not. I have no pride left at all.'

Lynn exhaled and laid her head back onto her pillow. She looked small, frail, beaten, her pale skin and soft hair lost in the vast folds of the pillow.

'Please go,' she said, more gently now and without lifting her head. 'To GENSUR. For me. As a favour to me.' She closed her eyes. The jubilation of moments before was gone. 'Please. Let me do this one thing.'

'Are you feeling ill Mrs Hunter?' Emily asked, this time meaning the question. She moved closer to the bed and felt her forehead. 'You're cold, and clammy.'

'Will you go?'

'Not – It's just—'

'Please.'

Suddenly, Lynn's insistence irritated Emily. Why should the old woman care what she did? Why did it matter? Emily wasn't used to mattering anymore to anyone. Nor did she want to.

'Leave me alone,' she muttered.

'Please,' Lynn urged again, this time opening her eyes and casting them at Emily. Her will shone through them, unassailable, despite age, despite infirmity.

And despite her exasperation, Emily heard herself agreeing.

This time, Lynn exhaled with relief. 'Good,' she breathed now in short, strained bursts. 'Go this afternoon. Straight after lunch. Luke will be back today.' Emily opened her mouth to protest but as usual Lynn's directions were not up for debate. 'You'll spend Christmas with us,' she continued. 'You'll stay here. I'll see you tomorrow.'

Emily couldn't help but smile at the woman's audacity. Even in her illness she was in complete command of herself and of everyone before her. She was so calm, so assured, so wise it seemed. She possessed such poise.

'Pass me those papers. From that top drawer. Before you go,' Lynn added, waving her pen like a wand towards a chest of drawers, as though she could conjure what she wanted.

Emily found them wrapped within a silk yellow headscarf. For a protracted moment she fingered the sunshine silk between her fingers, a memory of heat rattling somewhere deep inside her, then she brought the papers to Lynn. As she carried the thin stack she couldn't help but notice the heading on the first page. 'The last will and testament of Lynn Rebecca Hunter,' it read. Without meaning to, Emily frowned, then felt Lynn's eyes upon her.

'Don't worry. I'm not going anywhere yet,' Lynn scolded as Emily hesitated with the papers. 'I'll see you tomorrow. You'll tell me about GENSUR. Oh—' she stopped and nodded back towards the chest of drawers. 'And quite plainly, that headscarf must be yours.'

On the bus, Emily stared at the piece of paper in her hand for a long time. It had been many months since she'd heard a Rwandan voice, and even then it had been the Anglicised tones of Auntie and Uncle, who hadn't been there. She didn't know if she was ready to look into the eyes of another survivor, who would understand without words what her history entailed.

When Auntie had appeared in the refugee camp a year after the worst of the killings were over, and explained that she'd seen Emily's face on BBC coverage of the camps, her greatest gift hadn't been the promise to take her back to London; it had been the innocence in her eyes. She was a generation older than Emily and had seen things that Emily couldn't then imagine, but she had not seen her mother being bludgeoned to death, nor Cassien's severed head buzzing with flies. Unlike the people in the camp, Auntie's eyes didn't remind Emily of piles of dismembered limbs, or burning spires, or the smell of death.

By then, it seemed a lifetime ago that she'd given up hope: of Gahiji still being alive, of him finding her, of ever returning to her village where in any case if her house was still standing and if Hutus were not occupying it, she would have to live next to Ernest who might come one night to finish the job he had started. She lived day-by-day, pressed forward only by need: to feed herself, to avoid the still-roaming Interahamwe gangs who sporadically terrified the camps, to satisfy the anger that kept her alive. The future was behind her, and there was nothing to live for beyond the defiance of living itself.

Until suddenly, through the tents and pain and starvation, Auntie appeared. And all at once, there was an alternative. Not to be happy, that was a feeling long abandoned, but perhaps in another country, it might be possible to forget. She did not hesitate in agreeing to leave Rwanda.

Emily fingered the corner of the piece of paper and recalled Lynn's jubilant face on handing it to her. She folded it, then unfolded it, and folded it again.

On the steps to the GENSUR office leant a middle-aged woman, unmistakably Rwandan. She'd spotted

Emily on the other side of the road where she'd been standing frozen and staring at the building for the past half an hour. But the denim-clad woman did not wave or usher her over, instead she lit a cigarette and waited for Emily to take her own time. Another 10 full minutes later, Emily finally crossed the busy divide.

The woman welcomed her as though they'd made a pre-arranged appointment and led Emily inside. 'You'll be wanting to see Alice,' she informed her. They walked in step through the corridor and Emily allowed herself to be guided into a small office where another, younger woman was sitting behind a desk. On the walls, Emily noticed photographs of other Rwandans, some wearing traditional dress and standing within Rwandan villages, others clothed in suits and ties in front of London buildings, proudly shaking somebody's hand or holding a document in front of them. The woman who had led her inside waited while Emily examined the images, then smiled broadly.

'This is Alice,' she informed her, signalling to the desk-seated woman. 'I'm Gloria. We are both here full-time. Alice moved to London just three years ago. I've been here since Before. My family though, they were in Rwanda.' Gloria extended her hand and not knowing why, Emily took it. 'You can come here as often as you like.'

Gloria left and Emily hovered unanchored in front of the desk until Alice signalled for her to sit down. She did so slowly.

'Can I take some details?' Alice asked gently, sensing Emily's unease. Her voice was soft and melodic, and she posed the question as a genuine inquiry, possessed with understanding of how great a request this was.

Emily nodded.

'Your name?'

'Emily. Emilienne.'

At this correction, Alice switched to Kinyarwanda.

'What is your address?' Even in another language Alice's voice held its soothing tone, but the transition shook Emily. She lifted her hand to her fringe and patted it carefully down.

'Hendon,' was the most she was able to volunteer.

'What street?'

With trepidation Emily provided the name of it, then her building, her flat number, the name of the village where she had lived in Rwanda, and the names of her parents and each of her brothers, and the number of years she had lived in London, and confirmation that she was Tutsi. The words fell from her like teardrops, the first few slowly and one at a time, the rest in a fast flood. Names and numbers. Her head felt light and a little dizzy. A lot dizzy.

Alice looked up from the notes she was diligently taking. 'Gahiji, I know a Gahiji,' she mused quietly. 'He was with the rebel army during the genocide.'

'Oh,' said Emily. Her head was throbbing and

361

she was finding it hard to concentrate. More and more often these headaches were coming. She rubbed her fingers across her temple.

'Are you alright?' asked Alice.

'It's just a headache. They make me woozy.'

Alice made a note on her pad.

'Do you experience this a lot Emilienne? These headaches? This dizziness?'

Emily narrowed her eyes but didn't answer. She didn't like such intrusive questions, and Alice's understanding of this seemed to have disappeared.

'Emilienne,' Alice pressed on. 'Were you raped in Rwanda?'

Emily stood up. 'What?' Her chair shot a few feet backwards. 'How dare you? How dare you ask me that?' she attempted to shout, though her head was pounding so intensely now that she could barely manage a whisper. 'How dare you?' She backed away from the desk and felt the door against her back. She found the handle.

'Emilienne, I didn't mean to upset you,' soothed Alice. 'It's only, you see sometimes headaches like these are an indication of . . . But we don't have to talk about it now. Please, sit back down.'

But Emily could not sit back down. Her head hurt. She smelled her mother's cooking, and her head hurt. She heard the words of the rosary, and her head hurt. She felt her face hitting hard, evening soil. Lynn had been wrong. Laying it out did not rid her of the memories, or neutralise them. Her head hurt. And her heart hurt. And everything span. She felt nauseous. *Forgive*, Lynn had said, but how could she?

'How dare you?' she asked again, louder.

'Emilienne,' Alice urged.

But now Emily had turned, and was running again.

Outside her block of flats, a gang of young boys kicked a football to each other and showed off their various tricks. One of them, a lanky lad who stood head and shoulders over the rest, could throw the ball into the air and catch it on the back of his neck. Another could bounce it between his knees and feet seemingly indefinitely. A girl about their age with blonde hair scraped into a ponytail was standing just to the side, and it was for her that they jibed each other and let out ever louder and bawdy shouts. Not far behind them, Omar leant against a wall. He was conducting a deep conversation with someone at the other end of his mobile phone.

Emily swallowed hard. Lately, she and her neighbour had meandered well past hello into musings about the cold weather, crazed Christmas shoppers, and about her job and his family who seemed to call him on his mobile incessantly, breaking their increasingly comfortable flow. They never talked about *his* job or *her* family, but there was an obvious absence of both and so she supposed, no need. When, on occasion, there was the kind of pause in which one of these subjects was required, Emily scurried away on the tail of some excuse. But every time, she hoped this wouldn't happen, that their conversations might stretch a little longer, a little deeper than they did.

Sometimes, as she listened to him proudly describe how his brother would soon be returning from university – his brother who was studying law he always added – and how he himself was thinking about going away, Emily imagined Omar's arms around her. She had never thought this way about a man. Deliberately, she wondered if she could kiss him, and forced herself to envisage it, but always this was a step too far. The thought of skin on skin triggered, still, a physical reaction and shot pain and sickness throughout her body. But when their fingers brushed on the handles of doors, she felt a shiver of unfamiliar excitement rush through her. When he called her *sister*, her heart pounded a little bit faster. And for some reason, she hadn't thrown away the piece of paper with a list of books he had suggested she read. Although she had no intention of reading anything about the concept of god, even a foreign one called Allah, whose followers, it was said, were the only ones in Rwanda not to join in with the madness when it overtook other holy men.

Emily crossed the street and walked with her head down towards the stairwell. Omar called out to her, but she didn't turn. The past bubbled beneath her skin. Tears and rage and desolation pumped dangerously in her veins and she knew that faced with his kindness, she would not be able to stifle the hot flood of images. She reached for the stairwell door, but too quickly, he was in front of it.

'You're crying,' Omar remarked immediately. Emily wiped her face roughly with her sleeve. 'What's wrong?'

'Nothing,' she rushed, mortified.

'What's wrong?'

Emily shook her head but words refused to come. Her veins throbbed. Frustration gripped her. She'd been feeling so much better lately, so much more of this world, but now all at once she was stuck again, cut up and made un-whole.

'What's wrong sister?' Omar repeated with urgency.

'Nothing.' She paused. 'Nothing. Leave me alone.' She said it firmly, but could not move from in front of him, and Omar hesitated for only a second. Then he opened his arms and brought her close.

The unexpected warmth of his body enveloped her and she sank into his chest. Her legs were heavy and useless, but Omar effortlessly held her up. It had been so many years since she'd been hugged, since she'd been touched, it was so soothing, so tempting to let herself be comforted by him. But then her mind clouded with visions of other male arms and bodies, and evening soil, and suddenly she had to get away. She couldn't breathe. With force, she wriggled free.

'What's wrong?' Omar asked again.

'I can't—' Emily whispered.

'Can't what? Sister, you don't have to be afraid of me.' Omar lifted his hand to stroke her face. 'You can trust me.'

'I can't trust anyone.'

Bewildered, Omar stared at her and said nothing, then abruptly, the spinning in her head grew faster, her legs buckled, and he caught her again.

Drinking sugary tea, they sat in his small flat, which she discovered was an exact replica of her own, save for the fact that his was piled high with boxes it seemed he had still not unpacked. Emily shook. Omar placed a blanket over her but the frostiness was not in her bones. Her heart felt frozen. Iced over she supposed, to keep hotter things out.

Taking another sip of her tea, Emily inspected this new, curious state. She was not on the verge of tears, she did not feel sad, or fearful, or angry. Instead, quite abruptly, she felt no emotion at all. She liked this. It was a useful transition. An English barrier of ice. Omar put his arm around her, but it felt dead and too hot.

'Don't touch me,' Emily said.

'I'm only trying to help.'

Omar pulled back. Letting his arm fall his eyes betrayed a concern that days earlier would have quickened Emily's step and consumed her. But suddenly everything about Omar's presence frustrated her. It lit a flame and drew her back towards feeling.

'Don't touch me,' she repeated. 'I don't need help.'

Omar shifted so that their sides no longer touched. They didn't look at each other.

'Your brother will be arriving soon?' Emily asked in a conciliatory tone, though even she could hear the coldness in it.

'No, not anymore. He's going to New York,' Omar replied, unable to hide the disappointment from his face, nor the pride that followed it. 'On a scholarship.'

'Oh?' said Emily, but by now Omar had refocused.

'Allah can help you,' he offered carefully.

Emily spun towards him.

'Allah?' She was calm, but her eyes were severe. 'Who the fuck is Allah to me?'

Now it was Omar who pulled back. 'You're not a sister?'

'God is a fairytale for children,' she answered coolly. 'You are naïve Omar. There is no god. There is only humanity, and the devil, which is the same thing. We destroy ourselves in the name of some greater order.'

'You're not a sister?' Omar repeated, stunned.

'I am nobody's sister. Not anymore.' Her voice was flat and listless. 'I am nothing.' She stood up. The blanket fell from her. 'And I want nothing, except to be left alone.'

* * *

His door slammed twice: once when she left the flat and then again moments later. She heard it from her bed where she had fallen on entering her own dark cave. She heard his footsteps on the stairs, moving away. She heard him and the hope of him disappearing from her grasp. But it didn't stir her. Nothing did.

For two days, Emily slept.

PART III

CHAPTER 30

Vera's father picks her up from the station in his new Honda saloon. She misses, suddenly, the old, rickety jeep, and the sheepdog who was once the main occupier of its back seat. As her father approaches across the station yard, she misses too the sight of his moustache, which she notices has disappeared from its perch above his lip. She misses feeling entitled to tell him how naked his face looks now, how silly. But he greets her as he always has, as though it hasn't been months since they've last spoken, years since she's spoken truth. And when she bursts into tears, he wraps her in his arms.

The 20 minute journey to the house is familiar, though a few new shops have opened since she was here last and a row of houses have sprung up next to the Pitman farm. Somehow, the refuge of childhood places, the sanctuary of countryside space makes Vera tearful all over again. Against the back-lit sights of her youth, the darkness inside of her feels darker, the heaviness heavier. She does not know if she is coming home, or still running away. It has been three days since Venice.

In Vera's old room, her mother has replaced her single bed with a double that she's made up with new linen, positioned a bowl of tangerines on her night stand, and somehow managed to unearth the stocking Vera used to hang by the fireplace, now lain out ready for her on the bed.

'I made the spare room up too,' Vera's mother winks as she begins to unpack. 'In case Luke manages to make it down for a night. I'd like to meet him, before the wedding.'

'I don't think it'll happen, Mum,' Vera replies.

'Oh well,' her mother smiles, squeezing her tentatively on the arm. 'More mince pies for us then.'

It isn't until Christmas Eve that Vera initiates real conversation. Both her parents have been tiptoeing carefully around safe topics, and even after two days they have not strayed far past what her cousins are up to, the state of her mother's garden, and the weather. Vera is both grateful and saddened by their efforts. They should not have to feel so very thankful to have her home. They should not feel her presence with them to be so fragile. They should feel confident to demand the truth, the hard, breakable things. That is what she is here for.

She edges open the door to the living room and pads in slippered feet to the piano. The old mahogany instrument reminds her of the tunes of her childhood, and she lowers herself onto the leather stool gingerly. Her father looks up from his *New Scientist* magazine and nods approvingly at her hands caressing the keys. Her mother lowers the volume of the television, bursting with kitsch Christmas specials that somehow this year strike Vera with their brassiness. Vera allows her right hand to play a gentle scale, an exercise of preparation, then she closes the piano lid.

'I need to tell you both something,' she says.

Immediately the television goes off and her father's magazine is dog-eared. Again, Vera feels ashamed by her parents' eagerness to accommodate. 'We've been hoping you'd, well, maybe want to talk to us. Is everything alright with Luke?' her mother asks, but Vera's father flashes a warning look: *don't ruin it*, he is saying, *don't pry, don't risk making her stop*. 'Since you've come home, I mean, since you're here . . .'

'It's okay, Mum,' Vera says, and she takes a long, audible breath, filling her lungs, replenishing her courage. Her parents wait patiently, respectful of the pause, of the breath, of the world tipping. And when she exhales, even before she utters a word into the painful space between them, it is as though the dark heaviness is rushing out of her, the countryside infusing her instead with fresh, free air, un-riled by city clamouring. The truth, it turns out, when allowed, dances on the tiniest breeze.

'*The truth*,' says Charlie, 'Is that you don't have a leg to stand on. I'm the father. I've been there since the second I found out he existed. I *wanted* to be. You on the other hand left him for dead on a doorstep.'

'Not for dead, for a better life,' she protests.

'And you placed him into better arms did you? Made sure of better parents? Watched him take his next better bottle? Vera, you thought he was dead.'

'I wished he wasn't.'

'It's irrelevant.' Charlie gets up and opens the door for her. He has been persuaded to let her in by a short dress and contrite, fluttering eyelashes, but has not taken kindly to her suggestion of friendship, shared parenting, separate relationships, hers with Luke. Not that she has run any of this past Luke. Nor does she intend to until she knows for sure that she will be able to see her son. In Venice, the very mention of Charlie sent Luke reeling, so she knows that proposing they share their lives with his offspring, and hence with him, may be just too much. It probably will be too much. In any case, she and Luke haven't spoken since she left Italy without him. She wonders if he knocked on her bedroom door for a long time before stepping into its emptiness. She wonders if, when he found her gone, he was surprised, or regretful, or perhaps relieved. She wonders if what happened in the bathroom was indeed a well-meant test, or Luke's own wobble, or the beginning of the end. She knows that it may already be over. But the thought of this pains Vera deeply and she will not believe it is so. Despite frothy, foamy memories, the idea of a future without Luke in it makes her heart squeeze itself against her chest and her lungs feel taut again, the way they were for so long before that deep, tearful breath at St George's. Without him, even as briefly as it's been, time has started to slow again, to muddle, to pause. And the hands on her shoulders have become lighter, less apparent. She should not have shrugged them off so hastily. She does not want to lose that clarity. She does not want to lose Luke. She should, perhaps, have walked through the bathroom door. But she cannot again lose her son. And so she is here.

'Look Vera, the second you declare yourself his mother, the authorities will be after you,' Charlie continues. 'And you'll end up in jail. Is that what you want?'

'How is it any different if you and I are together then?'

'Because you'll be there as my partner. Nobody ever needs know there are real, biological ties between you and him.'

'Not even Charles?'

'Well, I guess – well he'll think that anyway, won't he?'

Vera remains where she is seated on the sofa and Charlie sighs by the door, reluctantly closing it.

'Look, I'm sorry V, but that's the only way I'm having it. If you want something else, you'll have to take it to the authorities. And you better do it quick 'cos my lawyer's confident I'll have him by the end of January.'

'Why?'

'What do you mean why?'

'Why? Why?' Vera hears her voice rising but cannot stop it. 'Why do you have to tie me to you? Is it punishment? Do you want to punish me? Here, punish me!' She begins tearing at her hair, a wild tugging that yields a handful of blonde strands before she stops, aghast at her own fragility.

For a moment Charlie stares at her in silence, then he sinks down into a crouching position on the floor. There is a small Christmas tree in the corner next to him, and a box of newly-bought decorations. She can see that one of them bears their son's name. 'I don't want to punish you,' Charlie says finally. 'It was both of our responsibility. I know that.'

'Then why—'

'Because you should be with me, alright?' he shouts suddenly. 'Wasn't that the plan? Ultimately? Some virgin messiah arrives and bowls you over and you just drop out?'

'Out?'

'Of my life. Wasn't the plan that we'd end up together, eventually?'

Vera furrows her eyebrows. 'It's not a plan you ever shared with me.'

'Yes, okay, I know that. But I'm sharing it now.'

Vera pauses. 'But I love Luke.'

The simple words resonate for a moment around them and they are locked in unfamiliar silence.

It occurs to Vera that in all the years they have known each other, there has never really been silence between them. Never quiet, always noise. She breathes awkwardly into the taut air, then Charlie stands up. 'Then, goodbye Vera.' His voice is soft but firm, and he does not look at her. 'I can't do it your way.'

'I just want to see him. I just want to know him,' Vera pleads.

But Charlie shakes his head. 'He'll be here in an hour,' he says. 'You need to go.'

'He's coming here?' Vera whispers this as though a holy secret.

'He's *been* coming here,' Charlie responds, just as solemnly. 'I'm serious about him V.'

Slowly, Charlie reopens the door and motions towards it. He waits, keeping his glance fixedly towards the door, but when seconds pass and Vera still doesn't move he claps his hand hard against the wall, then takes a deep, steadying breath and finally looks her in the eye. 'The chaperone will be with him. She's asked about you. Don't make me angry Vera.'

From behind a post box, Vera watches Charles arrive. He skips out of the car cheerfully and holds his chaperone's hand as they walk together up the path towards Charlie's door. A backpack much too big for his small body is slung over his arm and he is holding a piece of paper that even from her hide-out, Vera can tell is a Christmas card covered in glitter and glue. Standing on the door-step he asks to be allowed to be the one to press the bell. He has the confidence of his father. When Charlie opens the door, he shrinks back ever so slightly, but then beams under the manly ruffle of his hair, lets go of his chaperone's hand, and reaches up, to be lifted up. Vera thinks she can see him mouth the word 'Dad'.

'But as much as he's the dad, you're his mum,' says Vera's mother.

'Why didn't you tell us?' asks her father. 'We would have helped.'

'You're a mother,' her mother declares again, her hand never leaving her chest.

Her father stands up. 'That whole time you were pregnant. And that whole time you thought he was dead. And these past months when – we would have helped.'

'You can't just walk away,' says her mother.

'We'll call a lawyer,' decides her father.

'But wait, Vera can't go to prison,' says her mother.

'That's what the lawyer's for.'

'And what about Luke?'

'And what about our grandson?'

'And what about our daughter?'

Now her parents notice that Vera, who is sat between them on the sofa, is weeping. And smiling as she weeps. And fingering the Scrabble board on the table. And not storming towards the door and out of the house and out of their lives. Nor asking either of them to stop.

In the afternoon the three of them take a walk crossing the same fields they used to when she was still a child. From somewhere deep inside the hall closet, her mother unearths Vera's wellies and as they hike across the fields of her childhood she fixes her gaze on them. The last time she wore this particular pair she was 19 and sharing a tent with a group of university friends at Glastonbury. Swirling ink symbols whose meaning she can no longer recall stamp across them like insistent flakes of mud. Sticky reminders of the past. In them, Vera cannot understand why she feels so light-footed. *'The Lord is near to all who call upon him, To all who call upon him in truth'*, she hears in explanation inside her head, or through the wind perhaps. Vera smiles cynically, then laughs into the wind, amused that finally, finally she has read enough of the bible for her subconscious to quote a verse back to her. *Your subconscious, or Jesus?* whispers the wind again, and Vera laughs again, this time loudly, oblivious to her parents' confused glances. She laughs, but it is not an answer, the truth has not yet freed her. She is so far from being free. If anything, having laid it all out to her parents – the facts, the problems, the inconceivable things that have passed – the longing for her son and for Luke is more intense than ever, more paralysing with the force of desire. And although there is a fresh openness between herself and her parents, and despite gargantuan efforts on their part to understand, they do not like what she has asked of them: to wait. To wait until she knows what it is she wants to do.

She does not know if this will ever be the case. If she will ever see her son, if she will be arrested if she tries to, or even if, in a few weeks time as was the plan, she will be married to Luke. *'Don't be a martyr,'* her mother cautions, as though guessing her thoughts. But Vera's overwhelming sensation is that she owes something. She owes Charles a parent. She owes Charlie a child. She owes Luke a true, baggage-free, clean-slated life. Yet these are separate, mutually exclusive obligations. They cannot be given together. And if given, they leave her with what? Christmas is a time for generosity, but she is just one person, with just one heart to break. It would be so helpful if those guiding hands would return to their shoulder perch.

Without them, Vera strides ahead. *Truth, truth,* whispers the country wind insistently. Or perhaps it is saying *Luke, Luke.* Or *move, move. Don't pause, keep moving.*

Luke calls at 3.45 on Christmas morning. 'I think it's going to happen today,' he whispers. 'Can you come?'

CHAPTER 31

When Emily woke, she was thirsty and her clothes were drenched in a cold sweat. Vaguely she remembered someone banging at her door but by the time she had dragged herself into full consciousness, and to the door, the corridor outside it was empty. Perhaps it was Omar. Standing in a pair of threadbare socks she considered venturing across the few feet that separated their flats and knocking, but even if he was there, what would she say? The iciness was still with her, unmelted by sleep. If he needed emotion, she did not have it. If he did not, then what was the point?

Emily closed the door and sat on the cushion in front of the television. Out of the corner of her eye she could see a red light blinking: her answering machine. It flashed on and off, on and off, on and off. Outside, the sun must have been fading because the small light that crept through the window into her room was growing paler and less insistent. Day to night. On and off. On and off.

At some point, Emily rose from the cushion and without a glass drank water from the tap at the sink, then without a coat or shoes, she left her flat. She wasn't cold, or rather she was unable to separate the effect of the weather from the iciness inside her, and so she didn't notice the hairs on her arms prickling or her toes turning numb. Occasionally the people she passed in the street regarded her from beneath their hats and scarves with curiosity.

Hours later she found herself outside Auntie's house. A light was on in the kitchen and Emily imagined Auntie peeling sweet potatoes, boiling rice, drying fish, preparing the foods of the place she'd decided to leave as though this mitigated her abandonment. For a time, Emily had felt angry with Auntie for not having had the courage to stay and face the dangers she herself had suffered. But later, she had turned this animosity against her own dead parents who had not been foresighted enough to take her and her brothers out of Rwanda too. The problem with the dead is that they are not around to answer indictments, and so Emily's rage had had nowhere to flow and she was always so close to snapping. Or had been. If Auntie appeared at the door now, Emily wouldn't snap at her, or blame her, or plead with her.

The curtain in the kitchen moved. Then the hall lamp lit up the space behind the door revealing a small group of silhouettes. Perhaps Auntie had seen her. Perhaps she regretted turfing her out. Perhaps she didn't. The light went off. On again. Off again.

Emily moved on. After hours she hadn't bothered to count, she lost track of where she was going or how long she'd been going for, but the sun rose while she was still in the graveyard. At this time of day the quiet of the place was liberating, and the thud of it made Emily pause. She sat on top of a stone monument undisturbed and thought about nothing. Gradually, early morning rabbits crept towards patches of grass, birds sang brazenly in nearby trees without summer foliage to hide them, and a London rat flitted deviously between graves. Beneath the soil, there were probably chrysalises waiting to hatch into caterpillars.

Emily noticed that she was hungry, but she lacked the necessary precision of thought to do anything about it. Hunger was only another empty hole to add to the dark mass inside her. In a distant part of her soul there murmured a suggestion that she had missed or forgotten something important, but this conviction was barely formed and slipped in and out of the pervading emptiness.

One by one and then in loose bunches, people began to appear on the path: People bent against the cold and scuttling to work, mothers with prams and red-faced babies in them, children padded in gloves and marshmallow coats that might tear if they climbed trees. For a while longer, Emily watched them, unmoved, but at some point she lowered her sock-clad feet back onto the frosty ground and slipped into the march of pedestrians.

Walking on, she noticed with a marked detachment that she was passing all the places she had once known intimately: her school, the grocer owned by Uncle's friend Franco, the newsagent where Auntie let her buy sweets, a string of bus stops. It was as if her legs were taking her on a tour of her life in England, recapping it, or bidding it farewell, but even this she did with indifference, uninterested in whether she paused or persisted.

It grew dark again and she was somewhere unfamiliar. She sat on the steps of a building she didn't recognise and rested her head against the stone wall, though she wasn't specifically tired. Perhaps night turned to day. Darkness. Light. Noise. Silence. On again. Off again. When she closed her eyes a red light blinked, and at the back of her mind that nagging suggestion itched uncomfortably.

Emily stood up. It was daylight and nearby a bus was pulling up to the pavement. She got on it, fishing her Oyster card out of her jeans pocket. She stared out of the window and wondered what it was that should be on her mind. Was it Omar? What was her soul suggesting? It was a great effort to force herself to think, almost as though she had to climb out from underneath a pile of dead weight to do so.

The bus stopped at a red light and Emily stared at it until it finally turned green. The colour that the Hutu Power men had waved in the street, the colour of the bandana worn by the man who'd once slapped Cassien, the colour Jean had worn, the colour of grass. She thought of these disparate things without emotion and returned her gaze to the city that trundled by.

Some indefinable time later, she found herself back in her flat, sitting again on the cushion in front of the inactive TV. A tin of corn had made its way into a bowl, topped with chickpeas and a few cherry tomatoes that she should really have thrown out days earlier. She ate the concoction slowly, taking at least a small grain of satisfaction from the feeling of fullness that began to engulf her. She supposed that it was important to eat. In fact, perhaps that was what her mind should be concentrating on: determining which aspects of her existence were truly necessary. So far, eating was the only thing that seemed obvious. If she didn't eat, she would die. If she didn't drink, this too would kill her and quicker. And she should probably not sleep on the street again, at least not during the winter. She poured herself a glass of water and pulled on a jumper. What else? Was anything else important to her survival?

It didn't matter where Emily slept, only that she did, and so she remained on the cushion and drifted again into unconsciousness.

When she woke next, the phone was ringing. The red light was still blinking and Emily moved slowly towards it, letting her body and not her mind decide whether or not to pick it up, since it was of little consequence. Her body hesitated. The answering machine kicked in. Suddenly, the urgent voice of Lynn's youngest son invaded the room.

'Angel? Are you there? Emily?' He paused. 'Emily I hope you're alright, I've been leaving you messages for days, I'm sorry to keep calling, only my mother was expecting you, well, for the last five days actually. She's not doing too well so – anyway we could do with your help if you can. And of course today is Christmas Eve and I'm no good with a turkey you see and Luke, well, anyway, I hope you're alright, I'm not really sure where you've been, the agency said they've called you already so – look, if you can come, my mother would like to see you. Oh, it's John Hunter by the way.'

Emily's body took her into the shower and stood letting the hot water beat down onto its chapped skin. Then it planted itself in front of the small wooden wardrobe and dressed in a fresh pair of jeans and a heavy jumper, before packing an old canvas bag with a few extra items including her toothbrush. For a moment, her body paused and glanced at the still-flashing red light on the answering machine, but then it turned and made for the door, traversing the stench-filled stairwell and walking directly to the flower shop a few roads away where it bought a bunch of yellow tulips, because they didn't have daffodils. Emily's body then made its way onto a bus, packed with last-minute Christmas shoppers, and it hung onto the handrail until it reached the stop close to Lynn's house. It walked without diversion down the three roads that separated it from Lynn's door and suddenly, Emily found herself on Lynn's doorstep, aware that her body had just rung the bell. It didn't matter, she told herself. It was inconsequential, whether Lynn was well or not. Whether Emily went in or didn't.

John's face flooded with relief when he saw her. 'Oh thank goodness.' He lurched forward as though he wanted to hug her but then only took her bag. 'Luke's with her now.' Her stomach tightened. 'She's not talking much. I think she might need help getting changed but I didn't know how to, or she might need to go to the bathroom I think but she's too – I didn't know if I should . . .' His voice trembled and cracked. His usually debonair demeanour seemed crumpled, like a slept-in shirt. His head dropped. 'Luke's been handling things.'

Emily put her hand gently on his arm. 'I'll see what she needs,' she said simply and turned towards the stairs.

Perhaps the flowers were heavier than she'd realised because Emily found herself climbing the steps slowly. Although Lynn's state didn't really matter, she couldn't shake the feeling of being weighed down. And although she'd prepared herself for it, and it was irrelevant, when she finally reached the woman's room, Luke's face shook her. The unmistakable eyes. Not one thing or another. Or two things at once.

He stood up when she entered. Grey and Green.

Emily dug her nails into the palms of her hands, clinging to ice.

Both of them hovered uncomfortably on either side of the bed.

Somewhere beneath the folds of the duvet lay Lynn. Her thin, white hair was sprawled across the vast pillow and the tip of a pale pink night-gown escaped the blanket that had carefully been tucked in around her, but it took Emily a long time to locate her face. Turned to the side, it could easily have been mistaken for just another fold in the ageing bedclothes, yellowed slightly, the lines that had once indicated a lifetime of smiles hanging downward now, uncertainly, like a sheet that had been accidentally made up inside out. Lynn's eyes were closed but beneath the thin lids they darted this way and that. Her lips were dry. Her arms were wrapped up in a brown, threadbare dressing gown. Her breath was shallow.

Emily looked around the room and found an empty vase that she took to the bathroom and filled with water, before arranging the yellow tulips and returning with them to Lynn's bed. Luke had sat down again and placed his hand onto the covers near where his mother lay, though remaining always just beyond the space where their bodies might touch.

'Has she been eating?' Emily asked.

Luke sat up straighter, his shoulders taut, and shook his head. 'Not for two days. Occasionally she manages a sip of water.' He pointed to the glass with a straw sticking out of it on her night-stand. It made a ring on the pad that Lynn had used to write the address of GENSUR so carefully. 'Where have you been?'

'Has she been to the toilet?'

'She's needed help.'

'Did you help her?'

'The bed smells a little.'

Emily lifted the top blanket and a putrid smell wafted out.

Luke wrinkled his nose. 'You were meant to be here,' he stated, with a sudden violence, slicing the air like a knife. 'As it's Christmas the agency had nobody else to send. And she refused to let anybody else come anyway. And she said she needed you, she needed to – I couldn't help her.'

'I'll see to the bed.'

'It could have made a difference.'

Emily began to collect the empty glasses that had accumulated in the room.

'It wasn't meant to happen so fast,' Luke kept on.

Emily put the glasses back down. She wished that he wouldn't talk with such volume and venom. She wished his eyes would close. Or would not exist at all.

'Emily,' Luke said again as though she had an answer for his anguish.

She brought her finger to her lips and shushed him firmly. 'It wasn't my fault,' she said decisively. 'I didn't do anything.'

'It's what you didn't do.' His words came in angry whispers. 'It's what you didn't do and could have.'

'I couldn't have stopped it,' Emily protested.

'But you could have helped. Her. And us. We trusted you.'

'Well you shouldn't have.' Emily noticed that her voice had suddenly risen. 'You shouldn't trust anyone.'

Luke stared at her, his two-toned eyes darkening into similarity but intense and as penetrating as ever, his strong jaw angled upwards, his hands twitching. As anger infused him he seemed to grow in front of her, and when he raised his arm Emily was certain he was going to bring it down against her head. She flinched. But then all at once, his great frame crumpled backwards into the small, unsupportive chair, and everything inside him shrank, like a hot-air balloon deflated. The escaped air whistled around the room and silenced them both.

'I – I'm sorry for you,' Emily offered after many awkward minutes had passed.

Luke looked up. 'You're sorry?' Through his desolation he grasped her apology like a piece of evidence, proof of her culpability or at least his lack of it, and it seemed to replenish him. 'Sorry? Sorry's no good. What am I supposed to do with sorry? What's John supposed to do with sorry? Sorry won't bring her back.'

'She's not gone yet,' Emily reminded him.

As though she'd been listening all along, Lynn

opened her eyes. At once, both Luke and Emily flew to the bed. Lynn's breath remained laboured but with her eyes open, much of her old poise seemed to return. Her no-nonsense gaze darted between them.

'Mother, I'm here. Are you alright? I'm here.' Luke gushed urgently.

Lynn focused on him and took another series of breaths, with each intake looking as though she might speak but never quite harnessing the puff for it.

'You're doing well,' Emily told her. 'You're looking better.'

Weakly, Lynn smiled, and Emily gulped suddenly, surprising herself. When she looked at Lynn, she saw both the old woman and her own mother, and could feel her ambivalence slipping away. She hurriedly returned to tidying the room – glasses and blankets and things that didn't matter, and Lynn shifted her eyes back towards her son. Taking a breath she opened her mouth, but again nothing came out of it.

'What is it Mother? What do you need?'

Lynn's eyes closed. Consciousness and unconsciousness danced across her face. A slow waltz that for all the death she'd witnessed, Emily had never seen. For many minutes she and Luke hovered over her not daring to move, but then all at once Lynn took a deep breath that seemed to pull on every scrap of oxygen in her body, opened her eyes again, and with barely a tremor in her voice, she spoke.

'I'm sorry I won't be at your wedding, Luke.' He shook his head and began to protest but she continued over him. 'You must look after John though, won't you? You must tell him, tell him it's okay. When he comes to you, you'll do that, won't you? And tell Vera she should use the china, all of it. Don't be precious about it. Don't lock it away. What you don't use, smash.'

'Mother, don't talk like that,' Luke interrupted, unable now to take any more and grasping her hand tight before realising how fragile it was and weakening his grip. 'John's only downstairs, you can talk to him yourself. And Vera, I'll ask her to come. May be for lunch tomorrow?'

'I should have used the teapot with the crocuses.'

Luke looked to Emily for explanation, who nodded, but did not explain. With a gigantic effort Lynn raised her free arm and patted Luke's hand. Her skin was soft, almost translucent next to her son's harder palms. 'Don't stick to all the rules Luke,' she murmured. 'Some you can break. Don't be afraid to.'

A thin coat of pain flew across Luke's strong face. He tried to hide it by painting on an even broader smile, but when Lynn asked him to leave the room so she could talk to Emily, he couldn't hide his distress any longer.

'To Emily, Mother? Not to me?' But even as she lay sinking deeper into the folds, a single glance from Lynn was enough to move him. Obediently he closed the door.

On the other side of the room, Emily continued to tidy, furiously engaged with the unimportant. But the silence-sodden seconds were heavy. She turned.

'You went?' Lynn asked her. 'To GENSUR?'

Emily nodded and without speaking began to help Lynn out of her stained nightgown and into a fresh one. She rolled her carefully onto her side and manoeuvred the bed sheet out from underneath her pale, shaking body. Then she replaced it with a clean white sheet that she found in a disordered cupboard whose jumble revealed Lynn's final attempts to care for herself in the days in which Emily had been missing. Lynn looked relieved.

'You managed to forgive?' She inquired hopefully, sinking again into the pillow that Emily had plumped behind her and trying not to wince as her failing body settled thankfully back into stillness. Emily noticed that there was a dark bruise on Lynn's arm where she must have banged it or fallen.

'I told you my story,' Emily answered. 'I laid it out. I gave it to you.'

'But that was only the beginning. You must accept it Emily. You must forgive.'

'I told you that I couldn't.'

Lynn nodded as though she understood, but her weary brow crinkled, troubled.

'I brought you flowers,' Emily said to distract her, pointing to the vase on her nightstand. 'Tulips.

I looked for daffodils but it's not the season. Still, they're yellow.'

'Like on your hills in Rwanda.'

'Yes.'

'Put them on the windowsill then so they get some sun. They won't last long in the darkness.'

Emily did as she was asked, carefully rearranging the stems over and over.

'Forgiveness breaks every moral code of the universe,' Lynn whispered as if reading her thoughts while Emily was still facing the window. Her voice had suddenly grown raspier. 'It's hard. But without it, you will miss grace.'

'Grace?' Emily turned around.

'If you forgive, the wrong loses its grip on you, because you've put it into God's hands.'

'You don't believe in God anymore,' Emily reminded her.

'I have forgiven Life, Emily. I have done it.' She said this with a proud, overwhelming smile that shot light through her creases. 'It is okay now.' She stopped. Her breath had run out. It was many minutes before she could speak again. 'Only John—' she mused slowly. Then paused. 'Promise to try Emily,' she whispered.

Instinctively Emily shook her head, but then, she realised that it didn't matter whether she promised or not. It was not a necessity. 'I promise,' she relented.

Lynn's eyes closed. 'Okay,' she murmured. 'Okay. Okay.'

Motionless, Emily watched her. Next to the bed the empty glasses still waited to be taken downstairs, on the floor the stained linen lay crumpled needing to be laundered or at least removed from sight, and it occurred to Emily that perhaps she ought to run Lynn a bath or make her some soup; but she did none of these things. There seemed no point. And so she merely watched.

Until, inexplicably, the rosary began to circle around her head. *He shall come to judge the living and the dead.* Emily shook herself.

'It doesn't matter,' she whispered to the almost empty room, pushing the familiar words back again. 'It doesn't matter. She is just one more person. Why should I care?' But now the words of the rosary crept from her mind onto her lips and she lowered herself onto the bed where, careful to avoid Lynn's frail, fragile legs she found a space that felt like a grass-woven rug and leant up onto her knees. '*Forgive us our trespasses as we forgive those who trespass against us.*' She reached for Lynn's hand. 'You shouldn't have given up,' she told her. 'You should have tried. You should have kept trying. You should have come back the next day. You shouldn't have left me with nobody and nothing.' A hot tear rolled down Emily's cheek. Melting her. Melting her. She bent her head low and placed Lynn's soft, spindly hand onto the rough edge of her scar.

Over an hour later, Emily was still in this position when John pushed open the door.

'I have to talk to my mother,' he whispered urgently.

Though much older than she, John struck her suddenly as young, or at least in every way the younger brother.

Without a word, she stood up from the bed, and straightened her fringe.

Emily just about remembered what a full house sounded like, a place with sounds you could identify without having to see, with family and familiarity. Downstairs, Luke was clattering about in the kitchen. Emily followed the noise.

'Bloody fridge,' Luke muttered when he saw her standing, watching him attempt to rearrange the shelves so that the turkey, which Lynn had organised delivery of weeks earlier, would fit inside. 'I can't find the recipe Mother uses for the stuffing, but I know that's her favourite part. And John likes cranberry sauce but I don't think we've got any cranberries. Usually I carve. Since Father died. I've got the knife.' He picked it up. 'Mother always keeps it in this drawer, but the – I don't know, do I have to put the bird in now? I don't want her to be without her turkey. I don't want to—'

He stopped. Emily had moved forward, taken the long carving knife from his hand, and in grateful surrender Luke had let her. His jaw remained fixed in a slightly raised profile but the corners of it trembled. His eyes meandered away from her but were bursting with colour. He looked so much like Jean.

Emily raised the knife to his face.

Neither of them spoke. Flashes of grass and dirt and her mother flickered before her. She could feel her heart beating fast, adrenalin shooting through her arm and fingers into the metal instrument. Her scar pulsated. Green and grey and blood red danced before her eyes.

Then Luke started to shake.

Emily paused. But she had shaken too.

Luke's hands gripped the sideboard, and the pots on top of it rattled to announce his desolation. He laughed loudly, obscenely, because there was nothing else to do, but he could not control his spasms. It was a total physical collapse, and it was mesmerising.

'Sorry. I'm being pathetic,' he mumbled apologetically, waving her away in embarrassment, and only then did Emily realise that his shuddering was not from fear, at least not of her or her sharp-edged blade. Violence was a concept that never even occurred to him. Yet he shook.

And she had shook. And was all at once shaking again. The knife waved from side to side in front of her.

'I'm sorry Emily,' Luke said suddenly, through his own trembling turmoil. 'For before. It was unfair of me. None of it's your fault at all. It's my fault.'

Emily said nothing but gripped the knife more tightly, and finally Luke noticed. He let go of the side and slowly refocused his two-toned eyes towards her, observing as he did the way her body quivered, the way her own eyes flashed, the way her nails had turned white from the force of her clasp on the sharp, deadly blade. And now, understanding crept dangerously across his brow. It seemed to compose him. He stopped shaking, his jaw clenched and he looked strong again, he widened his stance and he looked powerful. He ran a weary hand through his hair and disordered it. She'd seen him do that before. Somewhere. Her head began to throb. Her two worlds scrambled. *I didn't have a choice.* 'You did,' she said. *I tried to save you. You are still alive.* 'Not really,' she answered.

Now Luke was scrutinising her closely.

'What are you talking about?'

Her head continued to pound. Clutching the knife harder, she put her free hand to her temple and rubbed it.

Luke moved a step closer.

'None of it was your fault Emily,' he stated again, eyeing the knife. 'My mother cares for you, you know.'

'I watched her die. I watched them all die.'

'What? Who?' She shook her head but abruptly Luke reached for the hand still working on her temple. He encased her palm within his own and held it still. 'Stop Emily. I'm sorry,' he repeated. Stunned by his touch, her head beat harder. Her scar throbbed. She needed it to stop. She needed to touch it, to calm it. She needed her hands.

Weakening her grip on the knife, Emily tentatively lowered it, then finally she put it down, raising her now free hand to find her scar, but Luke was too quick. He caught her wrist and held it aloft with the other one. 'I'm sorry,' he said again, holding her still, forcing her to focus on him. 'I'm sorry.' Without speaking, the two of them held each other's gaze, remaining this way for many long seconds until finally, trapped in his grasp, unable to escape, unable to avoid him or hurt him or pretend he wasn't there, Emily let out a deep, haunting sob. 'I'm sorry,' Luke said once more and now Emily stared up into his green-grey eyes. Not one thing or another. Or two things at once. Aggression and fear. Power and regret. Love and loss. Just like Jean's, though through the film of her tears they looked almost ghostly, almost gone. She held them in her sight until they disappeared.

'I forgive you,' she sobbed finally.

And then they kissed.

Afterwards, Emily sat alone on the orange-tiled floor of the kitchen and tried to work out how it had happened.

To start with, all they had done was hold each other and let their salty tears mingle with the other tastes of their mouths. He had clung to her as if in need of comfort, and she to him, each tenderly letting their tongues explore the other's as though this was a sweet first kiss and she again an untouched child. Gently they had inhaled each other's alien smells, leaning in close, steadying their breath, considerate, anxious not to expel too much force and blow the moment away. It had seemed, almost, like a natural extension of his apology. Sorry. But there were no more words. Silence had surrounded them and it was insistent. There was no TV blaring from the lounge, none of the old music chugging out of the gramophone, and now that Luke had stopped fumbling with the turkey and she had put down the knife, there was no clattering about of cupboard doors, or friendly, familiar sounds to remind them of the ground they were leaving behind. Upstairs, John may have dragged his chair a little closer to Lynn's bed, and Lynn might have been murmuring; but they had not heard these earthly sounds or chose not to.

Instead, Luke had touched his hands to Emily's face and held her a little away from him. She may have flinched slightly, but otherwise she did not move or try to move, standing instead wilfully paralysed by him. Luke had relished her paralysis as though she was some ethereal being. He examined her closely as he went, caressed the smooth dark skin of her cheek and pushed her fringe behind her ear so that with his thumb he could trace her long, lumpy scar. He let his fingers slide into her thick hair and felt the texture so much rougher than his own. He explored her small ears, traced a curve around her earlobes, cupped her dark, bony chin in his pale hands, and with his mouth tasted her skin. He paused. He looked. And then all at once he tugged roughly at her heavy jumper, lifting it in one motion over her head so that she stood in Lynn's kitchen in just her bra and jeans, which he quickly began to unbuckle, and with that movement, their early caution was over and there was no turning back. Now they were both overcome with a powerful momentum. Emily reached for the shiny black belt of Luke's trousers and the zip beneath it. Luke's shirt was already untucked but she scrambled with urgency to unfasten the buttons, one, then another, and then ripping off those that remained. He looked up as the white circles bounced across the floor, and for a moment she thought he was going to stop. But instead, he grabbed her wrists and threw her hard against the fridge, inside which the turkey was nestled, tearing her bra from her chest with an intensity that equalled her own. She fought back. Slapping him across the face and scratching at his shoulders she pushed hard until he backed away slightly, and then she pounced on him once more, trapping his face with her hands against the cupboard and sucking hard on his lip as they kissed again.

After that, it was hard to say who had taken the lead, or followed it. Together they had descended somehow onto the floor and brawled naked, tugging, biting, craving each other's raw flesh. His lip bled. Her breasts throbbed under the strength of his fingers, and she cried out in pain. But Emily felt empowered as they battled, high on the excitement of returning his roughness, of demanding it, of controlling it. She held onto his hair. A few strands of blond came loose in her hands, his pale, stubbled face rubbing coarsely against her thighs, that angular jaw and penetrating eyes beneath her, compliant. And then, as her fingers began to unfold and she writhed against the cold floor she'd mopped so often, he yanked her over and thrust his way inside. Deep. Intense. Within her.

Strangely, this was the moment that she felt her mind floating away. Flesh collided and took time and space with it. And from nowhere, Emily thought of Omar. Luke puffed on above her and her own body continued to contract and contort in a peculiar, detached pleasure, but she was no longer there. Instead, she was in Omar's box-filled shantytown, then watching him from across the road, then noticing how enchanting his smile seemed up close, how beautiful he was. How his eyes had continued to bore into her own even once he'd learned she was not a 'sister'. Luke grunted in satisfaction, but Emily was lying on a bed while her father read to her, she was looking at yellow flowers swaying in a cool breeze from between the gaps of her mother's fingers, she was laughing as Cassien chased her through the bushes, she was waving a greeting to Gahiji whose head tilted as he opened his arms for her to dash into, she was home. A current of warmth rushed through her body. The cell had been so cold, so hard, so numbing. But she was warm now. She was balancing on the branch of a tree, and she was warm. She was in a cage where her mother refused to move, and she was warm. She was looking straight up into Jean's face.

Her eyes locked with his. Green and grey, and the brown of her own. Still she was calm. He pushed once more, then with a final spasm collapsed on top of her, his face nestled between the curves of her bare chest, her arms around him. He exhaled. Her breath matched his. There was peace.

Fleetingly.

A moment later, Luke had released her and immediately they'd moved in simultaneous haste to opposite sides of the kitchen where they scrambled to collect the various layers they'd shed without premeditation, and stole glances at each other, in need of confirmation of their equal nakedness and equal compliance and equal sin. Emily didn't feel sorry. She didn't know what she felt, only *that* she felt, she was indifferent no longer. She pulled on her jeans and watched him, a new sensation brushing delicately across her face, one that she didn't recognise but made her smile. And lifted her up. By the hairs on her arms. By the spine in her back. By the joints of her legs and the soles of her feet until she would have sworn that only air was beneath them. Outside her body, the room glowed.

Now Emily considered the sin they had committed together. It was certainly a sin. At least it was something that her brothers and the priests and her mother would have disapproved of. She had slept with a man she hardly knew, who was engaged to an unsuspecting girl she'd never met but knew about and Lynn said he loved, a man who was clearly in mourning because his mother was sick upstairs and dying. Emily considered it all. Still, she felt no guilt. She was, she supposed, still more sinned against than sinning. Shakespeare. Her father had read it to her once. It was a story about a king. About madness. Or freedom maybe. Suddenly she felt freedom bestowed upon her, without qualification and without her asking. She felt renewed. And all at once, bruised and half-dressed, she realised that she had survived.

And Emily laughed.

With her head thrown back.

Like the girls from the café by her flat who sat outside on their cigarette breaks.

Luke tucked his shirt back into his trousers and dabbed at his lip with a piece of kitchen tissue. He stared at Emily as she giggled against the cupboards, as though viewing her for the first time, and he shook his head, mumbling to himself over and over, 'Like Bathsheba.'

'What?'

Luke looked away. He seemed not to want Emily to speak, for her to remain only a body. She didn't press him. Lowering herself back down to the floor, she noticed that one of his shirt buttons had rolled underneath the fridge and she picked it up, offering it to him.

Luke took it quickly. The noise of a door opening above them had wafted down the stairs, then John's footsteps creaked on the landing.

'I don't know why – I've never – I'm engaged,' Luke rushed suddenly, his angular jaw offset and awkward. 'I love her. She'll never forgive me.' He was crying now, urgently swiping the revealing tears.

'I forgive you,' Emily said calmly, repeating the words that seemed to have started everything, and as the syllables slipped smoothly out of her mouth, the room glowed a little brighter, more like the colour of a rising Rwandan sun.

Emily slept at the foot of Lynn's bed. There no longer seemed to be a need to hide her feelings from the boys, or from herself. They were simple: she did not want Lynn to die. Her whole body was brimming with the revelation that it was after all possible for her to care and love and feel again, and she would cling to Lynn for as long as she was able. Luke couldn't look at her, but did not ask her to leave, and John seemed grateful for her presence in the room, as though her being there somehow tempered the reality, made different the memories that must have been flooding them. John was wearing the velvet waistcoat, Emily noticed. The older woman sighed through shallow breaths.

Lynn felt peaceful. She didn't open her eyes but sensed Emily at her feet, her sons at her side. Somehow, without looking, she could see them all.

The yellow tulips on the windowsill stood proud, her favourite colour, their petals pushing further open with every hour that passed, opening, blossoming, dying. Unfulfilled stems. Unless of course, being there for her had always been their destiny.

Okay, Okay, Okay.

Who was Lynn talking to? Did she know that Emily was there? Was she trying to reassure her? Or was she talking to God? Letting Him know that she was ready now, that she understood? Or maybe to her husband, whose picture, Emily noticed, Lynn had removed from the frame where it had always stood and was now lying upside down on the mattress where it had fallen from her weak hand.

Okay, Okay.

The words came less frequently and in raspier tones. Lynn's eyes didn't open. The skin around them looked bruised and tired. Her hands that had once been poised enough to paint sweeping, delicate strokes, were lifeless now, contorted strangely towards her chest. Emily reached for them and felt the iciness that had invaded Lynn's bones. Gently, she rubbed the thin skin and squeezed the fragile palms between her own. Hot now. From the far corner of the room, John wept. Luke sat stoically on the other side of the bed. She noticed the buttons missing on his shirt. His hands twitched again and again and he moved forward and back, forward and back, in and out of the sphere of his mother, though still not touching her. Perhaps it was enough for him to feel her breath, to sense the rising and falling of her chest, to imagine her arms around him.

It was almost Christmas morning. The boys would be up wanting their stockings soon. Philip would be exhausted from spending too long wrapping presents until late, but he would sit up in bed when the boys came running in with their load, and read the letter that Santa had left them written on paper he'd bought especially from an Indian shop so that it looked as though it could have come from the North Pole. A lie they told them, to make things prettier. Full of possibilities. She should get the turkey in the oven. It needed to go in before they left for church and she should peel the potatoes before she put on her good clothes. Perhaps though, she would sleep for just a few minutes more. Something was rustling at the bottom of her bed and the gentle fluttering lulled her into a state of unusual lethargy. The boys would be in soon anyway, bounding onto the bed, and they would wake her. There would still be time for the turkey, there would be time. She would sleep for just a few minutes more, another few minutes. Philip was next to her, his body was warm, it felt good to snuggle up against him. She lay her face onto his bare shoulder and wrapped her arms around his waist, breathing in his familiar scent.

★　★　★

Night fell. John and Luke took turns sleeping on the couch in the living room while the other maintained a vigil at their mother's side. Neither one would go to their childhood beds. Emily rested her forehead gently on the duvet and held on.

At 5.30 am, the doorbell woke her. Both boys were camped out again in their mother's room, but didn't stir. The tulips had turned slightly away from the window that was now swathed in darkness. Lynn was no longer breathing.

Emily stopped breathing. For a full minute, through the dark, she watched, and waited, then finally she opened her hands and let Lynn's cold fingers slip from between them.

Downstairs, the doorbell rang again. Dreamlike, rising slowly and stretching her neck from where it had been hunched too long, Emily made her way down the staircase and acknowledged the swelling pain in her throat. Somehow, the sensation of it comforted her. She reached the hard, wood floor and padded across it quietly. On the edge of the doormat at the front of the house, Emily noticed another one of Luke's shirt buttons. She stooped to pick it up before opening the door. Later, she would give it to Luke to repair. Such little things would go on, they always did. The world that morning was unbearably sad, but at least it finally felt like a reality, the pain was at least fresh, and the universe was rational again.

Then, there on the step in front of her, was a young, blonde-haired woman she realised immediately that she had seen before. Emily struggled to place her. Her blue eyes were still, but nervous, her skin was pale but for a spattering of freckles. Her wispy hair flew about behind her. And then she knew. Emily had seen this woman not in the flesh, but on a canvas. The effect had been luminous. And the luminous woman said her name was Vera.

CHAPTER 32

Lynn lays lifeless, tiny amidst the vast swathes of linen on the bed, her terrifying, smothering presence suddenly as thin as the air. Vera feels her throat tightening.

Luke and John sleep on. Slumbering, Luke looks smaller than he seemed in Venice. The memory of leaving him there induces a pang of guilt and Vera thinks of the unheeded sobs from his side of the bathroom door. She doesn't want to hear that sound again. She doesn't want to be the one to wake him. She doesn't want to steal those last remnants of a world in which he and John still have a mother. Hovering, Vera wishes the carer would return upstairs and be the one to disturb the frozen scene, but she's already heard the front door close and footsteps on the pathway, and she supposes that the girl has done enough. It is after all she, Luke's 'fiancée', who should be there.

Standing close to Luke's chair, she waits for him to feel her presence beside him, and when eventually he stirs, he doesn't catch sight of his stony-still mother but looks straight up, gratefully reaching for her hands. Vera's heart wrenches. 'You came,'

Luke whispers as his eyes focus blearily on hers. 'I'm sorry. For Venice, and for judging you, and for – I've betrayed you.'

'Luke,' she hushes.

What follows seems to wash upon them without direction. They do not go to church and not even Luke suggests it. For most of the morning they sit in the lounge in their usual places, only Lynn's seat empty. Without agreeing, nobody switches on the television, or the radio, or the Christmas tree lights that John dragged out of the attic at Lynn's request weeks earlier. Vera makes them cups of tea, wondering every now and then if she should try to baste the turkey, or peel some potatoes, or abandon all such tasks that might remind the boys of their mother. On the fridge, magnets swirl in familiar floral patterns. Vera cannot quite place why, but more than anything that day, the sight of them is toppling.

Luke doesn't cry. A bible rests on his lap and occasionally he caresses the spine or edges a finger between the pages as if to open it, but then resists, in concession Vera figures to his brother whose own tears flow freely and without ancient texts. John mops his eyes with the back of his sleeve and shakes his head over and over. It is not for her to direct, but Vera wishes that one of them would move across the room and hug the other. When they don't, she brings them more cups of tea, and after a while they begin to look up for her exits

411

and entrances, everything seeming to rest upon this, the sweet liquid a drug to soothe their pain and lull them into normality.

Although this seems to Vera to continue for eternity, at some point one of them must finally have spoken because by midday the coroner has been called and arrives. Lynn's body – wrapped in a white sheet that does little to disguise her tiny frame – is carried downstairs by her two silent sons and into the waiting vehicle. Afterwards, they stand uncomfortably next to each other in the entrance hall. John's head is lowered, the back of his neck flushed raw red. Neither one moves. Luke breathes deeply and lets out two sharp bursts of air. Still they do not touch, but finally Luke draws breath again and this time manages to speak, his words reaching John as a carefully wrapped gift.

'You made her happy,' he says, slowly. John lifts his head. 'She always said that. Especially after Dad died. And even after you moved out. I was so jealous of you being able to make her laugh so effortlessly.'

For a second, John pauses, carrying the words carefully to his heart and fingering the edge of his velvet waistcoat. Then looking earnestly at Luke, he reciprocates.

'She told me you would never let any of us down.'

This time both men's shoulders heave, and they raise their sleeves to wet faces.

*   *   *

Vera begins tidying. She carries dirty teacups and uneaten meals downstairs and washes them up in the sink, fastidious with the beautiful china. She clears the makeshift beds from the lounge and straightens the cushions. She surveys Lynn's room and wonders whether or not it is too soon to strip the bed, open the windows to let out the lingering smell, and either wash or throw away the dirty laundry that Lynn will not use again. Such truths will of course need revealing, but perhaps it is too soon. Vera finds herself staring blankly towards the window, the sun outside mocking the sobriety of the day, and she feels winded, insufficient. Minutes pass, she imagines. It might be seconds, or hours. She doesn't know what to say to Luke. It feels a sham to be strong for him, to be his support, his shoulder, when if he knew the truth of what she has done he would most likely cast her away. She is going to tell him. The truth is already in the wind. But when? Of course not now, so when? When? Before or after they marry? Before or after Charlie gets custody and moves to New York? Before or after she is arrested and jailed and finally accounts for her guilt? Before or after she decides whether to fight for Luke, or to fight for Charles. She knows she can only pick one. Vera catches a glimpse of herself in the mirror of Lynn's dresser, hunched over, paused. Paused. Paused. She is so terrified of pausing again, of letting events colour her commitment to candour. And of losing faith. She straightens herself. The low winter light has

413

crept into the room and now it bounces off Vera's ring, filling the space with colour. She is reminded of the rainbow bestowed as a symbol of promise to Noah after the flood. And she stands straighter. Then, resolutely, without allowing another moment to pass, she moves with the laundry to the chest of drawers. She will hide the stained layers, but only for now.

The drawer she opens is overflowing. Scarves, tops, tights, underwear, all of Lynn's garments together. Sadly, Vera begins to sort it, but as she makes room her fingers brush against something firm. She pulls it out. In her hands lays a heavy stack of papers tied with a single piece of string. 'The last will and testament of Lynn Rebecca Hunter', she reads on the first sheet of the pile. And then in smaller lettering beneath it: 'To be executed by my son, Luke Hunter.'

Luke sits close to John with Vera opposite. He flicks through the papers and they can see at once the back pages filled with list upon list of the belongings for whom Lynn has designated an owner: the gramophone to John, the linen to her cousin Patricia who (she had noted in the margin) many years earlier helped her select the fabric, a small silver ornament shaped like an elephant to Emily.

'Let's come back to that later,' Luke says, looking to John for a nod of consent. 'There's a letter from her on the front, to you and me John.'

Already tears are streaming down John's cheeks again. He doesn't bother to sniff, or wipe them away. Luke begins, softly.

Darlings, don't mourn for me.

He looks up and Vera smiles encouragement.

Believe me when I tell you that I am a stubborn old mule and will only have gone when I was good and ready. I wanted only a say in the matter, and this is it: I want to be sure how you will remember me. As your mother I hope. As a woman who loved you both absolutely, who packed up your lunches, tended your scrapes, and picked lice out of your hair. As the woman who, for a time, knew you better than any other and knew the world through your eyes better than she did her own. Darlings, you are the life I chose, the life I would choose over and over, and this I want you to remember. My death however, is a different matter. Once, many years before either of you were born, I was going to be a historian. Did you know that? Did I ever tell you? I was going to be a writer of historical fiction, a creator of plot. Here is a plot:

There lived for many years over two very different centuries, a woman with three gifts: her Youth, her Love, and her Wealth. The first and second gifts were made in haste and bestowed greedily upon the same recipient, but there was never a better decision than this one that took moments and the heart alone to make. Because she gave them so freely, the man who locked them away gave her a gift of his own: Life. The woman was not aware that the man had sewn this gift within the creases of her dress and for many decades she was oblivious to the joys and passions and tiny wonders that unfolded softly from it. In fact, she was oblivious to its existence at all, and when at last she noticed, the stitching around it old and frayed, the Life inside was all but gone. But still she had her Wealth. The woman looked around and wondered, since her time left was short, to whom she should offer this final gift. The man who had given her Life had also bequeathed her two sons and so her first thought was to leave it tidily with them. But then she realised that these sons were in fact what her Life comprised, and so they retained the joys and passions and tiny wonders she had not noticed, and had plenty of gifts of their own. There was however another. A girl. She was poor and from a far-off land, and possessed little. The only gift she had ever known was difficult to carry, and the name of it was long and burdensome: survival. This girl did not ask for help, or for a different gift, or even for the one she had, but the woman could see where her Wealth would be a true blessing, and she decided to leave it to her.

Luke glances up. They all remain silent. He turns the page and carries on.

There are lists that follow this my sons, and I hope I have been thorough, but here in essence is what it comes down to: Luke, I leave you your father's watch so that you will always remember that time and order are only illusions, the heart is what is real. John, I leave you the house and hope it will give you the space to be who you truly are. The key to my art room is attached. The wrapped canvas inside it, should go to Vera. My money – my stocks, shares, the bank accounts – I leave them in equal parts to you, and to Emily. Please don't argue about this, it is my death after all, and I shall do as I please.

I must say goodbye now. Emily is here and will be up soon with my lunch. Don't cry John. Luke, don't bury yourself in your bible. Do not be sad and do not stop your lives because mine has ended. Your happiness is the only thing I ask you to give me. I am happy. I am with your father now. I'm young again and every possibility is before me.

Slowly, Luke lowers the letter.

'That's it,' he says, turning the page over again to check and fighting against the tremor in his voice. 'The rest is just lists and some legal stuff. Do you want me to read it now?'

John shakes his head. 'I suppose we'll need to talk to Emily.'

'Emily . . .' Luke practically whispers the word. He glances at Vera who smiles in what she hopes is a gentle, reassuring way. A way that says, *I am here, though there is much to say.* 'I mean, she's leaving so much, to Emily?'

'She *was* an angel,' offers John.

'But—' Luke's voice falters.

Vera raises an eyebrow.

'I mean we hardly knew her.'

'Mother did,' says John.

'But she's practically a stranger. And I don't – we should just let her into our lives? Into our . . .' He trails off.

John doesn't respond but looks at him curiously, and Luke says nothing more. Vera too studies him closely. If asked, she would have gambled that he'd give his whole fortune away in a heartbeat for someone in need. It was after all the Christian thing to do. His resistance makes her wonder, again, how he will react when she tells him everything. She wonders if she will ever tell him that she wants her son back.

'Shall I call her?' John ventures finally.

'Not today, surely.'

'Perhaps we'll tell her at the funeral.'

'Do you think she'll want to come?'

'Of course,' John stands up, He looks older suddenly. Anxiously, Luke stays his arm.

'John—'

John stops and Luke pauses solemnly, as though reassessing his brother, or his own question, or his whole life. In the end he says nothing, but allows John to pat him on the shoulder, John's hand lingering for Luke's affirming tap back. Then John clutches his waistcoat tighter around himself and climbs the stairs to Lynn's room.

With John gone, Vera and Luke say nothing for a long while. It is the first time all day that the two of them have been alone and now that they are, Vera doesn't know what to say to him. In the wake of Lynn's passing it seems wrong to broach any topic other than her, wrong to mention Venice, wrong to address anything other than the sadness she can see deep in the pool of Luke's green-grey eyes. Eyes that seem to be avoiding her now, sinking low in the silence.

'Of course she should give the money to Emily,' Luke mutters finally, glancing ashamedly up at Vera and then down again.

She wants to tell him it is okay, that a moment of selfishness on the day of his mother's death is allowed. That this tiny slip is not even what she has been pondering. But they have not yet found a way to pick across the stillness. His fingers fiddle with the clips on the papers he is still holding, then he reties the string as closely as he can remember to the way his mother's fingers had positioned it. He coughs, then looks at Vera, then shrugs his shoulders and coughs again. Finally he stands and picks up the rest of the paper pile. A key falls from within it, clattering into the quiet.

'Her art room,' whispers Luke, picking it up gingerly. It seems suddenly necessary to whisper. Vera is grateful to the key for giving them something to whisper about. 'She never let us in there.'

Vera stands up tentatively. 'Shall we see?'

Together, they walk to the room facing the garden and slot the key into the lock. Both of them hesitate before pushing it open, acknowledging that this is hallowed ground. If a spectre of Lynn remains, this is where it will be. The air seems to change as they enter. Vera hangs back allowing Luke to go in first, and stepping across the threshold he inhales loudly, his reaction as stunned as Vera's was when she first saw it. His mother's talent is overwhelming, and now that Vera has time to study the room more closely, she sees that the paintings dripping colour from the walls are filled with Luke, and John, and an older man who looks like John, and other images without shape but overflowing with emotion. They are so intimate that even now Vera feels as though she is trespassing. Stepping on a grave.

In the centre of the room is the wrapped canvas. Luke nods and Vera moves towards it, pausing for just a moment before unwrapping the heavy sheet.

She cannot help but gasp when she sees herself staring back from within the frame. And not just herself, but the best, most dynamic, most vital version of herself. The version she thought nobody could see. In the bottom right hand corner, Lynn has signed the piece. And in the left is a title: 'Myself'.

Vera exhales. *Herself? She who was so good? And thought Vera so bad?* But yes, she can see Lynn in the eyes, there is something in the front-facing sweep of them. Transfixed, Vera stands staring. Then ever so gently, she feels a soft weight creeping onto her shoulders. Without thinking she lets her shoulders drop, relaxing into the warmth of returning hands. She looks behind her for Luke, but it is not him. The hands nudge her forwards. Gently, she runs her own hand over the edge of the canvas, admiring the myriad of reds that layer and define and create a thousand shades. When her fingers reach the bottom, her ring catches something wedged into the corner on the back. Vera peers around the other side of the canvas and pulls out a loose piece of paper. Luke shrugs his shoulders, so Vera unfolds it, quickly, as though caught up in a hunt for treasure. Lynn's elegant script is artwork itself, but there are just three words on the page.

Vera, it reads simply. *Have both.*

Vera freezes. Both? A coolness prickles her skin as though she is being spoken to from the grave. But it is not possible that Lynn knew about her son. Unless Luke told her? Even then she could not have known that she wants him back, or that the circumstances are such that having one – Luke or Charles – seems so much to rule out the other.

Have both. Have both. Have both. Could she? Can she? It seems so unlikely, Charlie so unmovable, a legal battle so unwinnable. Yet amidst the sadness of the day, Vera dares to hope. Dares to summon strength for the fight. She turns to Luke and sees tears building behind his eyes as he continues to stare at the canvas, his mother and his fiancée rolled with red into one. She goes to him. It doesn't matter what happened in Venice. It doesn't matter that there is much to tell, much to navigate. Suddenly nothing seems to matter except that she loves him, and trusts him to love her too, all of her, even her sins. As Jesus loves them both.

Instinctively, Luke shrugs away her extended hand, but Vera whispers,

'Don't shut me out Luke. Let me be here for you.'

'I want you to be here,' Luke replies, his voice cracking slightly. 'More than anything. But – Vera, if you knew the things I've done, you wouldn't want to be. I've, I've . . .' he trails off.

'It's not important now.'

'I committed a great sin.'

'Stop.' Vera grabs his hand again before Luke can move it away and holds it tight. 'Stop Luke. Today is about your mother. Tomorrow, tomorrow we'll swap our truths.'

Luke smiles weakly, and she nods. And suddenly he pulls her hands inwards until she moves closer to hug him properly, her heart unexpectedly skipping a beat as she feels the needy wrench of his arms, and they melt into each other. It has been so long since they embraced this way. His frame is so strong, his chest so warm. Vera wraps her arms around his waist beneath his cardigan. And wants never to let him go.

'Marry me. Marry me today,' he asks of her.

'Tell me something true,' she whispers into his ear. 'Not everything, just one true thing until morning.'

'I love you,' Luke sobs.

CHAPTER 33

There were no buses on Christmas Day and so Emily trudged the entire way from Lynn's house to her flat in Hendon, thankful for the hours it took in which to think. Her insides were twisted in two, torn between sadness and mourning and regret, and something else, something brighter that made the streets look clean and vivid, despite the weak English sun.

There was no point in sorry. It would change nothing because Emily wasn't really regretful at all, and as her mother had told her once, forgiveness only means anything if you are truly full of remorse. She was sorry for Vera of course, and had she met Luke's fiancée earlier then perhaps she would have chosen differently, especially now she knew how much she must mean to Lynn. But the moment with Luke had transpired so rapidly she wasn't certain she had chosen it at all. It had seemed more like a necessity, in order to forgive Luke, or rather Jean, and the others like him. Had she managed it? She tested the words in her head: Hutu; uncle; neighbour; friend. No longer numb she felt the full clout of them, but the usual panic seemed to be gone, her scar didn't throb, she didn't shiver.

What would she do if she saw Jean now? If she bumped into him on the dull London street? Immediately, her stomach tightened. There was no pretending that she could ever be pleased by the sight of him, that she could ever again call him a friend, or an almost more than friend. No matter how much she wanted to she could not forget those horrific days and weeks and months in Rwanda in which everything was taken from her, and he was part of it. If only Cassien was alive, or her mother, or one single person that she loved, if there was just one. Infinite presence rather than infinite absence. Maybe then, maybe. Nevertheless, the hatred that had once consumed her had subsided. She did not want to see Jean, but perhaps she had finally escaped him.

'You are still in the cage,' Lynn had warned her. But she was out now. She was free. They both were. How could she be sorry about that?

Her thoughts drifted to Omar. She wondered if his brother had flown to New York yet, if his parents were visiting, if he was visiting them. She pictured the pride that dripped from his handsome face when he spoke of his younger brother, the student of law, and imagined that perhaps it was not too late for him to wear such a smile when he thought of her. 'Sister,' he had called her, unconscious of how much had hung on such a simple word, how much had been called up by it.

Would he still call her sister if he knew about Luke? She thought about Omar's long, elegant hands, the way he used them in broad gestures to defend her to his friend, the wave he always reserved for her. She could imagine a time when she would allow those hands to touch her.

When she arrived at her building, there was a collection of empty beer cans lining the front wall, a group of children playing with new footballs which they kicked right across the Christmas-quiet road, and a small cluster of teenagers displaying unblemished trainers while they chain-smoked and pretended not to care; but no Omar. Making her way inside, she embraced her disappointment, tantalisingly aware of what it suggested and wishing she could tell Lynn that she had, after all, been right.

As she climbed the stairs she was struck by the clamour of Christmas day, struck too by the realisation that for once she longed for quiet, for the chance to hear birdsong and the rustling of the wind.

When she rounded the last flight of stairs and made her way down the corridor she looked immediately towards Omar's flat, listening carefully for any sounds that might be evidence of him. So she did not at first notice the white paper envelope with her name, 'Emilienne', neatly printed on the front of it pinned to her door. Her first thought was that it was from him, and tearing it open, she allowed her mind to jump ahead to declarations of love, or concern at least, a Christmas greeting, a phone number, a promise. But as soon as she unfolded the paper inside, she saw the official letter heading of GENSUR. Underneath was a handwritten note from Alice.

'Dear Emilienne,' she read in Kinyarwanda, 'I am sorry for asking you too much. It was not my intention to probe. Please accept my apologies and contact us as soon as you can. I have some news. Alice.'

Before opening her door, Emily folded the paper carefully in half, then in quarters, and then once more before pushing it deep into her back pocket, as though if she folded it small enough, she could make it disappear. She didn't want to talk any more about the genocide. Through Luke, by confronting this apparition, she'd found a way to free herself from Jean, from the last memories of sun-red soil. Lynn had forced her to go back, but now it was time to move in the other direction.

Inside her flat, she noticed for the first time how small the room was, how dark and claustrophobic, and she yearned suddenly for a window from which she could see the sun. She imagined herself bathing in it, with Omar. Omar. He was the only kernel of her life that she wanted to preserve.

Emily showered, removing the last of Luke's aroma from her flesh. She cleaned her teeth, applied perfume, and smoothed her thick hair back from her face into Lynn's silk yellow headscarf, which had been scrunched up in the bottom of her bag. It was not dissimilar from the one her mother used to wear with her favourite red dress. The scar by Emily's eye seemed to cut ever more insistently into her face, but for the first time, she wasn't repulsed by it. It made her look as though she was running so fast that a streak of jet-black mascara was trailing in her wake. She liked the idea of that. The world wouldn't be able to stop her now. Pulling on a pair of jeans and the most brightly coloured top she owned – a navy jumper – she forgot to paint a smile onto her face but left the apartment wearing one.

Omar didn't answer. She knocked three times, but he wasn't there and the anticlimax of this drove the breath from Emily. She tapped again. On the other side of the door was silence. She sank slowly to the floor and peered underneath the crack into his flat, hoping for a glimpse of his white trainers or the wiry hair she knew lay beneath them. There were only some scattered flyers, and the bottoms of his shantytown boxes. Emily pulled herself into sitting and rested her head against the door.

The plan to wait for him wasn't a conscious decision, but Lynn was gone, there was nowhere else to go, and sitting there at least contained the hope of Omar's return. As she leant her head against the hard wood she noticed how sore and tired her eyes were. She had barely slept the previous night and memories of Lynn's tiny, gasping mound under the bed covers now danced in front of her heavy lids. Sometimes Lynn's face sat atop her mother's body, or visions of John slumped in his chair merged with images of Cassien, but the sorrow she felt washed over her gently, without shaking her frame. She opened her eyes. Omar had still not come, but perhaps he would appear a little later. Perhaps he would apologise for not understanding her desolation. Or let her explain. Perhaps he would say that they should leave this place together, move out of London, out of the city, somewhere she could see the sun.

When she awoke it was to the sound of a baby crying. 'Hush Mary,' she murmured, still caked in sleep, feeling the weight of something heavy in her arms and reaching in half-remembered habit to place a quietening finger inside her sister's mouth. The crying continued from further away. Slowly, Emily opened her eyes and gradually deciphered the shape of a book and not a baby in her lap. 'Allah can help you.' Omar had been.

Immediately Emily stood and knocked on his door. There was no answer. She tried again but the same stubborn silence from the day before pervaded. A dim morning light was inching its way through a tiny window at the end of the corridor. She jostled the stiff, graffitied frame and found that it could be nudged open. Below, a group of kids were already out again with their footballs, a hum of traffic crawled by, no longer subdued by Christmas, and there, standing at the bus stop across the road, was Omar. Emily dropped the book. A piece of paper fluttered from inside it. She grabbed it from the floor. 'From afar, you have been loved,' Omar had written. 'Not only by Allah.' Emily glanced again towards the window, and she ran.

The stairs were far too many and conversations in which Omar had mentioned his intentions to go away soon tumbled through her mind, as she flung herself outside the building and turned towards the road. She scanned the area, certain that this would be her final opportunity to see him, her last chance. Her frantic eyes found him still standing at the bus stop. His hostile friend was with him and the two seemed locked in deep, angry conversation. Omar's head was bent, and every now and then he shook it, but even hunched he seemed proud, unable to be beaten. Finally the friend pointed an accusatory finger at Omar, held it there, glared at him, then he threw his hands into the sky and turned away.

Omar smiled, defiantly.

From 50 feet away, Emily smiled with him.

Then, she noticed the suitcases at his feet.

A noisy grumbling bus came up the road and pulled heavily into the stop. Omar reached for the cases on the floor and boarded, waving a greeting to the bus driver. With the same wave he had once saved for Emily. Or perhaps not. Perhaps it only seemed that way because it was all Emily could see from behind the bars of her cage. The last of the waiting passengers got on behind her old neighbour. And Emily stood, still smiling, transfixed by the scene of him moving seamlessly through the present: settling his bags in the storage rack at the front of the bus, finding a seat, checking his phone, taking out a book, removing his good jacket, glancing out of the window, leaving. Leaving. Leaving.

'Omar!'

The bus hissed its doors to a close and sighed as it began to pull away.

'Omar!' Emily screamed. She ran towards it, fast, faster, her legs and arms flooding with acid, but somehow, the distance seemed only to grow. She shouted again, but no sound came out. She waved, but her movements were slow and minuscule. She ran. But with every metre she covered, the bus and Omar on it fell further away. An unreachable plane.

She stopped. He was gone.

A car beeped impatiently as she stood in the middle of the road. And he was gone.

On the pavement, a couple glanced at her curiously, interested but from a distance, without a stake in her loss.

Emily's heart hurt.

And life continued.

Outside her building, the kids from the estate continued to kick their football and, still standing in the road, Emily watched them, ignoring the succession of cars beeping at her as they drove wide and past. She recognised most of the kids, some only a few years younger than she, many with skin as dark as her own, but she didn't know their names. Had she once made such noise? Had she once been so raucous? Could she again? She thought back. She realised that she could think back. Even without Omar ahead of her. Cassien's football had once been new and shiny as theirs was. When they were children. Before.

'Goal!' Emily suddenly heard herself yell from the middle of the road as one of the kids scored between two makeshift jumper-posts. But she was not a child anymore, and when they looked up she saw the wonder in their eyes at her yellow-flowered interruption. The kids threw 'weirdo' glances at each other and carried on.

Except for one boy.

Behind the rest, her eyes were drawn to him. He was standing a little way back from the others, not shouting like they were, not raucous. He was taller than them too but his slim frame and baseball cap had masked his age so that it was only when she studied him more closely that she realised he was not one of them, not in fact a child.

Another car beeped, this time over and over. It stopped dead and refused to swerve around her, but Emily couldn't pull her eyes away from the man who was not a boy. His body was turned towards her building as he consulted a piece of paper, so she couldn't see his face, but there was something about him that seemed strangely familiar. She recognised the frame, the leanness of the arms, the slight tilt of the head. Somewhere, in a place far away and long ago, she had seen that tilt before.

She stopped breathing.

A car door slammed. Now a whole chorus of horns started up. Someone was shouting. Loudly. And taking heavy strides towards her. She heard words like *black bitch*, and *fucking retard* and other things that meant nothing, and were not *cockroach* or *Tutsi*, and came from a stranger who didn't really know. The horns grew more urgent, like a refrain of bullfrogs.

But the boy-man was still in front of her.

The boy-man was tilting his head towards the sun, peering through gaps in his fingers to consult his paper.

Something heavy was grabbing her shoulder.

And there was a pain in the back of her skull.

And bald skin and knuckles and tattoos.

Suddenly, from a strange, shifting angle, Emily noticed that the kids had stopped kicking their ball and were one by one turning towards her.

And as if in slow motion, the boy-man turned his head.

Emily saw his face.

Then abruptly the sun was obscured, and there was darkness again.

CHAPTER 34

His voice sang through the sirens like a half-forgotten song, whispering softly with words of childhood, and leftover laughter, and home. Emily blinked painfully. Her brother's face was older but the same. His skin, black as the night of the power-short village they'd lived in, was scarred and weathered, but smelled still of Gahiji. Blood was everywhere. Her arms were strewn nearby, not stumps like Cassien's, but contorted underneath her.

Ambulance men in yellow jackets appeared before her. They were trying to convey something but she could see only their lips moving and hear no sound.

She could feel Gahiji's leather-strong hand on her arm and if she closed her eyes, her mother was there too, with her fingers shielding her view from the unfathomable sights before her: police, and a man in handcuffs, and blood trickling into her mouth, tasting not of soil but gravel. Papa was nearby, unpacking his glasses and choosing a book, preparing to read it aloud. Simeon and Rukundo were cavorting around in the distance, cajoling her

434

to get up, to join in. Mary was in her arms, warm, giggling. And Cassien, her beloved Cassien was right next to her, his lean arms tired from climbing trees, his legs toned and bare, his hands reaching to steady hers, his face, as always, grinning. 'Climb higher,' he urged her confidently. 'Keep climbing Emmy. Gahiji will catch you.'

A general buzz followed her. If she kept her eyes squinted shut she could sometimes decipher individual voices within it, but they blended with her dreams and would not sort themselves into helpful groups like past and present, real and imagined, truth and merely hope. Often, Gahiji's voice invaded her sleep, but when she opened her eyes, she could see only doctors and nurses, and other beds with relatives gathered around them, and nobody at her own, so it was probable that his presence at other moments was only a result of her longing. 'Stay,' she wanted to tell her brother on the occasions that he was there. 'Don't leave me.' But her voice had deserted her, and so he drifted in and out, and so did she.

Sometimes a policeman hovered in her periphery. He said words like *stranger* and *road rage* and *assault* and *pressing charges*, and asked questions. But they all tumbled over her flesh like a rushing stream and didn't stick to it. And usually a melodic voice intervened until the man in uniform somehow melted away.

Once, Emily thought she heard a voice in the

corridor that could have belonged to John. Another time, she saw a doctor standing over her, furiously scribbling notes. When he noticed her eyes open he asked her if she had headaches often, dizziness, nausea, if she had ever been tested for HIV or Aids, to which she may have shaken her head or may simply have drifted again into her dreams.

It was possible that Luke had been there, although the face may also have belonged to Jean, and the screaming in the corridor that followed was too distant for her to decipher which was the most likely: Was it his luminous bride Vera who the man had been arguing with? Pleading with? Consoling? Or a nurse? Someone, she knew, had been crying.

'Emilienne, Emilienne,' a nurse urged her one afternoon, and she became aware of a spoon in front of her mouth, a bib underneath her chin, and a woman without a shred of impatience smiling generously, urging her to eat. She was sitting up, she realised. There were yellow tulips on her bedside table. She opened her mouth and allowed some of the soft substance to trickle down her throat. At the taste, she grimaced.

'She doesn't like mangoes,' she heard a woman to the other side of her admonish, and she could have sworn that the voice belonged to Auntie. There was a rustling of plastic bags and the voice came again. 'I have better food,' the voice told the nurse.

★　　★　　★

Slowly, the buzzing diminished and one morning Emily awoke to silence. She had been moved to another room. The walls around her were white and a large window let a high sun flood light across her. She turned her head and discovered that she was able to lift it. The door was closed but she noticed a call-button just inches from the bed. If she strained her ears, she could hear a low murmur of voices from somewhere far down a corridor, but she did not struggle to decipher them. The window was open a little at the top and if she tried it was possible to hear birdsong and the whistling of a sharp, winter wind. Gently, and with only a little pain, Emily pulled herself onto her side and surveyed the landscape.

The hospital was somewhere that overlooked an expanse of garden. There were no tall buildings to obscure her view and if she looked up, she could watch the clouds drifting slowly past. One cloud in particular caught her interest. It had a narrow beginning that stretched to the right before swelling into bulges and outcrops that blurred with each other to make it look as though the cloud was shedding bubbles, or raindrops, or leaves. In fact, if she slanted her head and turned the cloud the other way up, it looked just like an old Nim tree. Emily smiled. She imagined that such a tree would have a great story. It would be climbed every day by scampering children, it would be the test of their agility, their successes and failures traded between them; it would shelter their fears and keep the secrets they whispered through its branches; it would provide a lookout and a base from which to stage missions for stealing fruit. And a hiding place.

The cloud drifted out of Emily's horizon. She selected another. This one looked like a bird, thinking, and she was just about to give it a story when the door to her room fell open.

She turned.

She grinned.

And like the bird, the man standing in the doorway tilted his head.